The Balance

Chronicles of Aurderia

The Balance

River of Souls

Queen of Shadow

Chronicles of Aurderia
The Balance

J. Steven Young

To my Shrimpo-Shrimpo, for putting up with being sometimes ignored
during this process!

- 831

Chapter One

Living without the ability to wield the Essence once it is gone is distressing, but for Moona of Birchshire, that difficulty is transferred to those who are subjected to her thorny presence. Her days became filled with mixing potions she could not use and helping to moon mother sprats she could not have. Now she found herself mixed-up in the birth of children of the prophecy.

Moona was called to a small town in the northern reaches of Aurderia to look after a special young woman named Sulura during the last term of her pregnancy, expecting children of even greater importance. Moona grew close to the young woman in their time together, so when zealots from the Order of Chaos arrived to take Sulura to their sanctuary for the birth, Moona refused letting Sulura be taken without her. No one refused Moona's demands without regret.

"What a wretched place this is for bringin' new sprats into the world," Moona said. "Special consideration and better birthin' conditions they said, YAK SCAT!" Moona continued, drawing a deep take from her pipe. "If these ground tremors keep up, they's like to bring this place down."

Sulura pursed her lips but could not resist a half smile as she watched Moona fuss about the small cell. "Moona you must not fuss, and please do not swear or smoke that stinky weed around me. I have said, this place is where we must be if we are to see an end to the quakes." Sulura was tired and so expanded with the babies in her belly, she could not spend much time on her feet. She laid her head back down and tried to rest.

Moona continued to sweep straw and dirt from the floor of their small room while puffing on her pipe. She started a fire in the room's fireplace and put the kettle on, filling it with contents from various pouches she retrieved from various pockets in her garments. "Sulura, I don' doubt your gift but could ya be a'tall misled, perhaps this ain' the way of the prophecy?"

"No Moona, it must be this way. When the time comes, I am counting on you to do as we have discussed. I trust none above you to look after me." Sulura was unsettled by the prophecy surrounding the birth of her children, but she had to appear strong for Moona's sake. She felt sorry for any who crossed her moon mother. Even with the loss of her ability to wield the Essence, Moona was a force to be reckoned with.

"I ain' likin' this one bit, but I do as you ask except the pipe, it calms me." After another drag, Moona continued. "But what o' the father? Is he like ta return from this task ya set him on?"

"I cannot say with certainty," Sulura said and closed her eyes as she thought of her absent husband. "It is no easy journey he has undertaken. Aid from the seven races of man must be sought if my children are to survive." Sulura turned her head away from Moona so she would not see the glistening in her eyes as the tears began to flow. "I grow tired and need my rest."

"Sleep child, I shall be here ta bring your sprats into the world, as I have others for nearly two hundred harvests before you." With a final pat upon Sulura's head, Moona returned to her kettle at the fire and poured a cup as she looked back upon Sulura and sighed. When a shuffle outside drew her attention, she cursed the guard who poked his head in the door to check on them. "Plank off ya halfwit, no'un asked for ya to come pokin' 'round. She is sleepin' and too fat with child to run off. I have seen far more years than is your business ta know, so I ain' be waddling off either!"

The last cycles of Sulura's pregnancy continued without complication. One night late after the sun Utu fell below the horizon, a figure emerged from the darkness and approached Sulura while Moona slept. "Wake and speak young woman, we have much to discuss and little time to do so." The man approached without waking Moona, who was snorting like a swamp pig on her cot in the corner of the room.

"Who is there, what is this about?" asked Sulura while struggling to push her body into a sitting position and look upon the man. "Do I know you stranger? You seem familiar to me though I do not see your face."

He remained in the shadows, just out of Sulura's ability to see him clearly. "Who I am is not important now but I have come to bear witness to the prophecy and bring a gift from Nabusa."

Sulura's gaze narrowed. "What does my grandmother have that I should care to receive?" Sulura began to anger as the thought of Nabusa knowing where she was crossed her mind. "I left the Foresworn as instructed long ago and made my way in Aurderia without her help thus far," Sulura said. "My fate is sealed and her help is too late."

"The gift is not for you but one of your legacy. A gemstone that must be given at birth," he said.

"Which child is this for and why?" she asked. The woman she called grandmother was a powerful wielder of Essence and more ancient than any other in the whole of Ersetu. Though Sulura thought the prophecy would require a sacrifice, perhaps her vision was not interpreted correctly.

"You will know the child it must be given to the moment it is required of you. The gift will hide the child so that it may be taken away and protected."

"But I must give up both my girls to bring balance, that is the way of the prophecy," Sulura began to reach for the man using strength born of the hope she was mistaken about the fate of her unborn children.

"No Sulura, there is more to the prophecy. More I cannot say but you must give this gift to one child and someone you trust must take it away. I will meet Moona in the Stone Forest and we shall make our escape." He left a gift in Sulura's hand and stepped back into the darkness before vanishing.

Just as the mysterious man left, Moona awoke with one final snort that echoed off the walls and startled the guards outside the small room. "What was that?" Moona shrieked as she jumped from her cot far more lithely than one might expect of her advanced years.

"You woke yourself again, snorting like some sort of farm burden-beast!" Sulura snickered while wiping the tears from her eyes.

Moona began laughing heartily as she walked to the side table to get a tankard of wine.

Their moment of giddiness halted.

"OH," Sulura said and held her belly. "Moona it is time."

"Nonsense child you are at least two cycles from birthin'."

"No Moona it is now, my waters have given and I feel the contractions setting in." Sulura looked to Moona with a horrible thought. "It is as if the birth is being forced." She looked at the green gemstone for only a moment before stowing it in the folds of her dress.

Moona ran to the door and screeched at the guards. "Hot water and clean rags, not these filthy scraps you left for our bathin' neither mind you. NOW!"

The guards ran off in opposite directions before each turned and passed one another deciding where they needed to go for help and meet Moona's demands.

"Biddley-diddles, both of 'em share a single brain, and a weak one at that. Order of Chaos indeed." Moona slapped her hands together and moved to begin packing their bags. "Now then off we go, mind ya it took me a bit ta catch on, but ready I am ta make our escape. Them Order guards 'll not be gone long so let's get on with it."

"Moona, this is no plan, I am truly going into birthing and fast!" Sulura tried to sit up, but the pain of a contraction rippled across her otherwise pleasant face. She furrowed her brow and she screamed out from the pain.

Before Moona could respond, the guards returned with more of their ranks and several zealots from the Order of Chaos. She could not understand why they stood there staring at Sulura. "Oye Biddle and Diddle, she is going into full birthing are we gonna have a show o' it 'cause this room ain' big 'nough for the lot o' ya."

"Make ready the altar and bring them!" one of the zealots ordered as he gathered his wits and turned from the room. "Quickly, before the First of our order gets there. We must be ready when the Assinnu Isten arrives."

The guards gathered Sulura atop a carrying cot and led the way out of the room with Moona yelling franticly after them.

"Get your hands off o' me, you witless forest troll. I be too old for shoving. Get those rags and hot water and hand me my bags."

The growing contingent of zealots and guards made their way out of the keep and past the outskirts of Drakkfoth. They left secretly by way of old tunnels carved from lava tubes deep below the city above their hidden keep. When they finally emerged from the labyrinth of musty old passageways into the open, it was growing past dusk and into the dark of night. They quickly made their way down to the ancient Altar of Chaos.

The group was passing a large out-cropping of dark rocks jutting forth from the ground reaching many spans into the sky when the ceremonial altar and surroundings came into view. The entire area was dark beyond midnight even as the last rays of passing twilight were absorbed by every stone. A diamond shaped field of smoothed ground lay before them, undisturbed by the passing of time.

Several raised stones shaped into seats, surrounded the center of this forbidding place. In the center of it, all sat a dark bench of the blackest stone that existed, dragon glass and it was found only in and around the heart of Hell's Mouth volcano.

A bench sat beneath two large columns with a solitary lintel atop. The entire structure was one enormous piece carved from a single dragon stone. Flawless and forbidding, horrifying yet breathtakingly beautiful all at once, the altar radiated such power that many guards just stopped and stared transfixed and unable to move.

"Disgusting!" Moona whispered to Sulura.

"Moona please, we must see this through." Sulura was no longer able to hide her tears from Moona as the time to sacrifice one of her children approached. Sulura knew what was required to fulfill the prophecy and it was breaking her heart.

"Yes, Sulura. I may be old, but I still have my wits, more 'en I can say about that lot," she replied thumbing over her shoulder at the guards who now stared blank-eyed into the abyss of power radiating from the altar. "Are you certain 'bout this?"

Sulura squeezed Moona's hand and shook her head. She dared not try to speak or she would give Moona more reason to fire her tongue up with insults and cause trouble.

As they finally reached the altar, Sulura was placed upon the bench within the structure along with the water, rags, and other items Moona had demanded.

From beneath her clothing Moona produced a pouch and sprinkled some of its contents into a tankard of watered wine before approaching Sulura. "Here child drink this down, it 'll help with the pain both to your body and shi. There is no going back, now is there?" she asked knowing the answer.

Sulura just smiled handing back the tankard and taking Moona's hand. Pulling Moona close, she emptied the contents of her hand into Moona's and whispered so the others could not hear. "Take this and place it on the final child. When he is born, you must take him away quickly."

"What do you mean third, child these herbs are working fast," Moona interrupted.

"No Moona I can see clearly now. I carry triplets, the third a boy child. After he wakes to this world, you must take this gem and the child away into the Stone Forest where a friend will meet you and hasten your escape." Sulura wore a desperate face full of hope and sorrow.

Moona just looked at her with questions in her eyes.

"The gemstone will keep you hidden so that you can get away. The others do not know of this third child and must not find out or all is lost." She pushed the gem into Moona's hand and wrapped her fingers closed around it.

"How do ya s'pose I hide the birth itself, I am only a herb worker now? I can perform no such magics any longer." Moona asked the question but again knew the answer as she looked into Sulura's eyes.

"It cannot be helped Moona, you must I beg you."

Moona nodded and hid the gem as the first baby began to crown.

As the birthing began, the Assinnu Isten, leader of the Order of Chaos, arrived in a dark swirl of electrified air. "Has it begun?" he asked of no one and everyone at once. Without awaiting a reply, he moved to the altar as though floating on air. Looking to the sky, he saw two new stars on the horizon. He looked into Sulura's eyes, "It is a wondrous fate that has brought you here this eve child. For you shall play a great part in what is to come."

Sulura gritted her teeth as she bore down. "Do not confuse my acquiescence with willingness old man," she said. "And do not call me a child for I am much older than you!" Sulura spat at him while Moona's eyes lit up with hearing Sulura's words.

"You think so? I doubt that very much but no matter, you have no choice in this." He turned to Moona and his smile faded. "You will deliver the raven-haired girl child to my man at your side. The snow haired girl child shall not live. Now let us begin shall we. Light the torches and begin the spell working!" the leader bellowed as he turned to take the largest seat that surrounded the altar.

The chanting began as a low and barely audible murmur that gained in volume and intensity as the zealots repeated and droned on with their spell.

"BEL GIBIDALAL, SISITU MUZU EMUQ
PULHU ES-INA LAMAGIRI
LASANAN EMUQ ADI ANNU ABANASQUPPATU
ZU ASSINNA ILEQQE BILTU, SEMU!"

"Oh, seven hells, that be the ancient tongue Sulura! What are they sayin'?" Moona cried.

"That is more than just the ancient Sumerian tongue, what they are casting is darkest of all magics." Sulura was horrified. "They are calling to the Lord of Chaos and summoning his power. They want to bring terror to those who do not submit to the power poured into this altar by paying tribute." Sulura's breathing became erratic between contractions. "More to the point is that they are commanding it. Moona this is a full summoning and it scares me to think where they learned how to do this."

Full birthing came upon Sulura and the sprats were on their way into the world. A strained push saw the first girl child was upon them. Raven hair and emerald eyes already open to the world. She did not cry which made Moona suspicious.

The child was quickly taken by the zealots and ushered over to the Assinnu Isten. Already the snow-haired girl was birthing as Sulura was weakening from the efforts. By the time she managed to push enough for a full birth, her energy was spent.

As Moona cut the cord on the second girl, a zealot came to her and snatched the child away rushing to the altar.

"Moona quickly, now while they are distracted." Sulura's tears streamed down her face.

"Sulura is there no other way, surely you can push more," Moona pleaded.

"No, I am spent, you must cut the boy from my belly and flee before they sense his presence." Sulura looked upon Moona with urgency in her eyes.

Moona quickly produced a small sharp knife from her pocket and set about her undesirable task. As Moona freed the boy child she placed the gem upon him, the Isten began to turn his head toward them, but then turned his attention back to the altar when seeing nothing amiss. Moona kissed Sulura upon the forehead and fled into the darkness unseen.

"Do it now!" The Assinnu Isten instructed the zealot to sacrifice the girl.

Sulura whispered under her breath.

"NINTI DUL-INA GISHTIL, NADANUTE SHI BALU SARRATUM."

"Bel Gibidalal awaits his tribute!" Isten said. And with his words, the zealot holding the snow-haired child thrust a ceremonial dagger toward the child's heart.

As the blade reached the skin, there was a blinding burst of pure white light and energy as the tribute disappeared. At the same time, one of the new stars suddenly bursts in brilliance then dimmed to barely a twinkle. "What has happened Isten? Is this the way of it?" asked the zealot holding the dagger.

Isten bent down to the raven-haired girl and placed a gemstone upon her heart. "The power of light has waned!" Isten cooed then looked back startled. He stood and began to approach Sulura's bloodied form with a look of questioning mixed with concern. Suddenly he stopped and turned toward the altar, his expression changed to one of pure awe. The Isten closed his eyes, tilted back his head, and spread out his arms as energy began to flow from the altar into him.

The other zealots began to feel it as well. A smoky mist poured off the altar from out of the dark stone and fed the power hungry Order of Chaos.

When all the power was absorbed, the Isten opened his eyes and turned to the raven-haired girl child. The child was absorbing the last of the power from the altar.

Her eyes once a brilliant green turned to a deep black before him. Power beyond anything he had imagined emanated from her tiny form. The Gem he had placed upon her dissolved and joined her flesh leaving a rune marked upon her chest, glowing a deep red. "And now you are mine to control little one. I shall call you Salmetu, dark priestess. Yes, an ancient name of power for such a powerful tool," Isten said with a maniacal chuckle.

Isten turned to the bench whereupon Sulura, barely conscious, lay bleeding to death. "Where has your moon mother gone, child?" he said with a slight curl to his lip. "Has she bled you so that you may die quickly without suffering, much? Not to worry we shall find her, but not immediately. Someone must spread the word of what has transpired so that all will know this new power and submit without question."

Isten turned from Sulura and walked back to where Salmetu lay quietly observing her surroundings with wisdom in her eyes beyond that of a newly birthed child. He picked her up and carried her to an awaiting basket. Placing her within, he turned to the zealots. "Clear the area and return to your mundane lives until called upon. As always our identities must remain hidden until the time is right."

"What of the mother, Isten?" A zealot inquired. As if in answer, a howl echoed in the distance followed by replies from other beasts.

"Leave her to the wolves, she will soon breathe her last breath." As Isten turned, he placed a chain and pendant over his head and tucked it under his robes. As his features began to change he turned and disappeared with the child into a swirl of blackness.

Back at the altar Sulura was alone barely holding on as she turned to see them. Approaching slowing from the darkness surrounding her came massive forms. Red glowing eyes piercing the shadows to look upon her. As the wolves drew closer, their gleaming white fangs stood in contrast to the black fur of their bodies. One by one they arrived and surrounded her weakening form lying prone upon the obsidian bench.

Try as she might, she was unable to muster the energy enough to move or resist the inevitable. As the last of the beasts came to sit next to her, she noticed with silent fear that they appeared to wait for something. And then she saw it, another wolf coming from the misty shadows.

This wolf was different, smaller than the rest by at least half yet more powerful in its presence. The white wolf, female it appeared, approached Sulura and without pausing dragged its tongue across the wound in her belly. Raising its head to the sky, it let out a bellowing howl that shook the night.

Fear and exhaustion overtook Sulura and her world went dark.

Chapter Two

MMoona was already well on her way to the Stone Forest when she began to feel the darkness surround her. It was as if all the light was being drained from the heavens and pouring toward the place she had just fled. Off to the East she could make out the outline of Hell's Mouth looming in the distance. Even the deep red glow from its fiery maw seemed to dim to the barest of a shimmer.

"Oh, this does not bode well little one," she said looking down into the deep emerald eyes of the bundle she carried. Soon she found a place to sit and rest for a minute. She was certain the gemstone that Sulura had given her for the child was working, as she was able to walk right past the guards without them noticing her.

Once a guard turned toward her as she stumbled and made some noise, but he simply dismissed the noise and turned away.

"Let's have a look, shall we young 'un," she said handling the gem and turning it over. "Ah, this would be it, ancient runes be here. I'm ain' sure 'xactly what they are, but they work. I know someone who could tell us," she said with first a fond look then made a scowl. "Someday maybe if we must, but for now we need ta get moving. This friend o' your mama will not likely wait forever and we need ta get far away from this horrid place."

Then Moona heard the wolves and a shiver ran through her body as she realized what their presence meant for Sulura. "Oh Damkianna, save her shi," she whispered to the sky as she picked herself and her burden up, making her way toward the heart of the Stone Forest.

Hours passed as Moona finally entered the Stone Forest. The forest was once a beautiful place that stretched from the base of what is now Hell's Mouth to the outer borders of Drakk.

Within this forest once lived the tree folk who worshipped and tended the forest. Millennia ago before the Lalli Mah, the first attempt to balance the magic of Ersetu, a mountain burst forth liquid rock and fiery ash upon the surrounding lands. That was the birth of Hell's Mouth and death to the forest.

The tree folk were unwilling or unable to leave their forest home and perished with the onslaught of ash and fire that leveled the forest and petrified the outer area. The trees that remained turned to stone and many still bore the outlines of horror from the faces of the dryads once living within them.

The long ago beautiful forest now echoed horror and fear and the creatures now living within, are not the passive animals that once shied away from travelers.

"Well, we're here, but how far must we go 'fore this mysterious guide meets us?" Moona asked the baby. "Now what do we call ya, eh little one? A strong name I should think, something that rolls off the tongue, but shows the strength ya gonna need." As Moona pondered a voice called out from the shadows.

"Shuran," Andra said walking out from beyond a group of felled stone trees.

Moona gasped and began to open her mouth before she thought better of it.

"It is ok, I am Andra and have been awaiting your arrival." Andra left his head cloaked as he approached Moona and Shuran.

Moona made no reply nor did she move as Andra approached and sat directly in front of her and the baby.

"Odd that Sulura never mentioned you were mute," Andra stated and chuckled. "The boy child was named Shuran by Sulura when last we spoke. The name means strength of the people," Andra said.

"I have a tongue stranger I simply chose not ta use it until I assessed you," Moona said. "You wear a cloak of the guardians I see," she continued, more observation than a question.

"Yes, you are familiar with our work," Andra asked.

"Only enough to recognize the cloak and that members do not reveal their faces. Am I ta guess you still follow that second custom?" she inquired.

"You are correct. But also know that we pledge our lives to those we have been tasked with guarding," Andra stated. "That is the symbol of our multi-colored cloaks."

"Ok then, that be good enough for me. Hey! Wait a second, how in the name of Damkianna can you see me? No one else has," Moona asked.

"The gem you carry will fully conceal you from vision while obscuring sound and scent, but not entirely, and not at all from the one who created it."

"That is some powerful spell you did then and I thank ya for its use in gettin' us away."

"It is nothing really and not entirely a spell. We should be leaving," Andra said while standing up abruptly. "Drakkfoth guards approach, we need to go." Andra took Moona's hand and in an instant they all disappeared.

"Captain have you located the old woman?" a voice sounded from behind him.

"No, the trail has grown cold just inside the Stone Forest. It is as if she sprouted wings and took flight," the Captain of the Drakkoth guard replied.

"Return to the city and take your post with the rest of your men. You were not here," the man commanded.

"As you wish my lord Telalsu." Without another word, the Captain and his men headed back to Drakkfoth leaving the sickly man behind.

Telalsu entered the clearing where Andra, Moona, and Shuran had only just left. He stopped and placed his hands on the ground as he knelt. He looked up to the sky then stood and removed a piece of parchment from a pouch at his belt.

After scrolling a message he then blew upon the parchment, and the words flew to the wind and took flight in a puff of ash. His eyes were ruby red and glowed like fire as he whispered a curse beneath his breath and headed east on the barren roads toward Middleton.

Andra, Moona, and Shuran materialized near a barn on the outskirts of Middleton; a simple settlement of farmers and crafters. Andra dropped to the ground breathing deeply.

"What was that?" Moona cried with surprise.

"It was a far traveling spell but poorly done, we've only made it to Middleton," Andra responded breathily.

"Only to Middleton you say? That is at least a few days hard travel by horse, never mind by foot!" she said.

"Yes, but I had planned on taking us straight to Draventon where we were to plan out our course. I have little provision with us and am now too tired to attempt another working." Though Andra would not reveal his face, his voice carried a tremor of concern beneath the gasps for air.

"Andra that spell was no little thing. We can trade here for more provisions and a baby satchel for Shuran. I'd like ta free up the use of my hands," Moona said pulling out her pipe and lighting it with a grin.

"Provisions we can get, but it would be weeks before I could work a traveling spell again. Shuran will be hungry; I've goats milk in this sack," Andra said as he handed a large pack over to Moona.

"Good heavens I ain' thought, some Moona I'm gonna be forgettin' you need food!" she said to Shuran, who just looked up at her quietly. "So brave ya are little sprat, not a whimper this whole time." She took out a bottle of goat's milk from the sack and began feeding Shuran.

Shuran feed from the bottle without fuss or reserve.

"Oh, my how much milk you got in this sack Guardian, cause this sprat is gonna drink all of 'em soon at this rate. My teats are too old and dried up to try wet nursin'!" Moona said. She smiled down at Shuran and cooed at him.

"We can trade in a few hours. After dawn has come the markets will be opening in Middleton. Until then, we can rest here inside this old barn." Andra guided Moona into the barn, never taking his gaze off of Shuran.

The trio made their way into the old barn, which was empty beside some old hay and a few rusty old farm tools. They sat down in the hay pile and leaned back to rest while Shuran continued to eat and stare at them in turn.

Just before dawn the three left the barn and headed into Middleton. As they walked, Shuran slept, and Moona followed closely behind Andra.

"So this traveling spell, the crusty ol' leader of that witless cult did something like that when he arrived. He did it again soon after when he left. Why was he able to do so again so quickly?" Moona questioned.

"Either he was not going farther than a few hundred paces or he had a source stone to draw power from. My stone cracked from the effort of arriving in Drakkfoth directly from the Foresworn Territories. This is why I have not the power to do it again so soon or for very far," he replied.

"Biddley Diddles, all the way from the Foresworn Territories!" she said.

"You have no idea where that is do you?" Andra asked.

"Well, no, but I guess it is far since I never heard of the place."

Andra continued without slowing their pace toward Middleton. "It is far beyond the Great Sea, the lands where many of the persecuted fled during the Sikil Mah." Andra whispered the last words as though afraid the Great Purification would come again.

"You said many but not all fled did they?" Moona asked.

Andra nodded.

"Thought so! I always wondered why my kin always lived longer than we ought. Most Aurderian humans don' live beyond seventy or eighty harvests. And I been around three times that. Suppose that's why we always moved around; keep folks from getting nosey," Moona rambled. "It wasn' until I left to be on me own I even found I was part dwarf."

"Good thing you and your parents moved about so, otherwise you would likely have been tried and sentenced to death," Andra said.

"ANZILLU, the trials of abomination from the Sikil Mah!" Moona spat. "They ain' had one o' them since I was a sprat. There's them that throw the words around oft' enough but only out of ignorance and superstition." Moona shivered at the thought and they continued on to the town in quiet.

The Market in Middleton was already bustling with marketers and traders alike by the time they arrived into town. Stalls were setup along both sides of the streets and around the entire town square. There were farmers selling their foodstuffs and grains, town bakers, crafters, smithies, and fabric weavers spread throughout the square.

The delicious smell of fresh baked bread and meat made Moona's stomach rumble. "Well, if we can't find what we need then we ain' got our eyes open." Moona said looking at the food carts.

"Hopefully, we can get what we need, I have not much to trade that would be legal in these lands and not much coin," Andra said.

"Don' you be worrin' 'bout that, Moona has more in the folds of her coverings than lard." She grinned and pulled out a good-sized pouch. "You see as many harvests in Aurderia as me without learnin' to save for a poor crop."

Andra just nodded and they went about gathering supplies and goods. They purchased food, water, and garments and swaddling for Shuran.

"We can get horses and a goat for fresh milk down at the stables according to the baker," said Moona between bites "I will be needin' to freshen my supply of herbs as well if I can find a proper apothecary this far south."

Andra took Shuran from Moona hesitantly and said, "You get what you need and I will get us a goat, horse, and tack. I hope you are accustomed to sleeping in the saddle because we are likely being followed from the Stone Forest."

Moona nodded and headed off to look for a herb seller. Both Andra and Moona agreed to draw as little attention as possible and avoid the city guard.

It did not take Moona long before she found a woman selling herbs and concoctions from a covered wagon in the square. "Good morning young woman what wares have ya for health, hygiene, and relaxation?" Moona asked winking with the last item spoken from her list.

"I have plenty of all you seek ma'am," the herbalist replied. "Are you of the trade?" she continued.

"I am, but not from these parts. I wonder do you have any frost moss this far south?" Moona asked.

The young herbalist looked at her sideways and replied, "Never heard of it, but I do have dried creeping vine from the Stone Forest. It is good for the pains of age and helps one, shall we say relax." The woman smiled and Moona returned a broad grin.

"Are you traveling alone then?" asked the herbalist.

Moona turned to her and paused long enough to compose herself before becoming abrupt with the girl. "No, I am traveling with friends who already passed. I will be catching up to them on the road after I collect what I need."

With that last question from the woman, Moona felt it was time to go. She had been conversing far more casually than she ought to considering the circumstances. She paid the herbalist and gathered up her purchases before heading down the road toward the stables.

The herbalist watched after her, occasionally glancing at the silver moons the old woman had just paid her with.

Andra was going toward the stables with Shuran and noticed they were attracting some attention. Andra had been walking past stall after stall, collecting sideways glances from the proprietors. A mysterious figure in a cloak with the hood pulled up and carrying a bundle that was obviously a child, this was precisely the kind of attention that Andra did not want. Andra decided that it was time to appear less conspicuous and lower the hood of the multi-colored cloak, but not before shifting.

"I only hope I have enough energy to make this last." Andra sighed and after a brief shimmer inside the hood of his cloak it was lowered to reveal the features of a young woman. Andra was already feeling the strain of holding this appearance but noticed that the onlookers seemed more at ease with the presence of this new woman carrying a baby.

Andra continued down the main street toward the stables. Once at the stables Andra inquired about the purchases with the stable master who was more than eager to strike a sale since business had been slow.

"I have plenty of good stock young woman, let me show you around and see what you think," the master started. "Do you want horses for speed or endurance, one must choose best based on how quickly or how far they have to travel," he finished.

As Andra started to respond, the disguise began to waiver and Andra's head lowered as a sudden feeling of strength renewed the woman's features he wore. As Andra wondered what had happened, a knowing look came from the sparkling green eyes of Shuran, who had wrapped his tiny hand around one of Andra's fingers. His eyes shifted colors to red then blue and nearly white. Andra suddenly realized where the power was coming from and was awe struck. Not just by the power but that the child knew what needed doing.

"Are you all right dear?" asked the stable master approaching Andra.

"Ah, yes just a bit fatigued from our travels is all," Andra managed.

"Well, no wonder with a young 'un to carry and by the looks only a few moons new to the world," the stable master observed.

It was not until just that moment that Andra noticed the growth Shuran had shown in just a short time since he was birthed. Not exactly sure what to think of it, Andra decided to focus on the task at hand. "Perhaps one sturdy horse and a wagon might be better, along with a pack horse and goats," Andra requested.

"Think I have just the horse and wagon, but maybe a female yak is better than a goat and works both for pack carryin' and given up milk for the young sprat there." After a nod from Andra, the stable master accepted the gold suns as payment and set off to get all other supplies in order.

By the time the stable master had returned, Andra was setting about preparing the wagon and Moona finally waddled her way over.

"Well, breaking the rules with that hood-" Moona started, but was cut short as Andra turned around and she caught her words in surprise. It was Andra's cloak and Shuran in the swaddling, but she saw Sulura's head on the shoulders. "What in the name of Hell's Mouth is goin'-"

Andra signaled for Moona to keep quiet. "I was drawing attention and needed to remove my hood. It would attract more attention if those already weary saw my true self, so I adopted the last face I could remember seeing in this land that would work."

Moona suddenly saw the truth of it and with few apprehensions accepted the explanation… for the time being. "Right then, what is with the wagon?"

"I needed to cover for a mishap, I will explain later. This does seem to work better though and we received a very good price since the trade of horses is slow just now in this region."

Moona looked at Andra or Sulura or whatever the thing was and shook her head. She then turned to a couple of young stable boys running past. "You two, how'd you like to earn yourselves a few coppers?"

The boys eagerly took the coin and ran off to retrieve the various purchases Moona and Andra made earlier in the market.

Upon their return, Moona gave them each another copper to help load everything up and they were soon on their way out of Middleton.

Well, after they were far enough away from the town, Andra replaced the cloak hood and with a shimmer the illusion was gone.

Moona moved up front in the passenger bench, pulled out her pipe, stuffed it with some of the crawler vine she purchased and took a rather large draw before exhaling and addressing Andra. "All-righty then, now that the shock o' seeing the face of a dead woman has left me, what in the name of Damkianna is goin' on?" Moona said.

"I will explain but please keep it down as we are still passing a few travelers heading to town, and Shuran needs to rest," Andra whispered gesturing back into the wagon where Shuran slept upon a makeshift bed of sheepskins.

"Fiddle the travelers, and that boy ain' woke up since we left the stables, which is odd, and why is he so big already?" Moona asked. She had more concern now than her typical irritation.

"I shall start from where we parted ways in the market square." Andra retold the events as they occurred and about Shuran sharing power. It was at this point Moona finally interrupted.

"You mean ta tell me our little sprat back there can what, juice you up or something?" Moona asked.

"Something like that. There are stories about such abilities, but they have not been documented since long ago during the breeding program's final generations, before the Lalli Mah. There is no other explanation I can think of. The transfer is also why he sleeps now as it takes a toll and he must rest to recover. When he awakes, he will be ravenous."

"What about his growth?" Moona asked.

"It is rather rapid but not unheard of in multi-blood spratlings. I expect it will come and go before tapering off," Andra finished.

Moona just grunted and took another draw from her pipe and smiled. "Good stuff this creepy vine, or whatever it's called. You know we ain' discussed where we're headed," Moona said.

"I think it best we head for the eastern settlements or perhaps in the Northern regions," Andra started. "There is no doubt that the Order will be sending out searchers for you. They'll have wanted a witness but not a loose end."

"I hate to disappoint them half-witted goons but this old woman ain' spreadin' the word o' what they did. Folks 'll find out soon 'nough and I don' need to be leavin' no trail for them ta follow," Moona said. "As far as headin' northeast I think I know a good place ta be settlin' in for a while." Moona told Andra of her old cottage in the woodlands outside Birchshire.

Moona had not been to her old home in many years, but assured Andra it would still be there and attended by someone she trusted well enough. Moona had been the local herbalist and potion brewer in Birchshire. She only went when called to Rivenwood to attend some local outbreak and she stayed there for many years and began moon mothering the local women folk. She left for a short time but was called back to attend Sulura.

The people of Birchshire were a friendly enough bunch and most kin stayed put and settled new farms or found a trade in the town so everyone knew everyone else, as well as their business. Moona gathered she could figure out a cover for why an old woman would be coming back after all this time toting a swaddled sprat. It would be at least a couple moon turns before she showed up, so she had time to think it all through.

<u>**Chapter Three**</u>

Telalsu walked the streets of Middleton questioning merchants looking for information about an old woman who would have been through within the past cycle. So far his inquiries were amounting to nothing. Most of the people of Middleton kept to themselves and were leery of strangers asking questions. It did not help that Telalsu was a rather imposing and quite frankly, frightening looking man.

His skin was like rice paper, both white and translucent. His coal black spiky hair and black eyes set in a hard angled skull left no question of his allegiance to Chaos. Common folk did not welcome Chaos into their lives so they avoided its followers like plague. The one thing they will not be able to resist is an Inquisitor of the Council.

Once the Inquisitors are sent out, these tight-lipped pheasants will have no choice but to loosen their lips. Telalsu thought to himself. He was about to give up for the present, when a merchant at the far end of the market road caught his eye and then walked behind her wagon. As Telalsu walked behind the herb laden wagon the woman spoke without looking in his eyes.

"An old woman was through these parts not two days ago," the herbalist reported. "She bought various supplies and met up with someone, a younger woman at the stables before leaving town in a wagon. I never saw the young woman myself."

"Is there anything else?" he prodded sensing there was more.

"Yes, the younger woman had a small child maybe a few cycles, no more than a moon old. Also the old woman paid me in silver moons."

Telalsu smiled and handed the woman a small purse of coin, leaving her with a look of shame but stashing the coin without hesitation. He stepped into the shadows of two buildings before disappearing.

A man made his way down an unlit corridor toward a dead end. He reached out and with a wave of his hand the wall slid inward and to the side, stridulously scrapping upon stone floor. As the man moved into the opening the wall slowly slid back into place.

Inside the hidden chamber a luminous orb in the center of the ceiling came to life illuminating every corner of the space. The large room was walled with shelves of ancient looking tomes. At its center was a large stone table covered with various implements and tools used for magical workings and spell craft.

The man's destination was a cluttered desk at the far corner of the room where sat a large basin emitting a bright glow of reddish light. The man walked around to better view the dragon glass bowl filled with a viscous red liquid. Upon the surface of the blood filled vessel was scrawled a message.

Quarry location unknown.
Ancient spell weaving felt.
Tracking to Middleton.
Advise sending out the Inquisitors.

The man scribbled a message down on a piece of vellum and then lit it on fire with a snap of his fingers. Within moments, a little creature appeared from a puff of smoke.

"What is thy orders master?" asked the small imp.

"You will watch for now and report back to me. I must head down to the catacombs and await a visitor."

When Telalsu reappeared, it was within the catacombs of the Essence Academy, school for learning magic of the Essence and center of power for the realm of Aurderia. He waited as patiently as was possible for one of his kind, before his master finally approached from the shadows.

"What news do you have of the boy," the man asked. He remained shrouded in darkness and held his hand up to halt the demon's approach.

Telalsu was unaccustomed to being kept at arms length. For a Telal, being treated with anything less than fear or respect was unbefitting a demon warrior. "You summoned me from the Shadow to do you bidding, yet you keep me on a leash. I followed the old woman and the boy but they were carried away by use of ancient ways. I could have retrieved them had you allowed it."

"You will do nothing more than what I tell you so long as I control you demon." The old man tittered. "It is a shame what happened to your kind, serving at the hands of masters."

Telalsu roiled with anger but could do nothing against the one who summoned him from the depths. "You mock me. You promised to free me once I retrieve and deliver that ceremonial blade to the Order of Chaos and witness the escape of the boy. Now do as you promised."

"I promised you could seek your freedom not that I would give you something that is not mine to give." The old man stepped back in to the shadows. "You will report now to the Order of Chaos and their Assinnu Isten. Do as he instructs from this point but remember who ultimately controls your actions." The old man disappeared leaving the telal alone in the bowels of the Academy, fuming.

Telalsu left to seek out the leader of the Order of Chaos as instructed. In spite of the man's disguised form, he knew who he was and where to find him. He was within the very building Telalsu now stood. When the demon warrior found the Isten, he was with the girl child Salmetu.

"What are you doing here demon?" Assinnu Isten said.

"I have news of the old woman who left the site of the breaking of the Lalli Mah. She heads toward Two Bridges." Telalsu said looking at the girl. He saw recognition in her eyes that unsettled him and backed away.

Isten noticed the demon step back and saw the worry in his face. He could use this demon if his real master did not. "Do not fear of this child demon, she is but a tool for the Order to use, as are you." He moved closer to the demon. "You did well by bringing us that dagger and I did not question where you found it, but I do question who your master is?"

Telalsu looked from Salmetu to Isten. "I am to serve the Order of Chaos."

Isten narrowed his eyes at the demon with suspicion, but he could not pass using such a powerful tool. "Perhaps it was I who called you up from the depths of the Netherworld. Sometimes I forget all the things I have done to bring about this glorious event."

"As you say, master," Telalsu said as he spat out the last word. "What are your orders?"

Isten thought for a moment. "I want you to take the Inquisitors and find the woman and bring her to me. I would very much like to know how it is she came to be involved with moon mothering this child's mother."

"How is that relevant?" Telalsu asked. He watched the Isten carefully.

The Isten turned away before answering. "Your's is not to question demon. Your's is to do as ordered. Now go."

When the telal left, the leader of the Order went back to watching the girl in the basket he carried away from the ceremony to break the balance of magic. He watched as the darkness flowed across her eyes and settled back inside her growing body. The eyes that were once green were now speckled with red that would soon overtake her iris. "We have much to do my sweet, and through you I shall have all the power I ever desired."

Chapter Four

It was a good four days trip until they would reach Two Bridges, so Moona decided to make use of the time. "So Andra, I be assumin' you guardians are a secretive lot and all, but what can you tell me of the Foresworn and what is going on now?" Moona finally spoke up after they had traveled well out of Middleton and were on the road toward Two Bridges.

"I will tell you what is important and only what I can," Andra sighed. He was being guarded and secretive due to his position with the Guardians, but he was growing fond of the feisty old woman. And he was enjoying the presence of the child. He looked down at the sleeping bundle in his arms and smiled beneath his hood.

Andra began retelling the events that happened when the first group of hunted mixed-bloods formed and made their escape from persecution. When the Anzillu trials were well under way, a large group of mix-bloods who later called themselves the Foresworn, decided to leave the lands of Aurderia and held secret meetings to figure out where to go.

"""

After many visions by seers and expeditions, the group heard tell of lands far beyond the Great Sea they later called the Foresworn Territories. These lands were on no known map as no one had ever been there or ever returned from searching for land beyond the seas. No one had ever spoken of doing so, that is. Through far-seeing and other magic weaving the Foresworn were able to locate these lands and used a great magic and much energy to move the first group of refugees to their new home.

Over the next hundred years, a secret group from the Foresworn took to traveling back to Aurderia seeking others who wished to escape. This group would send those back to the Foresworn territories by way of rough and perilous route over the Orenthal Mountains and around the Northern most point of the Great Sea. A few other routes had been found over the millennia, however, but none was without risk.

Using magics and the Essence was far riskier without enough power and most who tried did not make it. For that far of a trip back then, it took a large group of great power to work such a travel spell. This was long before the creation of source stones, abnu emuq. When this group finally found and assisted all those they could easily find, they formed the Guardians. Guardians travel throughout Aurderia and help the Foresworn and their offspring, wearing multi-colored cloaks to represent the mixed-blood.

"You said Foresworn or their offspring, aren' they all offspring?" Moona asked.

"Many of the first Foresworn may still be alive," Andra answered.

Moona nearly choked on her pipe. "The first ANZILLU happened many millennia ago." She looked at Andra in wonder.

Andra understood her look of surprise. "I am offspring and not from the original to flee. I was birthed in the long after the first exodus."

The rest of the journey toward Two Bridges passed without incident. Andra and Moona took turns driving the wagon along with the various tasks involved with stopping to rest the animals and to look after Shuran. Andra told Moona all that the Guardian knew of Shuran and the prophecy, which was no more than Moona already knew from Sulura's visions except there being a third child.

In the four days it took them to reach Two Bridges, Shuran had grown more to appear the age of a sprat-ling of at least six moons. He slept less, and all of his attention spent with watching Andra as though he were studying the Guardian.

Two Bridges was a small trading town situated between two river crossings where the Napalkua River forked off toward Academy Lake to the East and New Draven to the South. The Town is sparsely settled as it was mostly inns, taverns, shops, and rented market stalls. Although there could be hundreds of people in town at any given time, most were travelers and traders who came and went throughout the market seasons.

The full time artisans, innkeepers, and tavern owners and their workers and apprentices made up only a small part of the population. The town was laid out in a grid system of cobbled roads running East-West with a few North-South streets and dirt alleyways. Two Bridges was relatively safe due to the proximity to the Capital New Draven, and the city soldiers were men of the Aurderian Guard.

The Aurderian Guard, or Lands Guard as they were commonly referred to, were responsible for maintaining order in larger cities throughout the Aurderian Baronies during times of peace. During times of war, the Guards returned to the ranks of the Protectors of the Realm and local order became a matter for each city to manage like the smaller towns and settlements. Even though cities had a magistrate like all other towns, the position was mostly for show and held no actual power to make law, only enforce the edicts of the Great Council.

Just before arriving at the first bridge that headed over to the town proper, Andra shifted appearance to resemble Sulura once again. Days earlier Andra and Moona agreed that to stow the conspicuous multi-colored cloak of a Guardian for a simple grey cloak would help keep up their facade. So the three made their way into Two Bridges with wagon and Yak in tow.

Four days on the Barron Road took its toll on their meager supplies. They needed to restock dried meats, vegetables, fruits, nuts, and anything else they could find, but only enough for the five-day trip to Dravenport. Once at Dravenport the plan was to sell the wagon and animals then barter travel by ship to the coast east of Birchshire.

When they finally entered the town, Moona and Andra left the wagon and animals at the nearest stables for tending and headed into the square. They decided to stop and check an inn named the Barking Troll for some fresh hot food and cold drink before re-supplying. They entered the nearby inn since it looked clean, and were then seated and served tankards of cider and bread while the server went to the kitchens to get them plates of food and fresh milk for Shuran.

Moona took the time to light her pipe and relax on the padded bench. They spent an hour in the inn delighting in fresh food and drink before paying and heading out to the market. As they went to the door, Andra stopped and turned around quickly, near knocking Moona to the floor.

"What in the… what's gotten into you?" Moona asked.

"Inquisitors!"

In through the door walked a thin and ancient looking man robed in grey with a bright red and gold treaded emblem embroidered on the chest. It was a Griffin in flight clutching a bundle of thatch in its claws. This was the official seal of the Aurderian Great Council. At his sides stood armored men with the same seal embezzled on their shields, the Land's Guard.

Moona's face flushed white when the word 'Inquisitors' finally registered in her overly relaxed mind. "Oh fiddle me, we need to move our rumps outta' here!" she whispered, eyes wide with fear.

She grabbed Andra by the wrist and whirled around, heading to the back of the common room they previously supped in. Located in the back was a draped off area Moona had noticed men and serving wenches entering and leaving earlier. Without ceremony she pushed Andra, carrying Shuran, beyond the skins partitioning the room and followed behind.

Shuran chose then as the first time he cried. Moona rushed over, took him in her arms and began rocking and shushing, trying to quite him.

"What witless wench has brought a squallerin' sprat in here to disturb our gaming?" a squat old man yelled from a table at the far end of what must have been a betting parlor. The man got up to approach the new arrivals, and source of his consternation.

Just then Moona rounded on the man without skipping a beat pushing Shuran into his arms she said, "Clap your trap Codger, we got trouble comin' with a capital C-H-A-O-S!"

Shuran immediately quieted in Codger's arms while studying the man's wrinkled old face and smiled.

"He likes me," Old Codger said.

"He like more to have passed wind, ya old fool," Moona said before making her way back to the skin-covered doorway where Andra was watching the common room.

"It would appear that Shuran's crying went unheard over the noise of the people supping and conversing," Andra said. The noise had already started dropping as the room's inhabitants began noticing the ominous presence of the Inquisitor and his escort. "We need a distraction."

Without missing a beat, Moona reached into her many folds of clothing and began rummaging around for something.

"Oh no you don' you squalid old harpy!" Codger cried. "I have a thinkin' what you got under them rags you call clothes and I'm haven' none of it in the presence of a defenseless sprat. You'll like to start a stampede outta' this place."

"Rubbish you ol' fool, you got any better ideas, then spit 'em outta that toothless mouth o' yours!" Moona retorted.

After a brief pause Codger grabbed a passing woman's wrist, "We need to be borrowin' your apron there missy," Codger requested of the bar wench. "What you got on under them rags Moony my dear?" Codger grinned back at her with a devious and toothless smile.

Andra exited the back of the Barking Troll, heading for the stables to gather their meager belongings and sell the wagon and animals. Andra thought it best that they not leave town with the same wagon they arrived, in hope that they might throw the Inquisitors off their trail.

The price was not fair since the stable man could tell that something was amiss, but the deal was done in short order. Andra then headed for the far Eastern area of town placing the Shielding Gem upon Shuran so that he may power the cloaking spell within the stone.

The plan was to all meet there where they would make for someplace on the coast. Old Codger said he had a boat anchored a few turns ride out of town.

The Inquisitor was heading for the back of the Barking Troll common room when a commotion within burst through the skins.

"OUI! You come back here ya sassy little troll of a wench! I'll be havin' that kiss ya promised!" Codger yowled, chasing the now painted up and costumed Moona out of the back room.

"Oh you rapscallions ol' fart!" Moona bellowed, playing along. They made game of chasing around the common room and past the guards out the front doors of the inn.

"I've seen everything now," said one guard to the other. "I hope I'm that frisky when I'm all shriveled like a sun dried briar fruit."

The Inquisitor returned from checking the back room. "Nothing, we need to move on. There are more of these hovels to check before day's end," he snarled as they made their own exit.

"Our things will be waiting for us down by my wagon when we get there," Codger said as he and Moona made haste to their destination.

"How can you be sure?" Moona asked doubtfully.

"Cus I trust the boy I sent on ahead afore we left, and I trust his want for the silver I promised when we get there," he replied between labored breaths. "You still got it Moony I have to hand it to ya."

"I'll be thankin' you to keep your hands ta yourself and shut it until we get where we need gettin'. Then I'll be havin' words with you," she promised, glaring at him with daggers in her eyes.

Old Codger started to say something and thought better of it. Quietly and as quickly as both their stumpy old legs could waddle them along, they made their way to the far end of town.

Moona and Codger arrived at his wagon behind a smithy. Moona had to admit that it was as good a location to meet, as the prying eyes of travelers and guards were far enough to the North near the main roadway.

Their little escapade had taken them across the East bridge to the few outer buildings and shops that did business beyond the central market. It was obvious by the fact that the wagon was prepared and the horses were already hitched, that Codger's young friend already made it to the wagons.

"Hey-ho Old Codger, I see you and the Misses made it ok," said the young boy with a grin that somehow seemed wider than his face.

"We made it just fine young man and I ain' his 'MISSES'!" Moona corrected.

"Well, now Moony dear that ain' all true," Codger retorted.

"Never mind that, where are my clothes lad?" Moona changed the subject.

"The name is Mallik, but friends call me Mally. Your things are already in the wagon Ma'am," Mallick replied. He bowed slightly after introducing himself and flourished his arms dramatically as he stood straight.

"Well, my thanks Mally for your help and here is that silver I promised along with a little extra. Now you should get back to town afore you're missed," Codger said handing a small pouch of coin over to Mallick.

"Keep your coin Codge I am comin' with ya," Mallick said before dropping his jaw in shock as Andra appeared out of thin air.

"I would say that there is no time to waste. You must all leave at once," Andra said handing Shuran over to Codger.

"What do mean? Ain' you comin' with us 'GUARDIAN'?" Moona asked.

Andra took hold of Moona's hand and slowly turned it over, placing the shielding gem in her palm. "The best way I can guard for now is through misguidance." Andra quickly shimmered out of the form of Sulura to that of Moona.

"And I thought one o' you was dreadfully difficult to manage," Codger croaked while taking his seat on the wagon.

"Shut it!" Both Moonas said in unison. With a brief and forced smile Moona nodded to Andra and climbed upon the wagon next to Mallick holding Shuran.

"Come see us when you can. You know where to find us," Moona called as the wagon pulled away and into the forested area to the East.

The Moona impostor made her way back through town making stops at various shops, inns, and taverns, making certain she was seen by purposely drawing attention. She found her efforts were finally paying off as several guards had come out of the places she had been and were closing in on her general vicinity.

When enough guards had begun pursuit and the Inquisitor drew near enough, she came stumbling out of her hiding spot in a nearby alley to allow being seen by them. She then darted down the alley with the guards in pursuit. The guards rounded the corner to find the that old woman had escaped and left a young boy knocked over near a doorway.

The young man, looking much like Mallick rubbed his bumps and bruises while pointing further down another alley. Once the guards left to trail their quarry. The young man stood, unhurt and walked away in the opposite direction.

Andra had kept this charade up for a few days before the Inquisitor grew suspicious enough to call off the search. It was then that Telalsu arrived in the city. Now Andra understood more of what was at stake when he recognized the one who had started this chase back in the Stone Forest.

A Telal, Demon warrior, this does not bode well Andra thought. But who is the master that called you from the depths of the Netherworld. It was past time for Andra to report back to Nabusa so he made his way back tot he Foresworn Territories.

Chapter Five

Moona, Shuran, Codger, and now Mallick, were headed toward the eastern coast by way of roads long forgotten and known by very few. According to Codger, these old trails were once highly traveled routes for trade within the old kingdom before the first time Chaos was let loose upon the lands.

The ancient Telukukal or First People, as they are commonly referred, once ruled these lands in peace and prosperity for thousands of years. They had magnificent control over all the seven powers of Essence and created the most spectacular structures using ore, stone, minerals, glass, and wood.

"There is little known proof they even existed," Codger told Mallick as they travelled along. "The only remaining history is in ancient tomes, spell books, and journals; most of which have been destroyed by the followers of the dark, or hidden away." Codger explained how he had seen some of these books.

They travelled a good distance out of town on the old roads and far north past the Essence Academy that sat on an island in the middle of a large lake. The sun, Utu was beginning to set ahead of them so it was less than likely anyone would spot them from behind at any distance.

It was well past the setting of the Utu, when the group finally entered into the forested land between Academy Lake and the East Coast. They stopped for the night in a small clearing off the old trail and made camp.

Shuran was fast asleep in the wagon after taking the skin of goat's milk that Codger had though to instruct Mallick to supply. As Mallick set about gathering kindling and branches for a fire, Moona sat on a large rock and pulled out her pipe.

"Time to spill Codge, what were ya even doing in Two Bridges and away from my cabin?" Moona demanded.

"A summons for sanctioning by that blasted Council brought me to New Draven," he responded. "Seems that since all of Aurderia has gone wibbly, they been calling in all the spellers, asipus, weavers and the like for re-registering and some been gettin' revoked or taken away someplace. Tis a fine mess the land is in Moony."

Moona just continued to stoke her pipe taking in what Codger was telling her.

Finally, Old Codger turned to her and asked, "What is this all about Moony? You turn up out o' the blue, carrying a sprat and bein' chased by Land's Guard and Inquisitors no less?"

"It's the prophecy Codge, or part of one, Shuran is involved and the Lalli Mah was broken," Moona began to sniffle.

Codger knew Moony's moods and this was not like her. He just sat and listened while she told her story and spat out her troubles.

"What is the Lalli Mah?" Mallick asked. While they were talking, neither Moona nor Codge noticed Mallick had returned and setup a fire ring of stones, placed the wood and brought out things to make supper.

"Oh fiddle!" Moona started and composed herself. "It is or was rather, the great balance of Essence. A magical weaving of powers was done millennia ago to put the powers of dark and light in balance. Don' they teach you sprats nothin' anymore?" she said.

"Not if it's 'bout magics. Them snoots at the Academy don' even allow folks to apply that ain' got family with sanction," Mallick said. "My folks both died a few years ago of I don' know what, and I ain' got any other family I know of. So I couldn' go to that school. I been too busy lookin' after myself to bother with mundane teachin'," Mallick finished.

"Do ya even have the gift boy?" Moona asked.

Mallick just looked at her sideways and pushed his hand toward the wood setup for the fire. He whispered 'BIL' to himself then smoke and flame grew from the pile in the fire ring as the kindling caught.

"Guess that would be a yes," Codger smiled.

The four travelers broke camp and set out the next morning before dawn. It would be two days through the forested hills in part because of the growth, but also that this long forgotten path was only known to few and not traveled enough to keep it clear.

To those who knew the way it was called the Smuggler's Passage. The name came from the fact that the way led directly to a secret keep in a cove hidden from the sea by the Serpent's Fangs, a vast outcropping of non-navigable rocks and spires thrust up from the seafloor.

The waters were not completely unnavigable, to those who knew the safe way through. Codger explained to Moona and Mally that there was an ancient fort on the shores of the cove where those who wished to keep their business private found safe harbor and passage, for a fee to the guild running Smuggler's Keep of course.

Codger went on to explain how the guild allowed travelers to dock and would hold their boat in keeping until such time as the owners returned to retrieve it. Payment for secrecy depended on what one smuggled in or out of the cove. So long as an agreement was made then total secrecy was adhered to on punishment of death.

The trip to Smuggler's Keep was uneventful. It was apparent that whatever Andra was up to, had been working to keep the Land's Guard and Inquisitors off their trail. It also helped that the Inquisitors were likely still looking for an old woman alone. Moona was unaware that they had been told of her being seen with a younger woman, sprat in arms.

During the trip Codger shared knowledge and spell words with Mally helping him find out just what he could do. He became better at producing fire on command and making small objects move by focusing on them and where he wanted them to go, then whispering the spell word. By the time they reached Smuggler's Keep, Mally had already become quite good and proved a fast learner.

Mally also had taken to Shuran and vice versa. In just the few days Mally became like a big brother, or sheesh, to Shuran and took to making himself responsible for his care. Shuran had also taken to wanting Mally carrying and feeding him as well.

Shuran grew even more in the few days since they left Two Bridges. His growth forced them to stop many times to hunt for game and wild vegetables to supplement the food they had since Shuran was now constantly eating and was the size of a two harvest old sprat. He was already walking and mimicking other's words.

Smuggler's Keep came into view late the third day of travel. Codger had to point it out to Moona and Mally as the keep was an ancient ruin situated among the cliffs that surround Smuggler's Cove. People never settled this area since long before the Lalli Mah.

It is believed this was once a settlement of the ancient Telukukal, and superstition had kept most away. The fact that the cove was both protected and blocked by the insidious Serpent's Fangs just added to the stories about the place being cursed.

Codger and the others approached the keep as the Sun was setting over the Great Sea and the last rays of light pierced through the Fangs, casting eerie light and shadows upon the keep and surrounding cliffs. As they neared a stone structure that appeared to be the stables and carriage house, a small group of men came out of the shadows to greet them.

"Who approaches?" A raspy voice called from the group of men still standing in the shadows.

"Old Codger. I've got a vessel here, and me and my folk intend to pack up and head out at Aknard's leave," Codger replied.

At the mention of Aknard's name, the group separated to allow passage to the piers and causeway to the guild's toll office.

"Old Codger!" bellowed Aknard as he walked the causeway down to greet the newly arrived wagon.

"Aknard by friend, how goes business since last I left?" Codger inquired in an overly friendly voice.

"Been lot's of folk arrivin' lookin' for passage seems times are gettin' desperate in New Draven and the area, for folks to brave this cursed

36

place," Aknard answered with a question in both his tone and face.

Aknard was a dwarf, full-blooded; once a prominent member of a leading clan in the Orenthal Mountains. The details of why he chose to leave the mountains and live among the humans he did not share.

"Turmoil has landed upon Aurderia my friend. Has the news of the breaking of Lalli Mah not reached you?" Codger asked.

"Oh, it has, but is just now confirmed. How bad is it?" he asked Codger.

"It is just beginning, but let us talk more in privy while my friends here get settled on my vessel," Codger said while tossing a bag of coin to a nearby shore-man and motioned for Moona and the others to head to the boat.

Moona gave a sizable portion of her coin to some of the shore-men to provision the ship with enough food for a full cycle of travel.

Aknard sat behind his desk and motioned for Old Codger to take a seat across from him. "Codge, you know I have no love for the Order, but they pay well for information," Aknard stated, making his point clear. "Why just days ago a man, or something masquerading as one, come 'round asking about an old woman traveling with a younger one carrying a new sprat," Aknard implied his suspicions.

"That be my Moony with me and our young charges, both too old to be a new sprat!" Codger said. Aknard was starting to irritate him. Though they had been friends for many years, Codger knew that Aknard's loyalty was to profit.

"Let's not mince here Codge. We have been friends for a long time, but I got a business to run here."

"What do you want pirate," Codger asked.

"I had me a look see at your fine vessel while you were gone," Aknard smirked. "No I don' be wantin' your boat friend, just the plans and purpose of the odd gear works you have workin' it."

After what seemed like half a turn, Codger cast his eyes down and replied. "Come aboard with me and you'll have what you asked for," Codger said.

Aknard responded by showing a toothy grin.

Codger's boat was a decent sized vessel. The outward appearance was that of any normal passenger and cargo ship. What was special about this ship was in how it operated.

Already onboard, Moona and Mally walked about the ship with curiosity, wondering what they were looking at. They found themselves in the pilot deck staring at the vast array of levers, gears, and wheels all made of a strong but light metal alloy. They were still there when Codger arrived with Aknard following close behind.

"Ah, good you are here. That keeps me from having to explain all this twice," Codger stated.

"I see you been busy with your tinkerin' while I been gone Codge," Moona said.

"This," Codger said gesturing to the pilot controls, "is a design based on ancient writings and diagrams I discovered some time ago. It is a working of gears and pulleys that power a paddle system." Codger went on to describe how all the workings fit together and both moved and steered the vessel at different speeds. The fuel source was a furnace that used heated water vapors to drive the entire system. As he described everything, Aknard and the others could not help but stare in astonishment at this marvel of creation.

"Where on Ersetu did you find a design for such a wonder?" Aknard asked. "Not even the most skilled of dwarves could have even dreamed of such a thing!" He held his tongue, but his expression showed that he saw ancient dwarven influence in the designs.

"Where I found it is of no consequence," Codger answered. Codger reached below a panel of gears and from within a hidden chamber produced a rolled parchment. He handed the parchment to Aknard. "Here is all you need to reproduce what I have done here." Reluctantly, Codger handed his drawings over to Aknard, who took them gladly and left the ship.

The Shore-men untied Codger's ship the Melammu Nanna, and then pushed them off from the dock. Codger opened the vapor vents from the already burning furnace and set the paddles in motion. Slowly and carefully the Melammu Nanna made its way out of the cove and into the Fangs.

Navigating the Fangs is a dangerous proposition at best. The jagged rocks and spires above the waves are bad enough, below the waves there are just as many dangers from more rocks that can tear a ship apart. Only one way through the Fangs is safe for a vessel of any size greater than a rower or raft. Codger is one of the few outside the smuggler's guild that knows the way through, only due to his old friendship with Aknard.

The going was slow but steady. Moona was amazed by the ease with which Old Codger navigated the vicious fangs edging closer to the mouth and safe waters. She remembered one of the many reasons she married the man so many years ago.

Mally was mesmerized but the whizzing and whirring of the many gears. More than once Codger had to pull him clear so he would not get burned by a burst of steam blasting from the pipes.

Shuran was giggling and taking turns being passed between the three of them to find the best view of all that was going on. The spinning of gears and whirring of steam from pipes, kept Shuran entertained.

After an hour of navigation, Codger finally eased the ship beyond the last spires and outcroppings.

<u>**Chapter Six**</u>

The ground shifted in protest as the battle between light and dark twisted within the Essence of magic deep in the heart of Ersetu.

Nabusa, the seer and leader of the mixed-blood outcasts of the planet Ersetu, replayed the vision from the Sumerian Gods. "I need a messenger from the Guardians, attendant. The miraculous children of the prophecy have been born," she said. While her attendant left to find a member of the shape-shifting Guardians, Nabusa steadied her body against the tremors that continued to shake the foundations of the world in greater frequency as the balance of magic shifted toward the darkness.

The patchwork multi-colored cloak of the man who entered Nabusa's chamber was the signature of the Guardians. His kind were among the outcasts of beings on Ersetu, who were not of pure bloodlines and the cloak reminded them of why they roamed the realms seeking to aid others who faced persecution. "I have come as you requested Nabusa, you have a message for me?" the Guardian asked.

"Andra, I had hoped you had returned to us here in the Foresworn Territories. Yes, I have a need for you to carry the message of hope in your travels." Nabusa beckoned Andra closer.

"How did you know it was I that answered your call as I only returned this day? Your eyes are yet clouded from your visions?" Andra kept his distance from the ancient woman.

Nabusa smiled as her gaze penetrated Andra and looked into his soul. "I do not need eyes to see who you are my child. You are meant to carry this message as it was gifted to me." Nabusa retold her vision to the Guardian Andra so he might take her words and instructions to the far lands of the East in the realm known as Aurderia.

"Much is happening, my child. The prophecy of the balance has begun and all of Ersetu will witness the presence of the twin stars in the heavens. These children will be the catalyst that brings the battle for the Essence to the surface of Ersetu. One child will be taken by the darkness and another to the light, that is what I always said. Now my vision and the prophecy have begun." A dark expression fell across her face. She wanted something relating to the prophecy and these children.

Andra listened to her message but watched her closely. "What are your instructions?"

"You must keep the boy child safe. Know that the Order of Chaos would sacrifice him to their dark lord. More I have not yet been gifted with foreseeing. Go now and see after the child." Nabusa's eyes cleared as she watched Andra leave her chambers.

The Guardian took his leave of Nabusa as the attendant stepped forward to bring food and drink to his leader.

"Is there anything more you need before I return to the Air Essence wielders city in the Highlands Nabusa?" The attendant set the tray down and gathered his traveling pack. He knew there was more to the vision that Nabusa was given and was waiting for instructions of his own. "Can you trust this Andra to do as he was told?"

Nabusa tittered at the man's doubt. "Kettanu, I trust that Andra will do as I have told him. I suspect he has his own agenda, but that will not interfere with my own. Go back to the Lil'Du people in Aluanu. There you will wait until the boy child will one day arrive seeking assistance from the people of the winds."

"I may never live to see the passing of so many millennia as you

Nabusa, but will I ever see the day when those of mixed-blood and talents with the seven powers of Essence take their rightful place above out inferiors?" Kettanu asked.

"One day my child, you shall see a time when your people will replace the ancient gods themselves," Nabusa answered. "I shall soon have what I need to fix the mistake I made when first I gathered the so-called impure and abominations to this land and attempted to fix them. One day the only anzillu will be those who do not have all the blood of the seven races of man flowing through their veins." Nabusa sat straight and crackled with power at her own words.

"What of the Kashshaptu in the Mist Swamps, surely their own seers will have had a vision of the prophecy?" Kettanu asked. He stepped back from Nabusa, seeing the look of menace that crossed her face.

Nabusa laughed, but her stare at Kettanu told him she was not amused. "Those weak-minded witches may scry all they wish, but they will never have a full vision afforded someone of my age and power. I have a friend among them and shall share with her what I see fit to reveal." Nabusa dismissed her agent as she approached a large basin in the center of her chamber. She retrieved a dagger from her table and pierced her thumb. A single drop of blood fell from her extended hand and created a ripple across the viscous fluid of the basin.

Nabusa's own reflection soon became replaced by something that resembled a cadaver well into rot and decay. "What news do you have for the sisters of the swamp Nabusa?" she asked.

"I have had another vision my sister. The demon warrior who claimed the Mi-Ib dagger was successful in persuading the Order of Chaos to use its power. The darkness has received its tribute and soon the Shadow will surface." Nabusa told the grotesque witch. "The demon is now working with the Order and will want the return of its real masters."

"Can we trust this cursed body snatcher?" the kashshaptu asked. "We are not sure of who controls him?"

"It matters not, it is likely the untrained asipu that called him from the Shadow did not protect himself and now the demon has taken his body. All that is required of the vile thing was to take that blade and share my words with the Order of Chaos. He did not share the origin of the message and for a Telal, the promise of freedom within a corporeal body is all the motivation we need to assure our interests are secure."

The witch glared back at Nabusa. "And how does any of this serve the interests of the kashshaptu? We have suffered the curse that keeps us in this swamp for long enough."

Nabusa lost her temper and reached through the liquid to grab the witch. "You placed yourselves in that swamp by your own deeds and getting caught."

The witch struggled to free herself from the ghostly hand that reached out from her scrying mirror and grasped her throat. "You said-"

Nabusa released the witch and retrieved her hand. "I know what I said." She sat back down and collected herself. "When the time comes, you will suggest to your Grand Kashshaptu that there is something the new Priestess can offer in the way of breaking your curse. You will offer to go retrieve a sample of her blood."

The witch hissed in shock. "You know we can not leave the swamp for long and to travel that far-"

"You will go or you will not, the choice is yours. Do not contact me again." Nabusa moved away from the scrying dish and pour herself a glass of wine. She knew that the witch leaving the swamp for such a length of time would likely kill her. It mattered little to Nabusa if a loose end took care of itself. A satisfied smile crossed her aged face as she sipped from her goblet.

Chapter Seven

The Great Sea was a vast body of water that stretched over one thousand leagues from the southern parts of Aurderia to well into the Frozen North beyond the Orenthal Mountains. The strong winds out of the West along with the strong currents made travel difficult heading north and impossible to the West. The warm waters from the South Sea mixed with the frigid currents from the Frozen North. The fast currents that resulted made travel from the North fast, but the same could not be said for the opposite direction. Their journey would normally take a normal ship two cycles or more to travel by wind and sail to the coast outside Birchshire.

The Melammu Nanna, however, did not use sails alone. The gear works and paddle system Codger had re-discovered allowed the vessel to counter the strong currents and added to the wind in her sails; journey time would be cut in half. The trip would not be without obstacles as they first had to get past the wildly unpredictable waters north of the Fangs. The way the coastline hooked to the West joined by the layout of the Fangs, the currents, and undertow of that area, caused whirlpools to form in unpredictable areas and times.

Forty leagues beyond the Fangs, Codger steered his ship in as close as he dared to the coast where the waters churned the least. Everyone except Shuran were on edge and listened intently for the telltale gurgling and sucking sound that accompanied a whirlpool. The churning waters made seeing the danger impossible until it was too late.

It appeared to Codger that they were to have a clear passing of the dangerous area and be saved from the fate of being pulled to a watery grave. His relief suddenly turned to terror, however, as a sudden sound on the edge of his hearing made his stomach sink to his feet.

The ship began to lurch and list to port. The sudden shift in the vessel brought with it a cacophony of sounds. The ship was groaning under stress. The paddles were slapping at the water in vain as the aft of the ship was lifting up out of the water, and Moona was screeching, and Shuran was giggling wildly.

Moona was doing her screaming while running to tie things down.

Mally was securing Shuran while holding on to the mast with all the strength he had in the one available arm.

Codger stood grunting in the pilot deck, white-knuckled hands gripping the helm.

As the aft of the ship began to spin starboard, the stern began angling to stare deep into the eye of the mother of all whirlpools.

Codger struggled to hold the helm. He let loose with one hand in order to reach for his belt and loose it from his waist. He tied one end with his free hand to the helm than with both hands he stretched the belt up to the control boards and tied the other end to a pipe. While trying to hold up his now sagging pants, he wiggled his way to the back of the deck to locate another secret compartment from which he produced an oblong crystal of quartz minerals. He struggled back to the control panel and reached out with the crystal in an attempt to affix it to a similarly shaped indented section. Several times the rocking of the ship threatened to knock him about, but he held fast to the pipe work and continued reaching. Just as he was losing hope, a forward lurch of the ship suddenly forced him forward and as he slammed into the controls, the crystal made contact with controls, nestling into the section Codger intended.

Just as suddenly as the shipped had been sent pitching about, the vessel began stabilizing and leveling.

Equal parts relief and confusion washed over Moona and Mally as they looked about them wondering what was happening.

The sea began to drop away below them as they realized the Melammu Nanna was lifting skyward. The sides of the ship that had appeared to only act as decorative wings folded out and down on each side of the ship. With a deliberate stroke, the wings flapped down parallel to the vessel.

Moona, Mally, and Shuran stood wide-eyed at the ship's side looking down directly into the mouth of the vast whirlpool that only moments early tried tirelessly to swallow them into its watery gullet. They looked at one another and then to the pilot deck where they could make out Codger standing at the helm with one hand on a glowing leaver the other on the helm. His pants were a sagging mess around his ankles.

As they made their way back to Codger, the sails filled with wind and were pushing on northeast past the monster whirlpool and into calmer waters.

"Codger?" Moona called. "What in the name of Damkianna is going on?"

Codger just smiled and gradually moved the glowing control crystal forward, thus lowering the ship back to the water. When the ship gently settled back down, he reengaged the paddle system and the Melammu Nanna lurched northward. He removed the crystal shard from its place on the controls and handed it to Moona. "That my dear is the one piece of information I did not share with Aknard. It is the only thing I cannot re-create and could not afford to loose it."

"I can feel its power!" Moona exclaimed as she examined it. Having lost her abilities, being able to sense power in an object meant it was strong and likely ancient.

"It is called 'abnu emuq' in the ancient tongue, a Power Stone," Codger beamed. "I found it with the diagrams I used to fashion this vessel."

As Moona continued to marvel at the shard, Shuran stared at it curiously and reached out toward the crystal. The quartz began to hum and color danced across its surface. Suddenly the stone leaped from Moona's grip and flew into Shuran's waiting hand.

In Shuran's grip, the stone began to hum and pulsate with a dazzling show of lights. The hum was almost musical, as various tones emanated from it in time with the flashing of colorful light. While the light grew in intensity, a glow began to inch its way from the crystal along Shuran's arm. Soon his entire body began to glow and the crystal began dimming in luminosity. In a sudden cry, Shuran released the quartz stone and fell back into Mally's arms.

Moona quickly moved to him trying to make sense of what just happened.

Shuran seemed knocked unconscious. His breathing was steady, but he had a faint glow along his skin.

"He is sleeping!" Moona said.

"What was that?" Codger asked.

"I have a thinkin', check that crystal; my guess is that it has been drained," Moona said.

Codger turned the crystal in his hand, having retrieved it from the deck floor after it was dropped. He nested the crystal in its place upon the control panel. There was no reaction from the shard. The control lever would not move. The crystal was completely drained of energy. "Well, I hope we don' have need 'cause this thing is D-E-D dead!" Codger declared.

"We need ta have plenty o' food ready when the boy wakes," Moona said as she took Shuran below decks to a cot in the sleeping chamber. "No telling how much he is going to grow from the power he absorbed out of that rock!" Moona wondered.

Shuran slept through to late the next morning, nearly a full day.

Moona had been watching him the entire time, when she was not sleeping herself. During his slumber, he grew to the equivalent of a sprat of ten harvests. Moona was just amazed and frightened by this sweet yet powerful boy.

"Up until now I had my doubts this child was the one o' prophecy," Codger told Moona. "But there can be no doubt."

"My belly hurts!" Shuran mumbled as he struggled to wake.

"Don' just stand there, get the boy some food you ol' fart!" Moona smiled at Codger while she said it.

Shuran sat up and smiled as he reached out to hug Moona and told her he was hungry.

She took Shuran topside where codger and Mally were setting about getting a spread set out for them to all break their fast.

Shuran tore into the food on his plate as though he had not eaten in a long time, talking around the food in his mouth. In reality, he had grown several harvests in age in just thirty hours. The power from the stone fueled the growth, but he still needed a large amount of food before he was satisfied. After he had his fill, Shuran ran about the deck pointing to things and inquiring about their name and purpose. He was a sponge soaking up information.

The next few days of travel were spent with Shuran taking in every bit of information he could glean from his caretakers. They taught him about the sea, the ship, and its workings. He took lessons on reading and writing from Codger.

Moona taught him about the herbs she carried and their uses.

Mally did not have a proper education and felt a bit useless with his education. He only played games with Shuran and told him stories. "I wish I could teach him things," Mally said one night to Moona.

Shuran was fast asleep after another long day of non-stop questions and lessons.

"You are teaching him my boy," Codger replied. "Your games teach him strategy and thinking out problems. Your stories, as you tell them, are from your own experiences," Codger continued. "You just keep that up and you'll be teachin' him more than you know."

Mally's spirits were lifted by Codger's encouragement and had suddenly developed an idea in his head.

The next morning Codger and Moona awoke to screaming and the pounding of running feet on the upper deck of the ship. Together they ran in a tangled mess above deck to witness Shuran and Mally pouring buckets of water onto the deck. They approached to find a smoldering smudge mark on the wooden deck and part way up the mast of the main sail.

"What happened here boys?" Codger and Moona asked in unison.

"Um, well you see, Um. I was just t-teaching Shuran stuff I know," Mally stuttered out. "He made a fire," Mally said.

"You taught him to spell fire?" Codger inquired with shock and wonderment.

"Not exactly," Mallick replied. "He never said the words and he did not wave his hands or nothin'. We just started, when I told him to imagine fire in his mind and then WHOOSH! Flames just appeared in front of us and leapt down on the deck from out of nowhere."

"He created fire from thin air not the wood," Moona realized.

"No he didn' create the fire, he called it," Codger marveled. Shuran had used the elemental magic of fire. "That be elemental Essence magic what comes from the blood of the Drakkian race," Codger explained.

Chapter Eight

The Drakkians he further told them were not the fire-breathing flying lizards of myth called dragons. They were, and possibly may still be, a human-like race of people who, through breeding programs, developed a flying beast of burden called the drakkon. It was in actuality, the rider's bond that created the fire ability in the drakkon. An un-bonded drakkon had no known abilities in elemental Essence.

This information sparked more questions from not only Shuran, but Mally as well. Codger now found himself educating them both on all he knew of the seven separate races of Ersetu.

He finished sharing the limited knowledge he had on the Drakkians with how they departed soon after the Lalli Mah. No trace of where most of them went existed. All that anyone knows for certain is that their lands were destroyed in Drakk when Hell's Mouth formed. Few remained in Drakk in the city they left behind known as Drakkfoth.

The Giants were a race that were a stronger, and taller version of humans that kept to a hidden valley that had been lost to time. The giants could control the elemental force of metal and ore. Much of the famed weapons of lore were said to have been Giant made, as their work on ore with Essence made them unbreakable. The weapons were also said to stand against the passage of time that would rust ordinary tools and weapons.

The third of the elusive races is known as Wind Walkers who called themselves the Lil'Du. Codger had even less information on them other than their control over elemental air.

Badur'Lu were people that long ago took to the seas. They live somewhere in massive cities built in the depths. The only written record of them is that their cities are built into seamounts. Badur'Lu are said to control the element of water.

The humans are the youngest of the seven races according to history both written and retold. The stories of where human origins begin differ depending on the storyteller. All accounts though refer to children of the Telukukal.

"It is told that humans were the last evolution o' those left behind when the Telukukal vanished from Ersetu. The significance o' this ain' never been explained and the Great Council banned study of the origins soon after the first anzillu trials of the Sikil Mah." Codger whispered the last words.

"Some humans had the ability to weave spells. Those who showed no talent in the Essence were considered Mundanes. Spell weaving was the art of using words of power to focus thought into existence. This was the raw form of Essence within everything. Where elemental magic manipulates the Essence within inanimate objects and forces, humans can alter their own Essence and move it outside themselves.

"The use of all Essence took a toll on the user, as they need to have energy equal to or greater than the result of their efforts. Many of a weaver destroyed himself or herself attempting spells far beyond the energy they had to draw on. Spell weaving was dangerous when not done in the exact manner required; it must be prepared and practiced until perfected."

For these reasons, Codger made the boys promise not to try more magic without instruction and definitely not on his boat.

The Dwarves on rare occasions could be found in Northern cities trading ore and gems with smithies and jewelers. They had the ability to manipulate elemental earth into their creations, making them stronger and unchanged by the passage of use and time. They live in the Orenthal Mountains deep within caverns both natural and dwarf excavated. The dwarves used earth Essence to build their homes and for extractions of precious gems and ores from the deep earth.

"What about elves?" Mallick asked.

"Elves are also seen on rare occasions when they allow traders into one of their settlements in Tarangale," Codger said. Codger explained how the elves control the element of electricity and can manipulate the electric pulses that run through the body and mind. This ability allows them to influence people's thoughts and movements. Most people are leery about getting fair trades with Elves for fear of being manipulated.

By the time Codger had completed answering a barrage of questions from both boys, the sun was high in the sky and hunger was again knocking on each of their stomachs.

Moona laid a blanket on the floor of the pilot deck and set it with plates of cheese, hard bread, dried fruits, and meat. They were in relatively calm water and sailing against a steady and straight current so Codger was able to continue while letting Shuran and Mally take turns learning to control the helm.

Codger decided he would teach them what he knew of the Telukukal after lunch. "Any actual lessons on reading or speaking the ancient tongue will have to wait until we get home," Codger said. "I can tell you about some history of what I know and perhaps some words I can remember easily enough."

Codger told them of his trip into the ruins of an old Northern outpost built before the Lalli Mah. He found beneath the ruins another structure. The ancient keep had been built on top of an even older ruin. Below the foundation was a labyrinth of halls and rooms. Most rooms contained nothing of value, but it was in one of the rooms he found the remains of a sealed up library and workroom. There he found the information used to build his ship as well as the now dead crystal that powered its flight. He spent months there in the ruins gathering knowledge and copying down what was not destroyed by the ravages of time and the elements. The journals, he told them, were back at the cabin hidden in a special place on the surrounding grounds.

Codger was a sanctioned spell weaver, and a long time ago was an instructor of the art. That was another lifetime, before the Essence Academy was started he recalled and changed the subject. Codger was much older than Moona and therefore lived through more of what led up to the events of the prophecy.

Codger did not speak much of his time lived before Moona came into his life, not even with his wife. Codger continued on, telling the boys about ogres, trolls, imps, and other creates.

Moona grumbled most of the time about being treated like a serving wench and cook. Secretly she enjoyed looking after 'her boys' as she was beginning to think of them.

Over the next few days of their trip up the coast, the boys spent time fishing and helping Codger take care of the boat.

Once in a while, Moona would continue lessons with the boys on herbs and concoctions. Some of the mixtures she made were the foundation of potions. She left out the instructions on how they were to have been activated, telling them that would wait until they were safely back to Birchshire, and her isolated cabin in the woods.

"Mind you I wouldn' object to a laugh we'd get out o' Old Codger there throwing a fiddle fit over magic working on the boat," Moona smiled.

The boys continued to absorb every bit of information provided by Codger and Moona. Mallick and Shuran became thick as thieves like an older brother and younger. It was hard for Moona to comprehend how only a few weeks ago she had helped birth this sprat, who was now as old as any of seven harvests. It was as though now only five harvests separated the two boys before her, yet they were not effected by the strangeness of it all.

Late on the last day of travel north, Moona and Codger found themselves alone in the pilot deck for the first time since the journey began.

"It feels like fate has brought us back together for a reason Moony," Codger smiled as he talked. "I know we ain' had the best o' times of late, but maybe we have a second chance with these two lads."

Moona turned to Codger and began jabbing him with her pipe. "Just you get this first in your addled thinker Codge, we ain' on the mends and I ain' 'bout to forget nothing' what happened back then," Moona screeched.

"Why you hard skulled, temper driven, harpy of a wench!" Codger retorted. "I ain' askin' you to forget nothin' nor forgive. Wha's done is done." Their raised voices drew the attention of the boys who were now heading over to the pilot deck.

"Is something wrong?" Mally asked.

"No dear you and Shuran run along and practice your lessons. Just me and Old Coder agreein' not to agree is all." Moona glared at Codger as she turned to follow the boys back out on deck.

"Moona, how long have you and Codger been wed?" Mally asked.

"Oh my, that be a very long time ago. We were married when I was but a woman new, over two hundred and twenty harvests past," Moona replied.

Moona continued telling the boys of how she and Codger met in her twenty-third harvest. Moona had an herb shop in Rivenwood and was working one day when, a then younger, Codger of Dravenport came into her shop looking for particularly rare and dangerous ingredients.

Never one to get involved in another's business, Moona naturally inquired as to why anyone in their proper brain would be looking for such things. She of course butt right into his business and after finally agreeing to acquire what he asked, told him to return in one cycles time. Moona being the self-professed expert in herb work and base mixing set about figuring out what he wanted them for. Moona actually had the requested items in her stock, but being both nosey and smitten had to keep this fine asipu around.

At cycles end, Codger returned to her cluttered shop with high hopes. She gave him the ingredients but told him that if he was looking for it to work it would not. He was after a love potion and she explained that business of the romantic kind could not be created to last. They argued into the late day and before long the spark between them was ignited.

"If you are wed so-o long, then where are your sprats now?" Mally asked.

"We were only ever able to have one sprat, a boy," Moona said blankly. "He was young and handsome, but only mildly talented in the Essence."

"Where is he now?" Inquired Shuran.

Moona stood staring at them for several moments before Codger interrupted.

"He was taken from us before his twentieth harvest." He left no indication that there was anything more to discuss.

Moona quickly changed the subject. "Now boys, we'll be reachin' home by this time on the morrow. There are some things we need ta set down as rules before then," Moona said.

She told them about the need to keep to themselves and not draw attention. "The Land's Guard will be still looking for an old woman and they mustn' be caught weaving or using the Essence. It is against the laws set by the Great Meddlin' Council, to practice without sanction and any under age of fifteen would be taken by the Council for testing and either trained or hobbled as they saw fit."

The boys nodded in agreement with no true understanding of the importance, but listened and intended to obey. The remainder of that day was uneventful and they prepared to arrive in Birchshire the next.

The Melammu Nanna lurched forward as it finally came to rest on the sandy beaches nearest they could get to what was to become their new home, Moona's cabin in the Birchshire woods.

Codger lowered the plank to a rocky outcropping that served as a natural pier, before heading ashore to tie down the ship. The party gathered their belongings and headed off into the woods for the long walk to the cabin. When they arrived, Moona was both excited and shocked by what she saw.

The Cabin looked the same as it had the day she left. There were animals in pens off behind the place and her herb gardens were hearty, if not a bit overgrown. She decided that would be the first thing that needed doing. She entered the cabin to find all her old things exactly where she left them. She systematically began checking every room, every cupboard, and every corner. Not a single thing had changed in over one hundred harvests since last she was here.

"Had friends look after the place anytime I left," Codger simply said.

"Don' think that gets you any special privilege if you catch me!" Moona said as she eyed him suspiciously.

"Smoke your pipe woman! I wouldn' want that wrinkly dried up ol' mess anyhow." Codger grumbled with a half grin as he turned from her and headed out of the cabin.

The next morning Bastien, from the family Codger had looking after the place, showed up to tend the cabin and animals. He was not surprised to find Codger at home since he had been down by the shore earlier in the morning. Bastien was a young boy of the same age Shuran physically developed into. Bastien was a mundane, having no gift for the Essence or it has not yet surfaced. Shuran and Bastien hit it off immediately.

With a look to Moona for approval, he ran off into the woods with Bastien to explore the area. Moona had already told Shuran to remain mindful of other people's business and that included not repeating his own. She did not think to worry though since Codger knew Bastien and the boys would be too busy with mischief to gossip as young ladies of leisure.

Shuran wandered around the forested area touching trees and picking up stones. Bastien and Shuran finally made it around to a rock outcropping that hid a small cave that Bastien recently discovered.

This cave would serve as their private hideout; no old folks allowed.

Shuran wondered at the dance of light against the crystal formations of the rocks inside the cave. This was a wonderful hideout he thought.

The newly formed family of sorts spent the next days getting settled. Moona and Codger grudgingly agreed to share their old room, but Moona insisted on changing the bedding arrangements. She separated the pushed together beds to opposite sides of the space. The boys claimed the other bedroom and went about gathering things to spruce up the room and make it their own sanctuary.

Over the weeks that followed the boys settled into a routine of early morning chores followed by lessons and lunch. Afternoons were spent with more lessons in the herb garden and potion making.

Codger built what he called a buffering ring in the yard some fifty paces from the main house. It was a deep trench dug in a circle around a central area he named the practice ground. He filled the trench with clay and baked it under conjured flame. The trench was then filled with saltwater. Codger explained that the water creates a natural barrier to the use of certain magics and would help keep what they did from being felt outside their new home.

Bastien came by every other afternoon when he finished his own chores at home.

Moona looked on at the boys playing outside and Codger grumbling at them to stay out of the garden half-heartedly. She felt a sudden pit in her stomach knowing for certain their joyful days were limited.

Life carried on and they would all spend the next few years enjoying a family life, while it lasted.

Chapter Nine

Salmetu was growing at an even more alarming rate than Shuran. Since she was taken by the Order of Chaos and elevated to become their Priestess, she was subjected to a multitude of dark spell weavings, potions in her food, and dark artifacts. The changes brought on by these efforts resulted in her maturing physically to that of a sixteen harvest young woman.

Female zealots of the Order were attending Salmetu since she arrived at the secret keep outside the city of Drakkfoth. She frightened most of those who served, educated, and attended to her every need. She had a short temper and could become easily enraged by the simplest of missteps. One thing was always able to calm her.

Her primary caretaker was an older woman who was employed to act as her mother figure. She also had a cat that she was given as a kitten. The old woman and the cat were the only friends she had, and that gave her comfort. She knew her mother died giving birth, but that was all she was being told about that night.

Where Shuran was experiencing growth, however quickly, by a less forced means, Salmetu was being forced into growth by spell work. From the time she was brought to the keep, Salmetu was fed enchanted food. She laid upon a bed carved from dragon glass, and was surrounded by zealots spelling power into her. The combination of these things caused rapid growth. Along with her growth in the body came the growth in her power.

As a toddler she began setting fires to things that would normally not burn, anytime she became upset. Deep fissures formed in floors and walls when she cried out from sleep terrors. Her powers were moving along quickly, but not so much as to please the Assinnu Isten. Something needed doing in order to speed her progress. Incentive he thought as he watched her play with her furry little friend.

The zealots of the Order fed Salmetu lie after lie about the nature of the world in which they lived. The people out in the world wanted to destroy order and discipline they would tell her. They wanted nothing more than to destroy the Order and all the good they perform.

Peace and order are the promises the zealots provide, but the people of Aurderia rebuked their gifts and choose to live under the thumb of the Order of Light, who did nothing to help those in need. She was taught that the worshipers in Britengate gave thanks and reverence to false Gods that did nothing to protect them.

Where the Order of Chaos offered long life, prosperity, and above all, justice, the Order of Light watched as people became sick and died. This she was told was why the Light let her mother die giving birth. The zealots explained how they tried to save her, but were stopped by the Light.

One day in particular Salmetu had a terrible time in her lessons of water. She was unable to force the contents of a large basin full of water to her will. The object of the lesson was to force the water to gather in the center and rise into a column. After several failed attempts where the water would begin to slash about the basin but not answer to her demands, in a fit of frustration and rage she screamed out.

The room burst with steam, and of the four weavers in the room with her, only two thought to shield themselves while she worked. The other two lay on the floor shriveled husks with all the moisture leached out of their bodies.

Later that evening when she was crying into her nursemaid's shoulder she sobbed. "I just wanted all the water to do as I said. I wanted it all in the center of the basin." Salmetu was fragile and still a young minded girl in her older body.

"We must harden the child inside the woman!" demanded Isten when reports of the latest in a long line of mishaps was brought to his attention. Isten was greatly impressed, however, with the manner in which the zealots had been dispatched.

Ideas began forming in his head as a wicked grin spread upon his face. "Setup for a dead rising spell. We shall see how well the girl performs this weaving when she has something to lose."

Shuran was also having a restless night. His dreams were full of scattered and horrifying images. Shuran found himself standing in the middle of a dark room. There were robed figures standing around a raised stone table.

One of the robed figures approached the table and pulled out a sack that wiggled and screamed a screech that sent shivers through Shuran.

The feeling of dread and despair overcame him as he watched the scene through another's eyes. The figure before him was an older man from what he could tell though his vision as it was growing cloudy as if looking through tears. Realization shot through him as the events unfolded in his mind. He heard himself crying out with a woman's voice to stop.

It was too late. The robed man took the animal out of the sack and stabbed it with a dagger.

"Now bring it back to you!" the man ordered.

Deep sadness began to mix with desperation. The feeling of power and life surged through his body and mind until it leapt forth from hands that were not his own and into the dead animal on the table.

Rage boiled on the edges of his disembodied visions. As he looked down at the reanimated cat before him, a realization that it was changed and no longer the same loving creature it had once been stirred more power. Flames erupted from all around and as he reached out to engulf everything in reach with hatred fueled fire, Shuran awoke surrounded with living flame and Mally shouting for help as he used powers to douse the Essence born fire that erupted around Shuran as he slept.

Once the fire was extinguished, and Moona fussed over Shuran, Codger called for all to come to the common area to talk out what had happened.

Shuran explained what he saw in his night visions. "It was so real, like I was there, but only someone else," Shuran sobbed.

Codger began to say something before Moona glared at him and cut him short.

"This may be a vision or simply a bad dream; it is too early to tell," she said. "Have you had others like this dream or vision?"

"I see things sometimes when I sleep but nothing so clear or so real," Shuran answered. "In the dreams I would be working Essence and moving elemental forces. Sometimes other things came in the form of nightmares." Shuran shuddered and did not elaborate.

Moona comforted him, and since no one was able to go back to sleep they all went about starting the day.

"Boys if you would meet me out in the yard I have a task we need doin' today," Codger said seriously. "We must surround the cabin similarly as we did the practice grounds. This will help Shuran sleep should more visions come unwanted," Codger said without further explaining.

The boys just looked on with confused expressions but did as they were instructed. Over several days, they worked at the hard packed rock filled ground.

On the fifth day, Shuran stopped digging and picking with a frustrated grunt. "This will take us 'til next harvest come and gone before we complete our task," he grumbled.

"You know faster methods of digging then please share or get back to it!" Mally replied between breaths while shoveling. "If we have not made progress when Moona and Codger return from town, Moona will give us both a good whack!" Mally said. His expression showed how serious he was about the threat on Moona's wrath.

Mally paused in his labors at a feeling on the edges of his being. He turned to see Shuran kneeling with his hands laid upon the earth, eyes closed, and mumbling to himself.

The ground began to groan beneath them as Shuran stood and lifted his arms. With a sudden burst, the ground surrounding the rest of the cabin rose forth from the edge where they had shoveled. The ringed ditch around the cabin was complete.

Shuran, arms still raised high in the air, gestured and the airborne dirt, rock, and clay moved over them to an area off to the end of the property where they had carted the materials they dug earlier.

Mally stood in awed silence as Shuran stood above the new trench. Without an effort Shuran separated the clay from the ground and brought it forth to a smooth form around the interior. He baked it hard with elemental flame. Next he called forth water from the shores of the Great Sea nearly two thousand paces away. A flowing stream of salty seawater poured into the trench. Another gesture and planks of wood previously cut flew through the air and lay across the trench at evenly placed intervals.

More planks and boards crossed parallel to the supports. Dirt and clay from the pile came up to cover the area smooth and then grasses, and wildflower sprang from the ground and blended in with the surrounding area completely hiding the deep salt water filled trench that lay below.

On the path back from town, Codger stopped his horse abruptly in front of Moona.

"Blast it," Codger shouted.

"What are you about ya ol' fool?" Moona yelled.

"Something has happened couldn' you feel it?" Codger puzzled.

"You know damn well I can' feel nothing since… For a long time now." Moona scowled as she hurried her horse past Codger toward home.

A look of regret and apology came over his face as Codger urged his own steed after her. "Sorry, Moony I just felt something odd. It was not terribly strong so it must have been far away."

"It could have been close as well and you know it Codge! Now move that horses arse and bring the steed with you!"

Mally stood in stunned silence. Only when Shuran fell to the ground did Mally snap back to his wits and run to his side. "Shuran! What is wrong? Talk to me."

"He will not wake for some time I suspect," Codger said, wearing irritation like a mask.

"What is goin' on here!" Moona asked frustration clear in her voice.

"The cabin is completely circled in a ring of salt water. I cannot feel things in the home that I should," Codger replied with a knowing glance at Moona that told her all she needed.

"You headstrong fool of a boy. What were you thinking?" she whispered as she motioned for Mally to carry Shuran into the cabin.

As Shuran slept, the others sat in the small common area supping on bread and rabbit stew with vegetables.

Mally explained the events of the afternoon with excitement and drama.

"Don' be so excited Mally my boy. That was nothin' compared to what that boy is capable of or will be when he comes to full power," Codger spoke.

"What do you mean Codge?" Mally asked, but it was Moona who continued the story.

She spoke of the prophecy and the events that brought them all together. Until the details of the prophecy were all revealed, Mally had just known they were escaping the Inquisitors who were still rounding up Essence wielders. He then knew the truth.

"You must not speak of this now. The time will come but not yet," Moona explained. "The visions he experiences are likely caused at times by a link he shares with his sister who lived." The rest of the meal was eaten in silence, and they all retired early without a word.

<h1 style="text-align:center"><u>Chapter Ten</u></h1>

Indra began Shuran's newest lessons in the Essence back to their origins. "Essence is all around us in everything there is," Andra said.

"I know this already. Why is Mally not taking lessons with me?" Shuran asked.

"Mally has learned much but what I teach you today is only something that you can do because you are different," Andra replied. "You are birthed of seven bloodlines, each of those having the makeup to harness one of the seven powers."

Shuran just looked at Andra blankly before responding. "What I did with the trench, it felt different than the weaving we have been practicing," Shuran said.

Andra smiled with pride. "Yes, you moved earth and water than called fire without using spells. This is dangerous for a weaver but not if the Essence was used to work the elements such as I suspected you did. Tell me what you felt at the time."

"I felt energy... power... life! It was as though I was calling out of need and what I wanted answered. I did not even think, I just acted,"

Shuran remembered.

"Did you hear anything?" Andra asked.

Shuran smiled and looked up at Andra smiling broadly. "I DID! I heard what was like music or singing and voices, but very faint. It was different with each. And the fire danced!"

Andra just smiled and started to explain what was known to the limited knowledge Andra possessed. "Elemental powers seem to respond and act in different ways to those who can communicate with them. Water ripples with musical tones. Earth rumbles and vibrates with deep drum-like beats. Wind whispers. Fire dances and swirls. Electricity buzzes and hums. Essence wielders of the elements must learn to listen and watch all around them and be able to separate the sounds, feelings, and images of nature in order to blend intent into action."

Andra further explained how most have difficulties controlling more than one element and those who can, must do so separately. Shuran seemed a natural for picking out the elements and bending them to his will and doing so seamlessly.

"It was not as though I was forcing the elements. I sort of told them what I wanted and asked the elements to help me." Shuran explained. "I did not even know what I was doing, I just sort of felt that help was there just waiting for the asking."

Andra was not certain how to approach this revelation from Shuran. It was not at all how he would describe things so he was unsure why Shuran would feel the elements differently. Andra decided they would go through lessons on concentration and isolating the different elements.

Before any of these lessons were to begin however, Shuran had to learn his limits and proper channeling of Essence. Up until then Shuran had been weaving spells from lessons that required little energy or concentration. Elemental forces that Shuran had wielded so far had been on instinct and without control, so they exhausted him and he would pass into a deep slumber.

Shuran's first lessons now would revolve around the flow of Essence and controlling it. He also needed to learn how to block it. Andra instructed him first to take the rest of the lessons time for that day to practice sensing the world around him and identify the Essence in everything.

It was not known where the Essence came from or why. There are old tales and stories of the origins. Some say that the Essence was a gift from the Gods when they created Ersetu, while others say that the Essence was stolen from the Gods when the people of Ersetu revolted and destroyed them. It did not matter the when, why, or how. What mattered was that they had it and must use it to survive. Only balance kept the world from tearing apart.

The Lalli Mah was created to forge a permanent balance of the powers of Chaos and Creation. Each bloodline of the seven races of man, had the innate ability to weave a certain aspect of the Essence. Those of mixed blood were often blessed or cursed with the ability to wield multiple gifts. But without balance, wielders of mixed-blood would often fall into madness or darkness.

Some wielders could not handle the power they could harness and ultimately destroyed themselves, while others could only wield to varying degrees of strength. Those who chose to allow themselves to be consumed with power gave in to the Chaos and were labeled abominations.

"There is no good or bad, there is only intent." Andra told Shuran.

"Are there some mixed-bloods that have no gift at all?" Shuran asked.

Andra knew where Shuran was going with his question. "It is rare, but sometimes a mixed-blood will show no gift. Why do you ask?"

"Moona has no gift but she is old beyond the lifespan of a mundane. I sense something missing," Shuran answered.

Andra raised an eyebrow. "That is something all together different, but not my place to speak on," Andra stated, clearly ending the conversation.

Shuran sat in the practice circle identifying the differences in the elements and communicating with them. He closed his eyes and began to meditate on his surroundings. He tried to concentrate on the elements but at first his mind was overwhelmed by everything at once and he lost concentration, falling over stunned.

Andra laughed as he helped Shuran sit up. "Do not open your mind up so wide and free, Shuran. Focus on opening up a little at first then slowly increase your awareness," Andra told him.

Moona had just come out from the garden and decided to sit a while with her pipe and watch Shuran.

As he slowly opened his mind, Shuran began to take in all around him in the practice circle. He reached down into the earth once he attuned to its rhythm. He felt the course dirt and sand mixture of the soil. He could feel the grubs chewing and digging as if they were under his own skin. This disturbed him at first but he regained his composure.

As he moved along through the ground using his connection, he ran into a barrier, which he quickly realized was the water ring dug around the area when they first created the practice ring. He quickly released the vibrations of the earth to join the music of the water in the ring. Once within the ring, Shuran sang along and traced its surface around to where he had started.

Soon Shuran left his song with water to jump into the embrace of the fire burning in the pit before him. He became entranced with the dance of the flame. It was exhilarating. He danced and danced faster and with ferocity that he felt himself growing and getting hotter.

WHACK!

"Ouch! What was that for?" Shuran asked turning to see Moona retreating with a switch in her hand.

"Two reasons I whacked you smart arse! One you were gonna' set this whole wood aflame if you kept it up," Moona said as she turned to walk away.

"You said two, what is the other reason?" Shuran asked.

"Because I could!" Moona smiled. "One thing, that shifty over there forgot to tell you, is if you open yourself up to all around you-" Moona started but was interrupted.

"You need to be able to sense sneaky old wenches creepin' up on you!" Codger finished.

WHACK! Moona cracked Codger across the backside with her switch. "Didn' see that one comin' either did ya old fool?" Moona laughed as she headed back to the cabin smoking on her pipe.

Andra turned back to Shuran with barely a hint of a smile on his borrowed face. "You are tired are you not?" Andra asked.

"Yes, I feel hungry as well, but I can keep going," Shuran insisted.

Andra looked at Shuran and wondered how far he could push himself so soon. "Good, what we will work on now will help how you are feeling I think."

"What do you mean, you think?" Shuran asked.

"I only know of this in theory since I have been unable to do so myself. You however, have already shown the ability to channel Essence when you were but days old."

Andra retold the story to Shuran of how with a touch, Shuran poured Essence into Andra allowing the shifting into Sulura's likeness to hold. "If you can move Essence out of yourself you should be able to take it in."

"From where?" Shuran asked.

"Think back to what I have already told you." Andra looked around them.

Shuran thought for a moment before smiling and looking up to Andra. "The Essence is in everything."

Andra nodded but then gave a look of great concern. "You must learn to take only what is safe. I will help you to understand."

Andra brought Shuran over to a large tree near the end of the circle. "I want you to focus on this tree. Feel the Essence within and draw it into yourself."

Shuran placed his hand upon the tree. He felt the smooth white bark beneath his fingers. Shuran stretched out his senses and located the tree's Essence immediately.

"Do you have it?" Andra asked.

Shuran nodded without taking his attention off of the Essence he now held with his will.

"Good now I want you to pull on it and draw it within yourself. It is said to feel as though you are consuming it."

Shuran tried to act as though he was feasting on the Essence, but it did not respond, but actually struggled to break free. Shuran fought back to hold onto the Essence of the mighty Birch tree. During his struggle, he barely noticed his own Essence moving out from his center and pushing toward the tree.

With a sudden jolt Shuran's Eyes opened and his head lifted up. He pulled the tree into himself. He fed on the Essence and savored the energy as it flowed effortlessly from the tree into himself. Shuran was consumed by the feeling of taking in that energy. He did not notice the bark of the tree shrinking and cracking below his touch. He did not hear the tree screaming in his head for freedom from the torture it was being subjected to.

Suddenly the tree cried out so loud that Shuran could not help but notice. It was too late. Shuran fell back in shock. Before him, stood the withered and dried up remains of the once mighty Birch tree. It was beyond dead. It was turned to stone. Shuran doubled over and released the remains of his last meal. He looked up to the sky as if looking for something. Sensing something, then closed his eyes tight.

"Do you understand now what happens if you do not learn limits, young Shuran?" Andra asked.

Shuran could only nod through his sobbing. Shuran felt horrible and tainted. He turned and glared and Andra. "Why did you let this happen? You should have told me!" Shuran steamed with anger.

"Hold young asipu. You had to feel this for yourself in order to learn to recognize the limits. This is but one tree compared to the world that is falling into the abyss of Chaos. It will not be the last before you fully understand," Andra answered.

"I will never do that again!" Shuran said.

"As you say. Then I suggest we move on to storing power so that you will have something to call on in need. I think you would like being rid of what you have stolen?" Andra inquired over a smirk.

Andra reached into a pocket and produced Codger's crystal shard. The shard was now dull and lifeless. He handed it to Shuran. "Release what you have taken. You had done it before when you gave power of yourself to me." Andra could see both anger and confusion on Shuran's face. "Let it go. Focus on the crystal in your hand and will the stolen Essence into the stone."

Shuran moved his glare from Andra and looked at the shard. It was a trickle at first, then a flood as Shuran poured the Essence into the crystal. It began to shine. The glow grew steadily brighter until it became difficult to look upon it.

"ENOUGH!" Andra shouted and knocked the shard from Shuran's grasp. "You only put in as much as you can. You already released what was taken and began adding your own strained Essence." He calmed and helped Shuran steady. "Each day you wake, fully rested, and you will add your own Essence to this shard until you begin to feel tired. Then you eat and begin your lessons."

Shuran just looked at Andra.

"Once the Crystal resists, it is full and can be returned to Codger."

Shuran nodded and went back to the cabin to eat and rest.

Chapter Eleven

◁𝖸

Andra began Shuran's newest lessons in the Essence back to their origins. "Essence is all around us in everything there is," Andra said.

"I know this already. Why is Mally not taking lessons with me?" Shuran asked.

"Mally has learned much but what I teach you today is only something that you can do because you are different," Andra replied. "You are birthed of seven blood lines, each of those having the makeup to harness one of the seven powers."

Shuran just looked at Andra blankly before responding. "What I did with the trench, it felt different then the weaving we have been practicing," Shuran said.

Andra smiled with pride. "Yes, you moved earth and water then called fire without using spells. This is dangerous for a weaver but not if the Essence was used to work the elements such as I suspected you did. Tell me what you felt at the time."

"I felt energy… power… life! It was as though I was calling out of need and what I wanted answered. I did not even think, I just acted,"

Shuran remembered.

"Did you hear anything?" Andra asked.

Shuran smiled and looked up at Andra smiling broadly. "I DID! I heard what was like music or singing and voices, but very faint. It was different with each. And the fire danced!"

Andra just smiled and started to explain what was known to the limited knowledge Andra possessed. "Elemental powers seem to respond and act in different ways to those who can communicate with them. Water ripples with musical tones. Earth rumbles and vibrates with deep drum-like beats. Wind whispers. Fire dances and swirls. Electricity buzzes and hums. Essence wielders of the elements must learn to listen and watch all around them and be able to separate the sounds, feelings, and images of nature in order to blend intent into action."

Andra further explained how most have difficulties controlling more than one element and those who can, must do so separately. Shuran seemed a natural for picking out the elements and bending them to his will and doing so seamlessly.

"It was not as though I was forcing the elements. I sort of told them what I wanted and asked the elements to help me." Shuran explained. "I did not even know what I was doing, I just sort of felt that help was there just waiting for the asking."

Andra was not certain how to approach this revelation from Shuran. IT was not at all how he would describe things so he was unsure why Shuran would feel the elements differently. Andra decided they would go through lessons on concentration and isolating the different elements.

Before any of these lessons were to begin however, Shuran had to learn his limits and proper channeling of Essence. Up until then Shuran had been weaving spells from lessons that required little energy or concentration. Elemental forces that Shuran had wielded so far had been on instinct and without control, so they exhausted him and he would pass into a deep slumber.

Shuran's first lessons now would revolve around the flow of Essence and controlling it. He also needed to learn how to block it. Andra instructed him first to take the rest of the lessons time for that day to practice sensing the world around him and identify the Essence in everything.

It was not known where the Essence came from or why. There are old tales and stories of the origins. Some say that the Essence was a gift from the Gods when they created Ersetu, while others say that the Essence was stolen from the Gods when the people of Ersetu revolted and destroyed them. It did not matter the when, why, or how. What mattered was that they had it and must use it to survive. Only balance kept the world from tearing apart.

The Lalli Mah was created to forge a permanent balance of the powers of Chaos and Creation. Each bloodline of the seven races of man, had the innate ability to weave a certain aspect of the Essence. Those of mixed blood were often blessed or cursed with the ability to wield multiple gifts. But without balance, wielders of mixed-blood would often fall into madness or darkness.

Some wielders could not handle the power they could harness and ultimately destroyed themselves, while others could only wield to varying degrees of strength. Those who chose to allow themselves to be consumed with power, gave in to Chaos and were labeled abominations.

"There is no good or bad, there is only intent." Andra told Shuran.

"Are there some mixed-bloods that have no gift at all?" Shuran asked.

Andra knew where Shuran was going with his question. "It is rare, but sometimes a mixed-blood will show no gift. Why do you ask?"

"Moona has no gift but she is old beyond the lifespan of a mundane. I sense something missing," Shuran answered.

Andra raised an eyebrow. "That is something all together different, but not my place to speak on," Andra stated, clearly ending the conversation.

Shuran sat in the practice circle identifying the differences in the elements and communicating with them. He closed his eyes and began to meditate on his surroundings. He tried to concentrate on the elements but at first his mind was overwhelmed by everything at once and he lost concentration, falling over stunned.

Andra laughed as he helped Shuran sit up. "Do not open your mind up so wide and free, Shuran. Focus on opening up a little at first then slowly increase your awareness," Andra told him.

Moona had just come out from the garden and decided to sit a while with her pipe and watch Shuran.

As he slowly opened his mind, Shuran began to take in all around him in the practice circle. He reached down into the earth once he attuned to its rhythm. He felt the course dirt and sand mixture of the soil. He could feel the grubs chewing and digging as if they were under his own skin. This disturbed him at first but he regained his composure.

As he moved along through the ground using his connection, he ran into a barrier, which he quickly realized was the water ring dug around the area when they first created the practice ring. He quickly released the vibrations of the earth to join the music of the water in the ring. Once within the ring, Shuran sang along and traced its surface around to where he had started.

Soon Shuran left his song with water to jump into the embrace of the fire burning in the pit before him. He became entranced with the dance of the flame. It was exhilarating. He danced and danced faster and with ferocity that he felt himself growing and getting hotter.

WHACK!

"Ouch! What was that for?" Shuran asked turning to see Moona retreating with a switch in her hand.

"Two reasons I whacked you smart arse! One you were gonna' set this whole wood aflame if you kept it up," Moona said as she turned to walk away.

"You said two, what is the other reason?" Shuran asked.

"Because I could!" Moona smiled. "One thing, that shifty over there forgot to tell you, is if you open yourself up to all around you-" Moona started but was interrupted.

"You need to be able to sense sneaky old wenches creepin' up on you!" Codger finished.

WHACK! Moona cracked Codger across the backside with her switch. "Didn' see that one comin' either did ya old fool?" Moona laughed as she headed back to the cabin smoking on her pipe.

Andra turned back to Shuran with barely a hint of a smile on his borrowed face. "You are tired are you not?" Andra asked.

"Yes, I feel hungry as well, but I can keep going," Shuran insisted.

Andra looked at Shuran and wondered how far he could push himself so soon. "Good, what we will work on now will help how you are feeling I think."

"What do you mean, you think?" Shuran asked.

"I only know of this in theory since I have been unable to do so myself. You however, have already shown the ability to channel Essence when you were but days old."

Andra retold the story to Shuran of how with a touch, Shuran poured Essence into Andra allowing the shifting into Sulura's likeness to hold. "If you can move Essence out of yourself you should be able to take it in."

"From where?" Shuran asked.

"Think back to what I have already told you." Andra looked around them.

Shuran thought for a moment before smiling and looking up to Andra. "The Essence is in everything."

Andra nodded but then gave a look of great concern. "You must learn to take only what is safe. I will help you to understand."

Andra brought Shuran over to a large tree near the end of the circle. "I want you to focus on this tree. Feel the Essence within and draw it into yourself."

Shuran placed his hand upon the tree. He felt the smooth white bark beneath his fingers. Shuran stretched out his senses and located the tree's Essence immediately.

"Do you have it?" Andra asked.

Shuran nodded without taking his attention off of the Essence he now held with his will.

"Good now I want you to pull on it and draw it within yourself. It is said to feel as though you are consuming it."

Shuran tried to act as though he was feasting on the Essence but it did not respond, but actually struggled to break free. Shuran fought back to hold onto the Essence of the mighty Birch tree. During his struggle he barely noticed his own Essence moving out from his center and pushing toward the tree.

With a sudden jolt Shuran's Eyes opened and his head lifted up. He pulled the tree into himself. He fed on the Essence and savored the energy as it flowed effortlessly from the tree to himself. Shuran was consumed by the feeling of taking in that energy. He did not notice the bark of the tree shrinking and cracking below his touch. He did not hear the tree screaming in his head for freedom from the torture it was being subjected to.

Suddenly the tree cried out so loud that Shuran could not help but notice. It was too late. Shuran fell back in shock. Before him, stood the withered and dried up remains of the once mighty Birch tree. It was beyond dead. It was turned to stone. Shuran doubled over and released the remains of his last meal. He looked up to the sky as if looking for something. Sensing something, then closed his eyes tight.

"Do you understand now what happens if you do not learn limits, young Shuran?" Andra asked.

Shuran could only nod through his sobbing. Shuran felt horrible and tainted. He turned and glared and Andra. "Why did you let this happen? You should have told me!" Shuran steamed with anger.

"Hold young asipu. You had to feel this for yourself in order to learn to recognize the limits. This is but one tree compared to a world that is falling into the abyss of Chaos. It will not be the last before you fully understand," Andra answered.

"I will never do that again!" Shuran said.

"As you say. Then I suggest we move on to storing power so that you will have something to call on in need. I think you would like being rid of what you have stolen?" Andra inquired over a smirk.

Andra reached into a pocket and produced Codger's crystal shard. The shard was now dull and lifeless. He handed it to Shuran. "Release what you have taken. You have done it before when you gave power of yourself to me." Andra could see both anger and confusion on Shuran's face. "Let it go. Focus on the crystal in your hand and will the stolen Essence into the stone."

Shuran moved his glare from Andra and looked at the shard. It was a trickle at first, then a flood as Shuran poured the Essence into the crystal. It began to shine. The glow grew steadily brighter until it became difficult to look upon it.

"ENOUGH!" Andra shouted and knocked the shard from Shuran's grasp. "You only put in as much as you can. You already released what was taken and began adding your own strained Essence." He calmed and helped Shuran steady. "Each day you wake, fully rested, and you will add your own Essence to this shard until you begin to feel tired. Then you eat and begin your lessons."

Shuran just looked at Andra.

"Once the Crystal resists, it is full and can be returned to Codger."

Shuran nodded and went back to the cabin to eat and rest.

<u>**Chapter Twelve**</u>

⟨ℿ

Salmetu sat in the center of a dim room barely lit by torches on the far walls. She sat in the room watching as Essence was drained from the tree. She could see the flow of energy like a stream of light from the tree, through the fingers of a boy. The pulses of light flowed up his arm and across his chest where they joined with his own Essence.

Salmetu groaned with delight as the tree began to whither and die. She heard its screams of protest and reveled in the agony it felt when it could not resist the draw of its last drop of Essence. Without any Essence at all, the tree could not hold onto its shi. The life force left it a dried and shriveled husk. So strong was the pull that the once thriving Birch turned to stone.

Salmetu pulled back from the boy whose eyes she had been looking through. As she looked around to see where she was, darkness suddenly took her and the vision was lost. "There is a boy somewhere in a clearing surrounded by white trees. He drained the Essence from a Birch and drank deeply," Salmetu smiled wickedly.

"We must find him," Isten turned from the room and joined Telalsu. "You will find this boy! He will join us or he will feed the Priestess."

Telalsu bowed as he left Isten then he disappeared in a dark shift of shadow and smoke.

***

Utu was high in the sky when Shuran was prepared to go back to his lessons.

Andra instructed him to continue reaching out with his senses and feel his surroundings. "I want you to take notice of the differences in the Essence in everything you feel. This will help you to understand what is around you and feel for what does not belong. You will also be able to tell if an old woman is ready to knock you about your head!" Andra finished with more humor as was capable of a mere Guardian.

Andra explained how reaching out with his senses, Shuran could learn to 'see' for greater and greater distances, to know what and whom may be around him. So this is what Shuran practiced for the remainder of the day until Utu began falling below the tree line late in the afternoon.

"Hello Bastien!" Shuran said as his friend walked out from behind the trees heading toward the practice yard.

"You have your eyes closed, how did you know I was here?" Bastien asked.

Shuran, realizing his slip, fumbled for a reply. "You are standing downwind my friend. Have you been rolling in fish heads?" Shuran jested as his friend returned the smile.

Bastien just looked at Shuran sideways for a moment before relaxing into a full laugh.

Shuran went to the side of the cabin to grab his fishing sticks and nets then followed Bastien out to the shore.

"There have been Land's Guard in the town recruiting," Bastien said as he worked to lay out the fishing net. "Adda says that they might start drafting if they do not have enough volunteers."

"Why?" Shuran asked knowing the true reason.

"Some sort of unrest in the realm. Folks are whispering of war with another realm or some uprising of an old enemy or something. All I know is that people are disappearing and some dark purpose is to blame," Bastien finished.

Bastien talked the entire afternoon about adventure and battles. He wanted to one day become a member of the Guard so he could travel the realms.

Shuran could not help but smile at his friend's naivety. There were no adventures to come, only destruction and death. Shuran did not have all the answers, but he knew what he felt, and what he saw in his night visions.

"Time to head back I suppose," Shuran finally said as the light was dwindling. "Let us gather up all our catch and head back."

Bastien and Shuran pulled in the last net and placed the rest of their catch of fish in baskets. As they started their long walk back, Shuran began opening himself to his surroundings. He examined the Essence that emanated from everything he passed. When he focused on Bastien, he began probing the Essence and sensed something odd in his friend.

He was not sure what it was, but he realized his friend was different. He thought it might be because he had heard Andra call him a mundane, but Shuran felt different. Something was changed, but he was not sure what it was.

Bastien suddenly dropped his burden and a quiver ran through his body.

Shuran immediately closed off his connection to the Essence and stared at his friend. "What got into you?" Shuran asked.

"Not sure, I just started feeling well… Sort of shivery. Ma used to call it, 'someone walking on your grave'!" Bastien responded. "Ever feel that?" he asked Shuran.

"Only recently, it is unsettling," Shuran replied not missing the connection between his probing his friend's Essence and the sudden shiver he felt. As they continued their walk home, Shuran noticed something different in his friend or perhaps in himself.

Bastien was giving off a slight glow that was not there before. The two friends soon parted ways as Bastien headed of the path toward his own home. Shuran continued alone for the last of the walk back to the cabin.

Halfway back home Shuran stopped still in his tracks. He felt a shiver, but it did not pass quickly. Shuran began to panic as something on the edge of his comprehension took hold. He was being watched.

An understanding from deep within him told Shuran he must block this, but how could he do it. Shuran began to imagine a wall surrounding his body. Slowly the feeling dissipated but suddenly returned stronger than before. In his mind, Shuran began to thicken the wall. The larger he made it, the stronger the shivers became. He had to change the wall he thought.

Quickly, Shuran began to turn the wall into metal and as he did the feeling lessened but did not stop completely. Shuran began to run through his mind a list of strong materials that could hold back the probing he now recognized the feeling was. Just as he was about to become overwhelmed by the weight of his apparent attack, he thought of the crystal he had been imbuing with Essence.

As suddenly as the thought came to mind, the attack stopped and was completely blocked. With a worried mind, Shuran looked around and searched out with the Essence but found nothing out of place. He grabbed his things, and ran as fast as he could back to the cabin to see Andra.

Shuran arrived back to the cabin out of breath and a look of worry over his face.

"Shuran! What has happened?" Mallick asked grabbing hold of him and moving him to a rock to sit upon.

"Someone was trying to find me!" Shuran yelled before he even sat.

Andra was there in heartbeats. "Who did you see?" Andra demanded.

"There was no one there it was as if someone was seeking me out. They were probing my Essence!" Shuran exclaimed.

Shuran went on to explain how he had been exploring the Essence on the way back from the shore. He told how he felt something different within Bastien and the glow he had after. Shuran recounted the discussion on the feeling of someone walking over one's grave that Bastien had experienced.

Andra only nodded in acknowledgement during Shuran's retelling of the afternoon's events.

Shuran got to the part about feeling the shiver himself and being compelled to build a wall around himself.

"You took the correct path Shuran," Andra said.

"We dunno what they was lookin' for," Moona said. "But they sure 'nough will be looking for ya again boy!" Moona finished.

"True, but from what Shuran retold, they do not have enough to be coming here for certain. We have time and we must use it wisely," Andra finished before they all went inside to take a meal and continue discussing the events of the day.

"If you are not too tired Shuran I think we can alter our training path tonight and start dealing with your Essence," Andra said as they stepped outside.

"Andra what do you think of the glow I saw around Bastien? I see the same glow around all of you now as well but less as much with Moona," Shuran inquired.

"You have learned on your own, the way to sense the ability to wield in others," Andra said.

"But that makes no sense. Bastien does not wield and neither does Moona," Shuran said.

"Bastien has not been awoken to his ability at least not until today perhaps thanks in part to you," Andra started. "As far as Moona, it is her tail to tell but she was once a wielder but no longer." Andra completed the last statement making it clear that there would be no more discussion on Moona unless from her directly.

"What do you mean in part from me as far as Bastien is concerned?"

"You may have hastened his awakening or enabled it all together by probing him as deeply as I fear you did," Andra responded. Andra went on to explain how the feeling of self-preservation that caused Shuran to build a wall, may have also been felt by Bastien to some degree and awoken his abilities when Shuran reached out to him. Andra further shared his feelings that Bastien may be more than he appeared.

"I want us to focus on guarding yourself against detection," Andra started. "The initial probe may have been a simple search for power. The Order has been looking for weavers to join them or to drain. Since you blocked their probe they will be vehement in their search for the one who blocked their probe," Andra finished.

Shuran just grimaced at the thought of now being hunted again.

Andra and Shuran worked in earnest through the night exercising Shuran's ability to block unwanted probing. They also practiced with Shuran's ability to probe Andra. Andra insisted that Shuran feel his Essence and find out what he was.

"Andra? What are you?" Shuran stopped and asked.

Andra turned to Shuran blankly while thinking of how to respond. Andra reminded Shuran of the stories of the Foresworn and the blending of bloodlines. "I am descended from parents who were birthed before the final blending. I am mixed of many lines so I bear the gifts of each in varying strengths. Above all I have the ability since birth, to shift. It is my easiest ability to weave," Andra finished.

"So you can become anything or anyone?" Shuran asked with wonder.

"To a degree yes, but I can be nothing smaller than I. Larger is not too difficult if I take organic material from around me to add to my own. To become something less would mean returning to less," Andra said.

"What if you stored the extra parts of yourself someplace, like I learned to do with Essence?" Shuran asked.

Andra smiled at Shuran's inherent understanding of Essence. "I have never thought of such a thing!" Andra responded with a look that showed contemplation of possibilities.

"I have lost him!" Telalsu yelled. "The boy has blocked me out. I could not get a good location and all I could see of him was fishing nets and a wooded path. His face eluded me." Telalsu was visibly angered. "We must split our search and focus on areas near water and forest. He will not likely be in a large populated area. Go and report back by scry daily. I want him found!" he said.

Telalsu dismissed the Inquisitor and turned to the scrying dish before him. "I have sensed the boy but lost the connection before a location could be ascertained." He said to the shadow in the bowl.

"Keep trying, and increase the weaver gathering. I want this boy found and we need more weavers to join our ranks or be drained."

"It shall be done mistress," Telalsu replied.

"Do not fail me Demon, or I will return you to a far worse place than you were called from."

And with those final words, the connection was lost. Telalsu grimaced out of fear and anger at being spoken too in such a manner from a flesh-ling. But the voice that she spoke in was ancient and familiar.

Chapter Thirteen

⟨𝄇

Hell's Mouth was a forbidding place. Since the time of the great eruption of the peak at what is now Hell's Mouth, the surrounding land appeared void of life; life on the surface that is. Although the great eruption destroyed much of the surrounding land, the many caves that did not collapse, remained.

There were still those who lived among them and refused to leave millennia ago when the mountain belched forth in fiery anger. These people are the Drakkians, and they did not, normally, mingle with other races since the Lalli Mah. The caves and former lava tunnels of the area created a natural metropolis for the Drakkians to live. They and their drakkon kept hidden within, and only ventured out to the East into the Highlands.

In a large chamber deep within the mountain, a gathering of Drakkian elders commenced.

"There is far too much stirring to the West!" an elder shouted.

"We do not know what is happening and cannot jump to conclusions," another responded.

"We cannot ignore what is happening," a loud and resounding voice said from deep within the recesses of the chamber. The source of the voice emerged from the darkness and cast far deeper shadows as it emerged. A drakkon of a deep and rich green stepped forward. "The prophecy is at hand, and we must act accordingly," it said and looked toward a figure standing off in the distance.

The figure responded. "I have already gotten involved. But we shall not reveal ourselves yet," he said as he turned and left the assembly.

"Will he prove trustworthy?" a member of the group asked after the figure exited the chamber.

"He will do what is necessary. He has more to lose than most for now," the drakkon said as it turned to look upon the young red drakkon sleeping off in the alcove from where it emerged.

In a cave deep within the ranges surrounding Hell's Mouth hidden deeper still, lay a secluded area. In the center of the area sat a young woman mumbling to herself.

The dark figure from the assembly walked up behind her. "How is our charge mistress?" he asked.

"As well as can be expected. There is little change. She stirs from time to time but nothing more," the woman answered. A light glow of light shone behind her as she spoke to the man. "What does the assembly say?" she asked.

"We are doing what must be done. Things are occurring as have been prophesied. Playing both sides has advantages," he finished and left the room.

The woman turned back to her charge. "Rest my dear, you will awaken when the time comes."

The Castle of Drakkfoth was a dark and formidable fortress built upon the ruins of an ancient city that existed in the same location and by the same name. The castle sat within the shadow of Hell's Mouth and was feared. It was a looming presence upon the land. Great dark spires of dragon glass shot forth from the ground along with walls and floors that made up the structure.

The dark ominous stone itself represented all that was dark to those who lived in its shadow. Upon the throne of the Castle Drakkfoth sat Baron Fallon de Drakk. The Baron harbored the Order of Chaos and worked with the Inquisitors.

"The Baron will see us now!" ordered an Inquisitor leading a group of Land's Guard.

"He will send for you when he is ready," responded the attendant feeling no intimidation. "You forget where you are Leacher!" the attendant spat.

Leacher was the term applied to the elite in the Inquisition, those charged with supplementing power and draining the gift from weavers who failed to pledge service to the realm. It was an ancient order that, besides being under the rule of the Great Council, aligned with Chaos.

Although the attendant is supposed to act in collusion with the Order of Chaos, he still felt disgust for those who drained the Essence from others. It is among the first rules of sentience that draining Essence of another is to be held highest above all crimes. This means that to take the Essence of another leads to damnation of one's shi. Even a member of the Order should not be cavalier to the ancient laws of the Telukukal.

The Baron opened his door at long last and allowed the Inquisitor entry to his chamber.

"Baron we invoke the right to request assistance," the Inquisitor said.

"I will give you what I see fit Leacher. Do not presume to speak to me with authority you do not possess," Fallon said. "What is it the Order want of me and my people now?" he demanded.

"Baron," the Inquisitor now humbly asked, "we seek only to request more able men to aid in the hunt for an unknown power beyond our reach," the Inquisitor said. It is not like an Inquisitor to show weakness to another, yet the Baron invoked a fear from the man that he could not explain to himself as he cowered. "We only bring the request of the Order Sir. We do not wish to insult you," the Inquisitor finished.

"What is it you wish of my men?" The irritation still covered the Baron's face.

"We seek a young man, a boy really. He appears to have a gift that the Order wishes to possess. That is all I know," the Inquisitor responded.

"I will send my men to find this boy, I will advise if and when we locate him," he answered. Fallon obviously had another agenda behind his eagerness, but he would not allow the Inquisitor to discover it.

***

Shuran woke with a start. "Someone has sent me an image!" Shuran screamed. Shuran told the others of what he saw in his vision.

A massive green drakkon smiling, a group of green-eyed and robed figures collected in a room, a young red drakkon, and an Inquisitor cowering before a dark figure. These images caused alarm in Shuran but he felt calm when he said, "These are images sent to warn us before we are discovered," Shuran said.

"How do you know this message was sent?" Andra asked.

"It felt as though someone was reaching out to me, but it was different. It felt like a request for permission to send me the images," Shuran said.

"It would be wise to limit your acceptance of messages in such a manner. A sending can easily be turned to a location spell. However, if it is as you say and a drakkon was there then perhaps…"Andra stopped speaking without completing his thoughts. "I must leave and check what is transpiring to the West," Andra finished and went out to gather supplies. Andra instructed Shuran to continue on his course of lessons and storing power in the crystal shard. Soon after, he was gone again.

Shuran spent the next several days going through his lessons and spending afternoons with Bastien. When he sensed the crystal shard would take no more Essence he put it away and went to the cave hideaway he and Bastien often spent time at.

Shuran many times sat within the cave staring at the multicolored quartz formations protruding from the walls. He had not thought much of them before, but now he wondered if they could be used to store Essence.

He searched around the walls for stones that would easily come loose. Every so often he would coax them out by asking the rock to let them go. He wondered at how easy it was becoming to work with the elements. He wondered still what the elemental power of electricity was as he had experienced it.

'Lightening is the purest form,' Andra had told him, but he still did not understand.

Shuran gathered his new crystals and took them back to the cabin.

He was tired from filling the rest of Codger's shard so he would not attempt trying anything with these until he had rested.

***

Twelve guards stood in the meeting room of Castle Drakkfoth. Fallon called them to task on behalf of the Inquisitors. They were dressed in black leathers from shoulder to toe. Upon their heads they wore helmets that conformed to the their skull. Only their green eyes and mouths were exposed.

Each carried a pair of long curved swords upon their back that they reached from opposite shoulders. These were the horsemen from the elite guard of Drakkfoth and they all pledged their lives to the Baron and his region.

The Baron entered the chamber and quickly scanned the group before taking position directly in front of them. "You all have been briefed by the commander. I expect that you will find the boy and report directly back to me. You are not to engage at this time." The Baron gave the men a final nod and they took their leave.

As the Baron turned to sit upon his throne, a large white wolf approached from the shadows and casually walked up to him. "You do not approve?" the Baron asked the wolf.

The great beast continued her approach and shifted from wolf into a fair skinned beautiful young woman. The think long white fur seemingly melted into her form to flow around her as a billowing gown of white silk. She took the seat next to the Baron and stared out to the guards leaving the throne room.

"It is not for me to question your motives nor your orders adda," she responded with only the hint of a smile upon her porcelain face.

"And how has your task been coming along Barurbe?" Fallon inquired of his ward.

"Little change adda as you know, but that does not mean she will not recover. I only hope that my uncle succeeds in his task. Has there been any word of him?" Barurbe asked as she turned to her father.

"His whereabouts are currently unknown. My brother does not always include me among his councils, but I trust in what he is doing. Everything hinges on him completing what he set in motion." The two got up from sitting and headed out of the throne room by means of a secret exit.

"What is our involvement with the Inquisitors?" Barurbe asked as they walked along the hidden corridors of the castle.

"We must collaborate with them in their pursuit of this boy. He is an ever changing variable to the success of our ultimate goal." Fallon forced a smile and continued to lead Barurbe down the corridor.

Fallon was uncharacteristically cryptic with his answers, Barurbe noted. "I will, as always, do as you ask adda, but I worry that defiance of the Inquisitors will not go well with the Great Council," she said.

"The Inquisitors do not work under the direction of those old fools of the council in this. They are taking their orders from the Order of Chaos and their dark leader, the Assinnu Isten." Fallon stammered in walking for a brief moment.

"What is it, father?"

"I am concerned with the shifting in the balance. Whatever the Order is up to, goes beyond what the prophecy spoke of I fear. This leader of theirs has not seen fit to share his plans and I worry they will interfere with our own."

Chapter Fourteen

The Order of Chaos leader was conducting a meeting of his own as the Baron sent out his men.

"The Baron has sent his men out as you requested Isten." The Inquisitor stood with eyes downcast awaiting further instruction.

"You will not report this to the Council. Our movements do not involve them at the moment. Once we understand this unknown factor in our plans, then I will solicit the Council's advice," Isten finished and then got up to leave the chamber. "I want you to watch the Drakkian Guard's movements. Fallon was a bit too willing to give the assistance of his elite," Isten said as he left.

"Do you fear treachery Isten?" the Inquisitor questioned.

"Treachery, although not beneath a Drakkian, is not something Fallon is capable of. The Baron will do as he is told and find a way to include his own agenda whatever that may be." Isten paused before dismissing the zealots in attendance. "I want reports on anything suspicious in the Baron's movements or those of his Elite Guard."

Before Isten could leave he sniffed the air and held his hand below his nose. "Step out and address the order, kashshaptu!" Isten said sitting back down.

A hunched figure approached the assembly and paused briefly near each zealot, eyeing them and making nods or sounds of surprise. She was taking in the full membership of this dark organization and who the leaders were. A kashshaptu from the Mist Swamps would not normally involve themselves with the affairs of Aurderia, but she wanted something and Isten knew it.

"Are you not surprised to see one of my coven here in your secret keep?" the witch hissed as she stopped by the fire set in a large hearth.

"I have little patience for games kashshaptu, nor do I wish to suffer your stench any longer than necessary. What is it I can help the coven with?" Isten, clearly agitated by the witch's presence, could not afford to offend the coven.

"We have had a vision. We know what it is you seek. We wish to offer our assistance." The witch stood staring over the fire, her wiry black hair streaked with grey and full of knots, dirt, and the occasional spider. She turned to face Isten and noticed his slight shiver as their eyes met. She smiled at him showing the few blackened teeth in her mouth as a deep cackle erupted from her mouth.

Isten dismissed the rest of the members from the chamber and came to stand as close as possible without being accosted by the stench of rot and filth that clung to the witch from the equally noxious swamps. "What is it you want? The coven does not normally leave the swamps nor get involved with Aurderian affairs." Isten was more than just irritated by the witch but needed to hear what the coven wanted.

"What we want is inconsequential compared to what it is you are doing. Your actions affect all of us Assinnu Isten and we want assurances. You will give us what we want and we will lead you to the boy." The witch shifted around to give Isten a knowing look.

"How do I know your information is useful?"

"You will not until your zealots get there, however I can tell you that he has been with the moon mother since his birth." The kashshaptu cackled at the look that began to fall upon Isten's face.

As the color drained from Isten's face as the witch let out another of her horrible cackles. "Yes, there was a third child and he grows strong."

"What do you want in return?" Isten asked while holding back his concern over this revelation.

"We want a small sample of the priestess's blood." The witch waited while Isten left to advise the search parties.

Isten found the men of the Land's Guard, Inquisitors, and Drakk Elite Guards assembled outside the keep's stockage. The yard was small but suitable for the keep. There was rarely a time when the stockades were used or needed since the Order worked in secret and the keep was well guarded by spells and few knew of its existence.

"You ride for Birchshire. The boy has been living with an old woman. I want the boy returned here, alive if possible." Isten glared at the Inquisitors and the Telal. His look was a warning to not leach the boy unnecessarily.

One of the Inquisitors stepped forward, "What of the hag or others in the boys company?"

"Kill them if they get in your way." Before leaving he paused and turned back to the men. "Leave the old woman alive." He did not explain further. Isten left them to their preparations and headed back into the castle to get the witch what she came for.

"What is the purpose of this sample?" Isten did not like this arrangement, but in light of the information, he had no choice other than to comply.

"Coven business is not your concern Assinnu Isten. We look after ourselves and will continue to stay out of your affairs unless they become a danger to us."

Isten noticed two things. One, the witch kept addressing him by his full title among the Order. Two, the witch shed her smug facade in favor of one displaying determination and urgency.

"Why do you address me by my full title?" Isten asked.

Without looking at Isten, the witch continued walking the dark halls, "It is what you are, is it not? Would you prefer I address you by your given name?" The witch gave him a toothless grin.

Isten found himself flushed of all color. Knowing that the coven knew who he truly was unsettled him, but it would not matter for long. Once the boy was taken or eliminated, nothing would be able to stop him from gaining the power he wanted. Isten turned at the noise. From where he stopped he saw, then dismissed, the shadow of a bird leaving a perch on the window and head out into the night.

"Let the witch come forward." Salmetu was sitting on a chaise chair next to a fire in a windowless room. Next to her lay a scrawny cat with dead eyes. The creature was growling instead of purring as Salmetu stroked its undead body.

Salmetu turned to face the witch and looked upon her with pitch black eyes. Her appearance was now that of a full-grown woman and her movements were slow and deliberate. "I understand you wish a piece of me kashshaptu." Salmetu spoke with a level and melodious voice that echoed throughout the chamber.

"Just a sample of your blood my dear, nothing more is needed." The witch studied Salmetu, noticing something otherworldly in her manner and movement.

Salmetu turned to Isten, "Leave us. I shall speak with the witch alone."

Isten only looked angered by being ordered out for a moment, but left without much hesitation.

"You cannot hope to achieve anything from the use of my blood kashshaptu." Salmetu moved past the witch without moving her head buy kept her eyes locked on her as she passed. She continued to circle around the witch, studying her.

"We wish only to gain insight. Our visions are cloudy and this will help us to watch the new world emerge," she lied. The witch was beginning to rot further and her face began to show the droop of flesh upon her face. She had little time remaining to achieve her goal and return to the swamps.

Salmetu could not read deceit from this witch woman, she could read nothing at all. She pulled up her sleeve and drew a dagger across her arm. "Take what you need."

As the witch moved forward, she produced a corked bottle from within her robes. After unstopping the bottle, she began collecting the blood as it ran from Salmetu's open flesh. "When this is over my coven would like its seat back on the Council. We have longed for the old ways to return." With her final request, the witch stepped to the fire and gave a knowing glance to Salmetu.

"It shall be done," Salmetu answered. She watched the witch nod and step into the flames then disappear in a column of brackish smoke up the chimney. She stepped from her room and to a large window where she watched as the last of the search parties left to hunt for the boy.

The group of guards and Inquisitors split into two groups to head to Birchshire. One group headed northeast on a direct path to a small village. The second group headed southeast for the Southern coast where they would take a ship along the coast of the Great Sea. Both groups should arrive in the area of Birchshire close to the same time.

The trip will take a full moon cycle at best, but there should be no worry of the boy leaving the safety of his current home. Fallon was concerned that the boy would resist and get himself killed by an Inquisitor or one of the Land's Guard. He could only hope that one of his own men would be able to intercede without drawing suspicion.

Fallon walked the dark labyrinth of corridors formed millennia ago by liquid rock flowing through the grounds. He had left the castle by means of a secret exit behind his throne. As he neared his destination, the corridors began growing lighter from the room lit up ahead of him. As he entered the chamber, a group of women stopped what they were doing and left him with his charge.

Only his secret guest and daughter remained in the room. "There was a third child born that night." Fallon was speaking to his daughter while watching the sleeping form below him. "My Elite Guard travel with the retinue from the Order to retrieve him."

"What does this mean father?" Barurbe showed her concern, not only for the woman she watched recovering, but for a child she only just found out to exist.

Fallon bent down to place a light kiss on the forehead of his resting guest. "I do not know. Perhaps when our guest awakens we will find out."

Chapter Fifteen

Shuran and Bastien spent the entire day together in the woods around their cave hideaway. While cooking a rabbit for lunch, Shuran showed Bastien how he was learning to use the Essence. Shuran knew that Moona and Codger felt strongly about keeping this a secret, but Bastien was his best friend. Shuran also knew that there was something inside Bastien, sleeping, and he wanted to awaken it for some reason.

"Shuran all I see is you staring at a crystal. You look as if you are going to crap in your britches." Bastien grinned at the expression Shuran gave him, and they both laughed.

"I suppose this does not really demonstrate anything. Pick up that crystal in front of you and tell me what you feel," Shuran instructed.

"I feel… I feel… like a dur holding a rock! Except how would a dur hold a rock with its hoof!" Bastien was laughing at Shuran.

"Here now take this one," Shuran said handing over the shard he had just finished filling with Essence.

At first Bastien just held the stone and looked at Shuran. Suddenly his expression changed to surprise. "It tingles. It tingles a lot!"

"I would not have thought of it as tingling but it is a start." Shuran was glad to have proven his suspicions. "You can become a weaver."

"What do you mean I can weave? I am a mundane!" Bastien was both shocked and frightened. "My adda says that it is not safe to be a weaver anymore. Sanctions are being revoked or worse folks are disappearing. How long before the rats in the Council spread out to the farms and remote homes to search for weavers?"

Shuran saw his reasons for concern. "Look Bastien, we have nothing to worry about here, and as long as no one sees us wielding or weaving, then what is the problem?"

Bastien was not convinced, but he sat down to listen to what Shuran had to say.

Shuran explained how he could learn to defend himself and hide his abilities to remain unnoticed.

Bastien eventually lightened up when he thought more about it. "Maybe there would be a place for us in the Land's Guard. They recruit weavers."

"I am not so sure about that since they are working with the Inquisitors, according to Andra. The Inquisitors are not to be trusted."

Bastien did not look convinced.

Over the course of the next cycle, Shuran and Bastien met each afternoon and all resting day, trying to see what Bastien could do.

He already learned a few spells well enough. He could start a fire and lift small objects with a word. Bastien was becoming very pleased with himself and Shuran was happy with his friend's excitement.

One afternoon Bastien was pre-occupied and not concentrating on what Shuran was teaching him.

Shuran made it look easy to weave the Essence and he felt this might be upsetting his friend, slowing his progress. Shuran had not shown Bastien any wielding of elemental magic since he could sense Bastien was not capable; beside he decided to keep that secret for now. He could not go back on all he had promised to Moona. "What is wrong with you today Bastien?"

"Nothing," Bastien seemed surprised by the question. "I mean I am just thinking about the Guards in the village. My adda told me this morning that a group of Guards and an Inquisitor showed up in town late last evening."

"What do they want?" Shuran was concerned.

"I do not know," Bastien lied but Shuran did not see his friend's face when he answered.

Shuran stood and turned to Bastien. "We need to go see what is going on!"

"NO!" Bastien stood to grab Shuran. "It's dangerous and Moona would strap us both but good!"

"Well, we will not tell anyone then. Meet back here an hour after Utu has set." Shuran ran off toward home leaving Bastien with knots in his stomach and worry upon his face.

Bastien headed home, not noticing his father watching from off the trail.

He headed to the village after Bastien was out of sight. "The boy will be in the village this evening." The old man told a guard wearing black leather, head to boot. They spoke quietly for several minutes before completing their transaction.

The guard handed the man a leather purse and sent him on his way. He turned to his fellow guards. "The boy will come to us. He travels with a mundane youth so you will be able to tell which is the one we want from his shi glowing. I assured the old man his son would be left unharmed."

The Drakk Elite would later disperse around the village, intending to wait for their quarry to come to them. As the men moved off into the nearby Inn to wait, an Inquisitor stepped out of the shadows and watched them leave.

"We shall find the boy first," Telalsu said as he stepped up behind the Inquisitor.

***

Bastien and Shuran skirted the edge of town looking for signs of the guards.

"This is not working. We have to go further into town perhaps the Inn or the town magistrate building." Shuran was on edge and Bastien just seemed nervous.

"We will be seen and we still do not know what they want here." Bastien was more than nervous, he was frightened.

"We can go in unseen but we must be quiet." Shuran pulled a green gemstone from his pocket and disappeared.

"Shuran!" Bastien whispered.

Suddenly Shuran was visible again and holding Bastien by the hand.

"DAMKIANNA! How did you do that? And why are you holding my hand?"

"If I let go then you will not be invisible with me any longer," Shuran said showing Bastien the stone in his other hand. "This keeps us unseen but not unheard. It was a gift from Andra a long time ago."

Bastien just stared in wonder and let Shuran lead him into town.

The boys still kept to the side streets and went around large groups of town folk to limit the chances of being discovered. As they approached the Inn, Shuran pulled himself and Bastien off to the side of the building where they could look into the common room from an open window. Soldiers dressed in black leathers sat throughout the room mixed with a few townsmen and other soldiers wearing the sigil of the Land's Guard.

"I do not see an inquisitor," Bastien whispered as they scanned the room.

"I cannot hear what they are saying. We have to get inside, but we also have not checked the magistrate's office."

With a nod of agreement shared between them, they moved off together down the alley toward the town center where they would find the magistrate's building. When they arrived, they found an Inquisitor standing outside the building talking to another man who had his back turned to them. The boys stepped off to the shadows and Shuran put his gem away.

"We need to split up. I will head back to the Inn and see what I can find out. I will meet you back here shortly. Just watch them and we can figure out our next actions when I get back." Shuran started to get up from his crouched position and fumbled finding Bastien was crouched and tangled in his robes. He soon recovered from the stumble and he headed off toward the Inn. Bastien stayed behind to watch the Inquisitor and his companion.

Shuran worked his way back to the Inn. He first thought of entering using his gem but thought better of it. The Inn common room was far too crowded to enter invisible without being bumped into. He did decide, however, to shield his shi.

Shuran took a deep breath and as he had been practicing, imagined a thick impenetrable wall around himself. He relaxed as the shield took hold and he headed into the Inn. Shuran was not known around the village so he drew a few stares from the local people, but their eyes did not linger. Shuran figured they thought he came in with the guards serving as a cook, a wagon driver, or other workers in their caravan. He moved over to a spot at the table and sat down where he could hear the conversation of a nearby group of soldiers.

"The two boys should be arriving any time now. We should be headed out to start watching for them. Remember the old man said that the one boy is not involved and we already know he is mundane, so look at the shi to confirm which is the one we want." The soldier got up from their table and exited.

Shuran was about to get up and follow when he noticed several Land's Guard get up to follow the black dressed soldiers out of the Inn. Shuran was horrified to find that they were here for him. He was also visibly upset to discover that it must have been Bastien's adda who let the men know about the boys coming to town tonight.

"How did Bastien's adda know we were coming?" Shuran questioned over in his head until he flashed back to what happened when he left Bastien at the Magistrate building. He reached into his pockets to find his shield gem missing. "Oh DAMKIANNA! Bastien what have you done?" Shuran ran for the door and as he exited ran right into Andra.

***

Bastien took the green gemstone in his hand and stood up. He figured now that he would be invisible, he could walk up to within steps of the Inquisitor and his dark companion in order to hear what they were discussing. When he got about halfway to where the men were standing the Inquisitor stopped talking and turned to look directly at where Bastien stood.

Bastien stopped in his tracks thinking that the deathly pale man had heard something. The man said something to his companion and the second man turned toward Bastien revealing a skeletal looking man with soulless black eyes.

"They can see me?" Bastien said to himself.

"Oh yes we can see you boy, though not as brightly as I would have expected." Telalsu said with an evil grin spreading across his face. "Did you think to shield yourself from us this close to you. You seem hardly the threat the Order has made you out to be."

Telalsu began making his way over to where Bastien stood shaking in his britches.

Without thinking to run Bastien created a ball of fire in his palm and hurled it toward the demon warrior stalking toward his position.

***

Andra was on the verge of worried anger. "Shuran why have you placed yourself in such danger by coming to the village?"

Shuran never saw the look of concern in Andra's eyes, nor had he witnessed such concern from the man. "We came to investigate and I just found out that they are looking for me!" Shuran struggled to get past Andra.

"I am aware of this and was heading to the cabin to hasten an escape. That is until I sensed your shielding gem nearby."

"Bastien has my stone, he took it from me when I left him watching the Inquisitor. Andra, his adda told these soldiers we would be coming here." Shuran suddenly knew what would be happening. His friend would try to use the shielding gem to go unnoticed and spy on the men. And the soldiers would be looking only for the boy who had a glow from his Shi. "Andra we have to go, NOW!" Shuran grabbed Andra by the arm and they made their way back to where Shuran left Bastien.

They were too late. When they arrived Andra had to pull Shuran back from running to his friend who was now lying on the ground writhing in pain, Telalsu standing over him.

Andra felt the pain for Shuran and turned to face him. "Stay here until I draw the demon away from your friend." Andra left Shuran to distract Telalsu.

"Did you think to over power a Warrior Demon, BOY!" Telalsu sneered down at Bastien lying prone at his feet and sent a shock of electric charge into his chest. "The Telal are far too powerful for the likes of some back woods untrained weaver." Telalsu was preparing to wield another bout of energy at Bastien when he was hit with a stream of fire. Knocked back several feet, Telalsu recovered to find another young man standing off to the side of the road holding glowing red flame in his hands ready for a fight. As Telalsu stood, the young man headed off into the village and out toward the river. Telalsu followed after him.

Shuran looked to see that the Inquisitor must have left as well. He quickly ran to his friend's side. He reached to turn him over only to get his hands soaked in the blood of his best friend. "Bastien, what have you done?"

Bastien gasped and spat blood from his mouth. Tears wee flowing freely. "Shuran I tried to spy on them but they saw me. Your stone did not work." Bastien handed the stone up to Shuran who took it into his bloody palm.

"The stone only works for me and those I am in contact with. It is my fault I should have explained that! Why did you not run away?" Shuran was shaking.

"My adda told me not to come here, I should have listened. I am sorry Shuran I thought I could scare them away." Bastien looked into the eyes of his friend that he felt he had betrayed then shuddered before collapsing in Shuran's arms.

Shuran began to burn with anger for the betrayal, not from Bastien but from that of Bastien's father. Shuran would find Bastien's father and find out what the life of his son was worth to him. He laid his friend's head down and before he could pick his body up to take it away, Land's Guard began running toward him. They could see him though he held his shield gem.

"I am sorry Bastien but I have to leave." Shuran left the lifeless form of his friend behind and ran.

After the Drakk Guard soldiers ran to follow Shuran, the Inquisitor stepped out from the side of a nearby building and headed toward the body left on the dirt road. He knelt down to the body and looked out toward where Shuran had run. With a gesture and a few whispered words of a spell, the Inquisitor and the body of Bastien disappeared in a shimmer of smoke.

Telalsu soon returned having lost the young man who attacked him. When he arrived to find the body gone along with the Inquisitor, he ordered the remaining Land's Guard to search the area for unsanctioned weavers and find the old woman who looked after the boy. After his final order was accepted, Telalsu placed his hand to the ground where the body had been and smiled.

"What are you up to?" Telalsu closed his eyes and abruptly disappeared as well, following the Essence trail left by the fleeing Inquisitor.

Chapter Sixteen

𒀭

Shuran ran with all his fading strength back toward home. He would have to stop and rest, and he did not want to lead any guards directly back home. He decided to go back to the cave that had become Bastien and his secret hideout. As Shuran approached the cave, he saw a figure sitting by a small fire near the mouth of the cave entrance.

"Who is there? Bastien is that you son?"

Shuran recognized the voice of Bastien's adda. As he approached the fire, Shuran pushed his hands outward, palms up, to show the blood of his now dead friend. "How much was the life of your own son worth to you?"

Bastien's father stood there, still, holding his breath as the realization set in.

"You told them we were coming and your boy lost his life because of it you old fool!" Shuran spat at the man who had betrayed not only him but his own blood as well.

"They only wanted you," the man stammered. "They were going to leave my Bastien alone and take you away. Things have not been the same since you showed up. It should be you dead now, not my Bastien." The old man was sobbing as he sunk to his knees.

"I should kill you where you are for what you have done. A man who would place his son's life in harms way for a few gold suns…"

Shuran raised his hands; his rage bubbled through him. The surge of power that moved through his body set all his hair on end. Through rage he was forming balls of electrical force in the palms of his hands. He felt the energy screaming to let loose. Shuran raised his hands above his head to let forth bolts of electricity.

"Shuran! You must stop. This is not the way." Andra grabbed Shuran's arms and brought them down before he could loose the energy he built up. The sparks and bolts immediately left his hands and he collapsed into Andra's arms weeping for the life of his best friend.

***

Moona and Codger were already moving to gather all they could into the wagons when Andra and Mallick arrived, leading Shuran from his confrontation with Bastien's father. Mallick had told Andra about the cave and that he might find Shuran there, after he suddenly appeared in the cabin an hour earlier. Andra explained to them what was happening and told them to get things prepared to make their escape.

Shuran made his way to his room to grab what he needed. He was visibly upset but he knew they had to leave. They managed to get some goats and a few cattle into a large wagon built for carrying animals. The other wagon was full of foodstuffs, warm clothing, and any other necessary items. They would have to get anything else they needed as they traveled, but they did not yet know to where. Shuran exited the cabin carrying just a sack filled with his clothes and another satchel filled with crystals and a few books.

Mallick rode with Codger and Moona with the animals, while Andra wanted to ride alone with Shuran for a while.

Andra tried to comfort Shuran. With the others he remained all 'Guardian' and stiff, but with Shuran he began relaxing. "This is not your fault Shuran and you must let go of the anger before it poisons you."

Shuran just looked ahead as they rode. He was racked with emotion over what transpired earlier in the village. To find out that his best friend had died out of fear and greed at the hands of his own adda, was more than Shuran could handle at the moment. It made him wonder about his own father. "If I had not sparked Bastien's shi, he would still be alive," Shuran mumbled.

"Shuran, whether you hastened his ability to the surface or not is but only a portion of what transpired. The blame truly lies with the Order of Chaos. It is they and their leader whom blame should be placed upon." Andra was not certain that Shuran was listening to what was said.

Before any further conversation could be held, Moona and Codger pulled their wagon to an abrupt halt in front of them.

"We need to pull off onto less traveled paths.," Codger said as he approached the trailing wagon. "There are men camped out ahead that look to be Land's Guard."

"You can bet your arse that they are looking for us!" Moona chimed in as she waddled up.

Andra thought for a moment and before he could say anything the group turned to a sound of movement off of the road to their right. The ground and vegetation was spreading apart to form a narrow path off to the North. They all turned to look at Shuran.

"I will clear a path and close it behind us. We should travel around north of the Mellamu Nanna and come back down the coast." His expression remained blank and emotionless.

Moona and Codger just stood there, mouths wide and questioning looks upon their faces.

Shuran just lifted a quartz crystal he was holding. "Quickly," was his one word response.

Mallick backed up the first wagon and once Codger and Moona climbed back on, he headed down the path Shuran was creating. As the wagons made their way down the path that parted before them, Shuran split his attention to return things back to their natural state behind.

The group went on through the woods as Shuran located and manipulated the ground into the best path they could use. At points the path was narrow and difficult but they pressed on until they finally reached a clearing near the coast north of the Mellamu Nanna.

"So much for a clear escape in spite of Shuran's efforts," Moona complained looking out at the large Aurderian vessel anchored not far from their destination. It was an old war ship of the Great Council, flying the sigil of the Inquisitors, illuminated by the soft glow of the moons.

"Perhaps we can use Shuran's shielding stone to mask our approach until they hear us?" Mallick asked looking to Shuran.

Shuran shrugged and shook his head. "The stone no longer works after I got it back from Bastien."

"We will worry about that later. I have an idea. Shuran may I have the use of one of your crystals, I assume you have more?" Andra looked at Shuran knowing the answer.

Shuran reached in his bag and produced a few shards. "I have found certain shards are better for different things. What have you got in mind?"

Shuran and Andra discussed options in private for a moment before turning to the group. After the five travelers conferred on the plan, they set it into action.

***

The guards and crew from the ship were huddled around a small fire near the Mellamu Nanna, drinking from a jug of wine and sharing stories. As the jug was passed from one guard to the next, it was dropped when a man stood and pointed north of their position.

A wagon came barreling toward them covered in flames. It took more than a few moments of panic and disorder before the guards even noticed that there were no horses leading the wagon. As the men scattered to avoid the flaming wagon, they did not see the group of travelers sneaking up to the odd vessel they had been camped near to guard.

It was not until one of the men saw the wagon pass through the area they just abandoned that suspicion grew. The blazing wagon passed without disturbing the camp; he called the alarm. "It is an illusion! There are people boarding that vessel. Stop them!"

The guards gathered their wits and ran toward the Mellamu Nanna, swords drawn and spells ready to cast. As the first guard threw his ball of fire, an opposite force of water immediately met it, resulting in a blast of steam.

Shuran stood at the foot of the gangplank ready to hold off attack as the others boarded the Mellamu Nanna.

"Keep them off as long as you can Shuran!" Mallick yelled as he and Andra worked hard to load all they could on the ship.

Moona and Codger were already on the vessel taking what they could secure, readying to leave quickly. Codger left Moona to continue stowing things as he headed to the pilot deck and fired up the boiler.

Shuran was holding his own with the attacks from the guards to the South when he heard a call of alarm from Mallick.

"More guards approach from the North behind us. They must have tracked us somehow!"

Shuran turned to look at the closing threat and missed an approaching fireball from the southern attack. The flames took immediately on the ground near the first wagon and spread quickly, spooking the horses and cattle still waiting to be led aboard the ship.

"Andra I need you to take over here while I see what our newest guests have to offer as a threat." Shuran switched places with Andra who was still holding the clear crystal shard Shuran supplied him earlier.

Shuran noticed that the guards approaching from the North were wearing black leathers. They were the men from the village at the inn.

They stopped and waited, seeming to be content with observing what was transpiring.

Shuran did not stop to consider what they were planning before he reached deep within his lessons to recall the spells for levitation. With the added strength from his crystals, he lifted the remaining livestock off the ground and onto the Mellamu Nanna.

There was no room for the wagons to be brought aboard so Shuran used them as a weapon. He quickly lifted them high in the air and hurtled them toward the southern assault that had positioned themselves about fifty paces from the ship.

As the guards saw the oncoming aerial threat they scattered and lost focus on the escapees.

Shuran and Andra quickly joined the others aboard the Mellamu Nanna and pulled up the plank.

"Get us moving Codge, we ain' got all night!" Moona yelled.

As they inched away from the shore, Shuran noticed the black-leather clad guards were still holding position and not interfering with their escape. He decided he would worry about that later. He noticed the emblem of a red dragon on one of their shields. HE had more pressing matters.

The Land's Guard regrouped and were sending fireballs and lightning toward them.

"Andra now would be a good time for you to put that crystal to good use. I am going to see Codger on the pilot deck," Shuran said as he ran off to see the old man.

Andra nodded and held out his hands, one holding the clear crystal that he had taken from Shuran. As he spoke the words of the ancient tongue, solid, yet invisible shield formed around the Mellamu Nanna.

"LILBAL BALEMUKU ZALAGBAD!" Andra said the words to transform the air around them into a clear shield. With the power of Shuran's Essence filled crystal, Andra was able to create a bubble of protection around them that would last until the power of the crystal ran out. Andra guessed that would not be anytime soon, sensing the power within the shard. "He has more power than he should," Andra whispered.

Shuran ran up to Codger in the pilot's deck, "Here, use this and get us out of here!" Shuran pushed Codger's crystal shard toward him. Seeing Codger's confused look, Shuran explained quickly, "I have spent weeks recharging it. We can discuss it later once you have lifted this vessels laden arse out of the water and get us away!"

Without another word, Codger placed the shard in its spot on the controls and smiled as it glowed. He then shifted the control lever into position.

As the Mellamu Nanna lifted from the water, the side sails unfurled into great wings to each side of the vessel and flapped once as the ship was hoisted over one hundred paces into the air.

The Drakk Elite Guard just looked on, stone-faced, as Shuran and his friends made their escape.

This did not go unnoticed to Shuran, but he was not done. In order to hide the direction they would take, Shuran set the air above the water to near fire temperature. Immediately, a thick misty fog arose all around the area and the Mellamu Nanna was lost to the onlookers on the shores of the Great Sea.

The Land's Guard continued throwing assaults of fire and energy at an unseen target.

The Drakk Elite backed away from the view of the Land's Guard so their captain could make his report to Fallon and await orders.

An eerie shriek filled the night as a gangly red-eyed black bird lifted from the branches of a nearby tree and flew off into the night.

Chapter Seventeen

The travelers busied themselves leading the animals and supplies below into the cargo holds of the Mellamu Nanna. Codger kept himself to the pilot's deck marveling at the ease of which the ship moved under a fully charged crystal.

Shuran arrived sometime later with wine, bread, and cheese. "Moona said she thought you might need feeding." Shuran saw the look of delight on Codger's face, "Of course, she said it in the same breath as tending to the cattle, horses, and goats!" Shuran laughed watching Codger's expression sour. "Where are we heading?" Shuran asked now that they were clear of the heavy fog he had created to mask their direction of escape.

"I' been thinkin' 'bout that young wielder!" Codger said with a look of admiration and pride in Shuran. "It seems clear to me that you are meant for far greater things, and knowledge will be your best tool."

Codger just looked at Shuran, then out to the horizon before him. With a slight shift of the controls, he adjusted their course back to the North. "I think I will take you to the ruins where I found the plans I used to build this here fine ship!" Codger beamed at the self felt genius of his idea.

Shuran was inclined to agree with the idea.

Now that they had a destination, and it was locked into the ship's controls, they all were able to relax a while and join for a meal and council.

"What I wan' ta know is where ya got all this power Shuran?" Moona asked accusingly.

"I did not suddenly get that much stronger, I have been storing Essence in crystals I found in a cave for many moons," Shuran said as he opened his bag containing dozens of crystal shards of varying shapes and colors.

"Through trial and error Bastien and I found that different crystals were actually capable of working better for various types of weaving and wielding." Shuran saw the looks of surprise and question on everyone, including Andra's borrowed face.

"For instance, this reddish shard enhances fire-wielding or weaving better than any other. Likewise the blue for water and green for earth." Shuran continued by showing examples of how a spell reacted, enhanced by each color shard.

"I have yet to find what some of the other crystal colors will aid in but I am certain that for some reason these colors represent a power somehow. I am confused though that I have found well more than seven colored shards." Shuran looked to Andra for an answer.

"I cannot be certain but perhaps the combinations of powers would make these other colors, so perhaps if you combined water and fire somehow, the purple hued shard would be helpful. Again this is all new to me even at my age and experience with using abnu emuq. I am happy to say Shuran has surpassed me in my understanding of power stones." Andra looked at Shuran with pride noticing Shuran's own look of accomplishment.

The group ate their meal and decided to retire early after agreeing to set a shift of watch over the night.

Codger determined that with a fully charged shard powering the Mellamu Nanna they would arrive at their destination by next midday.

Codger already expressed to Shuran that he was unsure how the ship worked, just that it did, but he wanted to know how. Perhaps the ruins would reveal more information than he found on his previous visit.

That night after Shuran finished his earlier watch he laid his head down for a long needed sleep. Rest did not come easy. His thoughts were full of images of Bastien and the Telal. Flashes of the Black-clad guards standing idly by during their escape and hope for what he would find at the ruins, kept restful sleep out of reach.

Once he finally drifted off to a fitful slumber, his dreams were replaced by visions. He saw two woman weaving and wielding Essence at one another. They appeared to be the same woman. The only difference was their hair and clothing. He saw himself standing between them attempting to halt their efforts. He awoke in a sweat and full of confusion over what he saw. When morning finally broke he found himself full of questions and worry. He went to break his fast with the others but remained silent.

"What has your tongue this morn Shuran?" Moona croaked as she drew deep on her pipe.

"Nothing," Shuran shrugged, and he ducked somehow knowing that a swing from Moona's free hand was coming toward the back of his head.

"OH! Got the power of sight now do ya!" Moona said recovering her balance from the missed swing.

"No, experience is a dear school!" Shuran smirked as he turned back from looking at Moona, who just grunted and smirked back at his response.

"So spit it out boy 'fore the feisty ol' dur gets it in her to knock it out o' ya!" Codger joked. He did not learn from experience as Moona's hand met with the back of his head.

After a laugh shared by all but Codger, Shuran retold the contents of his vision.

Andra and Moona briefly looked at one another but said nothing, and they played off the visions as nothing but dreams.

Shuran knew better by now, noticing their shared look, but he said nothing, for the time being.

After Shuran got up and headed off to check on the animals, Andra decided to have a talk with Moona. Andra and Moona sat in the pilot deck watching for their destination and deciding about what and when to tell Shuran.

"His visions are getting closer to the truth of his involvement in the prophecy. He must be told soon." Andra started the conversation direct and to the point.

"I know it, shifty! Just ain' found a good time is all. Suppose there ain' no puttin' it off much more." Moona did not wish to unset Shuran more than he was. He knew his mother died at his birthing but knew nothing much of his sisters aside that they were sacrificed. Moona had also told him she knew nothing of his father, which was not true. Sulura may not have told Moona where her husband and Shuran's adda had gone, but she felt he was out there somewhere on some quest for Sulura.

"I will tell him after we arrive and settle in." Moona was not looking forward to that time and shivered from more than just the cold air this far north.

It was not much past mid day when the Mellamu Nanna began her decent toward the decimated castle in the Northern forest east of the Orenthal Mountain range. As the ship angled downward toward the ruins, Shuran could see how this place had gone lost and forgotten for so long.

What once looked to have been a grand and formidable structure, was now overgrown and fallen to ground in scattered sections. Moss, fungus, weeds, trees, and all other form of plant had reclaimed the millennia old towers, turrets, and walls. All they could see however old it may be, was not what they were here to find.

Far beneath the structure was an even older ruin. A former building of the Telukukal once sat here and was covered by the builders of the visible ruins on the surface.

Shuran could not hold his excitement. Thoughts of scouring through remains from thousands of years before the Lalli Mah and perhaps finding lost artifacts or books, made him nervous with anticipation.

The ship was nearing an area close to what must have been the stockades of the old ruined castle. An odd structure was visible that looked similar to a dry dock for ships. Codger maneuvered the Mellamu Nanna onto the dry dock supports and with a final slight shudder, the Mellamu Nanna was safely nestled into her landslip.

Codger explained how he built it along with the Mellamu Nanna in this very spot.

Mallick and Shuran busied themselves getting the animals to land and into some old structures that could serve as a stable until other arrangements could be made.

Codger pointed out the safe areas within the fallen castle where he once made a temporary home. It appeared as though nothing had been touched since he was last there. At least that meant it unlikely they would have unwanted visitors as the ruins still seemed unknown to others.

Once the animals were settled in, the group made themselves as comfortable as they could inside what remained of a tower. The ground level was mostly usable, but the tower had long ago toppled over from a point just above the second level, leaving it full of rubble and debris.

They made short time of moving supplies from the Mellamu Nanna into the tower. There were partial walls separating a few sections to allow separating areas for sleeping and living.

Moona was able to get a fire started in what remained of the fireplace. The angle at which the tower above had fallen left the fireplace free of debris, although the birds and mice that came scattering out did not appreciate the intrusion.

Shuran and Mallick went off into the woods surrounding the area in order to check the terrain, gather wood, and set some snares. They had plenty of dried foodstuffs for a few weeks but they were not sure yet how long they would be staying at the ruins. Some fresh rabbit or other wild game would be preferred, and they could dry some meat as well for later since Shuran felt there would be rough times ahead.

The area around the ruins Shuran noticed, was rough and wild as any woodland would be. The land had been unsettled and lost to history for so long that it was completely overgrown. With access to enough wild food and fresh water, they could stay there indefinitely if not for the harsh cold that time of year.

Mallick and Shuran finished gathering wood and some tubers,

mushrooms, and roots that appeared to be edible, and headed back to the castle.

Moona caught Shuran's attention with one of her grunts. "Shuran, come help me check these plants you brought back while we talk," Moona instructed. She took a seat near the fire on a makeshift stool of stone.

Shuran immediately noticed the absence of Moona's pipe, warning him this was a serious conversation.

As they looked through and categorized the plants into medical and edible uses, Moona retold the story of his birth. This time she did not leave out any details. Shuran listened in silence taking it all in. Moona also recounted the time of her and Sulura's transfer to Drakkfoth and imprisonment by the Order of Chaos. While Moona was retelling a conversation held in the cell with his mother, Shuran finally broke his silence.

"You mean all this time I was not only believing I was an only surviving child, but that my adda is known to you and might be out there somewhere on some quest?" Shuran was angry.

Chapter Eighteen

The earth below Shuran began to rumble and energy began sparking on his body. Water shot forth from a crack in the ground and the fire at the hearth roared. Shuran saw the fear in Moona's face. He saw fear in everyone's faces, and he suddenly let go of the Essence. He closed his eyes for a moment then turned and ran out the hole in the wall that served as a doorway.

Shuran went off into the ruins, away from where they were making a new home. Although his initial shock had worn off, he was still seething with anger. When he was feeling angry or distracted, Shuran had always used the time to focus on storing energy in a crystal shard, but he left them back with the others.

As he sat alone, he began staring intently at a rock lying on the ground near him. He began to sink his thoughts into the center of the stone, willing Essence into it. What he noticed was that there was already a trace amount of earth power in the stone, so he began pulling on the earth and funneling more Essence into the rock. Suddenly the rock burst apart into uncountable pieces.

After he dusted himself off and recovered his wits, he tried again with another rock then another and soon began sensing the limits in the stones. He decided that storing Essence in them would not be suitable for use supplementing personal power, but they might be useful in other ways. He would have to work on a way in which to bind the stone together and hold the overflow of Essence until he wanted it released with a word.

Andra later found Shuran sitting among rocks and rubble covered in dust and staring distantly out into the wilderness.

Shuran sensed Andra drawing near. "You knew as well did you not?" Shuran asked Andra who came and sat down beside him.

Andra sighed as he sat next to Shuran. "I did. But you were not yet ready to deal with the burden," Andra replied.

"What of my sister that survived?" Shuran asked already sensing the answer.

"She is but a vessel and tool of the dark now. Any part of her that was your sister may have long been extinguished by the Order." Andra could feel Shuran's hurt and anger. "What you must focus on now is locating knowledge."

"You have the ability to wield the elements and weave Essence spell work, but that will not be enough. You must learn to use these gifts properly. Perhaps there is some lost knowledge here buried beneath us, but you will have to travel to the other races and learn from the masters." Andra looked at Shuran. "This will not be an easy journey. The races are untrusting of outsiders and also not all easy to find."

Shuran looked up at Andra. "That is what my adda is doing is it not?" Andra's nod was all that Shuran needed. Shuran realized that his father had gone on a quest to rally the seven races together and somehow became lost or worse. He had to find his father at all costs or finish what he started.

When Shuran and Andra returned to the fallen tower, the others had started dinner, and Codger has been busy with Mallick making things more like a home. They moved stones and logs around inside to make tables and chairs. Walls were setup to separate living areas and a special area created for Moona to work her herb-lore. Outside the shelter, a well was created from the earth around the spot where water burst forth after Shuran lost his temper.

"Who constructed this well?" Shuran asked.

"It was Codger and myself. Being part dwarf, Codger has earth elemental power in him as you know," Andra stated.

"But not much strength for it!" Codger finished. "I borrowed one of your green stones after Andra reminded me how you worked out the better uses by color. Ingenious boy!" Codger beamed like a proud grandfather.

Shuran realized in that instant that these people were also his family and only trying to help and protect him. "I had hints from the missing pages of the Iniminim Ma," Shuran said and Codger lit up knowing that Andra had returned the missing vellum to the book.

Andra returned the look with a slight nod and then they all sat to eat dinner.

The next morning Shuran was up early gathering water from the well to place in a large rock-lined basin he had created for watering the animals. He was curious as to where the water spring was coming from so he reached out with his shi to touch the water's Essence so he might know its origin.

As he followed the path of the water, he was amazed at what he found. The water here had been forced into an underground circle surrounding a defined area, before folding back upon itself at a deeper level and flowing underground far to the South. The source of the underground river was far to the Frozen North.

Over the years, the flow had diverted leaving this trickling spring but when Shuran lost his cool the previous day, he had inadvertently closed off the diversion leading the river back to the circle around the ruins. Shuran mapped the deliberate circle in his mind and discovered that this was created in ancient times since it only encircled a portion of the ruins and was very deep in the earth. He now had a reference point for them to focus searching for lost artifacts… or more.

All five started out late morning checking the circle that Shuran had mapped out as the Abzu Mu, or deep water, encircling a portion of the ruins. Focusing their search here paid off as Moona shouted for help with some stone slabs.

The group surrounded the slabs and began clearing away overgrowth and rubble. Across the surface of the stone, a broken layer of plaster partially revealed the remnants of an ancient text. As they carefully cleared away the plaster, they could make out forms of more writing chiseled into the stone.

Most of the writing was far too damaged or worn to read, but there was a center section that had been partially protected by a layer of the plaster. Once they cleared the plaster, they could make out a portion.

"Salamu Turzu!" Shuran whispered and smiled.

Only Andra and Codger seemed to understand the significance of Shuran's words.

"You can read that scribble!" Moona grumbled.

"I can but I'm not sure how. What it means is something like gathering place for safe keeping knowledge," Shuran said.

"I agree," Andra said while Codger nodded as well.

"If that is so, how can this have been from the Telukukal? It is not exactly hidden," Mallick said doubtfully.

"Hidden in full view, check the surrounding retaining wall. This was the basin for a fountain or pond." Shuran pointed out the area, and the others agreed with his assumption.

"With the plaster covering the markings, whoever built this castle likely overlooked the placement and incorporated the stones into a garden or other structure rather than try to move them," Andra finished the observation.

Shuran asked the others to stand back while he inspected the area deeper.

"There is a void in the ground!" Shuran said. "It is a deliberate block from my probing the elements. Something is preventing me from seeing anything but a circular chamber of some sort deep below this stone. There is a slant to the ground leading to the deep chamber north of our position."

Shuran motioned for them all to stand back as he realized how to open the slab. "I cannot lift this stone out of the way even with the aid of an Abnu Emuq. I think I know another way." Shuran breathed deep and began coaxing power to flow from the surrounding earth and into the slab. He found that the stone was resisting his attempt to overload it with Essence to the point where it would burst. "I am unable to burst the stone!" Shuran shrugged.

"What are you trying to do?" Andra asked.

After Shuran explained what he had discovered the night before, causing stones to burst apart, Andra realized what the problem was.

"This is not ordinary stone Shuran. If it resists your efforts then it must be gug."

The others all looked confused, so Andra continued.

"Gug is a special stone that has odd properties of attraction. The dwarves call it lodestone," Andra said to Codger's looks of realization and tossed a coin into the air and watched as the others gasped when the coin arched toward the stone on its way down.

"This stone has power alignment to the earth and is a natural shield. That is why you see it as a void as well Shuran."

Shuran moved closer to the slab and upon removing the coin he felt the force in the stone. "Now I think I understand," Shuran said and placed his hands upon the stone. Electricity began bouncing between Shuran's hands and the stone, but it would not move. On the verge of giving up, Shuran let out one more frustrated burst of electricity from his hands and shouted. "PETA!" The stone slab slid effortlessly open in and upward motion until it stood at a steep angle, allowing entrance to the enormous opening down into the earth.

Shuran explained to the others how he opened the vault, as they now referred to it as. It took the use of electric force element into the stone. The seal was kept all this time by the foundation lodestone being electrically charge opposite of the covering slab. Shuran had forced electricity into the stone but explained that all he was doing was reinforcing the seal until he shouted 'PETA' out of frustration.

"Peta is ancient for 'open for me' and must have triggered a spell that reversed the polarity in the slab, forcing it apart," Shuran said as they worked their way down the steep slanting tunnel. Every five paces there was a quarter pace drop in the tunnel floor making this a long slanted stairway.

"I believe that it required the word and the electricity to open. I will create a crystal key for the rest of you to use since I do not think it wise to leave the vault open when not in use." Shuran finished this last thought as he reached a solid wall.

Andra stepped forward and sent a globe of illuminated energy into the space above them.

"This is a large door, nearly the size of the tunnel entrance!" Mallick wondered as he ran a hand over what appeared to be seems in the wall.

Shuran stepped forward and placed a hand on the wall and almost instantly the wall moved inward and slid to the side revealing a wondrously large chamber on the other side.

Shuran and the others felt small within the enormous chamber. The Vault was easily two hundred paces from one side to the other if it were possible to walk directly down the center.

The middle of the room appeared to be an oversized pillar surrounded by seven pedestals. Each pedestal had a recess in the top and an unknown symbol. There did not appear to be any way into the center space. Shuran soon lost interest in favor of less puzzling items to explore.

The treasures of knowledge and history enclosed mesmerized each of the five, even Moona could feel the ancient spells and power that emanated from everything with preserving magic.

Shuran moved over to the statue he noticed against a far wall. When he approached the statue, he felt a spark of energy move between himself the sculpture.

In a sudden flash, the statue began to glow and others, evenly spaced around the chamber, began to glow as well. Nearly two score of these statues surrounded the room standing silent vigil for untold eons, now lighting the room and enveloping the occupants with a warm, comfortable feeling. Most of them were crude likenesses of men of women, but four of them were so lifelike it was unsettling. There were several empty alcoves as well.

"I could get lost down here for several life spans!" Codger exclaimed.

"We could follow the stench to find you!" Moona cracked back with a puckered grin. "Now let's see what we got here!" She cackled and started exploring the shelves of books and scrolls.

"I do not recognize this material that most of these book's pages are made of." Codger explained.

"It is a pulp from wood!" Shuran said. "I can feel the faint signature of some tree left behind, but I do not know what kind. The weaving used to preserve this chamber, and its contents are likely the only reason the pages are un-aged."

Mallick found a book of ancient spells and runes.

Moona found preserved samples of plants and notes on their uses.

Codger was rummaging through diagrams and models of the strangest yet amazing devices and gadgets.

Shuran found many items, but was focusing his thoughts on a loosely bound tome about living things. The large book was an examination of every creature and plant living now and in the past from what he could understand, but the language appeared older than the ancient tongue. Shuran placed the book down hoping to find a translated version.

He found what appeared to be a start to a translation and now he would have to finish it, perhaps with time and the started translation to help, he might be able to interpret its contents.

Andra was focused on one thing only; the layout and features of this room struck a familiar chord, but Andra could not speak on it until certain. He was focused on the center structure within the seven pedestals.

The others all gathered their favorite finds and met in a section of the room that held a large wooden table with high-backed cushioned chairs.

"Oh! An old fanny such as I got could get use' to these chairs!" Moona said with a sign of relief. As Moona began to pull out her pipe, Codger grabbed it from her with a look of shock.

"Evalria! What are you thinkin' you can' be smokin' in here around these books!" Codger yelled.

Shuran and Mallick turned to each other with goofy smiles on their faces each mouthing 'EVALRIA' silently.

"Sorry… habit!" she responded retrieving her pipe and putting it back within the folds of her garments. "And you two, it is still Moona. Got it."

The boys just nodded with a snigger.

"I think that although these items are spelled, that removing them from here is not wise," Andra started.

"I have found blank paper and writing charcoal so we can copy things we wish to learn more about," Shuran offered. "We should only take our notes from the chamber, and nothing else until we have learned more about this place."

The others agreed and since he found the place the others began to refer further to it as Shuran's Vault.

The various writings they found were of similar, but not exact languages. Shuran could decipher them, as could Codger and Andra, but it was slow going so they decided to create a translation key of sorts that would reference the basics of each the four unique languages they found written.

Once finished, the translations of each book they came across became easier. As the days past into moons, they all made their way through various tomes within the ancient chamber of knowledge, history, and magic.

Shuran was able to create what he called a 'Nabad' or keystone, for the use of others to open and close the door and slab of the entrances to what Shuran called 'The Vault'. He somehow felt that naming it after himself was premature and narcissistic.

Shuran made great strides with understanding the anatomy book of life he had been translating. He discovered the differences in the various pages were because each page was written on the pulp of the plant or skin of the creature that it described. Shuran was repulsed at the skins of what were once people, being used as a medium for the written word. He only hoped it was taken after a natural death.

The advantage of being able to place his hand upon the page and feel everything described on the pages outweighed his repulsion of the vellum. He also learned about the bodily makeup of all the seven races. He was uncertain as to how, and why this information was in a book that had been sealed away in a hidden chamber longer than these races supposedly existed. That would be a mystery to solve another day.

Chapter Nineteen

In the council chambers of Chaos Keep, Assinnu Isten was meeting with the Order members.

"How is it that this information has not reached us before now!" shouted one of the elders. "How long have you known of this and chose not to tell us?" he asked with suspicion.

"I only found out myself recently, and even then it was only information from a vision and had yet to receive verified," Isten replied with every bit of venom in his voice he could muster without outwardly insulting the other elder.

Isten may have been the first of the Order, but it was an appointed position, so he did not yet want to jeopardize his status until his plans came to fruition. "The kashshaptu shared information which we checked. It is yet to become proven but looks as though the mother somehow hid a third child in the womb and her moon mother secreted it away," Isten finished.

"How, I wonder, did all that transpire under the watchful eye of our exalted leader? You were there Isten, and yet you failed to sense the deception." This time the questions came from another elder. He was much older and at his side was a small red-eyed imp wearing a smug and toothy smile. Isten thought he recognized something about the little demon but brushed it off.

"I am certain, Nagutan, that there was some weaving at play. The mother was not without talent," Isten started. "I am further certain, that with the Essence involved that night, it was unfortunate but not surprising, that this happened. We were all of us present, filled with awe of the chaotic forces flowing during the ceremony." Isten glared at the old man as he spoke the last few words.

Isten turned from Nagutan to look at other elders gathered. "It is of little consequence, the boy has no place in our plans and based on reports he will be no threat to Salmetu." Isten thought he had set the matter to rest.

"You of all should know the threat family bonds could be to goals such as ours Isten. I should not discount this boy if I were you," Nagutan said as he got up to leave. Of all those present Nagutan was the only one Isten would not reprimand for his actions or exiting without leave.

"It is already being taken care of Nagutan, old friend and mentor. We have insurance against the boy's interference," Isten finished almost meekly to his mentor's back as he left.

"The boy's name is Shuran, I suggest you learn it. Much power can be found in a name, especially that name." Nagutan exited with a flourish and smoke but the echoes of his laughter remained and hung on the air for several moments after his departure.

Shuran was a name of protection and power, It was a name that meant protection to the people. Isten was visibly shaken.

Isten dismissed the meeting and decided to pay a visit to the Order's benefactor and landlord, the Baron De Drakk.

Fallon sat within his dining hall enjoying breakfast with his daughter on any other morning, but today he was being subjecting to the infernal blathering of the Order of Chaos. To make his morning worse he was to be questioned directly by the Assinnu Isten.

"Your Drakk Elite Guards were there when this boy Shuran and his crew of dissidents escaped. What do you have to say for their actions?"

Isten shouted from the chair opposite the Baron of Drakk.

The baron looked across the table at the cult leader, seeing him for what he felt he was. This Assinnu Isten was a fear monger and insecure in his position, and power hungry. Fallon also knew exactly what Isten was all about. "You may be important among your order, but to me you are a guest of my land. The Order for that matter has enjoyed the protection of my borders as guests. You step over the line of hospitality with your tone Assinnu Isten to accuse me openly of some transgression!" Fallon spoke smoothly and evenly.

Isten became visibly red in the face but held his tongue.

"My men did as I instructed and nothing more," Fallon said.

"And what pray tell were your instructions?" Isten asked only slightly calmer.

"My men were told the boy was preferred alive. They were told to follow the lead of the Inquisitors. And they were told not to engage the boy if they could not subdue him. They followed these orders to the letter." Fallon smiled mockingly back to Isten who became expressionless.

"He speaks truth plainly." Salmetu slinked in from the shadows beyond the main room.

Suddenly calmer, Isten motioned for Salmetu to join him. "Baron this is-"

"I am aware of who the Priestess is. I am pleased to make your acquaintance Salmetu." Fallon interrupted.

"Pleasure is not what I would call being out at this bright hour of the day. I only come at the behest of my lord the Isten," Salmetu said without emotion, but her eye twitched as she said the title. "May we leave now?" she asked.

"Momentarily my dear, Salmetu," Isten whispered. "Has the Baron left anything out?" Isten asked her.

She closed her eyes and paused while reaching her mind out to the Baron. She flinched slightly then opened her eyes in shock, recovering too quickly for Isten to notice as he turned to face her. "Nothing of consequence was left out of his testimony." Salmetu shared a final knowing glance with Fallon, who only nodded as his morning guests left his council chambers.

"Perhaps I shall regain my appetite by dinner." Fallon muttered to himself as he exited the chamber. He gathered himself after the brief encounter and decided a visit to his secret guest was in order.

Fallon made his way back to Drakkfoth and travelled through the hidden tunnels to find the room his secret guest was staying.

"Please come in and sit," came the soft voice with an effort from the confines of her sickbed.

"I do not wish to disrupt your rest my lady," Fallon said with a slight and respectful bow.

"You can dispense with formalities brother, there is no one around," she said as Fallon entered the room to face his guest. "What news do you have of my children?" Sulura asked as she turned her weakened form to her husband's brother.

"Events are unfolding as we have planned thanks to your foresight," Fallon said as he stretched for her outreached hand.

"And of my husband?" she implored.

"I am sorry, but there has been no word, but a mutual friend is watching for signs of his progress or at least his whereabouts."

***

Salmetu and Isten arrived back at the keep they held within the borders of Drakk.

The darkness inside Chaos Keep penetrated every corner of the structure even on the brightest of days. Salmetu was now so joined to the dark that she bathed in shadow and rejoiced during the setting of Utu.

Tonight was a special night for her. She would be gaining some insight into the boy who would have been her brother before she was reborn. "Bring the man child forward and place him before me," she commanded of the zealots in attendance.

Isten sat off to the side of the room observing the weaving that was beyond his power and comprehension. He was uncertain how Salmetu knew these new spells, but he was so transfixed by the power, he dismissed concern.

When they found this boy, he was barely breathing. Only through weaving was he kept alive and prepared to be brought before the priestess so she might use him. Tonight Salmetu would breath chaos into his shi and make a tool out of him.

Salmetu placed a hand on his forehead and looked deeply into his empty eyes."KUKU-MA, SI NE BUR, TAMUSU BAMU!" With the weaving and a flourish of her hands, Salmetu's shi glowed and a stream flowed from her to Bastien in an attempt to join them as master and slave. She stopped frustration and anger on her face. "It still cannot be done. Take him to his cell until I find what to do about him." Salmetu said as she wavered slightly and sat back at her throne in the main chamber of the keep. Something was preventing her spell work. She was furious. "Isten! I have need of food." She shouted and the usually dominant Isten acquiesced to her command and left to get her what she ordered.

Chapter Twenty.

Shuran sat at a large table in the vault reading through his translations of the anatomy book he became obsessed with. He had already exercised running through each of his foster family's bodies with his mind and was able to match what the book referred to as genetics, to sections of the book. He could see why each was able to perform certain Essence weaving or wielding.

It was built into their genes. What he could not understand is why the same genes were somehow damaged in Moona. Moona had been elusive in her reasons for not submitting to Shuran's tests and at first he excused it as Moona being… Well, Moona. His curiosity got the better of him and he finally learned to do a probe by having just a piece of her hair. What he found was nowhere in the book. He found similarities to genes shared of all the races but where markers should have allowed wielding or weaving the Essence, he found corruption of the cells. He finally worked up the courage to confront her.

"Moona, I have a transgression to admit," Shuran said when he could get her alone at her workstation in the Vault.

The Vault was separated into areas of subject and Moona secluded herself in the area dedicated to the knowledge of plants.

"Before I whack you for probing me without permission is there something else you wish to admit!" Moona did not look up from her work.

"You knew?" Shuran asked with surprise.

"Just 'cause I no longer have the abilities I once had, don' leave me without certain strengths. Never underestimate the power o' seein' what be goin' on around ya, young wielder." Moona looked up and gave Shuran a smug look. "Yes, I was once a wielder and weaver. I have the blood of dwarf and human, both of my parents were powerful in their own right, and I inherited it." Moona took out her pipe and stuffed it with a sample of something she found in a jar. "This is some really good stuff," Moona said taking a drag and after slowly exhaling continued her story.

"Growing up a mix blood ain' as difficult as it was in the first centuries of the Sikil Mah, but we all still had ta hide. We became adept at blendin' in and stuck to our own. Codger was a fortunate marriage ya see. Not that I didn' love 'im mind ya. It's just, well we stuck to our own and I had little choices. Just happens we met by chance. Dwarf men get ta be a thorn in your arse after a hundred harvests or so." Moona caught herself drifting off subject and continued.

"We had a sprat of our own, Codge and me. Our beautiful baby boy was the center of our world, but soon we realized he was different somehow." She paused briefly before continuing and wiped her eyes. "Most o' the gifted don' develop until after their first ten to fifteen harvests, but Vardoran showed nothin' of a spark 'til he was nearly twenty harvests, and even then it was not... normal. He became so obsessed with makin' us proud, that he got mixed up with some bad dingir cult, Xul followers.

"He paid someone to call up a Telal to reveal its secrets. All of what he learned, I do not know, but there is one thing I do..." Moona stopped and shuddered slightly before continuing. "He learned to steal another's Essence." Moona finished the last statement with a glisten to her eyes. Shuran apologized and did not press her further, knowing she would share more in her own time.

"Shuran come here and look what Codger and I have found!" Mallick yelled from the other side of the chamber.

Shuran, feeling somewhat rescued from an awkward moment, nodded to Moona, who smiled at him and went to join Mallick and Codger. "What has your britches in such a bunch Mally!" Shuran joked as he approached the table they were working at. He noticed several crystal shards from the cabinet laid out on the table in front of them with an old text open before them as well.

"This text describes how things are made up and you can break them and they are still connected!" Mally said excitedly.

Shuran just looked at them with a confused look.

"That is the simple explanation my boy," Codger beamed at Shuran. "Come read this and see what ya think."

Shuran read the text and understood how it described things as being made up of small particles, too tiny to see, but he already knew this because he could feel them. If something were split a certain way, these parts could still somehow remain tangled together even over great distances. Shuran just exhaled at the vast complexity of the knowledge stored in this chamber before recorded time. "This is truly the knowledge of the gods!" Shuran said.

Shuran, Codger, and Mally went about testing and experimenting on crystals based on the texts with mixed results. In a moment of frustration Shuran, holding one half of a split crystal, looked at it and out of frustration spat out an ancient word. "PAD!" And instantly the crystal and its twin both shattered into so many uncountable pieces.

Shock and understanding shook him at the same time. "The crystals need to be spelled first with a purpose before they are split!" Shuran said.

Mally just looked at Shuran confused but Codger understood and immediately brought Shuran an assortment of shards from which to choose.

Shuran thought of something useful from the Iniminim Ma, and set about weaving it into the shard while at the same time gathering Essence into the stone to power the spell. He then placed the crystal in the device used to split them and spoke the words to separate the shard.

At first nothing seemed to happen but then Shuran's eyes lit up. "Look at them closely. Open yourself up to the rhythm of the Essence in the stones.

"They are pulsing but in the opposite of one another!" Mally shouted.

"They are... tangled." Codger said in a whisper. "What do they do?"

Shuran sent Mally outside of the vault taking one half of the shard with instructions to speak a specific sentence once he was well outside the main entrance. After what felt like an eternity Codger nearly lost his patience.

"What are we waiting for boy!" he shouted.

"Just a moment, Codge." The half crystal in Shuran's hand started to glow with pulses of light.

"They are working," Shuran started, touching the stone and saying, "Kin'Ge!"

"Shuran, come here. I want you." Mallick's voice came from the crystal.

Codger jumped in shock at hearing Mallick's voice sounding from the glowing stone in Shuran's hand.

Shuran just smiled and lifted the shard to his mouth and said, "Thank you Mally, now come back inside! Kin'Su." Shuran beamed with accomplishment and Andra stood behind him smiling, which is not something anyone ever saw before.

Moona saw it.

In the ancient Vault beneath the ruins of the old kingdoms, Shuran was working hard at learning all he could. Now that he knew of his sister and the prophecy, he wanted to do everything he could to be what he must to put his family back together.

"Shuran your progress is unprecedented," Andra exclaimed. "I feel that there is nothing more for me to leave you with, but one tool before I must go."

"What do you mean leave?" Shuran asked.

"My time with you has always been simply to set you on the proper path for now. I have done this and more. It is time I return to my duties and prepare for what is to come," Andra said more cryptically than usual.

Shuran read this to mean he would get no further explanation. "What do you wish for me to learn my dear friend?"

"You must learn what it is to shift and what a shifter truly is." Andra held out his hand.

Confused, Shuran took Andra's extended hand, allowing him to fully explore the being that was not part of his book of anatomy. What Shuran felt was nothing he had yet experienced? His own body began morphing from form to form. Each face he took on was so different from the next, that he began to weep. Shuran felt what it meant to never have a true shape. He felt the emptiness of being destined to mimic everything while claiming no identity for oneself.

Only then did Andra take back its hand looking into Shuran's eyes with a shared understanding.

"Is there nothing that can be done?" Shuran pleaded.

Andra stood and looked at Shuran. "My fate is to be, what I must for as long as needed and nothing more, for as long as the Essence flows within me. One day perhaps I shall become that someone I can keep as myself."

The sadness nearly overtook Shuran before he gathered himself. "I shall miss you."

Andra shared the tears, but did not allow Shuran to see them.

Andra left the next morning with only Shuran to see off his friend. They went into the Vault alone, and Shuran closed the entrance behind them as they entered.

When the others woke to find them not in the tower ruins, Mally went out to find them. He showed up at the Vault entrance to find Shuran exiting alone, with a glossiness in his eyes.

"Andra has left for home. I do not know if or when we might meet again," Shuran said as he passed Mallick. Before Mallick could question him, Shuran called out for him to follow to the clearing around the corner. When Mallick rounded the corner, he found an Inquisitor standing before him.

Shuran worked in earnest practicing his newest skill of shifting into other forms.

Mallick helped by finding a spell to transmute his garments, as well as his appearance. He was convincing most of the time and after the initial shock of being confronted by an inquisitor, Mallick was becoming more helpful in suggesting where Shuran was having problems.

"You are too big to be Moona or Codger!" Mally said.

"I know but that cannot be helped. Andra said that I could borrow Essence to become something larger."

"Yah that snow bear you did earlier nearly scared Moona out of her wrinkled old skin," Mally interrupted.

"You be careful who you be callin' old smart arse!" Moona yelled from across the room.

"I kinda like your wrinkles." Codger whispered next to her.

Moona just grunted as she smacked Codger in the back of the head. Then she smiled to herself.

Shuran shifted back to himself from Codger's form. "The problem is to become something less is to give up something of myself. I would have to be able to store that part of myself somewhere safe in order to get it back," Shuran finish with frustration.

"Ah!" Mally said as he got up and ran to the shelf to retrieve a book. "What you need is a keepsafe!" Mally said. "As I understand this, you create a spelled chamber of gugtu, or magicked lodestone. With a proper binding, you can send and retrieve anything from this location with a thought. Perhaps it would work with your... Extra bits?" Mally questioned.

Shuran thought about it and finally answered. "It might work if the vessel is protected. And where does someone go about finding lodestone?" Shuran asked.

Mally just grimaced and gestured. "You are standing inside it you dur!"

Shuran just stared in shock at Mally's suggestion.

"I would literally lose myself in this place!" Shuran gasped.

Mally just shrugged. But together they read through the instructions and decided to try it on the chamber.

Shuran placed his bloodied palm on the door to the chamber over the new inscription of his name in the language of the first people. He intoned the spell to bind his will to the room and immediately felt the overwhelming rush of the chamber's inventory run through his mind. He passed out cold.

Later when Moona pouring iced water over his head awakening him he jumped up with a start and head-splitting pain.

"What happened to you?" Mally asked.

After several moments Shuran finally gathered his sense enough to answer. "When I bound myself to the room, everything in it became mine. I know everything that is in the chamber." Shuran said in shock.

"You mean you understand all this?" Codger asked.

"Not exactly, I know the contents I can reference the available texts by title and inventory of artifacts, but I do not understand everything outright. I still need to learn more of the language and history of the first people," Shuran finished, as if the others should understand what he just said.

Later that evening the group ate dinner and talked of what was to come.

"It is time I left to follow the path that my father laid out before me," Shuran said.

"What path boy? You think 'cause you are all mighty powerful now you can take on the Order alone?" Moona held a scowl on her face that would make a forest troll cower in fear.

"He will not be alone," Mallick answered before Shuran could speak.

"Oh, so now both you spratlings got your brains all addled!" Moona said.

"I do not know what my father was doing but it had to be important. So I must find out if he is still out there and help finish what he started," Shuran said dutifully.

"Once you figure out what it is, you mean." Codger finally spoke up. "Moony dear, we won' be stoppin, 'em from goin' best we can do is be here for um learning what we can and keepin' things safe. We have the talking stones now."

After dinner, Shuran practiced storing and retrieving items from the vault. He only moved things in and out that were not part of the original library so he might protect them from damage. He still was uncertain what would happen to anything if it were removed from the protection of the vault's spell work.

For now, he would rely on copies of originals and hopefully not need any artifacts that he was yet unsure of what they did, if anything. He was not yet ready to try storing part of his Essence there yet and thought it something only done in extreme need. For now he was content with sending crystals, notes and supplies.

"This will certainly make traveling easier not having to carry everything with us," Mally commented.

"How much energy does it take from you?" Codger asked.

"That is just it, I hardly feel a draw at all. It is as if the room is now part of me and I can just reach in as though placing my hand in the pocket of my garments," Shuran answered. "Codger perhaps you could do some reading on the subject?" Shuran asked and Codger nodded back in reply.

"Are you going to tell us why Andra left?" Codger asked.

"He said he had to prepare the Foresworn for what is to come. What that means he did not explain," Shuran answered.

"He did not leave on foot, did he use one of your crystals?" Mallick asked.

Shuran looked up at his friends and sighed. "Not exactly, he found something in the vault or rather something about it. I am sworn not to speak of it yet," Shuran said before anyone could question him on it further. "I was not even certain it worked until Andra sent a message by stone from the second set I created. I have made new ones with Andra's help."

Shuran pulled back his sleeve to producing an arm brace of silver alloy. Set in the brace was two gemstones. He then reached out with a thought and produced three more items with similar features but only one stone on each. "The red gem on each is for communication-," Shuran said before Codger interrupted.

"And the clear stone? I assume the second on your brace alone is for you to speak with Andra." Codger said rather than asked.

Shuran nodded and handed Mallick an arm brace and a pendant to each Moona and Codger.

Mallick and Codger put on their articles and they immediately flashed with a glow settled over each of them before dissipating. "I have also created the stones so that only we could use them and will return to the vault if they were to somehow fall into the wrong hands. If something were to happen to the owner and your Essence drops below acceptable levels, the artifact would transport you into the vault."

"Well, that is all well and good for the rest o' ya but you forget somethin' Shuran," Moona said feeling somehow less than she should. She had not yet placed her pendant around her neck.

"I have a solution for that if you are willing." Shuran gave Moona a slight smile.

They went inside the Vault, not knowing they were being watched.

"What are they doing now?" asked the dwarf to his companions. "This duty bites more than the cold,

and Utu is making my eyes ache!" he continued to complain.

"Stop your complaining Avrank. When the elders deemed us go watch Durangug, that is what we do." Dvargan and Grafdrik said.

"Hand me the wine skin I have a thirst," Avrank continued as they watched the man-lings down at the ruins of what was once a castle built upon the ancient home to the watcher of the lands, the Shin'Ar.

Dvargan closed the spyglass and tucked it into his satchel. "I am thinking we have enough to take back to the elders. The time we were told about seems to approach. Only the chosen one could have entered the chamber." The three dwarves picked up their things and headed back to the cave entrance behind them.

Chapter Twenty-One

≪𒁹

Shuran led Moona into the Vault alone, where he asked her to stand in the now open central interior chamber.

Moona noticed that each of the pedestals now held a crystal shard. Each shard a different color that corresponded to the element represented by a symbol carved into the pedestal.

He reached out for her hand and placed his over top of hers. Within moments his mind was racing through her, locating and repairing the corrupted markers in her genes. By the time he finished, he was sweating and visibly tired.

"You have exhausted yourself. Why didn' you use one o' those fancy rocks?" Moona said trying to hide her gratitude behind sarcasm.

"The first part had to be done without excess power. It required finesse and concentration that I have not mastered yet using an abnu emuq. However, this next part requires no delicacy and it will likely sting a bit." Shuran looked up at Moona sideways and she sneered back. "Ok, it will sting like Xul is sticking you with dragon-stone needles or burn like Kibalga!" he admitted.

"Just get this over with," she cringed.

Shuran stepped out of the chamber and walked over to the earth stone and placed a hand on it. Immediately the shard began to glow and pulse. He then walked over to the pedestal containing a shard of green crystal.

As soon as Shuran touched it, the chamber Moona stood in went pitch black then a steady stream of green light burst up from the floor and engulfed Moona. She screamed.

Moments later Shuran helped Moona out of the chamber and onto a cot in a secluded section of the vault. He laid her back and then brought a waterskin to her lips. After a couple sips Moona opened her eyes and looked up at Shuran with tears in her eyes.

"Thank you!"

Shuran nodded back.

"Now get that water away from me and get he some of Codger's brew. That hurt worse than birthing a sprat!"

Shuran smiled and left Moona to get what she asked.

After he left, Moona reached into one of her many pockets and pulled out her pendant. Slowly she placed the chain over her head and immediately gasped when it activated. "DAMKIANNA! Bless that boy!"

"What is that thing… the chamber?" Moona asked Shuran after she had rested enough to regain her strength.

"From what I can understand, it is, or was, used to concentrate the seven powers. Each pedestal channels one of the energies and can only be used by someone who can wield that particular power," he replied.

"So it would take seven people to work? One for each power?" Moona asked.

"Yes, perhaps even multiple abilities combined in any number of individuals or just one who can wield them all. I was able to activate each pedestal so I assume I could work it alone. Its ultimate purpose I do not know, as the language used to describe it is different from all the others we have encountered in this vast library except the book of living things."

Moona looked at Shuran. "Is that device what you used to send Andra home?"

A nod was the answer that Moona received from Shuran.

After spending a few hours testing the speaking stones, Mallick and Shuran began helping Moona and Codger move all of their things into the Vault. They would spend all their time there so it made sense that they live inside as well.

The animals were brought into an area outside the main chamber where there was space large enough to corral them and create a stable of sorts. The group had no idea as to what was to come, and they felt that being over cautious was better than not.

The chamber, when closed, somehow provided breathable air and the antechamber had a fountain that brought in fresh water from the Abzu Mu. The main chamber had several empty sections that were converted to living quarters and storage.

Shuran designated an area for sending in new things and showed them where he or Mally would appear should it become necessary. He also found an empty place to arrange all the abnu emuq he created in Birchshire as well as new ones he found in the library. He packed away a few he would keep with him, as well as a few devices he found useful that still worked when he took them outside the vault.

Shuran and Mallick began packing up the supplies. Some basic provisions of dried meat from one of the cattle they had slaughtered, cheese, and dried fruit. A water skin each and a medical belt that Moona had provided.

"No need wastin' energy healin' a blister my boy!" Moona said.

The belt contained herbs and ointments for healing and pain management. They all agreed that when they could not find food or water on their own, they would send the empty sacks and skins back to the vault to retrieve full ones that Moona would keep fresh and ready.

They each took a blade and dagger from the weapons rack found in the vault. They took the plainest ones they could find but even those were far more ornate than necessary.

Mallick had thought ahead to bring their bows and full quivers when they escaped Britengate so they only needed to put together sleeping rolls.

"Shuran! Look at this traveling shelter I found. It looks like an ordinary tent but I do not know this material. It is so tightly woven I do not think water could even penetrate it."

"It seems heavy but might be useful. I will call for it if there is need," Shuran said flatly and turned.

"Just like that… I need this or that and ZAPPO, it just appears. This is going to be amazing!" Mallick spoke with far too much glee for Shuran's current state of mind.

"Mally look, this is not going to be any ordinary adventure. There will be danger and the unknown to face. We still have no idea where we are going and who is waiting for us," Shuran snapped.

Mally was not taken back by Shuran's tone. He knew his friend, though younger in actual age, he was now aged and wise beyond his years. And yet he was still just a boy. "I know this Shuran. We are in this together since the start."

Shuran calmed and grabbed Mallick's shoulder in a gesture of brotherhood before moving on to finish preparing for travel.

***

Meanwhile Andra returned back to the Foresworn Territories before schedule. He had things to set in motion and hoped to move about without impediment, but he was called to the Nabusa.

"Andra! Why have you returned so soon and without notice?" Nabusa was both pleased and concerned at the appearance of her agent in the antechamber.

"I apologize for my sudden arrival Nabusa but things have progressed so rapidly and in a direction we did not foresee," Andra said as he knelt down to kiss the grandmothers hand in greeting. "Shuran has found the chamber of Shin'Ar," Andra said.

Her expression light up with a broad smile. "I assume he has opened it as well?" she asked.

Andra noticed her excitement. "He used the central chamber to send me home," Andra said looking to Nabusa for answers.

"We must convene a council to discuss our next steps. This changes much but it is not a bad thing. Not a bad turn of events at all my child." Nabusa reached down to rest her hand on her Andra's head.

"You were correct," Andra added. "He carries the ability to shift as well."

Her eyes narrowed. "It is as I suspected. Shuran is more than just the blending of the seven. Something or someone has meddled with him," she said.

"How is that possible? Surely not the Old Codger, Moona, or the boy Mallick?" Andra asked.

Nabusa played along with Andra's ignorance. "I fear this was done before he was birthed, and I wonder at what was done to the girl child." Nabusa carried a look of concern that Andra had never seen.

Nabusa was not the only one concerned over Shuran.

Isten was angry at the fact there was no sign of Salmetu's brother Shuran. The Great Council, for failure to produce proof of a threat, had suspended his use of the Land's Guard and Inquisitors. Now he had to figure out his next move.

"Why are you so upset Isten?" Salmetu asked as she turned her chair from the fire to face him. She sat with her undead cat in her lap scratching it behind the ears. "So the high and mighty Great Council has halted its pursuit of Shuran and his companions. That does not mean we have no recourse." Salmetu looked up at Isten and smiled.

"What are you thinking my delightfully devious child?" Isten asked in a slightly perked up tone.

"We have Bastien and we could, use him. Perhaps make some undead forces with weavers to control them. And there are always the ogres and trolls," she said as she turned back to the fire.

Isten saw the truth of it, but he also knew something needed to be done about the Council. He must find a way to take control of it once and for all.

Chapter Twenty-Two

⟪𒀭

Shuran and Mallick finished everything they needed before setting off on their journey to an unknown destination. They spent the night going over maps of the known realms of Aurderia. The closest destination they decided to try was within the Orenthal Mountains. The maps indicated that this place was once the ancestral home of the dwarves.

Codger agreed that this was a good place to start. Although secluded, the dwarves held no true ill toward humans in general, and they would likely ignore them before being outwardly hostile.

Shuran figured if the dwarves of Orenthal were anything like Aknard, then they would at least be able to barter for information if nothing else.

Although Moona and Codger both had dwarven blood, they knew little of the heritage or history of full-blooded dwarves.

Aknard is the only dwarf that Codger was familiar with and Moona had only ever done occasional trading in Rivenwood with the few dwarves that would enter the human settlements to trade for goods.

According to Aknard though, his people enjoyed their ale and wine. Codger promised to cook up some more of his home brew and have it available in a designated spot of the Vault if Shuran had need. There was also the vast store of aged wine and brandy already in the Vault.

Moona was like a sprat in a candy shop once Shuran repaired her ability to wield earth element and weave spells. She was busy now making up for the time the others had spent pouring over the library contents. She was translating spells and putting them in categories of usefulness.

She found some books too distasteful to read and avoided them all together. "There is some right nasty stuff in some of those books!" she said returning an old tome to its place on the shelves. "If ya ever need to do somethin' nasty to someone, I'll know what books ta look in. We have one last night together so I thought we should all have a nice dinner and talk or somethin'," Moona said with a smile.

"What has gotten into her?" Mallick asked Codger.

"Kinda scary right?" Codger whispered. "I think she must have found somethin' in those jars and smoked it."

Shuran just looked at them and laughed knowing she was just overjoyed at having her abilities back. But he had to admit, seeing Moona the least bit cheerful, was frightening.

The four of them ate a hearty stew of rabbit caught in the snares with wild vegetables and mushrooms.

Codger poured ale from some of his supply that he always kept on the Mellamu Nanna.

The mood was jovial, and Shuran felt well, while at the same time held fear for the future. He had no idea what was to come, but he felt that there would be much trouble in the world before this ended. He was not convinced it would end well either.

"I sure am gonna miss this," Codger said. "I've enjoyed having a family again."

Moona dropped her glass at Codger's words.

"Oh, yak scat, now I've done it. Moony dear I didn' mean-"

"It's all right Codge. You only said what I been feelin'. These boys turned out good, and now I know it wasn' our fault Vardoran turned out the way he did." Moona was well into her cups by now.

"That's right Moony," Codger motioned for the boys to help him get ahold of her and lead her to her bed.

154

"Whatever she smoked didn' mix well with your brew Codge," Shuran said.

"Don' talk about me like I'm not here," Moona shouted in a brief, coherent moment. She just as quickly went back to babbling under her breath as the three men in her life helped her get to her bed.

"She is not going to feel well in the morning," Mally said.

"I think it best we be gone before she wakes," Shuran said and nudged Mally.

"Cowards!" Codger said to them both and smiled as they watched Moona roll into her bedding and begin snoring, loudly.

Before long the men decided to take to bed as well since it would be an early morning. Shuran was off to sleep quickly but not soundly. His night was filled with visions that were more vivid than ever before. Later he would realize that sleeping within the vault heightened his awareness.

In his visions, small furry bears carrying clubs and sticks were surrounding him. The next moment he was in a grand cavern surrounded by dwarves and confronted by a figure with a double-edged hammer.

Suddenly he is in a large wooded area surrounded by silence with Mallick and a dwarf who seemed stunted wearing a crown. Arrows began raining from the skies and pierced his companions through their leathers.

The woods around him began to shake, and the trees were falling around him as giant heads appeared from above the falling trees. Fire began raining down from the skies and engulfed him. Suddenly he was raised into the air and dropped. Just before hitting the ground he woke suddenly in a sweat.

Shuran decided that sleep would not come again soon and it was only a couple hours before Utu broke above the horizon. He decided to go get some air outside the Vault. Some quiet time away from Moona's snoring would be welcome also.

He walked the grounds past the dry-dock where the Mellamu Nanna was resting, and off into the clearing nearest the tower ruins. After just a few moments of enjoying the quite, he heard the snapping of branches then silence again. Someone was out there.

Immediately Shuran formed a shield around himself and tried to remember if he had closed the Vault entrance. He turned to head back to the entrance when the first creature came out of the woods toward him.

It was one of the furry creatures from his vision. It seemed it was moving toward him deliberately but in no hurry.

Shuran moved to try and circle back around but saw that another fur-covered creature blocked the path. The moon was currently behind the trees so he could not make much out. He began to gather Essence and thought to frighten the creatures away. He let loose a few bursts of fire and lightening.

The creatures stopped and one of them lifted a double-edged axe into the air and the noise came out of it.

"SHIN'AR!" and the other creatures repeated the sound.

Shuran was confused until he decided to look deeper at the furry things closest to him. He could see the Essence and power of the Earth element about them.

Shuran approached a fur-covered animal only to discover that it was fur cloaks being worn by a dwarf. They were all dwarves. "Who are you?" Shuran called out and waited on an answer. After what seemed like an eternity, Shuran thought to sidestep the dwarf, then there was a response.

"You are the Shin'Ar returned. We have come to escort you to the elders who wish to look upon you," the dwarf said as a duplicate bundle of furry dwarf came to stand beside him. "My name is Dvargan and this is my brother Grafdrik."

Shuran could not tell exactly where the furs ended and the dwarf began. What showed of his head was covered in a thick beard and bushy eyebrows that reminded him of fuzzy leaf eating crawler bugs, only much larger. Two rather large eyes where all he could see. Behind those eyes were kindness and excitement. And next to him stood his brother, a mirror image.

"I am Shuran," he managed to say.

"Shuran Shin'Ar, it would please the king if you would accompany us to Duranekur.

"I think I need to sit and drink," Shuran said.

Shuran sat with his new companions around a fire set outside the Vault tunnel entrance.

They told him that they had been watching the site of the ruins for as

156

far back as the Dwarven history records extended. As Dvargan and Grafdrik began to recite the history, finishing each other's sentences, Shuran interrupted.

"Please, before you go on would you meet my friends and let them share the story?" Shuran got up and motioned for them to enter the Vault with him.

"ELITUR!" the five dwarves all said in shock. "Shuran Shin'Ar, we cannot. It would be sacrilege for any, but you or your Zidu'Si to enter," Grafdrik and Dvargan said in unison.

Shuran was confused and he did not understand the Dwarves. These were nothing like the dwarf Aknard, whom he met at Smuggler's Cove. Shuran drew back his sleeve and tapped the red crystal on his arm brace. "We have honored guests, please come outside the Vault. Kin-Su," Shuran said as the dwarves all made sounds of awe at seeing the Shin'Ar weaving Essence.

Moona was the first to waddle out of the Vault entrance. She looked miserable from the night before and it was evident in her disposition.

"What in the name of DAMIKANNA is so blasted urgent... ARRRGG!" Moona caught site of five furry creatures with eyes glowing from the firelight and was caught ill prepared.

"Biddley-Diddles! Are those? I mean them fuzzy bundles. Are there dwarves under them furs?" she finally spat out.

Shuran just laughed and motioned her, and the now arriving Codger and Mallick, to join them. "Everyone this is Dvargan and Grafdrik along with their traveling team. They will be leading us to the Dwarven Capital City of Duranekur," Shuran said.

Dvargan and Grafdrik told the story of their history keeping watch over the Library of Shin'Ar. It is told that as long as Dwarves have lived they have been charged with keeping watch for the return of the Shin'Ar, Watcher of the Lands. In the most ancient of their history stories was told of how the ancients left this world, all but one.

The Shin'Ar stayed behind because he loved the people of Aurderia and was rumored to have actually sent the other ancients away deliberately to save Ersetu. Shin'Ar lived for thousands of years watching over the peoples of the lands but one day disappeared.

The dwarves were the first to arrive at this exact location looking for their protector. What they found, was Shin'Ar's trusted apprentices and faithful companions from the seven races, the Zidu'Si. Shin'Ar had closed himself off in his library and the Zidu'Si could no longer enter.

They were told that the time of Shin'Ar was at an end. One day he would return in the form of another, but not until he was truly needed. The Zidu'Si all returned to their homelands and the dwarves made TAMU'TUR, a sacred oath to stay and await the Shin'Ar's return.

"Nearly ten thousand years later Shuran Shin'Ar returned as only he found and opened the Library!" one of the dwarfs said.

"Seven races? That would mean giants were part o' this Zidushi group?" Moona asked.

"ZIDU'SI. And yes they were." Grafdrik answered.

"Ah you can speak by yourself! That talking at the same time thing gives me the wibblies!" Moona looked at them sideways. "Are you two twins?" she asked.

"Yes, we are," they said together. "Very rare for a dwarfess to birth more than one sprat and rarer still for identical twins," they said speaking every few words in turn.

Moona shivered at the 'talking as one' thing and turned to Mallick. "That is gonna cause ya ta jump from the peaks of Orenthal, mark my words Mally!" Moona pulled her pipe and began to light it when one of the other dwarfs jumped to light it for her. Moona gave him a sideways look and just the slightest nod of thanks.

"Giants! Never seen one but that explains the size of the vault." Codger said.

"Nobody has reported seeing the giants in thousands of years. Not since the Great Council created the anzillu and the seats of the council became held by all humans," one of the dwarfs spat.

"It is said that they went back to their ancient homeland in some hidden place beyond the Frozen North," Mallick said.

Everyone turned to him as though he had stepped in something left behind by a beast.

"What? I read it in the vault library," Mallick admitted.

"The Zidu'Si speaks true." Dvargan said.

158

"Why do you refer to Mallick as Zidu'Si?" Shuran asked.

"He and your other Zidu'Si can enter the chamber. They have traveled here with you and we have watched how they are devoted to you. This is the way of the Zidu'Si. It is honor above just family," Dvargan and Grafdrik said.

"Do any of you other shorties talk?" Moona snapped.

"Of course they do just no one ever gets much chance to speak when we are around," the twin dwarves said together.

"Imagine that!" Moona said looking at Mally and mockingly acted out a person jumping from a height, walking her fingers off her other hand.

Mallick grimaced and Moona just cackled at herself.

"I think we should get you boys and dwarfs fed and on your way!" Moona said jumping up to head back into the vault.

"What is her hurry?" Mallick asked.

Codger thumbed toward the newcomers. "I think she is not used to 'not' being the shortest."

From the vault came a screech that was undeniably Moona. Codger was blown backward by the force of a rather large ball of snow that fell from out of nowhere. Moona loved having her magic back.

"I do not envy you being left here alone with her," Shuran said with a grin.

Codger just smiled back. "It will help that she found some frost moss growin' on the East walls of the tower ruins!"

Moona made omelets out of eggs gathered previously from wild snowbirds. She added onions, reconstituted peppers, mushrooms, and meat.

Mallick fried up some sliced potatoes and apples.

Codger gathered plates, cups, utensils, and wine from within the racks inside the Vault.

Shuran used his new ability to instantly bring it all out onto a setup table and chairs from the Vault as well.

The dwarves were all amazed at seeing the power of the Shin'Ar. They ate well and talked until Utu was well into mid-morning. When they were finished Shuran and Mallick spelled the table clean and Shuran returned everything to its proper place.

The day was wasting and Shuran could not put off leaving any further. With glossy-eyed farewells, the boys set off on their quest, lead by five fur covered dwarves.

Shuran thought back to his vision that started with furry things coming out of the woods.

Chapter Twenty-Three

≪ 𝅘𝅥

The seven travelers made their way through the forested lands along the path the dwarves had used to come to the ruins. They would be taking this route to the Eastern base of the Orenthal Mountains where they would make the trek up an age-old route toward the first of the dwarf clan settlements.

They were making good time to the base since the heavy snows had not yet started in the Southern ranges. The depth of the snow was well over the heads of the dwarfs, and it was lucky that the path they had used followed a riverbed where the depth was manageable. They decided that due to their late start from Shuran's Vault, they would travel as far as the mountain base, then camp for the night before starting the climb in the morning.

"Dvargan, you say that your people have been keeping vigil over the Vault for all this time, what was the castle that now lay in ruins on the site?" Shuran asked.

"There have been two castles built upon that spot according to our histories," Grafdrik started.

"The ruins that currently remain are from an old monastery built by the Followers of Light before the Lalli Mah," Dvargan finished.

Mallick's smile at the dwarfs back and forth way of talking together was already fading. He thought that Moona was correct in her prediction. If this back and forth babble kept up, he would find himself stuffing his ears with cloth, jumping from a cliff would be a last resort. "Shuran, no matter how I plead, do not let me jump to my death once we begin our climb."

Shuran just looked at him with confusion.

The dwarfs told the stories, as they knew them, on the history of the site they refer to as Durangug, Magic Stone Fortress. The first Shin'Ar lived in his underground dwelling along with his Zidu'Si. There were only basic stables and a few housing and storage buildings on the site for visitors that were not allowed into the below-ground dwelling.

Once the Shin'Ar departed, and Durangug sealed, the site was abandoned and long forgotten to all but the dwarfs. Over time, hunters and travelers used the unnatural clearing for breaking camp. The site soon became a hunter's refuge of sorts, until a new King of the North from Dravenport, built a hunting lodge and summer retreat upon the spot.

Dravenport was the old capital of the lands long before the Lalli Mah, and sat on a large bay on the Great Sea, south of the Orenthal. The King was killed under mysterious circumstances in that castle, and after his eldest son took the throne, he also died in a strange accident while summering in the royal vacation home.

There was no male heir, so the first King's eldest daughter took the crown as Queen and fearing a curse, insisted the castle be destroyed, and the site abandoned.

Many centuries later a ruling council replaced the monarchy. Once the lands began to shake and fault, religious cults began to form and worship various ancient deities, looking for hope in a world that was collapsing.

The two largest groups were the Cult of Creation and the Cult of Chaos. The Cult of Chaos later became what it is today, the Order of Chaos. The Cult of Creation built their monastery upon the site of Durangug. During the destruction before the Lalli Mah, the monastery was leveled by earth shakes and the cult dispersed. They regrouped during the great balance to build the Altar of Creation in Britengate.

Throughout the time, the dwarfs watched over the site; its occupants and occasional plunderers never stumbled upon, or appeared to know of the Vault's existence.

"We always suspected that the Creationists knew of the location's significance, but they never threatened the Vault. They harbored mixed-bloods and practiced old magics. Some say that it was they, who were responsible for the balance falling apart after a failed experiment, but there is no real proof."

"That might explain why Old Codger found an abnu emuq and ancient plans for his..." Mallick started and stopped not wanting to reveal the Mellamu Nanna.

"You refer to the Magurmu that the old man built?" the twin dwarfs asked.

Mallick looked at Shuran who nodded.

"We watched him build it. It is of an ancient dwarven design actually but the part that allows flight was not part of the original plans. The creationists must have found some ancient knowledge and modified the design," one of the other dwarfs, Avrank said.

Shuran knew of the ancient books Codger found as well, so the theory was sound.

"After the Lalli Mah was performed, the Creationists moved to Britengate, we have little knowledge of their practices since. They are Followers of the Light now and only send out their priests occasionally to trade in Tarangale, and they do not speak much to others."

The group trekked on through the deep snow toward the area where they would make camp for the night before heading up into the mountains. They arrived at the mountain base shortly after nightfall.

The dwarfs pointed out a crevice in the rock face that provided some shelter from the freezing winds that began blowing from the North. The dwarves all made fast work of collecting firewood and building a stone ring to create a fire.

Shuran noticed however that they did not light the wood.

"Shuran Shin'Ar, would you call forth the fire from the wood?" the twins asked. "We have not seen elemental fire used."

Shuran though it a small request but he could see the excitement in the eyes of his new friends. Calling forth the element of fire was easy enough for him but he feared the simple act would disappoint the dwarfs.

With an over exaggerated expression, Shuran pushed his hands out toward the pile of wood in the ring of stones. He extended his fingers and began to wiggle them slowly. Suddenly, Shuran lifted his hands above him while following the movement with his head. Shuran spared a quick moment to wink at Mallick before a large ball of flame burst into existence above his hands and began licking at his fingers. With an equally ostentatious movement, he sent the flame to the fire and left it to feed on the wood a few moments before settling it into a steady warming burn.

The dwarfs stood in quiet awe for several moments as Mallick moved closer to Shuran.

"Seriously sheesh! You are worse than a charlatan at the harvest fair," Mallick joked.

"What? They wanted a show," Shuran protested half-heartedly.

"Whatever; we need some food and unless you are going to pop it in here wastefully-"

"I'll get my bow," Shuran said as he smiled. "I agree, unless we are in absolute need, we should not call things from the Vault."

Shuran and Mallick headed off into the nearby woods to look for game that the dwarfs said was in plentiful supply. They left the dwarves marveling around the fire and arguing about who had the best view of Shuran while he created it. Shuran just shrugged at the scene as Mallick elbowed him along.

Shuran and Mallick wandered the surrounding woods for nearly and hour without any signs of wildlife. They were about to give up and head back to camp before Mallick noticed something.

"What do you make of these tracks Shuran?" Mallick pointed to large prints that disturbed the otherwise pristine blanket of snow.

Shuran approached and knelt before the large grouping of tracks left in the snow. "They look like no creature I have ever heard or read of." The prints were larger than a grown man, and showed impressions of three toes.

"I do not like the feel of things out here Shuran. We should head back and ask your fan club what they think."

The joke was not lost on Shuran, but in light of his current concern he chose to ignore it. He reached out with the Essence to locate the fastest route back to the dwarfs rather than backtracking their path. As he felt for their life forces he stumbled upon something else, something large and dark, several somethings he did not recognize.

"Mally, we need to move now, and fast. We are not alone!"

The two ran for the camp at full speed without stopping. Behind them, they could hear the cracking of branches and crunching of snow that sounded like a herd of cattle stampeding behind them.

"Shuran! Do something, whatever they are we cannot lead them back to camp!" Mallick yelled.

Shuran stopped dead and turned to face the oncoming threat.

Mallick came to a skidding stop next to him and could already see the glow of Shuran's shi as he worked the Essence. The ground beneath them began to shudder, growing into a deep rumble.

As the two young men could see the shadows of several enormous creatures striding out of the shadows toward them, large boulders began breaking through the ground to form a wall of jagged stone between them and the oncoming heard.

"That will only slow them down, we need to get back to camp and ready a defense. There are creatures riding those beasts," Shuran shouted over the rumble of Earth magic being worked.

They turned as one and ran for camp. When they arrived at camp, the dwarfs were already prepared for an attack.

"We felt your working, Shin' Ar!" the dwarfs cried out. "What has caused your alarm?"

"Riders on great tusked beasts chase us. I have slowed them, but they will arrive soon," Shuran told them.

The twin dwarfs turned and held a council before turning back to the others. "Forest Trolls! They ride great boars and hunt the Northern woods. They do not usually travel this far south until deep winter."

"As I see it we have but two choices, stand and fight or climb in earnest. They will not follow into the mountains," the smallest of the dwarf said, speaking for only the third time since meeting at Durangug. His name was Avrank and was small even by dwarven standards. He was sent along with the group as part of an initiation into the watchers, and this was the first time he had ever been away from his mountain home.

"Avrank! You know it means certain death to attempt a climb in the dark of night!" the other dwarfs scolded.

"And to face down a Forest Troll hunting party means what?" the small dwarf said back in a calm and collected tone.

Shuran thought for a moment. "Why would these trolls be chasing us?"

"They are territorial, but they normally would not waste time or energy chasing us unless they saw us as a threat," the twins said.

"They are not the most intelligent of creatures and rather lazy. It is not likely they will continue after you thwarted their charge with Essence weaving," Avrank said.

Chapter Twenty-Four

This did not hold true, however as the sounds of crunching snow under heavy weight slowly drawing closer, broke the relative silence of the camp.

"So much for normal behavior!" Mallick whispered.

"This makes no sense. Trolls fear Essence more than most creatures in all of Ersetu!" Avrank said.

"Then something has them frightened even more, but what?" Mallick asked.

"Chaos," Shuran answered flatly, "they are working for the Order to find us."

"How can you know this?" the twins asked.

"It is the only thing that makes sense. The Order will stop at nothing to find me. These trolls may not know who we are, but they are likely out looking for anyone out of place. Now that I have used Essence against them, they will be certain to follow," Shuran finished.

"Then we must stop them. They cannot be allowed to notify the Order of our movements," Mallick said.

Shuran just nodded and headed toward the approaching trolls, glowing brightly to eyes that could see his shi.

Mallick and the dwarfs all shuddered and blinked back from the vision of Shuran surrounded by a brilliant red glow. He was angry.

"You come human! We take you… Leave others alone!" the troll in the lead said.

"Why do you give us chase troll!" Shuran demanded.

The mounted trolls began to form a semi-circle around Shuran. They were hairy half human looking creatures about shoulder height to the average man. Their eyes were huge in relation to their wrinkled and wart covered faces.

The lead troll just stared back at Shuran with his row of pointed teeth showing behind his snarled lips. "YOU COME OR BE DEAD!"

Shuran just stood there waiting and watching with his senses extended to feel the other trolls around him. They were frightened beyond measure, but not just of Shuran. "Who has called upon you to give chase to humans?" Shuran asked again.

The troll did not answer with speech. He made a motion of his hands, and the surrounding trolls began to dismount their boars and close in on Shuran's position.

"I do not wish to harm you but I will defend myself!" Shuran shouted back.

That was when the first rock flew.

Shuran extended his mind to stop the stone, but nothing happened, and it grazed his shoulder as he finally dodged to the side. He was confused by what had just happened but had no time to think, as more stones began to arc toward his position. He rolled, ducked, and dove out of the way trying to repel the falling rocks. He attempted to construct a shield around himself, but the stones fell right through unimpeded.

Shuran was lying vulnerable on the ground after one of the projectiles hit him in the head. As he tried to gather his wits, the troll leader moved to stand over him.

The troll lifted his club above his head preparing to pummel Shuran when the first arrow struck the troll deep in the back. His body fell limp onto Shuran with a load grunt.

Shuran looked out from where the arrow had come and saw Mallick and the dwarfs sending volleys of arrows into the troll gang. Then darkness took him.

Shuran woke several minutes later to a splash of water to the face. Once he realized it was Mallick standing over him he took a moment to gather his senses and look out at the carnage that lay before him.

Twenty trolls lay dead around him and his friends. The bodies were a horrid scene of charred remains and lifeless pincushions.

"What has happened?" Shuran managed as he rose to his unsteady feet.

"You were knocked unconscious Shuran Shin'Ar!" Avrank said holding a stone. "They used these against you." Avrank handed the stone to Shuran, who immediately felt the void of energy and dropped it.

"What is that?" He asked feeling repulsion for the rock.

"On the surface it is just gug, but it has been tainted," the twins said. "We do not know how but it is obvious why," they continued. "They were sent after you, or more likely pressed into service to help search the realms for a wielder. Someone gave them the altered lodestone."

"These things will not be reporting our whereabouts," Mallick said.

"They will eventually be missed," Avrank said.

"We will pile the bodies then, and destroy them." Shuran reached down and plucked another tainted gug stone from the ground and placed it into his satchel.

The seven travelers went about piling the dead trolls in an open area some distance from their camp. Shuran and Mallick worked Essence, rendering them to ash by calling forth elemental fire and spelled flame. Once there was nothing left but soot and bits of bone, the dwarfs finished the job by splitting open the earth below them and swallowing up the remains.

Avrank was visibly taxed by the effort as he wavered and nearly fell where he stood. They all slowly made their way back to the campsite.

"We must make for the mountains sooner than planned," Shuran said.

The others did not relish the thought of climbing in the darkness of night but they did not argue. The trolls would be missed and sooner or later another band of the ugly creatures would come looking for their absent comrades.

"It will be light in a few hours. We will take it slowly and carefully until we can see better," Shuran decided.

Shuran and the others broke camp and eliminated the evidence of their presence. Shuran called forth winds from the North to erase the path left from their approach to the mountain base. The snows were coming but they were not heavy yet and would have taken days to cover their tracks unaided.

The climb started slowly and awkwardly as Shuran and Mallick stumbled on unseen obstacles along the path. The dwarfs being familiar with the mountain trails were less hindered. The going was slow but before long the sun was brightening the skies enough to see better and they were able to quicken their pace.

The added advantage of climbing the western face of the mountain meant that they would be obscured in the shadows of the mountain until midday. The climbing gave Shuran time to think on his failure to face the trolls alone. He was deeply concerned and rather humbled by the events that rendered him useless and vulnerable.

If not for the actions of Mallick and his new dwarven friends, Shuran would have been beaten to death by the trolls. How could an attack by stones have had such an effect on his growing abilities with the Essence?

After the first couple hours of travel Avrank was showing signs of complete exhaustion. When questioned he shrugged it off and refused to stop.

Shuran had to admire his tenacity. Being undersized as he was by dwarven standards, the young dwarf must feel that he always has something to prove. This time Avrank would push himself too far.

As the group moved around a bend in the path, they reached a narrow ledge that would force them to shimmy one at a time to a wider path beyond a sheer drop into a chasm. Each in turn, began the crossing. Backs to the mountain, they sidestepped along the ledge. Shuran had insisted the dwarfs go between him and Mallick. Progress was slow but steady. As Mallick and the first four dwarfs had finally made their way across, Shuran noticed Avrank's fatigue. The small dwarf was wavering as he struggled to make his way to the other side of the chasm when he stumbled and slipped from the ledge.

Those on the far side of the ledge, save one dwarf, just looked on in horror and shocked silence as Avrank slipped from the overhang and free fell into the chasm.

Shuran acted on instinct and reached out after him. "Lil'Il!" Shuran spoke in the ancient tongue to lift with air. He strained to maintain concentration as he felt Avrank's fall slow to a halt.

Slowly he began to rise up toward the ledge. As he reached a level with the others Shuran, visibly tired, pulled on the whispers of the wind to push the motionless form of Avrank over to his friends waiting on the opposite side of the deep crevasse.

Once Avrank was safely settled among his friends Shuran let loose of his grasp on the Essence and fell to knee. Mallick made to call out but Shuran reached into his pocket while lifting a hand to signal his wellness. Shuran pulled himself up as a faint but recognizable glow of Essence wrapped him in energy.

Mallick knew at once that Shuran had forgotten to use the stone to aid in his weaving but used it now to replenish his own strength.

Shuran made good time in reaching the others and making straight for Avrank.

"He lives but is breathing shallow," Mallick said.

Shuran knelt down to examine the wounds his small friend had received slipping from the ledge. With one hand on the stone in his pocket, he placed the other upon Avrank's head. "Dug Kalag-Ga!" Shuran intoned as he closed his eyes and reached into the unconscious dwarf to begin healing him.

As the other dwarfs watched on in stunned silence, Mallick as well, was awed by the ease with which Shuran was able to manipulate the Essence and heal the wounds upon Avrank. This was the same man who Mallick had to stand over to protect while he was laid out cold, from a rock to the head.

Avrank's color returned quickly and his breathing deepened as his eyes fluttered open. "What happened?" he asked as Shuran removed his hand and sat back to open his water skin and offer it up.

"You took a bit of a fall. You will be ok now," Shuran said as he held the skin while Avrank drank deeply.

Dvargan and Grafdrik both snorted at that statement. "Bit of a fall he says! You went head over arse into the chasm is all, and Shuran snatched you back up as easy as picking a berry," the twins said in unison.

"You two really need to stop that or there will be another 'bit of a fall' before long!" Mallick smirked remembering Moona's warning again.

Shuran held out his open hand and in an instant a sizable piece of dried meat appeared. "Eat this and have some more water to level yourself."

Avrank took the offering and began chewing on the meat while looking up at Shuran with a deeper respect. "It is no small thing to save the life of another with us dwarves," one of them said to Mallick. "And saving the life of Avrank makes it that much bigger."

Mallick was not sure what that last statement inferred, but he was certain they would soon find out.

"If you are feeling better Avrank, perhaps we could continue on now. The sun is high and we want to be within your E-Kur before any trolls or whomever they answer too comes looking after their missing ranks," Mallick said as he helped him to his feet.

"I feel well. In fact, I feel better than before-" he started.

"It was foolish of you to put such great effort into burying the remains earlier," one of the other dwarfs said.

"I am sorry sheesh, but I was only trying to help," Avrank said.

"Just because we nursed at the same teat does not make us brothers, Tur!"

Avrank cringed at the slight. The other dwarfs were visibly uncomfortable but said nothing as they all continued on their way.

Shuran hung back with Avrank at the rear of the company as they continued to climb. The group made good time, stopping only occasionally to rest, eat, and drink. That night they found a small cavern in which to spend the night.

While the dwarves collected dead brush and branches from the bushes that clung to the cliffs, Shuran retrieved foodstuffs and Mallick setup the bed rolls. It was not long before there was a warm fire burning,

172

and a pot of stew cooking. Shuran took a seat next to Avrank and offered him a wineskin that he also pulled from the Vault.

Avrank accepted the skin and a warm smile spread upon his face when he realized what was within. "Now that can surely lift the spirits!" he said after taking a hearty swig of Codger's brew.

After Shuran took a drink and handed it back to Avrank, he decided to find out what was going on with Avrank and the other dwarf named Brakvar.

"He is not all bad you know," Avrank said looking at his older brother sitting nearer the fire across the cavern. "He is just angry that our father insisted I come along to meet you. He feels like he is my nurse made because I am much smaller."

"And that name he called you?" Shuran asked.

"Tur, it is not a nice thing. It means, to be small. To a dwarf it is not welcome to be called small by other, larger races, but to be called 'Tur' by a fellow dwarf is the deepest of insults." Avrank was holding back his sorrow.

Shuran could not understand how a brother, a sheesh, could act so unjustly toward his own blood. "It seems to me that with what you did to help clean up the troll's mess, and your quick thinking, you are quite a big help in my eyes. I am honored to call you friend."

Avrank was truly touched by this and it showed upon his ruddy little face.

Chapter Twenty-Five

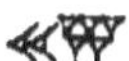

The next morning saw the seven up and off long before daybreak. Brakvar was still keeping distance from Avrank, but he was not openly hostile any longer. They were nearly halfway up the mountain by now and Shuran noticed Mallick getting visibly wary of the hike.

"Do you need rest Mally?" Shuran asked.

"No, I feel fine but breathing is getting a bit taxing."

"The air thins the higher you go," Shuran said.

"What do you mean it thins? It is already invisible how much thinner can it get!"

Shuran just sniggered and continued. "I read in the Vault library about things called particles. They make up everything when combined in certain ways. The air has different particles in it that we need to breath. The further we travel toward the sky, the fewer breathable particles there are, so it becomes more difficult to fill our lungs," Shuran finished.

"You will be breathing easier soon Shin'Ar. Inside the caverns of Duranekur, mosses and plants grow on many surfaces that make breathable air," Avrank said and smiled as he stopped before a large outcropping of boulders.

"And when will we arrive?" Shuran asked.

"Follow and you shall see," said the twins.

The men followed the dwarves around the boulders to find before them a doorway beyond the scale of even the tallest of mythic giants. On each side of the enormous door stood matching totems of dwarves standing upon the shoulders of another. Each dwarf was carved intricately into the hard granite wall and each held various weapons.

The bottom ones held war hammers. The next held axes. Another set held short swords and the following a spike headed club. There were crossbows and daggers and so on. What struck Shuran the most, was the top dwarf on each side held no weapon, merely a book.

Before he could ask after the significance of the entry, the great doors began to slowly and silently swing inward. When they finally opened enough to allow light to enter, Shuran was surprised at the contingent waiting within. A long procession of dwarfs of all shapes and sizes were cheering the arrival of the Shin'Ar.

"Ah Shuran, I think they mean for you to get into that cart drawn by those oversized hairy goats," Mallick teased.

"Oh no, Mally, as a member of my Zidu'Si, you may have the honor of staring at the same hairy arsed beast while we ride!" Shuran jested back.

Mallick only mocked defeat as he climbed aboard and sat next to Shuran. "I hope these things have not been eating beans," he said as he pulled the stopper off his wine skin and drank deeply. "The talkie twins tell me it is a long ride to the capital where we will audience with the King."

Shuran took the wine skin and drank deeply as well. Surprisingly, the ride in the cart was smooth. Shuran was already feeling a pain in his neck as his head was turning back and forth to nod and great the assembled dwarfs they passed along the unnaturally large passage.

"I would assume that this grand passage is the work of your people using Earth Essence?" Shuran asked Avrank who was running on his short legs to keep pace with the cart.

"It is, but this is nothing compared to even the most meager of our clan villages. Just wait until you see the grand chamber of the capital."

176

Avrank could not hide the pride of his people if he tried.

As they travelled along, the beauty of painted frescos on the walls amazed Shuran. There were scenes of what appeared as daily life as well as past wars and major events. On several occasions he would recognize what must have been the same figure of a warrior or a king holding a great war hammer and leading a battle, or sitting head of a banquet table, or other gathering. As he took in the artistry, as well as the scenes, he could not shake a feeling of familiarity. He decided to put it out of his mind for the time being. As they drew nearer their destination his nerves began to rattle at meeting royalty.

"Shuran you have been more quiet than usual. What has hold of your tongue?" Mallick asked.

"Mally we are about to meet the King of the Dwarfs. Are you not in the least bit nervous?"

Mallick just shrugged and turned to his friend. "The way I see it, we are being treated as honored guests. Hairy goat pulled cart aside, I think that it may be the King who is nervous at meeting the Shin'Ar reborn!" Mallick held no humor in his expression.

This alone made Shuran struggle to hold back the impetus that threatened to force him back the way he came. "At least breathing is easier," Shuran finally said looking at the patches of plants and moss growing around the wall base.

Before long, the cart they rode, and most of the greeting party following, passed through the grand arched entry into a vast chamber deep in the mountain. They had arrived at Duranekur.

Shuran and Mallick alike where stunned silent with the majesty of what they saw. To say the chamber was big or even enormous would be akin to calling a speck of dust miniscule. If he did not know better, Shuran would have thought they just arrived at the home of giants, not dwarves.

Avrank came up breathless, to find his people's most honored guests staring around slack jawed. "Beyond beautiful is it not?" Avrank asked them.

Shuran and Mallick just nodded as they continued taking in the sight. Along the outer walls ran tall columns that reached into the heights of the chamber before arching toward the center point of the dome. Giant torches lined the walls and were spread throughout the complex on buildings and atop posts that lined the roadways. Buildings were aligned in a grid pattern following the circular plan of the chamber.

What finally caused Shuran to catch his breath, was the structure at the center of everything. It could only be the Royal Palace and grounds. The palace was a towering castle with twelve turrets and what seemed hundreds or terraces. The palace and the surrounding buildings all looked as though it was carved from a single block of stone. It appeared as if the entire city had been built by simply removing what was not needed from the center of the mountain.

Even more onlookers met the procession to the Royal Castle.

"Do you see all the Dwarven maidens throwing flowers down from their balconies? I think more than a few are vying for the attention of our guides," Shuran said.

"How can you tell they are maidens?" Mallick asked only half kidding.

"They wear what might pass for a dress," Shuran said.

"I used to know an old man in Two Bridges who looked better in a dress than these dwarven maidens. At least he shaved his legs," Mallick jested.

"He likely shaved his face as well I imagine," Shuran joked back.

"I suppose you think your women are so beautiful to behold?" Brakvar said as he stepped up beside the now stopped cart.

"Sorry no offense meant," Mallick stuttered.

Brakvar smiled. "It is as you say. I think some of our dwarven maids could stand for a waxing of the lip." He chuckled as he walked ahead to meet the guards at the castle entrance.

Shuran and Mallick watched blush faced, climbing off the cart, as the guards stood back to open the gates and allow the five dwarves and the two of them into the castle grounds.

"Aknard, is there anything that Mallick and I should know before we meet the King?" Shuran asked.

Avrank looked at him in surprise. "In what regards?"

"I have never met royalty, neither of us has. We would hate to make

178

some gross breach of etiquette and insult your King," Shuran said.

"I would not worry over much. The King is quite personable and down to earth if you pardon the play on words," Avrank said.

As if on cue, the doors before them opened to the main castle and standing before them was the King of the dwarves. The King was a hearty and imposing figure for a dwarf. He was head and shoulders taller than Brakvar reaching just below the chin of a grown man. He was dressed rather opulently with silks, jeweled belts, rings, and crown.

"Welcome honored guests, I am Vraduun, King of the Dwarves. Please… please, come into the palace. We have a welcome feast awaiting and I want to get out of this jester's suit my Lady Wife insisted I wear to meet you."

Vraduun looked at Shuran. "I do not mean offense my young asipu friend but a little of this goes a long distance." He finished tugging at his ruffles and sash.

Shuran smiled back and nodded in understanding.

The King led them into the main chamber where they were met by staff to take their things. "My staff will take you to your rooms where you may wash your travels away and freshen for dinner. I will see you a turn hence in the main dining hall. I would have preferred something less grandiose but again my Lady Wife insists on keeping up on appearances for the dwarven court," Vraduun said as he gestured for the staff to gather their things and take them to the royal guest rooms.

"Thank you your highness," Shuran said.

Vraduun just grunted and smiled. "Unless we are in formal proceedings I insist you call me Vraduun. And save your thanks until 'after' you have been subjected to the court and my lady wife!" With a wink, he turned from the weary travelers and headed for his own royal rooms.

Shuran and Mallick followed a housemaid to their rooms.

"Is it true?" the dwarven maid asked Shuran. "Are you truly the Shin'Ar returned to Ersetu?"

"So I am led to believe," Shuran muttered.

The maid clearly did not catch what he said.

"Yes, he is and I am of his Zidu'Si. He is called Shuran and I am

Mallick at your service fair dwarven maiden."

The dwarven maid giggled and might have blushed had it been possible to see beneath the layer of fuzz on her face. She motioned for the other dwarves following with their meager traveling bags and fresh water to go about their work.

"This is the main sitting and greeting room of your suite. You will find bedchambers on each side of this room. I will return within an hour to show you to the dining hall." With courtesy and bow of the head, she backed from the room and shuffled on her way giggling.

"What is with the fair maiden hoo-ha, Mally? She has more hair on her knuckles than you can manage growth in a moon turn on your chin," Shuran joked as he mockingly punched his adopted brother on the arm.

"Regardless of who the hair maiden… I mean fair maiden be, one should always be gentlemanly." Mallick returned the punch and went off to his room to freshen.

"I will retrieve suitable clothing from the vault and have one of the chamber men set them out in your room." Shuran went off to his room as well.

Shuran entered his oversized room and immediately noticed the average human-sized furnishings. It appeared to him that the rooms were specially prepared for non-dwarven guests. He wondered at the craftsmanship of the woodwork and the tapestries that hung about the room.

The dwarven attendant cleared his throat and motioned to the now filled bathing tub.

Shuran nodded and undressed. The feeling of the hot soapy water was heavenly against his road worn skin. After he thoroughly scrubbed and washed his hair and body, he emerged from the tub and refused the offered towel, preferring to call forth fire and wind to heat dry himself.

The dwarf gasped in surprise and awe, then bowed. "Shin'Ar!" he said in reverence.

"Please, just call me Shuran." Shuran called forth clothing from the Vault suitable for dining with the royal court. He was not sure they would still be fashionable since they were part of the contents of the Vault for at least the last few thousand years, but it was the best he could do. He did not know at the time that he would be wearing the clothes that once belonged to the original Shin'Ar. "Please take this other set of clothing and lay it out for my friend," Shuran said as he handed the bundle to the dwarf.

"As you wish Shuran Shin'Ar."

Chapter Twenty-Six

Shuran and Mallick stood in the greeting room, pulling and tugging their clothing, trying to adjust to the strange garb.

"We look foolish. I can now see why the King dislikes what he met us wearing," Mallick said.

"We are not wearing crowns or enough jewels to ransom a duchy," Shuran groaned back. "Still I hope we at least look the part."

"You look majestic and lordly as befits the Shin'Ar and his Zidu'Si," the dwarven maid said as she entered the room.

"These clothes are not out of fashion?" Shuran asked.

"These garments are timeless, and besides we do not see humans dressed as anything other than traders of craftsmen in villages, so I would not worry over much." She smiled and motioned for them to follow her from the room.

They followed her down the grand stairs back through the grand hall and into the dining hall.

As they entered the room, the attendant announced them. Immediately the dwarven court assembled, stood and applauded them.

Nearly half of them gasped.

At that moment, Shuran noticed several things. First, Avrank and Brakvar were placed to either side of the King and his Queen. Second, the King's appearance struck a cord of familiarity to the dwarf in the frescos he saw traveling to Duranekur. Finally, he noticed the same dwarven ruler in a fresco beyond the dais. Standing next to the King's likeness was a man with a striking resemblance to Shuran.

Shuran was now wearing the same clothes as those on the man in the painting. The applauding began to wane as the King lowered his hands and took his seat. Shuran and Mallick were led up to the dais to seats beside Avrank.

Mallick noticed the painting as they passed and nudged Shuran.

"I see it, just fasten your lips would you. We can talk about it later." Shuran sat down and smiled out to the court, and readied himself for what was bound to become a feast of discomfort that rivaled his feelings about the clothes.

The feasting itself was not unpleasant, as dwarfs take their eating and drinking quite seriously. The spread before them was vast. Vegetables and fruits of uncountable varieties along with meats from at least a dozen animals filled the tables beyond capacity. Wine and ale flowed freely, and it was consumed like water.

Shuran restrained from over indulging in the libations but certainly ate his fill.

Mallick, on the other hand, was well into his cups speaking boisterously, and with great animation on tales of his experiences since leaving Two Bridges.

Shuran was certain the King would want a private gathering after dinner and suggested that Mallick slow down. This suggestion was met with only the slightest acknowledgment. Although Shuran was not one to take overly of the cup, he had often seen the results of the morning after in Codger. Mallick was going to be sorry in the morn should he keep up this pace is all Shuran could think.

True to Shuran's assumption, the King bid his guests continue and enjoy the evening while he retired. He then requested Shuran and Mallick join him and his family in the private sitting rooms for dessert. The King wanted a private conference.

The sitting room was far less grandiose than the dining hall. There were simple yet comfortable furnishings, a large fireplace, and a table for private dining.

Vraduun took the largest seat nearest the fire and across from the Queen, then motioned for Shuran to join him. "Shuran, you have not been properly introduced to my lady wife," King Vraduun said. "Shuran Shin'Ar, may I present the love of my life and just about the finest dwarven maid to have-"

"Oh husband do shut up!" the Queen interrupted. "Shuran Shin'Ar, I am Levdrianda and am so very pleased to see your return," she said looking from Shuran to the image his double in a painting above the fireplace.

"I must admit the resemblance is uncanny your majesty," Shuran managed.

"Fiddley Biddles! There is no doubt my boy; you are he, Shin'Ar returned. Why would you have chosen those clothes to wear? How do you explain all your abilities?"

"Your Majesty-" Shuran started.

"And do stop the hoity-toity monikers and call me Levdrianda."

"I must admit that a rational answer escapes me your highness… I mean Levdriana."

The queen smiled broadly at the familiar use of her name.

"And please if we are to speak as the friends I hope to become, call me just, Shuran."

"Shuran, it is nothing short of prophecy that you should come along now and in the likeness of the Shin'Ar before you," Vraduun said. "All the pieces fall into place so you should just accept who are and move onward."

"I know nothing much of the Shin'Ar. I have full access to the knowledge of the Vault in Durangug, but there were no personal writings among the library volumes," Shuran admitted.

"Well then, we can fill you in on answers to many questions. I of course was not around five thousand harvests ago but my great grandsire twice over was there and well acquainted with Shin'Ar the first."

"Is it your grandsire then in all the frescos I have seen?" Shuran asked.

"Many of them yes, my clan's blood is strong as is our looks. I am the image of my father before me as he was to his and so on," the King answered. "The images of my great grandsire two times would be those holding the Menasutur, the ancient war hammer of the dwarfs given our ancestors by the Telukukal, the first people." Vraduun said with a tinge of sadness.

"After the Menasutur was lost to our people, Vraduun's ancestor soon died and the dwarfs life spans lessened. Where once we lived in a measure of as much as a thousand and more harvests, to reach five hundred is now rare," Levdrianda said sadly.

On the other side of the room Mallick was sitting with Avrank talking. "Why does your brother sit alone and treat you the way he does?" Mallick asked glancing at Brakvar sitting alone drinking in the corner.

"Brakvar is proud and stubborn," Avrank whispered. "My sheesh, was next in line for the throne until I was born and he resents me for it."

"Forgive my ignorance of dwarf customs, but why would you be named successor?" Mallick questioned.

"It was no decision of my father. Many years had passed without any new dwarven births. As you can imagine with our stunted life spans compared to thousands of years ago, the dwarves do not have the numbers we once did. That changed twenty-five harvests ago when I was born. Since then more dwarf sprats have been birthed than in generations before."

"And this is good I would imagine?" Mallick pressed.

"It is not a simple answer to say yes," Avrank continued. Avrank told Mallick of how all the new young were somehow stunted or small at birth even by dwarven standards. The term 'Tur' became derogatory, to describe those of the smallest stature. The Dwarven elders however, saw this as an omen for a return to the old days.

In ancient times dwarf young were much smaller at birth and did not reach full growth until well after one hundred years of age. Part of ancient dwarven prophecy has said that a time would come when the dwarven life spans would return to that of those times gone.

"Since I am of the royal line and small, the elders felt I should be placed in succession rather than my sheesh. He was not happy."

Mallick now understood Brakvar's resentment. "Perhaps he will grow out of it?" Mallick said.

"I had hoped so but now with the return of the Shin'Ar, the prophecies are coming to pass and it has caused a great divide in my people." Avrank looked at his brother when he finished to find him glaring back.

"What happened to the hammer?" Shuran asked as he stepped up to look closer at the painting of his doppelgänger and the ancient King of the Dwarves.

"No one knows after the Zidu'Si were dismissed it was gone. We know that this weapon was the first and the Zidu'Si later created other similar weapons. The only other account is a final writing of the then King," Vraduun said.

"Menasutur Gigi, Mummu Shin'Ar," he recounted.

Instantly Shuran knew what it meant and realized why so many things were familiar. "War hammer will be returned by the Shin'Ar reborn!" Shuran whispered. In an instant he closed his eyes and reached within himself to that place connected to the Vault in Durangug. He retrieved an item he barely remembered seeing but instantly knew its entire history. Shuran stood before the King of the Dwarfs and his Queen and held out the Menasutur for them to take back.

"How? What? Where?" Vraduun stumbled over the right words then took a long drink from his goblet of ale.

Shuran could see both his confusion, and his joy.

"It has been in the Vault," Shuran said. "I knew the first time I saw it in the paintings that it was familiar. Although I never saw it in person I have a connection to everything in the Vault and can call it forth at will," Shuran said and instantly called forth a keg of the ancient wine stored.

"You may want something a bit stronger. Let us drink from the ancient wine stores of Durangug and celebrate the return of what belongs to your people." Shuran set the keg on the table and an attendant began filling glasses, taking a full gulp for himself to steady his nerves. It is not every day a dwarf sees prophecy fulfilled in person.

As the glasses were passed around, Mallick and Avrank joined the others from their private council. Brakvar finally joined them as well.

"That was quite the gift Shuran!" Mallick said as he patted his friend on the back. "According to the King's sons you have as much as joined the clan!"

Shuran was confused momentarily when Mallick referred to the King's sons. This fact quickly made sense, having seen them sitting at the dais during dinner.

"You have dwarven blood to be able to work earth Essence! You could already be of our clan!" Avrank said.

"Shuran Shin'Ar, you have brought great honor and pride to our house by returning the Menasutur. You will be forever a member of my clan." The King was nearly in tears. As the King held the ancient artifact in his hands, he trembled with understanding of what this might mean. "You must return the hammer to its proper place, in the hands of a dwarven Zidu'Si," he said. "I will call for a ceremony and celebration of both the return of Menasutur and the adoption of Shuran Shin'Ar into our clan. If you would do us that honor Shuran?" Vraduun humbly asked.

"I would consider it a privilege and an honor sire," Shuran said.

"Excellent, now on to another point of business. What do you know of your father's quest?" King Vraduun asked.

Shuran was dumbstruck.

Avrank smiled with great pride and excitement.

Brakvar's expression was blank, but Mallick could sense he was not overjoyed at this turn of events.

"What do you know of my adda? I only know he was on some quest and I need to find him or complete what it is he has started," Shuran spoke in earnest.

"Dalgon was here many years ago," the King said. "I must now conclude that he was your adda for he spoke of the prophecies and that the seven blood son would call on my house at some future time. All things considered I believe the time is now and you are he!" Vraduun let out a hearty laugh and clinked his cup with Shuran's wine goblet before downing his own.

Chapter Twenty-Seven

Shuran woke the next morning sick with drink for the first time. The events of the previous night hit so hard that he turned to the cup for clarity. He realized now how wrong that decision was. He lifted his head from the soft bed and sat up. The fast change in blood flow had an immediate and violent result. Shuran doubled over onto the floor from a spinning head and heaving stomach.

"You look positively green Shuran Shin'Ar," the chamber man said. "What you need is a good cold bathing. Into the tub, I will clean up what remains of last evening's festivities."

Shuran grumbled and crawled to the tub. After struggling to remove his garments, he unceremoniously dumped himself in the bathing tub. The shock of the cold water was evident in the girlish screech that came out. Immediately Shuran called upon fire to heat the tub. The resulting effort to weave, and the sudden warming of the tub combined to relieve his symptoms completely. "Now that is better!" he cheered.

The chamber man just laughed and finished cleaning up the pile of sick Shuran left beside his bed.

After finishing his morning ablutions, Shuran dressed in some less formal attire and walked out to the central chamber where he found Mallick nursing a mug of coffee and moaning in discomfort.

"GOOD MORNING!" Shuran shouted.

Mallick threw a biscuit at the object of his auditory assault. "Are you mad?" he spat through clenched teeth.

"Do not order the ale if unable to settle the tab my friend," Shuran laughed.

"How are you so chippie this morn? You drank as much as I?" Malick asked.

"I simply tolerate the drink better than you," Shuran answered.

The chamber man exited Shuran's room and grunted while carrying a bundle of soiled rags.

"What is that smell?" Mallick asked.

"The remains of the young asipu's tolerance!" the dwarf remarked with humor.

"AH! Truth bender! What herbs did you take?" Mallick demanded.

Shuran just nodded negatively.

Mallick moved to place Shuran in a hold but lost his footing when Shuran dodged and laughed.

"When you pick yourself from the floor you might try stoking the fire." Shuran inferred.

Mallick did not understand at first but then the suggestion dawned on him and he turned to the hearth. With an outstretched hand, he called to the spelled fire and ignited the logs in the fireplace. Instantly, relief showed on his face. "Ninkashi!" Mallick breathed with a smile.

"How fitting to call out to the Goddess of ale and wine!" Shuran laughed.

A knock on the door broke their shared laughter.

"Come," Shuran said.

The door opened to reveal Vraduun and Avrank. They entered the room and took seats at the table in the center of the room.

"Good morn my friends, how does this grand day meet you?" Avrank asked as he struggled to get climb into the seat.

"Slowly I would guess from the taste for wine you both had last eve. I could use a bite from the same goat myself this morn," King Vraduun admitted with a smile followed by a grimace as the chamber man banged the door closed when he exited chuckling.

"Ah, well a bit of weaving burnt threw the sick," Mallick admitted.

Vraduun's expression lit up, and a slight rumble and shake of the foundations brought an expression of relief to the dwarf King's face. "Why has no one tried that before? I feel wonderfully better already?"

"What brings you here this morning, I thought we were to meet and break our fast in the royal dining room?" Shuran asked.

"I thought it best to keep private matters that way. My staff is loyal, but their lips move before their brains form thoughts," Vraduun said. "I wanted to talk more about your father's visit."

Vraduun spoke of a secret visit Dalgon paid Duranekur several harvests past. He came to speak to the King about receiving his yet unborn son. This child, grown quickly to a young man, would need the assistance of the seven to heal Ersetu, that was his message. "Dalgon spoke of his quest to announce your arrival at the seven realms of the races, seeking knowledge in the ways of their wielding, so you might somehow fix whatever is happening to Ersetu," Vraduun said.

"What has happened, is the ruddy zealots of Chaos have broken the balance? How do you fix that?" Mallick muttered.

"It is more than that, I think Mally. The balance has never been the answer," Shuran responded.

"What do you mean?" Avrank asked.

"The balance has fallen at least three times now from the history we know, and I think even more than that," Shuran started. "I do not know yet what needs to be done but I feel it somehow, that I must figure that out as I go about this journey." Shuran turned to his adopted dwarf father before continuing. "What was he like?"

"All business, your father was. He came to say his words and left after only resting a night with us." Vraduun stroked his beard a moment before returning to his story. "He looks very much like you in the face but with bright blue eyes. He is tall for a human. Being mixed blood, I would guess he is of Drakkian, Human, and Giant decent in the least."

"Your father is part dragon?" Mallick asked.

"Not dragon, Drakkian; recall Codge's stories about who the Drakkians are, fire wielders and their steed of choice is some hybrid lizard beast that flies," Shuran said, and Mallick nodded, recalling the story.

"Just so Shuran," Vraduun chimed in, "so if you are bound to go on this quest you will need at least two things from the dwarves my adopted son. I will personally teach you all we know of Earth Essence," The King said.

"And the other?" Shuran asked.

"Why dwarf warriors to join your Zidu'Si and guard you," The King answered with a prideful smile.

Shuran, Mallick, Avrank, and King Vraduun met the Queen in the royal dining room for a hearty meal to break their fast. Having finished their meal, the four men went to Vraduun's personal library to begin Shuran's lessons on Earth lore and Essence.

"This library contains all the collective knowledge of Earth wielding we dwarves have. It has been compiled since the histories were first written of my people." Again the King wore his prideful smile and straightened up as though he were ten spans tall.

"What does your history know of this?" Shuran asked as he produced a gug stone he collected during the troll attack.

"That would be one of the stones the trolls were slinging at you then?" The King took the stone from Shuran's hand. "Nasty creatures them trolls. The Gods saw fit to give them more warts than brains. They could not have made this stone," Vraduun said.

"You have seen its like before?" Shuran asked.

"Oh yes and you will likely see it again, but at the tip of an elven arrow!"

"It is gug, but a twisted kind of lodestone." The king went on to describe how gug is a charged stone that can attract metal and lines up to the pulses of energy deep in the world. This malformed sample is found in areas where the world has been damaged by the unbalance in the Essence. It is rare and not found in samples larger than a goose egg.

"The elves use it to fashion arrow tips. We will send a contingent of dwarves to collect what was left behind during your encounter. Even more rare, are samples found large enough to make weapons such as the Menasutur."

The King smiled at Shuran's surprise. "Had you held it any longer you would have noticed. Which brings up another fact, your dwarven blood is that of my clan or you would not have been able to hold it at all." Shuran just sat silently for a moment; he was not sure that was why he was able to hold it. He would not contradict the King.

Shuran retold how he was unable to block the stones using Essence or weaving a shield.

"Have you ever heard the saying, 'it takes a mountain to move one'?" Vraduun could tell from their expressions they had not. "You can put out a small enough fire with water or smothering it with earth, but sometimes you must use the same force against itself. This stone has chaotic energy; two powers joined but not harmoniously. So in order to fend it off you must learn to focus your Earth Essence with a bit of a spark that opposes the gug."

Shuran looked even more confused.

"We dwarves may not be able to wield the Essence of Electricity or lightening but we can sense it in the ground."

Shuran suddenly started to understand.

The remainder of the day Shuran practiced locating the pulses of energy in the Earth that were formed by electric lines of power. After several hours he was able to track the lines, similar to veins of life's blood in his own body.

"They are everywhere but in varying sizes and strengths, interrupted in some places by odd imbalances I could not identify," Shuran discovered and told Mallick.

"I will take your word for truth sheesh, but I fail to see how this is helpful. Are you not here to learn Earth lore?" Mallick asked.

"This is part of it, I know there is something more that I must need, but it is a start." Shuran handed the stone to Mallick, who took it with a confused look.

"I want you to throw it at me."

"Say again?" Mallick asked.

"Throw the gug stone at me. I have a thought."

Before waiting a beat, Mallick threw the stone, fast and hard.

"OUI-CH! I was not yet ready!" Shuran said grabbing the stone and handing it back. "This time wait until I say."

Mallick just grinned. Shuran walked several paces away and let his shi reach for the Earth. He separated the heartbeat of Ersetu from the buzzing of the electric flows of lines through the packed ground and rock. With a nod to Mallick, he was ready.

Mallick threw the stone, and when it reached nearly two hands from his face, Shuran stopped the stone dead in the air before him. Then he sent the stone flying back in the direction it came from.

"HEY!" Mallick barely ducked in time as he felt the breeze of the stone passing his ear to hit the wall behind him.

"Weapons from gug were a rare and coveted addition to the armories of all the races during the wars of ancient times. The fact that the trolls had these stones in abundance is worrying," Avrank said.

"What is it you are thinking my son?" Vraduun asked.

"You said it yourself. They are not the sharpest arrows in the quiver. Someone has armed them for the purpose of fighting Essence wielders," Avrank said.

Shuran saw the same wisdom in this that the King did.

"This means that the Order has employed the lower races to hunt you Shin'Ar." Vraduun said.

"Perhaps, but they do not yet know that I am anything more than a wielder and perhaps of my true origins. Who else knows of your prophecy of the Shin'Ar?" Shuran asked.

"That is a guarded secret of the Dwarves. It is not likely that my people would have passed that legend off to outsiders. There is only one outcast among my people, and though he feeds his greed, I do not see him betraying his people so deeply. Only a few actually know of the existence of Durangug," Vraduun said with a downcast expression.

"Aknard, is he the outcast?" Mallick asked.

"How do you know of him?" the King asked in surprise.

"We had to 'barter' with him to escape from Inquisitors many harvests back. He was a ruthless negotiator but likable." Mallick answered.

"My brother does have his good side when not chasing profit."

Shuran spent several days pouring through books on the history of dwarven Earth lore and wielding. It was not until just before giving up that something dawned on him.

"Vraduun, what does it mean to you?" Shuran asked.

"What are you asking Kimmatu'du, my adopted clan son?"

Shuran smiled at the endearing term. "What does it mean to be a dwarf and an Earth Wielder?"

Chapter Twenty-Eight

"This is not a simple question to answer. For a dwarf living in a world where everything is made for bigger men, we are often overlooked and even looked down upon. What do you see when you look down but the Earth at your feet?

"It supports us and it provides nourishment. The Earth can provide shelter. She can also move mountains and hold back the fires beneath. She is gentle, and she is fierce. She is a mighty dwarf. For a dwarf, wielding Earth Essence is something bigger than all else yet small enough to be thought unimposing." Vraduun was glowing with more pride than Shuran though possible.

"I have found what I needed. It was never in these books my King. It is in every dwarven heart," Shuran said.

"You are truly one of us Shuran Shin'Ar to have known where to find your answer."

That afternoon the castle was all buzzing with excitement over the celebration set for the same evening. The castle grounds were opened and setup with uncountable tents and tables. Wild boars and goats were set to roast in pits. Kegs of ale and wine were plentiful. Decorations were strung from poles, and banners lifted to mark the occasion.

Shuran was being pronounced Kimmatu'Du and Shin'Ar reborn, returner of the Menasutur. Shuran spent the afternoon talking with Moona and Codger using his communication stone. He brought them up to date on all he had learned and been through.

"I could have taught you what it means to wield Earth magic if you had fixed me sooner!" Moona shouted.

"It is not the same, you are only part dwarf. Besides I think, this is something I must do. Also, you do not need to shout," Shuran answered.

"I ain' shoutin' sprat."

"Ignore her Shuran. Where are you headed next?" Codger interrupted.

"I think it will be to find the elves if I am to follow my visions."

"Makes sense. Just watch yourself around them wily bastards. They like to mess with your brain. Had one make me walk around brayin' like a dur once," Codger said.

"Ha! I always said you was a jackass Codger!" Moona said.

Shuran said his good-byes and promised to keep in touch more. He missed the two of them already.

The celebration was already underway when Shuran and Mallick met the royal family in the private greeting room before heading to the ceremony.

"Your majesty Queen Levdrianda, you are a beauty to rival the Goddess of Light," Mallick said with a flourishing bow.

"I see someone has hit the cups early," she replied with a blush.

"You do yourself dishonor my Queen," Shuran said.

"Careful you do not rile my husbands jealousy Shin'Ar!" she answered, still blushing.

"I love you my lady wife, but this boy shoots fire and bolts of lightning from his fingers," the King jested.

"You would not fight for me?" she asked indignantly and playfully at once.

"Always my Love!" then the King jumped as Shuran sent a tiny spark at the King's backside.

After a hearty laugh by all, they made ready to exit the castle and into the awaiting crowd.

"Shall we then?" Avrnak said with excitement.

Brakvar was more sullen than usual.

Cheers and shouts greeted them as the palace doors opened onto the gathered dwarfs. Thousands of dwarfs from all the clans had been arriving for the last few days to join in the festivities. The group moved to a platform setup with a table and high back chairs for them.

Mallick and Shuran sat at the end with human-sized chairs as not to tower over the royal family who sat in boosted seats at the tall table. The seating of the head table was the signal for all in attendance to begin the feast. Dwarven custom dictated that the feasting had finished before the ceremony began. Entertainment would round out the evening as far as the royals were involved and the rest of the guests would drink on through the night. Shuran knew Mallick would like being among the all night revelers, but he understood they would be leaving early the next morn.

After eating their fill, the King signaled the beginning of the ceremony by having an attendant blow into a long horn that appeared likely the remains of an enormous tusk from some unknown animal. The crowd immediately quieted down.

"Honored guests and fellow dwarves. We have gathered this evening to celebrate the most wondrous of events. This event comes to us with three blessings," the King started.

"Vraduun stop dragging your tongue," Levdrianda whispered. "He has such a flare for the dramatic, you would think he was a court player in the acting troops," she said to Shuran.

"The Shin'Ar has come to us. He has returned to us the Menasutur. He has delivered it with his own hands."

The crowds roared with excitement. All the dwarves knew what this all meant. Shuran Shin'Ar had royal dwarven blood and by returning the ancient war hammer he had returned their long life spans. The King motioned for Shuran to stand.

"I present to you my Kimmatu'Du and our Shin'Ar, Shuran Shin'Ar."

Every dwarf in attendance cheered, except for one, Brakvar.

Shuran spent much of the next few hours meeting various clan leaders and representatives. He limited his partaking in wine since he wanted to keep a straight head, but Mallick was not following his example. There would be a hearty fire in the hearth the next morn.

Shuran was finally free of the crowd when he noticed Brakvar sitting alone. "Brakvar, may we speak?" Shuran asked.

"If you must, but you will not find me swooning at you like some maiden at her first dance," he answered.

"Have I done something to you?" Shuran asked as Brakvar stared at him blankly.

"You exist!" Brakvar said as he got up and walked away.

Shuran stood their stunned.

"What was that about?" Mallick asked having heard the exchange.

"I have no thoughts, but whatever it is, I am certain it is nothing I have done and cannot dwell on it."

Shuran and Mallick turned to follow the King and Queen with Avrank, back into the palace.

"Shuran, in the morn when you prepare to leave I have instructed two dwarfs to travel with you as both guides and fighters should you need them. I think you will be collecting such comrades during your quest," Vraduun said.

"If he wishes, I would ask Avrank to accept placement in my Zudi'Si. That is if you have no objection," Shuran requested.

"It would be an honor upon the entire clan, but the decision is his alone," Vraduun answered.

"I ACCEPT!" Avrank said as he entered the room.

"I am honored by your acceptance, Avrank. I am uncertain of what is proper protocol for being inducted into the Zidu'Si. We will put off the formalities for now," Shuran responded.

"Avrank, you know what this means do you not?" Levdrianda asked.

"Brakvar will stand in as heir apparent while I am in the service of the Shin'Ar," he answered. "And I will be taking the Menasutur with me."

The next morning Shuran, Mallick, and Avrank prepared to leave and were met by the two dwarves that King Vraduun assigned as guard and guide.

"Well, the 'talkie twins' I wondered what had become of you two. Come to see us off have you?" Mallick asked.

"No, we are to travel with you." Dvargan and Grafdrik answered in turn.

Mallick had no response and Shuran just laughed and walked over to greet them. "Well met again, my friends. You are most welcome among our merry troop," Shuran said as he gave Mallick a crooked smile. "Did we pack rope? I think perhaps Mallick will need to be anchored as we climb down the mountains for fear of leaping a ledge."

Everyone laughed, except Mallick who just smirked. "Har-har!"

The King and Queen soon arrived to see them all off. It was an emotional scene. Vraduun and Levdrianda both let the tears flow freely at seeing their youngest son go off on his adventure.

"You come back to us whole," Levdrianda said. "And you, Shin'Ar or not, look after my boy!" she ordered Shuran, who merely nodded and bowed his head in acceptance.

The King had seen fit to overload them with supplies and was about to order pack goats be brought out when Shuran spoke up.

"Your Majesty, that will not be necessary. We will travel light. All that we need is but a thought away." With that statement Shuran walked among the supplies and at his touch, sent everything to the Vault.

The trip down the Eastern slopes of the Orenthal Mountains was easier than the climb. Not simply because they were headed down but because this was a regularly traveled route for the dwarves who practiced trade with the humans of Elmwood and the elves in Tarangale.

They would be meeting a ferryboat at one of the feeder rivers of the Napalkua called the West Pass feed. It was named this because it originated beyond the Orenthal Mountains in the Frozen North, and flowed along the Western side of the mysterious break in the ranges that provided a means of passing to the North.

A dwarf captain would take them along the Western Pass feed beyond Elmwood into the main branch of the Napalkua River. He would take them as far south as safety permitted and drop them west of the Forests that bordered Tarangale. Travel too far south along the Napalkua would mean venturing too close to the rapids just before the great falls of Zig'Mada. There was a branch of the river that flowed directly into Tarangale, but that would mean passing Rivenwood.

Shuran did not want to risk traveling to his mother's home village for fear of spies watching for him.

They made it to the feeder river and met the ferryboat before Utu reached mid-sky the next day. The ferryboat captain was a jovial fellow and excited to have the Shin'Ar and his companions on his rig.

Knowing that he would have such passengers the day before, the captain provisioned for a comfortable and well-stocked journey on his best boat. It would be a two-day journey to Elmwood then another day and a half to their departure point. The Napalkua ran much faster than the feeders so they would spend less time on the longer stretch of the journey. After getting settled onboard, the ferry left the Orenthal Mountains behind and headed south.

Shuran spent the first half of the trip toward Elmwood talking to Codger and asking him to research gug weaponry.

Moona reminded Shuran to remain on guard for elven trickery and keep his mind shielded unless he wanted to think he was a dur like Codger had.

Shuran relayed this warning to the others. The dwarves could not shield themselves the same as Shuran and Mallick, but they assured him they had ways of protecting their minds from elven influence.

As they finally approached Elmwood, it was well after dark. The town appeared asleep and there was little to no torchlight in the windows. Had they passed the village during light, they would have noticed the town was actually all, but abandoned. The only residents left were those having no place else to go or looters picking over what was left behind when the majority of the inhabitants fled for safety.

News would reach Shuran and his companions soon enough. A force of warriors was on the march through the lands of Aurderia. They were not entirely human and not taking prisoners. They had but one order; to find and capture, or kill the human known as Shuran of Rivenwood, son of Sulura and Dalgon, ANZILLU of mixed blood.

Chapter Twenty-Nine

The ferryboat sided along shore in the best spot the captain could gain without threat of running aground. He was not close enough to let down a plank, so Shuran and company would have to disembark the boat many paces from shore and swim.

"We will not need to swim." Shuran raised his hand and one by one, levitated his friends over to the shore. When it was just himself left, he jumped off the boat and descended slowly to the water, which parted below him. He walked to shore as the waters parted in front of him and folded back behind.

"Bit of a flare for the dramatic, even for you Shuran," Mallick teased.

"I have not yet got the trick to moving myself by levitation. I can lift myself up but have yet found a way to use opposing force to move," Shuran answered.

"Why not use the wind to give you a push?" Mallick asked.

"Try as I might, I have yet to be able to blow myself about," Shuran said with all seriousness.

Mallick turned and walked away with the dwarves who all laughed heartily.

The companions had to travel nearly all day to reach the tree line. Once they reached the forest Shuran called their trek to a halt. "Have any of you traveled to Tarangale from this direction?" he asked.

"We have never been to Tarangale from any direction Shin'Ar!" Avrank admitted.

Shuran reached out with his shi to locate signatures of the Essence. He stretched his senses to their limits without using a power stone. He found nothing human. He boosted his power with a stone to widen his range. He finally located the trading settlement.

"I have located what must be Tarangale since I sense no other human life around. It feels odd though," Shuran said.

"What do you mean sheesh?" Mallick asked.

"There are very few people about and none appears elf."

The group trekked their way through the forest toward the sense of life that Shuran followed. Shuran stopped suddenly.

"What is it Shuran Shin'Ar?" the twins asked.

"DOWN!" he responded and reached out with hands and Essence. He immediately sensed a disturbance in the area around them. Dozens of empty spots were the best way he could describe it to himself. Before he could investigate further, dozens of arrows came arching toward him from high above.

Instantly he tugged on the energy of the nearest line of energy in the ground and then on another of opposite charge. He wove the forces together and formed a powerful net of energy to snag the arrows several paces before they reached him. More arrows flew and met the same net of force.

"You can loose arrows all you wish, they shall not reach me or my companions," Shuran yelled then turned to face the nearest void in the Essence. "Reveal yourself elf before I send these arrows back the way they came!"

"HOLD!" The elf cried out then stepped forward.

Shuran turned the arrows the way they came. "Explain why you attack us without cause?" Shuran demanded.

"You are not from the army," the elf said half question half statement.

"Do we look like soldiers you pointy-eared shoemaker!" Avrank said.

The elf glared at the dwarf and turned his eyes back to Shuran. "You are the mixed blood we have heard tell about." This again was more statement than a question.

"He is Shuran Shin'Ar, and you should show respect!" Avrank said. "And I am Avrank son of Vraduun, King of the Dwarves. You will show us all respect and stop this needless waste of our time," he finished.

During this exchange, Shuran used the distraction to adjust his senses. He was now able to see the remaining elves as they moved in to circle him and his group. With a slight movement, he adjusted the aim of the arrows.

"I see you," he said.

The elves who just arrived all revealed themselves and lowered their bows.

Shuran let the arrows he held with Essence fall to the earth. At the sudden appearance of the elves, Mallick and the dwarves all jumped with surprise and began to point their weapons at the new threat.

"Lower your weapons, they will not harm us," Shuran said and he turned to the elf that first came out of hiding. "Why would you think we were soldiers?" he asked the elf.

"Forgive the mistake Shin'Ar. We were warned of a threat arriving from the North. We took you for a scouting party since you arrived by wood and not from the river feed into our settlement." he answered. "These are unsettling times. Come we will escort you to the village. My name is Orian."

"You spoke of a warning of an army marching?" Shuran asked.

"We received a bird not two days past telling of an army marching across Northern Aurderia. They have been laying waste to settlements and villages along their path including Elmwood," Orian said.

"There have been no open hostilities between realms in centuries, where are these troops from?" Avrank asked.

"Unknown, the only people who have survived the raids are those who were not around during the attack, or travelers who came upon what was left. There are no signs of troop movements, and there have been no sightings of soldiers anywhere. They just appear randomly, destroy, then move on leaving no trace," Orian Finished.

"How is it that you then received warning of army movement along the Western line of the forest?" Shuran asked.

"Our message came by Guinea Hawk." This statement was directed to the dwarves.

"Those are the messenger birds of the Dwarves!" Avrank said. "We had no knowledge of an army when we left Duranekur, four days past," he said.

"Perhaps someone saw us passing Tarangale by ferry?" Mallick suggested.

"Or perhaps someone wanted us attacked," Shuran spoke to no one in particular.

As the group walked along the path Orian led them to, Shuran extended his senses again to look for signs of the elves now that he knew what to look for. He gasped with surprise. He could sense hundreds of them around in the forest and at the settlement he first felt only mundanes and weaving humans in.

"You have discovered our true numbers in Tarangale," Orian said. "Only elf blood could have felt past our shielding." Orian smiled at Shuran.

"I am of seven bloodlines," Shuran answered.

"Perhaps…" was the only response Orian made.

They all walked on in silence as they made their way to Tarangale. Only Dvargan and Grafdrik were chattering to themselves endlessly about who would have sent the Guinea Hawk.

Mallick was doing his best to block them out.

As they came to the end of the tree line, Tarangale came into view. Before them, spread across a clearing of no more than three hundred paces, was a town of log built houses and shops surrounded by a stockade fence of thick pilings.

They headed for a simple entrance that was large enough for two men side by side or a single man on horseback.

"Sneaking in the back like thieves are we?" Mallick asked.

"On the contrary, we are conveniently entering by the guard's entrance that is closest. We also do not wish to get caught in a crowd," Orian started. "Unlike the trained elves of the rangers that were with me in the forest, most elves are far too curious for their own good, and would cause a display in the trading center were we to enter by the main gates."

Orian led them to a large structure toward the back of a row of understated cabins near where they entered the village.

"This is our main meeting house in our Southern settlement," he said.

"You have other settlements then?" Mallick asked.

"Many; we elves do not call Tarangale our mother home. This is but our place of trading and center of communication within the realm of humans."

Orian took them to a large room where several older elves sat around a table deep in discussion. At their arrival, the elves quieted and met Shuran's eyes.

"Elders, I bring you the one they call Shuran. He may be the mixed blood we have been expecting."

Before Avrank could interrupt, Orian continued. "The dwarves claim him to be the Shin'Ar."

At this statement the elder elves began whispering among themselves, apparently upset.

"Come forward Shuran claimant of the title Shin'Ar, we would test your right." The oldest looking elf by far was addressing Shuran on behalf of the council. "We are the eldest of the elves and carry the burden of living among humans," he said.

"I do not pretend to know what right I have to be called Shin'Ar, but I know what responsibility has been thrust upon me by prophecy or the Gods or whatever it may be. I am a man at only the age of over eight harvests. I can control forces I barely understand. I do not ask for this. I do not want this. I accept this as what I must do," Shuran said with all his heart.

"And why do you accept this fate?" the elder asked.

"If not I, then who shall stand in my stead?" answered Shuran. When there was no reply Shuran continued. "My mother gave her life that I might live. My father went out in the lands to foretell my coming before I was birthed to this troubled world. I must go where the path leads," he finished.

"Your words are heartfelt young man, but before we allow ourselves to commit to your cause, we shall test you. Dalgon was a friend and I trust in his words but we need more to trust in his wisdom," the elder elf finished.

Shuran was thrown by the mention of his father's name. "You have seen and spoken to my adda and yet you question my identity?" Shuran asked indignantly.

"Oh, we have no doubt who you are Shuran son of Dalgon. We question what you are and what you will become. We are not alone in this." The elder rose and spoke out to all in the room. "On evening fall next, we shall test his claim, to see if he stands worthy. The Shin'Ar is a heavy responsibility. Many worship his memory. The elves do not!" With this last statement, he turned and left, the other elders followed behind.

"Do not concern yourself overmuch Shuran Shin'Ar, son of Dalgon," Orian said. "Elder Voreen is weary for good reason. He is nearly five thousand summers of age, by far the eldest of our race. He only reaches this age as a direct descendant of a member of the first Zidu'Si."

Shuran had a sudden flash. "He is from the line of Grastrell!" Shuran said.

Orian was shocked by Shuran's revelation. "How could you know this?"

"I had a flash of knowledge that is not of my own living experience," Shuran said. It was only a half fallacy. As the Shin'Ar reborn, he also had access the vast knowledge inside the Vault. He did not remember ever reading records of past Zidu'Si, but he could not dismiss the possibility he was gaining memories of another.

Chapter Thirty,

Orian took Shuran and his companions to a cabin where they would stay as guests of his family. "Shuran Shin'Ar, you honor my house by sharing our roof and bounty. Please make my home yours for as long as you stay," Orian said.

"You call me Shin'Ar. May I inquire as to why you do so when your elders insist I prove my worth?" Shuran asked.

"Do not judge us all or even the whole of the elders by the words of Voreen. He is wise and weary, but also proud. It was considered disgrace when his great grand sire returned to the elves, and the Zidu'Si disbanded. It did not matter that the Shin'Ar disappeared to some unknown place or purpose. It only mattered that he was Zidu'Si no more," Orian said.

"Perhaps when he learns the truth he will be less prideful and more full of hope." Before Orian could question Shuran, he continued. "I will not say more until my test."

They ate well that evening. Orian did not have a mate, but his sheesh lived with him, and was mated and adda to several elf sprats. They were more than excited to have guests of any sort. To have the one who may be the Shin'Ar reborn to Ersetu, was more than they could stand.

The elfin sprats all ran about making crafts and pictures to gift Shuran and his friends. Orian's sister by mate joining to his sheesh was making every elfin delicacy known and several that were not.

Orian brought out nectar wine, bottle after bottle.

Shuran drank freely. He held concern about the tests.

"Do not worry so much about these tests Shuran Shin'Ar. You will pass whatever they throw at you," Avrank said.

"I might be able to provide insight Shin'Ar," Orian said. "Perhaps we shall speak in the morning."

The next morning Shuran met privately with Orian in a room that served as a study. "There are many books here on elfin use of the electric forces around us."

"I do not think they will be of use," Shuran said.

"You believe yourself a master of this ability then?" Orian asked him.

"No, but to master a thing I must first understand it. What I need is to feel it, experience it, harness it."

"Then let us begin," Orian said with a sly smile.

They stayed secluded in the room all morning. When they finally came out Shuran looked completely drained while at the same time elated.

Mallick came up to him with concern in his eyes. "Sheesh! You look like a heaping pile of yak scat!" he said.

"Thank you my chosen brother. As usual you find the words to point out the obvious. I am fine, just need some food and a bit of rest."

Shuran took a mid-day meal and then rested for a few hours before receiving a communication from Codger. He conferred with him for several minutes before cleaning up and changing his clothing.

Orian came to lead him to the elders for trials of right. "They are ready for you Shuran Shin'Ar," he said.

As the others began to follow, Orian turned to face them. "You are all welcome to follow, but like myself, we will have to wait outside while Shuran faces the trials alone."

They accepted this poorly but understood. As a group, they started

210

out for the council meetinghouse. A sizable crowd gathered and followed. Elves are consummate gossips; therefore everyone in the village knew what was about to occur.

"We will be here waiting for you Shuran," Mallick said.

"I hope you packed a meal and bed rolls my sheesh, because this may be a while," Shuran said with a forced smile and turned to enter the council room. The door closed behind him with a thud and a slide of the brace that locked the chamber.

"Shuran, son of Dalgon, you stand here to answer the right to the title, Shin'Ar," Voreen said. "Prepare for your first test."

Shuran took the chair set in the center of the room. Before he could adjust to the seat, he felt an attack on his mind. Images of his past flashed before his eyes. They were a jumble of past experiences and knowledge. He nearly lost himself before he was able to begin controlling the flow of information and direct it. Slowly he began placing barriers around the most sensitive of memories.

Gratefully the onslaught did not reach his knowledge about Durangug or the extent of his abilities. The only information that surfaced was irrelevant experiences. Except for one. The memory of Grastrell was accessed. Voreen gasped in surprise and the onslaught halted.

"What is this memory!" he demanded.

"What memory might that be elder Voreen?" Shuran asked without emotion.

"Do not trifle with me mixed blood!" Voreen spat back. Voreen then sent an electric pulse toward Shuran.

Shuran lifted his hand and effortlessly palmed the pulse. He turned it to look at it. Slowly he opened his fingers to allow the sparks of energy to dance upon his open hand and down along his arm. The sparks scattered across his body without effect.

"Your great grandsire would be ashamed at your actions Voreen. He was Zidu'Si. He was never released from duty, only set on a different path," Shuran answered.

"What path? How do you know these things?" Voreen implored.

"His duty was his alone and between him and his Shin'Ar. I am new and my path is different."

The council conferred for nearly half a turn before resuming. "You will show us a final demonstration of worth. Something was not returned when Grastrell left the service of the Shin'Ar," Voreen said.

Shuran raised his hand to stop further speaking. "I am aware of the Agal Kastu. You wish to have it returned." Shuran said flatly.

Gasps came from the elders.

Voreen stood and moved toward Shuran. He had a look of longing for peace and forgiveness on his face. "Please Shuran, son of Dalgon. If you be the Shin'Ar reborn, then you have it in your power to return the Mighty Bow," Voreen pleaded.

"It is not my intention to keep the Agal Kastu from your people. I only question that you have and elf among you, worthy to receive it on their behalf." Shuran said with a sideways look and tilted head.

Voreen was taken back by the statement and felt shame. He now understood that he stood before the Shin'Ar, back amongst Ersetu. He bowed before Shuran.

Shuran exited the chamber less than two hours after he entered.

Orian had a look of surprise on his face.

Shuran's expression was blank.

"What is the outcome Shuran?" Mallick pressed.

Shuran did not respond at first. He pointed for Mallick to hand him his wine skin. Shuran drank deep before handing it back. "We will finish this in the elven capital city before your Queen Mother," Shuran said as he walked on toward Orian's home. "We will leave in the morning for Entensiama."

Orian was again shocked silent.

"What is Entensiama?" Mallick asked.

"It is the elven capital and home of the Queen Mother as Shuran stated," Orian said. "You are honored to be invited, no outsiders have ever been allowed near its borders," he said.

"Oh we were not exactly invited, and you are coming with us," Shuran said.

"You mean to just arrive uninvited to the elven capital?" Mallick asked. "Are you looking to start a war between the elves and the whole of Aurderia?" he continued.

"There will be no hostilities my friend. Voreen will be sending word ahead of us by bird announcing our intentions," Shuran answered.

"And what, if I may be so bold Shin'Ar, is intended by this visit?" Avrank asked.

"I shall be pronounced Shin'Ar reborn to the elves as I present the Queen Mother a gift of faith." Shuran started. As he looked at his friends who wanted more, he turned to Orian who was beside himself with concern. "Do not worry my new elfin friend. All will be well."

"I am sure you will be accepted, but an elf not on the council must be a resident, or granted access to the home of Queen Mother. I cannot simply show up as your escort," Orian explained.

"You will not be escorting us, Voreen will. I hope you would be accompanying me as a member of my Zidu'Si, someone must become the bearer of the Agal Kastu."

Orian bowed his head in acceptance.

"It would appear that whatever Orian shared with you helped during your tests?" Mallick asked.

"Yes, in part, but I think what worked best was knowing what kind of man Voreen is," Shuran answered.

"And what kind of man is that?" Avrank wondered aloud. "He seems like a cantankerous old toad!"

"He is a wise elf, but with a damaged pride. Pride can make a man do dangerous things, imagine what the pride of an elf the age of Voreen could get up to," Orian said.

"I do not imagine he gets 'up' to much of anything these days," Avrank cracked.

The others just sniggered uncomfortably.

"Voreen seems manageable for the time being, but once we are in the Northern forest home of the elves…" Orian did not finish his thoughts.

Shuran just nodded having discussed this situation with Orian earlier in the day. "We shall just deal with things when and if they transpire. For now let us get some rest and in the morning we will visit the market square before preparing for our journey." Shuran finished the wineskin that Mallick had with him and they all headed back to Orian's home.

"Shuran Shin'Ar, why did you offer a place among the Zidu'Si to Orian? You barely know the pointy eared cobbler," Avrank asked.

"You do not trust him?" Shuran asked.

"We dwarves have little trust for the elves. They are a shifty lot and use deception and persuasion in every dealing with outsiders," Avrank answered.

"I spent a great deal of time with Orian this morning, he seems different then the other elves, more dedicated and trustworthy," Shuran said.

"Deception and persuasion Shin'Ar, be careful," Avrank said.

"I appreciate your concern, but since our first encounter in the woods, I have bested their abilities to deceive," Shuran said.

"Yes, but how will you hold against the bulk of the elfin population in their Northern home?" Avrank winked and walked off to get some sleep.

"How indeed?" Shuran muttered to himself with a tinge of worry on his brow.

The next morning saw Shuran up early and Mallick setting the fire in the hearth. "Stayed up drinking again last night did you?" Shuran asked Mallick.

"Had too, the two tongued bane challenged me to a test of tolerance," Mallick shrugged.

"And?" Shuran inquired.

"I do not know how those two could shut up long enough to drink me under the table!"

Shuran just laughed at Mallick. "Dwarves have very strong livers my friend. They can process liquids and filter the spirits much better than you or I," Shuran said.

"You read a few books on 'anatomsy' and suddenly you are a healer and internals expert!" Mallick mocked.

"It is 'anatomy' and I am no expert but I have learned a great deal more through probing with the aid of the Essence and using the books as a reference," Shuran answered as he helped himself to some food to break his fast.

Orian and his family were awake earlier than the rest of them and prepared a bounteous spread. "Since we are leaving for Entensiama soon I thought it best we have a hearty meal to start the day. There is a great deal to do in preparation, especially if the elders are to accompany us," Orian started. "Shuran Shin'Ar may we speak privately when it suits?" he asked.

"Yes, and please just call me Shuran, we are among friends," Shuran said as he finished his biscuit and followed Orian out to his study.

"I am honored by your offer, but I am not certain I could accept," Orian admitted.

"You have no direct ties, no mate or young to look after. Your brother and his lady wife can do without you, no offense."

Orian acknowledged there was no insult taken.

"What reason could hold you back, unless it is that you do not wish to accept?" Shuran asked.

"It is no small matter to accept such an honor. The elves have long memories and you recall how they treated Voreen's great grand sire when he was returned from service. It may be that the Queen Mother would refuse me the offer in place of another. She may be displeased with any elf accepting without her approval." Orian bowed his head in embarrassment.

"Orian, I will not be told who I shall accept into my Zidu'Si. It is not a service but a brotherhood of most trusted friends and comrades. Let me deal with the Queen if she disapproves." Shuran grabbed Orian on the shoulder in friendship. Orian smiled, but he was nervous, and Shuran could sense it. He was suddenly not very keen on this visit to Entensiama.

Chapter Thirty-One

After visiting the market, buying herbs for Moona and extra supplies they could not get near Durangug, Shuran was tiring of the elves. He was in part to blame for the added attention. He insisted on sending every purchase directly back to the Vault. Every elf around, that was not busy with bartering, gathered to watch the spectacle of Shuran and his Essence working.

"Elves hear stories of adventure and the uses of Essence in the South, but we do not see asipu here in Tarangale or in the Northern settlements," one of the merchants admitted.

"I suppose not, truth be told as I hear it, not much Essence working happens even in the South these days. Exception to that rule is the Essence Academy or the few asipu seen worthy to be sanctioned by the Great Council," Avrank said.

Shuran nodded and moved on quickly toward the stables where he was to meet Orian and Mallick. Avrank and the twin dwarfs trotted along behind trying to keep up with Shuran's fast pace. Before he reached the stables, Orian met Shuran.

"We will not need the steeds," Orian said with a smile.

"And how exactly are we to get there, walk?" Mallick asked sarcastically.

"What the council can do will be more than you imagine. We will be in Entensiama moments after we depart Tarangale," Orian smiled.

Shuran was intrigued.

"What are you prattling on about shoe maker?" Avrank spat.

Shuran placed a hand out in a motion to tell Avrank to settle down.

"Speak plainly friend, I have no humor for riddles this day," Shuran said.

"Voreen knows an old method of travel, knowledge from his great grandsire's time as Zidu'Si many suspect. He has shared it with the other council members. Together they will travel us all by way of the energy lines of Ersetu, directly to the center of Entensiama." Orian smiled at the light in Shuran's eyes.

Shuran needed to reach Codger and Moona, they had some research to do in the Vault library. When the time to leave arrived, Shuran had already spoken extensively with Codger a number of times.

The Council gathered in the meetinghouse and prepared themselves for the traveling. It was not quite a spell or regular wielding according to what Codger was able to find so far. It was a union of the body and shi with the energy flow of the lines. Shuran was not entirely sure how that worked or how they could move with purpose and direction, but he was determined to find out. Shuran opened his senses and examined the Essence and kept the flow steady. He concentrated his attention on Voreen. He began to feel a shift of force in the ancient elf.

The council clasped hands and ordered all traveling to place a hand on one of them.

Shuran sidled up to Voreen and rested his hand on the elf's shoulder. Shuran could sense the elf knew he was present even though his eyes remained shut. In an instant there was nothing but light and energy flowing over him, through him.

When the flow stopped suddenly, Shuran felt dazed and confused.

"The feeling will pass Shuran, son of Dalgon," Voreen said with a smirk and turned to leave them in Orian's care.

"Come we will rest and make ready to greet the Queen Mother, the message will have reached her of our arrival by now."

Shuran and company followed the elf to a staircase that seemed to emerge from the side of a mountainous tree. Now that his senses were coming to, he was able to take in the scenery. Looking back where they had arrived, Shuran saw a center courtyard surrounded by flowerbeds and small ponds.

He could feel a chill in the air, but the flora and fauna betrayed how north they had traveled. From what he was told of Entensiama's location, they should be far enough north for snow, yet everywhere he looked was green and lush. "It is amazing!" was all he could manage.

They climbed the stairs that wrapped around the large tree winding up into the canopy. It was a long climb. Once in the canopy, the true beauty and artistry of the elfin home came into full view.

The great limbs and branches of the massive trees served as a foundation for huts that seemed woven out of the branches. Leaves appeared to gather upon the top of each hut to form a roof.

Mallick let out a whistle of appraisal.

"This is beyond beautiful!" Shuran said.

"Seems you pointy ear snobs are good at making more than shoes," Avrank admitted.

"I am glad you approve," Orian said smirking at Avrank. "Perhaps you would like some food and drink while you rest. I can also help find some suitable clothing for Mallick and yourself, Shuran Shin'Ar. I am afraid we have nothing to fit children." Orian threw back the jibe at Avrank personally for the shoemaker cracks.

"We have proper attire. Lead us to where we can settle please," Shuran said.

Orian looked at Shuran wondering where they were packing clothing and what condition they would be in. He had to trust that Shuran Shin'Ar knew what he was doing. Orian had not witnessed Shuran's display in the Tarangale market, sending things back to the Vault.

Shuran retrieved the clothing required from the Vault. After refreshing and changing into proper attire, Shuran, his yet incomplete Zidu'Si, and the twin dwarfs Dvargan and Grafdrik all made their way back down the tree to the central gardens.

"These tree houses are fine but they could do with a lift system. The stairs are murder on little legs!" the twins said.

"We have lifts, but prefer to use the stairs unless time is against us. Walking the stairs provides time to reflect and take in the splendor of our surroundings," Orian said walking up to greet them. He gave the group a once over and nodded his approval of their appearance. "I do not understand how you do it Shin'Ar."

"Secrets of the Zidu'Si that you may yet discover my friend," Shuran answered back to Orian.

"Let us not keep the Queen Mother waiting," Orian said and turned to lead them to the Royal Bitmu, tree house.

As they walked the paths toward the great tree where the Queen Mother received visitors, Shuran noticed the elves here, unlike those in Tarangale, seemed far less enthused with his presence. Shuran wondered if that had anything to do with Voreen.

The tree they approached was bigger, by far than any other they had seen. Rather than stairs leading up the massive trunk, intricately carved doors were set in the base of the majestic tree. The doors opened inward where they found an audience chamber containing rows of benches along each side leading to the throne and dais at the far end.

The Queen Mother sat upon the throne expressionless as they made their approach.

Shuran reached the proper distance from the dais when he bowed in respect, and his companions, save Avrank, did the same.

Avrank merely lowered his head briefly; after all he was royalty in his own right.

"Stand and be recognized by the reverent Queen Mother, Sovereign of all elfin kind, keeper of the great garden," the herald announced.

Shuran and the others stood before the Queen waiting for her to address him.

"You have come a long way young asipu and presumed Shin'Ar reborn," Queen Mother said. Her voice was soft yet commanding. She sat upon her throne, draped in layers of fine ivory silk, decoratively embroidered with threads of gold and emerald in patterns of leaf and vine. Her entire body radiated a powerful glow to Shuran's Essence assisted vision.

"It is as you say Queen Mother, a long journey that is barely begun," Shuran responded.

"Then let us not keep you needlessly. You have come to present your claim on the title Shin'Ar, do so," she said.

Again her tone and posture gave away nothing of her feelings.

"I present to the elfin people, the Agal Kastu, mighty bow of the elfin Zidu'Si," Shuran said as he held out his hands and within, appeared the Agal Kastu in a flash of light and energy.

The Queen Mother now stood and approached Shuran. As she stepped forward, Shuran bowed his head and something on the bow caught his eye, a symbol, the symbol that represented his name as Shin'Ar. Before he could think on this new detail, the Queen Mother took hold of the bow and lifted it from his hands.

Her expression now changed. She could feel its power. She knew it was the true bow. "So you have returned to us what was once lost in betrayal," she said as she returned to her throne.

Shuran looked up to see her challenging look. She was testing him, daring him to speak out in defiance to her statement. He did not have the opportunity to respond.

"You are Shuran, son of Dalgon. He was here you know, some many winters ago. He spoke of a son yet to be birthed, who would reunite the races in a final bid to save Ersetu from destruction," she said. "Before me stands a young man, human in form, who appears to have seen far more harvests than would fit Dalgon's prediction," the Queen finished.

"My growth belies the true passing of my days. I grow differently than most, I am truly younger by half or more, of what I seem," Shuran answered.

"Yes, Voreen has told me of what he gleaned from your mind, and what he could not." Again the Queen was testing him.

"Should answers be required, I would gladly answer in truth that which I am able. I will not, however, suffer the raping of my mind without challenge," he stated.

"No, I suppose the Shin'Ar would not. The Shin'Ar you may be, but I will think on what that means for my people." The Queen blinked and looked at the herald who announced that dining would begin. During the dinner, a troupe of elfin players acted out a history while another recited the story.

"In days of long past, the elfin lives and pride be vast. The Telukukal leave save one who guards, his power strong beyond words. For five millennia he watched over the land, trusted were those who he would call, right hand. Mighty the power of the Zidu'Si was told, Power that came from the weapons they hold.

"Fashioned for peace, not a war did they wage. Not until the day when came the dark mage. The warriors they fought with great power to bare, The dark one they wrestled whose shi was not there. To trap or destroy him was fruitless thus far; it would take a great joining and death of Shin'Ar.

"The warriors they could not do as they were commanded, the Shin'Ar took back their weapons and the Zidu'Si disbanded. What happened thereafter not a story is known, the Shin'Ar was gone and the lands left to their own."

"A bit sing-song for my taste," Avrank said.

"What do you suppose it means, Shuran?" Mallick asked.

"I have no thought. We do not know anything of what happened when the Shin'Ar first disappeared," Shuran said.

From behind him Voreen spoke. "We know all that is necessary. The Shin'Ar abandoned Ersetu and left us to the dark asipu before he disappeared as well. Since then, this world has been in turmoil and poisoned," Voreen said. "You wish to start this cycle again and make what is bad worse by far."

"That is but your interpretation. The hurt pride of your people stands in the way of seeing the truth." Shuran stood and challenged Voreen's words. That is when the attack came.

At once, Shuran felt the weight of a thousand and more minds intruding on his. Through the dizzying attack, he could see his friends being taken away and bound. They were unable to withstand the onslaught of the elves in their heads. Shuran fought to place a wall up against the intruders but was unable to hold them back.

As he began to fall to the knee under the pressure, he did the only thing he could think to do. He reached for the line of power below the Earth. He allowed it to surround him and ease the pain of the mental attack. Suddenly he was engulfed and swimming in a river of electric force. He struggled to keep his mind together and remember what Codger had read to him from a book in the Vault library.

"Focus on the flow and let it join your thoughts, wrap your will around it and it shall obey," Codger had said.

Shuran stopped fighting and started to focus. There within his reach he sensed the flow of energy and he grabbed it. The wash of power that engulfed him was staggering and yet it steadied him. He pulled back and then dove into the flow.

He emerged just behind Voreen and placed his hand on either side of his head and surged power into him. Through the connection, he was able to reach all the other elves. They had joined their minds to make the attack. Shuran lashed out and sent enough power out to render them all unconscious.

The attack was ended.

Chapter Thirty-Two

"Release them," Shuran commanded the elves holding his friends in bonds, including Orian.

They hesitated too long.

Shuran waved his hand and instantly brought his friends to his side through the lines. Shuran reached out and called the bow to him, but the Queen held tight and struggled against the pulling force. Shuran then changed the mental grip he used to call the bow, and suddenly it was his.

"What is the meaning of this?" the Queen yelled. "You take back what you gave. The very prize that was taken by the first Shin'Ar so long ago." she trembled with anger and fear.

Shuran steadied himself and calmed, but power still danced upon his skin. "You mistake for a gift, what was only a loan. The gug weapons were never the belongings of the separate races. This bow belongs only to the Zidu'Si elf who stands by the Shin'Ar's side, and only so long as the Shin'Ar allows." Shuran spoke with authority he had never before commanded.

Voreen began to stand and gather his wits. "Voreen, great grandson of Grastrell, betrayer of Shin'Ar, you were right to feel shame for your ancestor's disgrace. He abandoned the Shin'Ar as did the other Zidu'Si," Shuran said.

"No. The Shin'Ar left Ersetu to the fate of the unbalanced Essence and dark asipu," Voreen answered back.

"Understand your own story told this night. The Zidu'Si refused to obey the Shin'Ar, and he faced the dark alone to his own demise. He did not abandon you; he sacrificed himself despite your ancestor's failure," Shuran finished.

"Enough of this," the Queen Mother said. "The attack was the final test Shuran Shin'Ar. And it was poorly executed. I wanted to see how loyal you were to your comrades and those you call Zidu'Si, including Orian," she admitted. "You have proven your right… and your strength.

"Never before has any man of the seven races been able to stand against such an attack, never mind best it. You conquered the line without training; you used the concern for others as your motivation." She paused while rising to her feet then bowed before Shuran. "You are truly Shin'Ar reborn. We are at your service."

Shuran rested a hand upon her shoulder. "Rise please, I do not wish to be treated as anything more than a man," Shuran said.

"No man known to us would act for the good of others as you have, you risked everything to enter the lines as you did, all to protect your friends and those who serve you. That makes you more than any man," she said.

Suddenly Shuran felt more uncomfortable than ever before. He shivered visibly. "Has it gotten colder?" he asked Orian standing beside him.

"Not in the least," he responded.

"Then why, am I so cold? Is it a result of traveling the lines I wonder?" Shuran asked.

Voreen came to put a blanket around Shuran. "Yes and no, your first use did not bring out all you took in!" Voreen smiled.

Shuran suddenly realized he was half naked, wearing burnt and tattered strands of what remained of his clothing.

After Shuran had dressed in clothing offered by the Queen's staff, he joined the Queen at her table for dessert and wine. His Zidu'Si, the twins and Orian were also in attendance.

"Again I wish to apologize for the deception Shin'Ar, it did get a bit out of hand." The Queen Mother was now presenting herself in a relaxed and informal manner.

"Consider the matter closed Queen Mother," Shuran responded.

"Thank you, and please when just among friends I wish you to call me Florisia," she returned.

"And likewise Shuran will suffice," he smiled back.

"If you will allow it still, I approve of Orian among your Zidu'Si," Florisia said meekly.

"It would please me if Orian will accept," Shuran admitted.

"It would be my greatest honor," Orian answered.

Shuran materialized the Agal Kastu and handed it to Orian. "Then this is your burden and weapon so long as you serve the Zidu'Si."

Orian took the bow and felt its power immediately and that of the other Zidu'Si. And the Zidu'SI felt the power of Electricity flow through their bodies.

"Feels good right?" Avrank asked Orian.

Orian just smiled.

Later that evening Shuran and his friends sat up planning their next moves. It was decided that in the least, Shuran would send Dvargan and Grafdrik back to Duranekur. Shuran no longer needed guides since he made it to the elves. The truth was since they were not to become Zidu'Si Shuran did not wish to risk them.

"I can take you to the base of the mountains where we boarded the ferry," Shuran said.

"That far!" they gasped.

"Truth I could probably take you further but I would not like to risk exiting the lines in the wrong place. Those mountain caverns your people created seem to warp the lines natural paths," Shuran answered.

"Close enough," they both answered not wanting the risk of dropping into a chasm or a fiery pit.

"Avrank has the hammer called Menasutur, I have the Agal Kastu, what weapon does Mallick carry?" Orian asked.

"Mallick is not assigned a particular weapon, he is first among the

Zidu'Si, my commander of sorts," Shuran answered. "His weapon would be his knowledge, and there is something else," Shuran said and suddenly a ring appeared in his hand. Handing it to Mallick, he said, "Wear this, and you shall have access to the Vault's library of knowledge. Seek out information while focusing on the ring, and if the answer is there, the ring will give you access to it." Shuran told him.

Mallick slid the ring on his finger and instantly felt the tingle grow to a pulse as the power joined him.

"How did you know of this ring?" Mallick asked, and suddenly the answer was in his thoughts. "Ninkashi!" was his standard response.

Shuran spoke of his visions before bedding down for the night. His visions have been growing in strength and intensity. He had already encountered the dwarves and the elves as his visions revealed. By the repeating pattern of the visions, he would next encounter the giants somewhere in a valley where the trees, plants, and creatures made the tallest of men feel like a dwarf ten times over. Otherwise, he would be surrounded by fire. Both things seemed to happen in a different order each time he had the visions.

His sleep that night would see the same vision of the giants, but this time the vision expanded. Shuran stood before a broken altar made of clear, pure crystal. Around him his friends and many elves were engaged in battle, but not amongst themselves. They fought an army of large deformed manlike monstrosities, ogres. The ogres were not alone; they were following a legion of soulless men. An army of undead was being led by a dark robed figure. Shuran ran to confront the leader, and as he approached, a force of darkness knocked him back. As he looked up toward his attacker, he was pulling back his hood to reveal his face.

"Bastien," Shuran cried out as he woke.

Shuran could not get back to sleep. He went into a small sitting room and retrieved a book from the Vault Library that he had once stumbled upon about dark weaving. He wanted to know if it were possible to raise the dead. His vision of an undead army disturbed him deeply. He could not get the images out of his mind therefore he risked removing the tome from the Vault. He was relieved to find that it did not disintegrate.

The undead looked fully alive but no light in their eyes. They weaved

Essence, so they had to have a shi he thought. Then there was the image of Bastien. He could not shake the feeling of dread. He saw Bastien die, did he not? Bastien did not have the same dead eyes, but they were not his own.

The book told stories of resurrection, but none produced anything more than mindless creatures unable to move unaided. He found a reference to possession by demon. This possession required a body with a shi. Another entry stated that to reanimate the dead, would require a spell to control it by mind along with the darkness to power it. Shuran was tired and worried when the others woke and began to enter the sitting room. He sent the book back to the Vault and prepared a meal from food left in the larder.

After taking breakfast, Shuran spent several moments transferring the twin dwarfs home to the Orenthal Mountains and then returned to Entensiama. Upon his return Shuran, was met by Voreen.

"Shuran Shin'Ar, may I have time to speak with you?" Voreen asked.

Shuran held no ill toward the ancient elf, but he did not trust him either. "We will be leaving soon, what can I do for you?" Shuran asked as he motioned for Mallick to stand down.

"I hope there is something I can do for you. I wish to share something that was passed down from my ancestor." Voreen approached slowly but without intending harm.

Shuran was unsure how he was suddenly able to read the intentions of another. Shuran nodded and Voreen to continue.

"It is said that before the Zidu'Si was disbanded, they prepared for war with the dark abisu," Voreen said.

"This much I know, what is it you can add to this telling?"

"There was never any history recorded of anyone ever facing this dark one directly. He or she worked behind the power brought against the light."

"Are you of the mind that this powerful foe is once again behind the actions of the Order of Chaos?" Shuran asked.

"I cannot answer for certain but the Followers of Light in Britengate have gone to ground. We have seen no sign of them in houses of worship or doing trade in Tarangale," Voreen said.

"Thank you," Shuran turned to leave.

"There is something else," Voreen started.

Shuran turned back to him.

"My ancestor learned the power over the mind and body from the teachings of the Shin'Ar. He passed this story to his sired elves. He always said it would be needed one day to fulfill the promise made when the Shin'Ar might return." Voreen stood for a moment then turned and left.

"Mallick look for that knowledge in the library, we leave for Britengate before nightfall. I wish to see what is going on there before we track down the giants."

Chapter Thirty-Three

Shuran and his Zidu'Si headed out toward Britengate, directly South of Entensiama. By foot, it took them until a few hours before daybreak to arrive. Shuran did not wish to travel by line. He wanted to check the land for signs of passage or hints of where the Followers of Light may have gone.

Throughout their journey, they were all on alert for an ambush. Shuran shared with them most of the details of his vision. He did not speak of seeing Bastien. Shuran was unsure if this was not part of his regret of loss, bleeding into the vision. Shuran often felt that Bastien would have been a candidate for the human weaver among the Zidu'Si.

The Zidu'Si needed a member of each race in the least to become complete. Additional members could be inducted, but there were seven weapons of power for wielding by a leading member of each race of man and another for an Isten to the Shin'Ar.

As they neared the outer borders of Britengate, Shuran could sense movement and halted his approach. He signaled the others to halt as well. After several moments, Shuran turned and said, "I see you."

With that statement, the elfin rangers came out of hiding. There were nearly fifty rangers spread out among the forests around them.

"We have followed from Entensiama," the ranger admitted.

"I have been aware of your presence, I just do not understand why you tried to remain hidden," Shuran said.

"The Queen Mother was afraid you would be insulted by our joining you. She wanted only that we observed and report back your findings."

"I warned the Queen of my vision and still she sends you?" Shuran asked.

"She says that to attempt to alter a vision is only to invite far worse. Fate takes measure to correct its course," Orian said.

"You knew they were sent?" Shuran asked indignantly.

"I only suspected until I felt them approach some time ago."

Shuran just rolled his eyes at Orian and turned back to the village of Britengate.

"I sense no life among the city except that of a few woodland creatures that have ventured within," Shuran said. "Let us spread out among the buildings and check closer then circle back to the altar in the center of the city," Shuran said and they all fanned out among the buildings searching for signs of recent activity.

Shuran walked around the shops and stalls that until recently were likely teaming with activity. He rounded a corner and was met by a vision that sent his skin to pimple. He had wandered to the center of the settlement and now stood before the Altar of Creation.

Standing beneath the lintel topped uprights flanking the altar, stood a young woman bathed in a pale light. She was sobbing.

"Ho there mistress!" Shuran whispered as not to startle the girl.

She turned to face him.

As she turned, Shuran caught sight of a large crack running up the center of the crystal altar stone. A portion of his vision came back to mind.

"You have come!" the apparition said.

"Who are you?" Shuran asked.

"Who I was I only begin to recall. I am split and lost. I must find myself," she said before sobbing came upon her again.

"What has happened here?" Shuran asked.

"The light has been taken, and the altar destroyed long ago," she replied without looking at him. She hid her face behind the long flow of snow-white hair that waved on an absent breeze. "I knew you would come. I saw it, and here you are," she said in a childish voice. Her sweet and innocent demeanor changed instantly.

"THE BAD HALF HAS DONE EVIL THINGS!" she yelled then suddenly returned to the docile sobbing girl he first saw. "She must not see me now. It is not time."

Shuran could not help but feel sorry for this young girl.

"They have left to hide from her evil death walkers," she continued. "You have come. I knew you would," she repeated.

"Do I know you maiden?" Shuran asked.

"You did yes, but not in this form." Suddenly she looked out past Shuran.

"The death walkers come. Save the light sheesh!" she said and then was gone.

Shuran was brought back to his senses by a scream of pain.

Shuran could hear sounds of steel and twanging of bowstring. As he turned back from the altar and left the structure, his vision came to life.

Undead soldiers were approaching from all directions.

The elves and Zidu'Si had arrived back to the Altar grounds as the attack began.

"Shin'Ar! They are unnatural!" screamed Orian.

"They are the undead I saw in my vision," Shuran began. Before he could say more, a stream of fire shot forth from several of the attackers that met with unprepared elves. The screams of the elven rangers now burning to death was more than Shuran could stomach.

He turned and ran to the nearest attack. With his hands outstretched he sent walls of earth up to separate the death walkers from his Zidu'Si and the elven rangers. The wall did not hold long as it melted from the heat of the fire being streamed at it from the undead wielders.

"They work the Essence! How? They have no recognizable shi. I cannot read their energies!" Orian said.

"Use your gug weapons!" Shuran yelled.

Shuran called forth a sword and shield from the Vault armory for himself and Mallick. The two went about slicing at the undead with limited success. Every act of magic they sent against the creatures was met with equal resistance.

Mallick decided to alter his attack. He dodged around a spear and came up behind an attacker then struck.

Shuran saw the body falling as the head rolled forward.

"That works," Mallick said with a cocky grin.

Shuran then noticed a dark mist seeping from the now headless body. "Demons!" Shuran knew what he read was in use. Someone was controlling these dead creatures using darkness to power the body. "Mallick! Hold them back I need to find who controls them!" Shuran yelled.

Mallick saluted and went back to slashing and hacking at the death walkers.

The elfin rangers were holding their own. They were able to confuse whatever lie behind those dead eyes with their use of electric pulses and sparks or balls of energy. For every elf to fall, five or more of the undead were taken out. Their bodies writhed and shook on the ground as they sizzled from bolts of energy the elves were sending. This could not go on for much longer. These elves would tire soon enough.

The Zidu'Si would stand longer being strengthened by weapon and the bond of service to Shin'Ar. Shuran ran around finding exhausted elves to re-energize through Abnu Emuq he was pulling from the Vault. He could not do this indefinitely. He had to find the source controlling this unnatural force of men. He needed something more.

Shuran reached out with his senses to locate his Zidu'Si. Once he found them in his mind he tried to send them all a message at once, but something strange happened. Their energies merged then separated.

Avrank was suddenly pulling molten rocks from the ground and thrusting them at his attackers while running beneath their grasp slamming the Menasutur into knees and shins, forcing them to the ground.

Mallick was likewise firing fire and lightening in turn as he got close enough to behead his foe. Orian melted the ground to liquid rock beneath foes. Shuran had joined their abilities.

This distraction did not last for Shuran. A looming presence appeared from the tree line. Four massive and monstrous hulks of flesh lumbered toward him, ogres. Shuran had to hope the Zidu'Si and elves could hold their own now.

The first of the ogres came for him. It brandished a club the size of a small tree. The ogre swung in an effort to take Shuran's head from his shoulders.

Shuran was not there to meet the blow. He entered the lines and concentrated on mapping them. He felt out with his senses to the furthest edges of the energy currents veining the continent until he found what he was looking for. In an instant he was out and standing upon solid ground.

As he gathered himself he felt the wave of heat. A wall of flame surrounded him. He was confused at first because this was not the mage flame the death walkers had been throwing. This was elemental flame. Shuran reached out and joined his shi to the flame and tamed it. Standing before him was the robed figure. Behind the figure, the ogres loomed.

"Nice trick! But not very effective at making your escape, Anzillu!" the man said in a forced and raspy voice. "You will not stand against the darkness," he continued.

"Who are you?" Shuran asked.

"You ask the wrong questions. I will give you one answer to one question before my ogre friends make breakfast of your innards."

Shuran thought hard about what to ask but did not have the courage to face the answer. He decided to ask something else.

"Who stands as the force behind the imbalance?" Shuran asked.

"Ah! A difficult question to answer since the imbalance has never been fixed," the mysterious man hissed.

"Your answer!" Demanded Shuran.

"The force behind the imbalance was and is the dark half of the whole," the robed man laughed.

"Speak plainly!" Shuran yelled.

"I answered true, finding the meaning is up to you," he giggled and turned. "Should you get past my pets here, perhaps I'll answer another question, Shuran."

The first ogre reached out for Shuran but never took hold.

Shuran was angry and did not wish being toyed with. He ducked and placed his hand on the ogre's arm as its grasp past him. Instantly the ogre was gone. One by one Shuran dispatched the other three ogres before running off to find the robed man. He found him standing near the cracked Altar of Creation, controlling his death walkers as they closed in on what remained of the elves and Shuran's Zidu'Si.

They fought well but were visibly exhausted and out numbered ten to one. Shuran let his anger boil and lashed out at the robed man with waves of powerful fire and electricity.

The figure was well prepared for it and met the challenge with a wall of dragon glass.

Shuran could not understand where the glass came from. Suddenly shards of the glass broke from the main body and shot through the air toward him. Shuran threw a spell at them, "PAD!" he yelled and they broke to pieces and dust.

"Impressive, but how will you handle this?" the man said as he threw a ball of pulsing dark energy at Shuran.

Shuran tried to sense the attack but it was a twisted form of power and all he could do was dodge the assault.

"Tsk, tsk, tsk, here I thought you a challenge, having dispatched my ogres so quickly. What ever did you do with them I wonder?" he mocked.

"They are swimming, in the fiery pool of Hell's Mouth!" Shuran offered. "Would you care to join them?" he asked the dark foe.

"I think not, I do like a warm bath but I also believe that would be a bit uncomfortable."

Shuran's distracting the wielder had an effect of slowing the death walkers. Mallick and the rest of the fighting force were able to gain advantage and dispatch more of the lifeless soldiers.

The robed man took notice and renewed his assault on them.

Shuran could see his attention could not be split and remain effective on both fronts. "Tell me stranger, what do you expect to gain by this?" Shuran asked as he began to circle around behind the man. Shuran employed the art of deception the elves used on him. He obscured his movements from the man.

The robed figure darted his hooded head back and forth trying to locate Shuran. The effect it had, showed immediately by the slowing of the death walkers' attacks again.

Shuran continued to goad the man. "Does your master expect you to win the night? Will he or she reward you somehow for taking down the abomination born in Drakkfoth?" Shuran continued.

Chapter Thirty-Four

"Reveal yourself mixed-blood, you only prove that you are ANZILLU!" he screeched.

"HA! That is a bold statement coming from someone controlling the bodies of dead men!" Shuran called back in echo from all around the altar. Shuran had succeeded in thoroughly angering the man. It was time to strike.

The robed man had backed himself into the center of the structure surrounding the altar. A dozen raised crystal stones surrounded him.

Shuran pulled forth energy and earth causing the electric lines to pulse up into the crystals and inward to the center of the shelter where the man stood. Shuran approached the smoking mass in the middle of the altar shelter. He kicked at it to find his foot going right through it. Off in the distant trees he could hear the angry and wounded shouting.

"I will see you again Shuran, son of Dalgon. You will pay for your past transgressions, and I will see you put down like the abomination you are," the voice yelled.

Shuran spared less than a moment on the man as he turned to see the death walkers slowed to a crawling unorganized mass. Without the direct control of their master, they were harmless.

The Zidu'Si and remaining elves made short work of taking their heads.

Shuran gathered himself and made for his comrades position. "How many were lost?" Shuran asked a Ranger.

"We lost nearly half our number, twenty-four dead, another seven wounded. We are not certain they will make it," the Ranger answered solemnly.

"Take me to them," Shuran said.

Shuran spent nearly two hours working on healing the seven wounded elves. Two of them were nearing the point where nothing could be done, but Shuran prevailed. He had to take extra time, as he was least familiar with elfin anatomy, but he found in remarkably similar to both human and dwarven make-up. Shuran wondered how the people of Ersetu could be so outwardly different yet inwardly alike.

Exhausted and feeling beaten, Shuran gathered the remains of his impromptu fighting force to finish disposing of the dead 'again' bodies. When they had cleared the battlegrounds of the foe, they gathered the elfin bodies so that Shuran could transport them back to their home for a respectful service and burial. Shuran escorted the Rangers and their fallen comrades home, spoke with the Queen Mother then returned to Britengate.

"What says Queen high and mighty point ears?" Avrank said.

The jest-full relief from what had transpired brought a smile to even Orian's face.

"She understood the risk and was grateful for the lives that were saved. She also stands ready to aid our cause when called," Shuran said. "This is just the beginning I am afraid. The sorcerer who controlled these poor soulless creatures got away," Shuran added.

"Who was this dark bastard?" Mallick asked.

"I am unsure," Shuran started, unable to convince himself. "We must prepare for what is to come. They now employ trolls, ogres, and undead bodies of innocents possessed by darkness. There are evil forces at play, and we must find out how best to oppose them," Shuran finished.

"Let us leave this place. What once was a place of beauty and light is now unseemly and unclean!" Orian said.

Shuran nodded and placed his hand out for the Zudi'Si to grasp. He 'zapped' them away, as Avrank had taken to describing travel by Emmuku'Gu, the power rivers of the world.

After they had vanished, a number of people began to emerge from the forest and into the clearing near the Altar of Creation. They gathered in a group near the altar looking at the ruins of their holy place.

"It is as the Lady of the Light spoke," one of them said.

"She spoke of a powerful young man and his companions, this is true to what we saw. Are we to see this as the coming of the prophecy then?" another asked.

"Now which prophecy would that be?" a new voice said from the darkness. She came out into the open, and moved gracefully over to the cracked altar. "Nasty business this imbalance, and such a waste of good fighters," Salmetu said as she ran a hand over the now powerless altar. "Take them, I need replacements," she said as a group of zealots followed after her.

"What do you make of this latest development, Priestess?" Isten asked Salmetu when he appeared from the shadows.

"It is a slight stall to our plans, nothing more," she answered.

"And what is it that happened to your army?" Isten asked impatiently.

"We will find that out just as soon as we find my pet abisu. Come out pet. Where are you hiding?" she asked in as sweet a voice as possible. Her frustration and anger were beginning to surface.

From the opposite side of the clearing, shuffled the robed figure of the man who controlled the death walkers.

"Now then pet, what has happened to my lovely fighters?" she asked walking forward to meet him.

"Destroyed Priestess. The abomination found some way to defeat them. And the elves fought beside him," he pleaded.

She looked at him much as a mother would her child, then she struck him with a bolt of dark fire.

He incinerated on the spot.

"You have destroyed your newest pet Salmetu," Isten said.

"Pets are a distraction and replaceable, you taught me that." She recalled the memory of her sweet kitten that Isten killed in order to force her to use the resurrection spells. She gathered her moment of sorrow into a mask of anger, then smiled and turned to Isten. "I shall need a new general Isten. Find me a new one please, someone from that academy of yours perhaps?" she asked sweetly.

"That will not do I am afraid. All the students of promising talent have been drafted into service of the council," he informed her.

"Then replace the council!" she demanded.

Isten began to feel concern over what Salmetu was becoming.

***

Shuran and his Zidu'Si appeared in the clearing outside the entrance to the Vault of Durangug.

Mallick proceeded to lose the contents of his stomach. "I will never get used to that," he said.

"At least our Shin'Ar has learned to keep his clothes," Avrank said with an uneasy laugh.

"Let us go inside and freshen. We can then meet in the dining area and have something to eat and discuss our next moves," Shuran said as he approached the slab of stone that marked the Vault first entrance.

"What is this place?" Orian asked.

"Welcome to Durangug, Orian. Ancient home of the Shin'Ar and site of a number of other inconsequential structures," Shuran said brusquely. He looked at the stone slab, and it opened.

"Shuran did you just open that?" Mallick asked, noticing that Shuran did not place his hand upon the stone.

"It is no longer necessary for me or any of us to touch the doors to enter. This is our home, we may enter and leave as we wish!"

They made it to the second door, the one leading to the Vault. It stood open already with Moona in the opening holding her pipe to her pursed lips and wagging a finger.

"You think ya' could o' called ahead an' told me there'd be guests for supping!" she scolded.

Shuran just ran to her and took her into an embrace.

She was at first surprised and overwhelmed. "Now then what in Damkianna's name is this all about?" she asked as Mallick passed by and gave her a nod. Orian and Avrank followed Mallick in and nodded to Moona as they passed. "Shuran my boy, what is all this about?" she asked again not releasing him.

"Moona, it is all I can do not to loose myself. Everything is happening far too quickly," he said.

Moona just pulled him back into an embrace.

Codger came out from beneath a stack of books at the sound of Moona crowing across the Vault. "What are you mooing about ya' silly ol' cow?" Codger said.

"Mallick? When did you… How… Weren' you halfway across Ersetu just this past day with Shuran? And who is this elf with you? Oh, Hello Avrank," Codger said nearly stumbling into the dwarf.

"What does a dwarf have to do to get a drink around here?" Avrank replied.

Codger led him, Mallick, and Orian to the table where he told them to sit while he fetched some cups.

Shuran and Moona went off to a quiet corner to speak before joining the others.

"Shuran, what is this all 'bout now?" she asked.

"It is all right, I am fine enough. Let us go join the others, and we can speak of what has happened since we last spoke."

"Just you sit your arse back down! I'll have a word or ten afore we finish here boy lest I redden your tail!" she said.

It was good to be back with Moona he thought.

Shuran and Moona talked about things left unspoken for far too long. Shuran has been carrying around guilt over what happened to Bastien, and it has been boiling over. He has become far too serious and guarded.

He did not feel himself. He felt as if someone was taking him over. He experienced memories and feelings that were not his. Abilities came to him as though he had spent a lifetime in training.

"I don' pretend to understand what has been happenin' to you my child, but I know your heart. You are good and kind and the truest friend Bastien had. What happened was not your fault. You want to be placin' blame; you look to the bastard what started this imbalance," she finished.

Shuran did not respond to this last statement. He still blamed himself for some reason he did not understand.

"Sometimes I think Ersetu would be better off without magic," Moona said. "'Course, not 'til I been long since eaten up by worms in the ground." She smiled, and Shuran smiled back.

Shuran and Moona soon joined Codger and the rest of his Zidu'Si at the table where Codger had laid out bread, cheese, some dried fruits, and a stew he started earlier in the day. A keg of wine sat at the end of the table and Mallick was well into his cups along with Avrank.

"Zidu'Si full-fledged eh?" Codger asked. "The fine elf here, Orian has filled me in on a bit of what has happened," Codger said. "Not sure I understand it all. I know you were rebuilding the Zidu'Si of course but this thing with the weapons and now somehow they share abilities?" Codger was asking for more information.

"I am unsure how it happened, I suppose we shall have to research it," Shuran stated.

"No need Shuran Shin'Arse!" Mallick jibbed.

"Ha-ha sheesh, what information have you found?" Shuran asked as he smiled.

"Well, the Library has quite a bit of information on the formation and binding of the Zidu'Si," he started. Mallick noticed the confusion on Moona and Codger's faces. He lifted his hand to show them the ring. "Shuran's gift to me as his Zidu'Si Sanu, sort of like his right hand and second in command," he explained.

"The ring gives me the weapon of knowledge. It, along with the overtly lethal weapons of gug, are meant to be tokens of membership, and weapon of choice for each member of the inner circle Zidu'Si," he said.

Mallick continued on to explain about how the original Zidu'Si was composed of seven primary members plus the Shin'Ar and his second. Each of the seven races held a place in the Zidu'Si and lived extraordinarily long lives in the service of the Shin'Ar. They worked to understand, and battle a growing threat of darkness.

All seven members working Essence together created the weapons constructed from gug. They fashioned them after the first made by the Telukukal, the Menasutur. The weapons were bound each to their wielder and could only be fully used by them or their kin by proxy. At some point during their work they found it necessary to deepen the bond of the Zudi'Si. They bound their gifts together allowing them each to wield the same Essence as the other.

"Shuran by accident rebuilt that bond," Mallick said.

"Was it accident or SIMTU, I wonder?" Codger asked.

"Simtu?" Moona asked.

"Yes, the ancient word for fate. I believe this all, is happening as it must," Codger said before gulping down the rest of his cup.

"Perhaps, or something is guiding things along." Shuran offered.

"What makes you say that?" Mallick asked.

Shuran looked around the ancient vault. "Just a feeling."

<u>Chapter Thirty-Five</u>

Morning brought renewed hope and faith in what they were facing. Shuran and Mallick went out to hunt for fresh game while Avrank and Orian worked their way through the secrets of the library. Codger was nursing his head after a night of drinking. Moona was making all the noise she could, to help him with his headache.

"Serves you right, you yak's arse. You ain' gonna keep up with them young men drinkin'," she said, loudly.

"Dwarfs are suppos' to be able to hold their spirits. I'm part dwarf ain' I?"

"Yes, I 'member which part!" Moona cracked. "Now get your wrinkled old bottom up and help me get some food cookin'!" she yelled.

She was glad to have her boys back, Codger could tell by how spirited she became the moment they arrived. Now with another two adopted children, she was a mother hen to them all.

Mallick and Shuran walked the woods resetting snares and collecting a few rabbits caught.

"What has been bothering you Shuran?" Mallick asked.

Shuran did not answer immediately. He was not certain he should share his concerns.

"If it effects you, it does so to us all, sheesh. Unburden your shoulders, it weighs you down," Mallick said.

"I have not shared a piece of my latest visions," Shuran started.

Mallick stopped walking and turned to Shuran. "If a snake has bitten you, suck the poison and spit it out!" he said to Shuran.

"The robed figure controlling the death walkers, in my vision it was Bastien!" Shuran said.

Mallick was not expecting this news. "Bastien is gone Shuran. You are just mixed up in your head."

"Am I? I am not so certain. I thought him dead but with what we have seen, perhaps the Order has done something to his body," Shuran admitted.

"I would be a fool to tell you that is not possible, but you would not be responsible if they have," Mallick tried to convince Shuran.

"Would a resurrected Bastien feel the same, or would he blame me?"

"If what you think is true, Bastien could not be truly dead if it were he controlling the death walkers," Mallick reminded him.

"I remember, but I also doubt that it was Bastien at Britengate. He knew who I was but not in the familiar sense. I think my visions are telling me what may be a possibility," Shuran said.

Mallick could see the pain in Shuran's eyes. Mallick and Shuran were like a brother to each other, that is why they call each other sheesh, but Bastien was his best friend.

"If he is out there we will find him. Together the Shin'Ar and Zidu'Si will save your friend," Mallick assured Shuran, though he had his doubts.

The two of them continued on into late morning tracking game. They returned to the Vault with several rabbits, a few game birds and a large stag.

Shuran enjoyed the physical labor of building a sledge and hauling the game rather than using Essence.

Mallick complained of course, but he too needed to work his muscles.

"'Bout time you two hauled your arses back here! We were 'bout to eat without you!" Codger complained through the pain of his headache.

Moona had forbidden Shuran or Mallick from telling Codger how to 'burn-off' his hangover. They both decided that Codger's pain was less of a problem than the ire of Moona.

"We reset the snares and hunted more game. There is a sizable stag outside the Vault door that will need dressing after our meal," Mallick said.

Shuran dug into his meal. Moona noticed the change in Shuran. He was not slouching and the light had returned to his eyes somewhat. She caught Mallick's attention and gave him a wink and a smile.

This was not lost on Shuran, who knew they had conspired to get him talking. He smiled at the feeling of love for his family. "So what have you two been up to this morning?" Shuran asked Orian and Avrank.

"We poured over the books in the library looking for anything useful," Avrank said.

"And what have you found?" Mallick asked knowing that he could immediately access anything he questioned. He simply was not yet skilled at asking the right questions.

"Did you know that elves make pointy shoes?" Avrank said jokingly.

"Ah yes, and little dwarfs are confused with brownies, because they always bump their heads into normal sized men's arses!" Orian retorted.

"Ah, the blending of gifts has given the elf a sense of humor!" Avrank smiled back.

"According to what we have found, the giants originated from a deep valley somewhere north. Nothing here indicates where or gives description, not even a map," Orian said.

"But there is an interesting mention of a reference book held once by the Edubba Lamadtu," Avrank said.

"Pardon my dwarvish but what is that?" Moona asked.

"It is not dwarvish, it is the ancient tongue for school of learning magic," Codger said.

"So am I to assume you think this book would be in the possession of the Essence Academy?" Shuran asked.

"It makes sense, they were known to have collected all the materials from all the old schools after the Lalli Mah, when they consolidated and began sanctioning weavers," Orian added.

"So what is this reference book?" Shuran asked.

"A ledger of sorts. It recorded all the ingredients for ancient spell work and where they could be found. There are spells created by the giants for working metals. Some of the items needed are likely from their homelands. If there is a record it may indicate where to find them," Avrank said.

"So how do we get our hands on this book if it still exists?" Shuran asked.

"I can get it." Codger said.

"What are you on 'bout Codge?" Moona barked.

"Quit your mooin' cow, and let me finish," Codger grumbled back.

"Dur!" Moona scowled back.

"As a sanctioned weaver, I have privileges to the Academy library," he said.

"You had privileges. We have no knowledge of what has transpired in New Draven and the Academy. Word is they have closed the city walls!" Orian said.

"Well, that won' be a problem. I know a certain smuggler who has ways between the walls," Codger said.

"And what may this smuggler extort for payment this time?" Moona asked.

"You know he did not get all the plans for the Mellamu Nanna," Codger implied.

"That is your plan, you want to hand over the full plans on building magurmu over to a dwarf pirate?" Shuran asked.

"I was not planning on givin' 'im the means to power it!" Codger added.

"And if he were to hold you until you did?" Shuran asked.

"Hey, perhaps he would hold you instead Shuran. You could become a pirate. They could call you Shin'ARRRGH!" Mallick joked.

Even Shuran laughed this time.

They boarded the Mellamu Nanna early the next day. Since they planned on flying her down to smugglers cove, they needed to make certain the ship would be warded against multiple threats.

The night before Mallick accessed the Library, searching for spells of protection they could imbue upon the magurmu, flying boat. They used the knowledge gained to add a cloaking spell, a shield, fireproofing, and spelling the sails against damage.

Codger suggested the fire proofing, remembering the accident Shuran had that scorched the main deck and mast. Runes etched into the control panel on the pilot's deck would trigger the spells. The shield and cloaking spell could be triggered with a spelled charm as well. They packed only essentials so to keep the load light for speed.

Shuran could call forth anything they needed.

They settled aboard the vessel and with the aid of the recharged Abnu Emuq, they lifted into the air and headed south. They engaged the cloak before clearing the trees as not to attract notice by anyone that would be near enough to see a boat flying through the sky.

Rather than head out to fly over the Great Sea, Mallick suggested they fly low over the land to get a sense of what might me happening. They headed southeast toward Birchshire and would fly along a path that would take them near the largest settlements and villages. Using spyglasses, they were able to see well enough to determine the state of the realm.

As they traveled past Birchshire, they could tell that thus far it remained untouched. Perhaps, having been visited by the Inquisitors and Royal Guard already, the need for the town being sacked was overlooked. Of course there was no reasoning for what the Order was up to. The death walkers were rampaging across the realm, destroying everything in their path.

Further east they flew past Elmwood. They already heard of the devastation, this was a chance to both confirm and appraise the damage. Elmwood was a burnt out shell of a village. Little was left of the town square. Every building was burnt down or blown to pieces. Here and there, a stray animal ran about, but there was no sign of the villagers that once lived here. Those who had escaped were not likely to return any time soon.

Traveling the countryside by magurmu, would normally be exciting and an adventure. Seeing the realm in such a state of upheaval sapped the joy out of the trip for everyone except for Avrank.

He jumped and ran from side to side of the deck looking at everything there was to see. "I have never been this far south. I am also unaccustomed to this warmer air," he said.

As much as Orian and Avrank teased each other, they were becoming best of friends. Orian moved some crates to create steps and a platform for Avrank to reach the rail and see over the sides.

"Signs of the death walker army and ogre movements are nonexistent as they must travel by some dark magic," Mallick said.

"There is no 'dark' magic Mallick." Codger said.

"Weaving is all about intent. If you intend something dark then the working is dark and the opposite if you intend good," Mallick said in a trance-like state.

Shuran looked at him sideways.

Mallick held up his hand and wiggled his ring finger.

"How could resurrecting the dead ever be anything but dark? The shi has left the body," Shuran asked.

"A shi can be anchored to or trapped in an object. You would need to bring the body back to life and reverse the damage of rot, but you could put the soul back," Orian said. "I read something about it in the library as well," he added.

Shuran assumed that Mallick had shared their conversation about Bastien.

They continued south along the Napalkua River where they passed the Zig'Mada falls. It was an unnatural break in the river that formed into a waterfall when the ground rose up.

Shuran took a moment to feel out with the Essence. He had sensed the falls a few days earlier when searching the Emmuku'Gu to find a place to drop the ogres. When he felt the falls, there was something there he could not take the time to explore.

"Codger can you move us a bit lower and closer to the falls? I would like to check on something," Shuran asked. When he reached out to feel for the oddness of the falls, he explored what first drew his curiosity. There were tunnels behind the falls and they were lined with deposits and something else.

"We will have to come back here when there is time. Beside gug and crystal deposits there is a full tunnel system that is not natural. The gug is preventing me probing deeper," Shuran shared.

New Draven crept into view over the horizon soon after they passed Two Bridges and Castleton.

Codger took the ship a bit higher making certain to clear the turrets and towers of the buildings and castle.

"Codge, activate the shield," Shuran said.

"Are you expecting trouble Shuran?" Orian asked.

"No, I plan to avoid it, the shield will block out any spells designed to detect intrusion. Unless someone knows to look for a shielded vessel they will not sense us. If someone looks close enough they might see a ripple in the sky, but if we are higher it is unlikely to be detected."

Shuran took out a spyglass and began examining the goings on in the Aurderian capital city. "There are Royal Guard everywhere. And the gates are sealed shut."

"It is not but two hours before Utu sets below the horizon, why would they close up the gates?" Mallick asked.

"Because they are under order to keep everyone out," Codger said. "We're off to see the smuggler," Codger said as he turned the Melammu Nanna west toward the coast.

<h1 style="text-align:center"><u>Chapter Thirty-Six</u></h1>

The sight before everyone's eyes was surprising. The once nearly empty bay of smuggler's cove was full with ships that were a near double to the Mellamu Nanna.

"That sneaky little bastard!" Codger spat.

"What did you expect scat for brains!" Moona whispered. "Time for a laugh!" she continued as she released both the shield and cloak spells.

The ship glided over the docks to the nearest slip available. Luckily there was one near the office. A crowd of dockworkers and smugglers gathered after they gained their senses. More than a few had wet their breeches.

Codger began the decent into the available slip. The wings folded in and tucked up alongside the ship as the vessel came to rest in the water. The dock was crowded with onlookers, but they cleared quickly when the smuggler's guild leader came barreling down from his office.

"What is the meaning of this? Who are you and what is this..." he stopped in mid bark when he saw Codger standing ready to disembark the vessel, now docked in Aknrad's personal slip.

"Codger you old bastard, I knew you left something out of those plans but I had no idea!" Aknard said.

Codger stood staring at the dwarven guild leader as the Zidu'Si set out the gangplank. He wore a grin from ear to ear as he headed down to meet his old friend.

"Of course I didn' give up all her secrets, fool! I only left out an important bit or two," Codger said.

"I should think you left a bit more off the list than that you scoundrel," Aknard replied.

"All right, you two dullards shut it and get up to that office. We got business, and time is shorter than Avrank!" Moona yelled as she pushed past them.

Shuran, Mallick, and the Zidu'Si followed behind. As the last member passed, he nodded.

"Hello Uncle!" Avrank said to Aknard as he scrambled up the pier chasing after the others.

"What is going on here? And why is my nephew out of the Orenthal and among the likes of you? He is royalty for Damkianna's sake!" Aknard scowled.

"I am Zidu'Si now Uncle, my brother sits as heir apparent," Avrank said as his uncle took him into a huge embrace.

"Oh, how I have missed you, my little turd!" Aknard said.

"TURD?" Orian, Mallick, and Shuran all said in unison.

"That was my little name for him when he was young. Being so small people got to calling him 'tur' meaning small in the ancient tongue. He always acted the little mischievous shit as well. So I began calling him turd!" Aknard said.

"HA! You are a little shit! Bumping into arses!" Orian laughed.

"REGARDLESS!" Moona said. "We have a need, and you have the means, Aknard. Let us get to business!" she took charge.

"So let me get this through my mind, you want to break into the city, or you want to get into the Library of the Academy?" Aknard said.

"Ultimately we only need access to the Academy," Shuran interjected before Moona could continue bullying Aknard.

Aknard was somewhat relieved. "You want to break into the most secure magical institution on all of Ersetu?" he asked.

"Not the most secure, but yes," Moona said.

Shuran shot her a glance, and she immediately understood her misstep. This was not lost on Aknard.

"We hope to use Codger's right as a sanctioned mage to gain access," Mallick said.

"Well, that will not work alone. You would only get an audience if you submit an apprentice for sanctions consideration to even get in the doors these days," Aknard replied.

"Why?" Codger asked.

"Because they need weavers to help with those dead things popping up all over the realm," Aknard answered.

"So they attack here as well?" Shuran asked.

"I would not say they attack here yet, but they have been seen about," Aknard answered.

The implication was not lost on everyone. Somehow the Academy was involved with the Order.

"Take me to the Academy!" Shuran said.

Codger started to object.

"It only makes sense, if there is trouble I can get us out," Shuran said.

"They will separate us likely, and put you to test before I can locate what we need Shuran," Codger said.

"Let me worry about that, you forget what I am now," he answered.

"Wait just a… is this the young babe in arms that you secreted away all those harvests ago?" Aknard asked.

"Aye, he is something more than he appears," Codger admitted.

Aknard looked at Avrank remembering the comment about being Zidu'Si and added it together. He bowed. "Shin'Ar reborn, your need is my duty to provide," he said.

"That'll be 'nough, all o' ya!" Moona said. "We got things to do and a ledger to find. Get on with it already. Aknard as adopted mother of the Shin'Ar, I command you to find me something to smoke!" Moona screeched as she poked him with her pipe stem.

"It is gonna cost you!" Aknard said looking back at the Mellamu Nanna.

Shuran engaged the shield.

***

Aknard got them into the grounds and near the entrance to the academy. They approached the guards at the doors and presented themselves.

"I am here to present my apprentice before the grand masters," Codger stuttered out.

The guards glanced at him then Shuran. They ignored them. Shuran lifted his hand and sent fire to the ground before them then water to extinguish it.

After their shock wore off they opened the gates and sent a page to announce them to the council. The page returned to meet them in the gallery and escorted them to the council chambers. They entered to find the Great Council in session.

"Who presents a candidate to the council this day?" the center member asked.

"Codger sanctioned mage of the second order. My papers are up to date," he added as the guard moved toward him.

"We will see to your apprentice," the councilman said. "You may wait outside."

"Might I be permitted the library while I wait? I have been testing a theory on the collapse of a re-animation spell?" Codger said working in a bit about the undead army hoping to help his request.

"By all means!" the oldest looking councilman replied quickly.

Shuran and Codger were sent separate ways. Shuran nodded at Codger and they parted.

Shuran was taken to a room not far from the chamber he had just left. Inside he was instructed to sit down and wait. "You will be tested young abisu. You will be placed if you pass," a voice called out.

"And if I do not pass?" Shuran asked.

"Then you shall be placed… Elsewhere," the voice returned.

From a door behind Shuran, a figure entered. Shuran had his shields up and could feel his approach. Shuran was not surprised by the initial attack. His shield deflected the fireball thrown.

"You will have to do better than that," Shuran said. He planned on keeping the testers busy, allowing Codger enough time. He would wait until he received a signal.

Codger entered the Library and walked up to the desk of the Librarian. "I am looking for some information on spells of giant metallurgy."

"Aisle seventy-four, row one hundred fifty-four, on lower level seven," the Librarian replied.

'Holy yak scat' Codger thought to himself. "Stairs or is there a lift?" Codger asked.

"We do not allow elemental powers or conveniences here, you will find the main staircase to your left. Next," the Librarian said, even though there was no one else waiting.

Codger made his way to the stairs and recited the location in his head over and over so he did not forget.

"Impressive!" The attacker said. "You can shield, that is advanced. How are you at offense I wonder?" the tester asked. "Throw me a ball of fire!" he ordered.

"What kind?" Shuran asked.

The tester hesitated. "What do you mean 'what kind'? There is only fire."

"What are they teaching here?" Shuran asked, "Witch fire, hell fire, earth fire, iron fire… You see there are multiple ways to defend," Shuran replied. "Is there someone more… experienced to test me?" Shuran asked hoping to stall for time. He had gained only one hour before someone new entered the room.

"I hear you are over confident in your abilities. I shall stub your ego boy!" the new tester exclaimed.

"Give me your best!" Shuran said.

Codger worked his way through book after book, leaving a mess behind him. He finally came upon a section that was roped off and held a closed case with a single book enclosed. He signaled to Shuran, "I will raise an alarm!"

"Only if you are certain," Shuran replied.

"What did you say initiate?" the tester said.

"Get on with it, unless you are frightened?" Shuran prodded.

The new tester prepared a volley of various types of fire from different directions.

Shuran was well prepared for the attack. One by one the balls of fire flew toward him from different directions. Shuran met each with a spell of opposite force. The test went on with attack after attack, until finally someone else entered the room.

"I will take over," the new figure said.

Codger broke the charm protecting the ancient tome. As soon as it happened an audible alarm was raised. Codger hit his charm and alerted Shuran.

"I will send you to the Mellamu Nanna," Shuran said and then Codger moved through the lines to the vessel.

"Who were you talking to?" the new tester asked.

Shuran was still unable to see anyone else in the room, but he could feel them.

"I was just wondering what lackey they have sent now. Why not just set me against the death walkers?" Shuran asked.

"What do you know of the death walkers?" came the response.

"They are an abomination to the face of Ersetu!" Shuran called out.

There was a long pause and then a response. "It takes one to recognize another does it not…ANZILLU!"

Codger made it back to the Mellamu Nanna with the book from the library. He sat there for nearly an hour before realizing that Shuran was not to follow.

"Moona is going to kill me!" he said aloud. Codger stowed the book in the ship before heading back to Aknard's office. "Shuran is in trouble!"

Immediately Mallick reached out to Shuran mentally through the link of the Zidu'Si. "Shuran what is happening?"

"I will be there soon. I taunt them to see what they truly know about the threat to Aurderia. I suspect collusion," Shuran replied. "What? I do not understand?" Shuran said to the new tester.

"You thwarted that last test without the aid of a spell. Either you wove the spell without a spoken word, which is highly unlikely, or you worked elemental magic. You are either not a human man or anzillu because you do not have the look of a Drakkian," he said.

"You think it impossible that I could wield without a word? Speaking a spell is the true weakness. If you cannot control your thoughts you should not be a weaver," Shuran said.

"Anzillu, I will see you destroyed. It is likely you, who sends these undead creatures to our peaceful settlements, destroying everything in sight," the man said.

"Prove your claim and I will submit; otherwise you will regret your accusation," Shuran threatened.

Chapter Thirty-Seven

"We are ready!" The ancient kashshaptu croaked from the cauldron. "For too long we have been forced to live in this wretched swampland!" she continued. "No longer will we be forced to stay within the borders of the misty swamps, lest the rotting curse set in."

The crone moved from behind the cauldron and placed a gnarled hand on the head of another witch. She was the one who met with Salmetu, and acquired the sample of blood. She was falling apart. Her face was loose on one side, and her hair falling out in clumps.

"Our sister's sacrifice in leaving the swamp for the sample will not go unappreciated," the witch said before heading back to the cauldron. "There was a time when we walked openly throughout all of Aurderia. We were beautiful and respected weavers," she reminisced. "We will be again, and we will track down those who cursed us, and repay the favor."

"That was long ago Grand Kashshaptu. Who shall stand blamed for an ancient curse?" the rotting witch asked.

"The same one responsible for our salvation!" she cackled as she dumped the container of Salmetu's blood into a cup of the brew.

As the witch swallowed the potion, a spasm overtook her body. The shaking of her form brought a chorus of high-pitched screeches and cackling from the coven. The old crone fell to the earth, writhing and shaking until, at the apex of her roiling, a final scream of pain mixed with relief sounded above all.

She rolled to her side and slowly stood. As she made it to her feet, her skin began to lose the pale green tint. Blemishes, wrinkles, warts, and spots disappeared. The once old and hideous creature was now a stunning specimen of womanly beauty.

The coven's cackles of delight resumed as the old crone, made young, discarded her tattered old robes and dress. She opened a package to her side and removed a crimson and black-laced gown. With the help of her sister witches she dressed and primped herself.

"Now I travel for the capital, where I shall take what is owed us by that fool Assinnu Isten and his Order," she said.

The witches knew that the sample of Salmetu's blood was only enough for one. They needed to acquire more of the blood from her line, in order to break the curse for the entire coven. As it was, the curse cast so long ago, has kept the witch coven alive in a state of perpetual rot. The vapors and mists of the swamp kept the worst of the effects at bay, so long as they stayed there.

Now the Grand Kashshaptu, Penelle, could leave the virtual prison indefinitely without fear of wasting away. Her intentions were hers alone. She did not share what she was planning beyond working from within the realms governing council, and acquiring the means to cure the remainder of the coven.

She did not have the power to take on Salmetu, nor did she want to. Although the Dark Priestess would be a means to an end of the curse, she also served the greater plans Penelle designed. It was not enough to break the curse. She was mad with vengeance, but she needed power to enact her plans. Time was on her side now; soon she would see Salmetu, as well as the brother.

"Is the carriage and the items I require ready in the border village?" Penelle asked.

"The driver stands ready. If I might ask, why travel by mundane means?" the witch asked.

"A new face requires a new impression. The people of this realm see only the surface and I will use that to my advantage," Penelle answered. "By the time our true motives and nature is revealed, it will be too late. I must present a different image of kashshaptu to the realm, it will make my goals, that much easier to achieve," Penelle finished as she continued walking to the outskirts of the swamp.

"This is where we part ways sister, you do not want to venture to near the border." Penelle turned to walk from the marshy land out into the dry lands of more civilized inhabitants.

The mists cleared before her and she felt the rays of the sun, Utu, on her skin for the first time in many thousands of years. She tilted her face to the sun and drank in the light. Only when she heard the clicking of the carriage driver bringing the horses to a halt before her, did she snap out of her silent revelry.

"Are you ready mistress?" the driver inquired with an admiring look in his eyes.

"Yes, will you provide a hand kind sir?" she said as she approached the carriage door.

The driver and his companion both scrambled to help her aboard.

She smiled and nodded as she entered. "This is going to be easier than I foresaw," she said to herself as the carriage drove off toward New Draven.

Penelle arrived at the gates of New Draven to find them closed and guarded.

"State you business!" demanded a guard.

"I am Council Member, Penelle, and I would very much like to be admitted to the city," she said in a sweet voice that nearly brought bile to her mouth.

"I am sorry mistress, but the city is under military law. No admittance without prior authorization," he said apologetically. He was softening up to her as she continued to spell him.

"But you see I am authorized," she said handing him a parchment.

The guard unrolled the parchment, read it, and handed it back to Penelle. The guard ordered the gates open.

"Sorry for stopping you, Council Woman Penelle, please enter without further delay."

Penelle nodded and smiled sweetly as she returned the blank parchment to her bag. Her carriage entered the big city and headed toward the building that housed the Great Council.

Penelle walked into the Council building with an air that belied her authority for actually being allowed within. She knew where she was headed since she already knew the layout of the building from her use of scrying. She continued on, until she reached her destination. With a determined posture, she opened the door and entered the room.

"What is the meaning of this? This is a closed session madam you do not belong here!" the man at the head of the table said.

"I have every right to be here. I stand before you, to reclaim the reserved seat of the kashshaptu," Penelle said. Her eyes met Assinnu Isten and she smiled and gave a slight nod.

"Who are you to take the seat, certainly not a kashshaptu?" one of the members said.

"I am, and I will have that seat back," Penelle said as she cast a spell shifting her appearance, from the beauty to old rotting crone and back again.

"I thought your ilk could not leave the swamps? How?" Isten asked.

"We were granted a gift that allowed me to break the curse. That is all that is necessary to share. As the Grand Kashshaptu, I have arrived to retake my coven's seat." Penelle saw that Isten understood she was calling on the bargain made in Drakkfoth with her sister witch.

Isten and Penelle met in private after the meeting broke up.

"Your arrival could not be more serendipitous," Isten said. "We are about to hold a trial of Anzillu," he continued. "We are holding the boy thought to be Shuran, son of Sulura."

"How did you capture him?" Penelle asked.

"He came to us. I am told that he came with an old man to be submitted for sanctioning," Isten told her.

"What of the old man?" She asked.

"He was said to have gone to the Academy Library but has not been seen. I am not certain there ever was an old man, but an illusion of some sort. We have no idea what this young man is capable of," Isten said.

"Young man? Shuran should be just a boy yet," Penelle said doubtfully.

"We have seen to Salmetu's rapid growth, what is to say someone did not do the same with him?"

"No, he was with no one who could work such spells when last we were able to scry him. He is either far from here or dead. What of the boy your demon claimed in Birchshire?" she asked.

"That was not Shuran. We know nothing of who he is, since he still lies comatose, only enough of a shi to keep him alive."

"Well, shall we go and see to this young Shuran? I assume he is at the Academy?" she asked.

Isten nodded and then offered his arm to Penelle. "I must say, I approve of the new look." Isten said just before they disappeared in a swirl of brackish smoke.

***

Shuran sat in the gug lined cell, eyes closed as though in a trance. He attempted to send a thought to the Zidu'Si, a feeling that he was fine. He hoped that would be enough to keep them from mounting some sort of rescue plan. Shuran wanted to gather information, and this opportunity could not be lost.

Though gug would normally prevent a weaver from using Essence, Shuran was able to manipulate the stone to allow him escape should he need. He sat there for long enough that night had come and gone before soldiers appeared.

"Get up!" they ordered as they opened the cell. "Someone is here to see you, anzillu!" The guards escorted Shuran through the maze of hallways and climbed several stairways to reach the main level where the guards led him to a room, where two people were waiting.

"Good morning, I hope you have been treated well?" Penelle asked him. She approached him with a look of recognition. "You remind me of someone," she said.

"What is it Penelle?" Isten asked.

She shook the memory from her mind. "Nothing!" she said abruptly. She looked over Shuran again before turning to Isten. "When will he be tried?"

Isten looked past her to Shuran. "On the morrow he shall be put to the test and then executed," Isten said with a smile.

Penelle walked over to a table near where she found Shuran's belongings laid out.

"Those were found on him when he was taken," Isten said.

"What are they used for?" she asked.

"We have not been able to determine a use for them. They are imbued with Essence but seem to be useless," he said.

Penelle picked up the gem-inlaid band and placed a finger on the red gem and tried to use a spell on it. The band vanished in a bright flash. "What just happened? Nothing should be able to leave this room!" she insisted of Shuran.

He just shrugged his shoulders.

She had started to anger before she looked at him closer, and a memory stirred. Her anger abated and her expression softened. "And if I touch the green gem, will it also vanish?" she asked.

"It is a useless keepsake, nothing more," Shuran half-lied. True it no longer served its original function, but it was more than a keepsake he began to suspect.

Penelle examined the gem, running her fingers over the runes. She recognized them but said nothing to Isten. She handed it to Shuran against Isten's visible objection.

"It is harmless, he should keep it. Take comfort in your last few hours under this roof young man," she said as she turned and left with Isten.

Chapter Thirty-Eight

Isten was concerned about the disappearance of the armband, but he would not allow Shuran to see.

The Guards took Shuran back to his cell in the lowest level of the academy.

When he got to the small dirty chamber, he entered and heard a muffled yell before turning to find Mallick, dressed as a soldier, subduing a guard while Orian dispatched the other. "What are you two doing here?" Shuran asked. "Did you not sense my thought I sent?"

"We did, but we needed more information," Orian said, not convincingly.

"You fell victim to the nagging of Moona?" Shuran asked with a smile.

"It was unbearable Shuran, she was ready to come herself. She said she would shake the place apart with Earth Essence if she had to," Orian said.

"I believe she would," Shuran chuckled. "I am unharmed but not finished here," he added.

"What is it that has your attention that you risk a trial of anzillu?"

Mallick asked.

"You have heard about that? No matter, it will not be an issue, I plan to make an exit before they can execute me," Shuran said.

"Why have you not communicated?" Orian asked.

"They took my band. Earlier it was sent back to the Vault when a woman tried to activate it."

"What woman?" Mallick asked.

"I do not know her, she was with an older man. They came to question me. I think she just wanted to see me for herself for some reason. She looked at me as though having seen me before."

Shuran told Mallick and Orian to explore the academy before heading back to Smuggler's Cove to report what was to take place. He wanted the two of them back in the morning for the trial. He was interested in knowing more of the Anzillu trials, and he wanted to determine who was on the Great Council. Shuran moved to the cot to lay down and get some rest when he heard a noise in a dark corner of the cell.

"Who is there?" Shuran asked.

From the shadows, a small creature emerged. It was the size of a cat but walked upright to spite the fact its head was far too large for the trunk. Large pointed ears framed its oval face. It blinked its large round red eyes. "I have a message from my master," it said.

"Who is your master?" Shuran asked.

"Nagutan wishes to warn you. He says that you must not allow the beautiful lady to sample your blood at the trial," the imp told him.

"Why is this a concern, and who is this Nagutan?"

"You will see him on the morn. Remember the warning wielder. The woman is not what she appears and must not have your blood." The imp blinked again and disappeared in a puff of smoke.

"You delivered the message?" Nagutan asked his imp servant.

"Yes master, though I am not certain he will follow your warning."

"We shall see on the morn. Perhaps I can intervene if necessary," Nagutan said.

"You would risk exposure, master. What is this young anzillu to you that you risk yourself?" the imp asked.

"It is not for you to be concerned about, my little friend. What is important is that the man has a purpose to fill, and it is in my best interest to see him proceed." Nagutan turned the pages of an ancient book that lay across his lap. He stopped on a page that had an image painted on it. A young asipu was standing before a group of other men, each of a different race of man. They all wore the same blue cloak bearing a symbol.

"That looks like the young man in the cells below, master," the imp said.

"Yes, it does." Nagutan said.

"What is that symbol on their cloaks?"

"That imp, is the sigil of the Shin'Ar and his Zidu'Si. This portrait is over seven thousand years old." It was then the imp noticed the ring on his master's hand was also on the hand of a man in the painting.

***

"What?" Moona screamed. She was not happy with the information that Shuran sent along back to the keep.

"He is going to face the Council and stand trial for anzillu?" Codger asked.

"He said he would not allow it to get that far. He wants to find out who sits on the council and anything else he can." Mallick said.

"Madness..." Moona started. "No one ever left that trial chamber that was accused of anzillu. Even if they are found innocent they could not be allowed to know who the council members were. They will not allow him to leave." Moona cried out.

"I would like to see them try to keep him. They never tried a seven blood weaver," Codger said with a wry smile.

Moona calmed somewhat, remembering exactly what Shuran was.

They all sat aboard the Mellamu Nanna and ate dinner. Aknard provisioned them some food since they had not packed much, thinking this was a simple job to fetch the ledger.

"What price has Aknard placed on this little favor?" Moona asked.

"Nothing," Codger said.

"Nothing? He will want something," Mallick said.

"The matter is a favor to me, my Uncle will require nothing directly, though he did ask about the power source for the vessel," Avrank said.

"I bet he did," Moona remarked and glared at Codger.

"Orian, have you found anything useful in that ledger?" Codger asked, changing the subject.

"Yes actually, quite a bit. There are trade routes mapped out. They seem a bit wrong though," he answered.

"How so?" Mallick asked.

"According to this, the giants are somewhere to the Frozen North or beyond. There is nothing north but ice."

"Have you been there?" Avrank asked.

"No." Orian answered.

"Thought not. Stick to making shoes, not geography." Avrank joked. "You two just make sure you get in there in the morning, and be ready should Shuran need assistance," Avrank finished.

"We will be aboard the Mellamu Nanna floating as near as possible," Codger said.

"We will signal you if we need help, but I have a feeling it will be the Council needing assistance," Mallick said.

"Just be prepared to swing over and get us. Shuran said he can transport us from the room but not to the ship since it will not be on or near ground," Orian said.

"We will be ready, just send a signal or wave your arms about." Avrank smirked at them.

"Turd," Orian whispered to Mallick as they left to get rest.

"I heard that!" Avrank yelled.

***

Isten and Penelle reached her room that was prepared for her while Isten took her around to see the building.

"This will do nicely. I see you had my things brought up as well," she said to him.

"Will you join me for dinner Penelle?" Isten asked as his eyes followed the line of her curves.

"I would be delighted. Allow me to change and freshen before I join you," she said.

"You will find me in my private chambers. I thought it best we dine privately so we might discuss the matter of your reclaiming a seat on the council. And also please call me by my given name away from the Order's keep, Vardoran," he said, then turned and left smiling.

Penelle closed the door and moved to the dressing table where she sat and cast a scrying spell upon the mirror. "I am positioned within the council building and will be soon, sitting our proper seat," she spoke to the witch in the mirror. "There is also a development," she continued.

"You do not seem concerned, what is this news?" the crone asked.

"The boy, Shuran, is being tried tomorrow for Anzillu. He will not allow himself to be executed, but he is up to something for certain. I will make sure I am the one to administer the test and draw his blood," Penelle said with a smile.

Penelle arrived at Isten's room, dressed in a low cut fitted dress of deep emerald green. The dress flattered her youthful appearing figure and made her red hair appeared on fire in the firelight of the torches in his room.

"You look stunning," Isten said.

She smiled and took the chair he offered.

"I assume that the blood you took from Salmetu was used to achieve this transformation?" Isten asked as he sat.

"Right down to business then?" she said. "Yes, but it was not a transformation. It was used to remove the curse that has kept us from leaving the restorative mists of the swamps. This is my true appearance with the curse lifted," she said, making a seductive shift in her position.

Isten nodded approvingly at her. "Tell me of this curse. Who placed it?" he asked.

"The curse is as old as we can remember. The history of it is lost to time I am afraid," she lied. "How do you plan on getting a seat vacated on the council? A member is not likely to volunteer."

"The matter is being seen to. It is past time a certain member retired, I am just moving that decision along," Isten said. "You will be seated by cycle's end."

"May I attend the trial tomorrow?" she asked sweetly.

"I am afraid that only current council members are allowed to attend, beyond the accused and he that stands as a witness," Isten replied with a sympathetic tone.

"Perhaps I could stand as A'Su? I am a trained physician, someone must draw and test the blood," she offered.

"Yes, that would be allowed. I will make the arrangements," Isten said raising his goblet of wine in salute.

***

A knock came to Nagutan's door. He slowly raised from his chair to return the ancient book he was reading, to his desk. He picked up a cloth and used it to cover the vessel of blood on his desk. "Come!" he called.

"Councilman Nagutan, I have brought your dinner from the kitchens," a young soldier said.

"Where is my normal attendant, I do not know you?" Nagutan said.

"He has fallen ill and asked that I stand his place this night," Nagutan was not fooled.

"Put it on the table near the fire."

As the guard passed with the tray of food, Nagutan reached for a vial on his desk, followed him, and took his seat. "What seems to be the young man's trouble? He seemed in top health this morn?" he asked as he poured a drop of the vial contents into his soup when the guard turned away.

"Something he ate likely. He complained of a sour stomach," came the rehearsed response.

The soup foamed-up as Nagutan stirred it. "And was it he who shared that I was a member of the council, or the one who sent you with a poisoned meal?" Nagutan asked.

The soldier reached for his sword but was not fast enough.

"Haza," Nagutan spoke and the soldier was held fast in place. Only his eyes moved, darting around trying to figure out what had occurred. "You think an old man unable to defend himself?" Nagutan asked as he rose to his feet and approached his would be assassin. "You are not the first to attempt to kill me boy! And will not be the last."

Nagutan moved to his bookshelf and removed a tome. The shelf slid aside to reveal a chamber on the other side. With a wave of his hand, the statue form of the soldier slid into the room.

"You stay put now and do not move!" Nagutan chuckled to himself.

"I will decide what to do with you later."

"Master, what is this about now? Have you stolen another man's woman again?" the imp joked.

Nagutan chuckled at the jibe. "I may be old imp but I still have a way with the ladies! No, this is a move of desperation. Someone wants my seat on the council and I will give you one guess who," he said.

"The kashshaptu?" the imp asked.

"Most certainly, and that fool Vardoran is trying to give it to her."

"She has a claim of a seat, why kill for it?" the imp asked.

"She has a claim yes, but even so there must be a vacancy. Nine seats fill the council and there is no precedent for removing a member who is in full capacity."

"That did not stop the humans from removing members after the Lalli Mah."

"That was different, they dissolved the original council when the races could no longer agree on how to handle the mixed bloods, and the fear of their power. Humans remained and took up the vacant seats. The governing rules were altered and then came the Anzillu trials of the Sikil Mah. It was a dark time in history and they look to bring that all back." Nagutan was getting angered. "Not while I am still around!" he said.

"Why do you finally act master, after all this time?" the imp asked.

"Things are different now, the Shin'Ar has returned."

<u>Chapter Thirty-Nine</u>

◄◄◄▦

Morning arrived, and Shuran was eager to get a look at the Great Council. Shuran did not have to wait long. It had been light out for only an hour when two guards came to retrieve him.

"Ready?" Mallick asked.

"As ready as I can be. I had a visit after you left last night," Shuran said.

"Speak quickly we have not time to dally!" Orian said.

"An imp came on behalf of his master, Nagutan. He warned me about letting some woman get to my blood. Find out if you can, who this Nagutan is."

Mallick nodded and as they left the cell he said to Shuran, "Try not to bleed."

They entered the trial chamber to find a long table with nine empty chairs. Guards lined the walls behind the table and flanked the door they just entered. Another door beside the table opened, and eight council members filed in and each took a seat leaving the center chair vacant.

The last member walked in, Shuran recognized him as the man who came to see him the day before. He paused before approaching the table when he looked at the member at the far end. He seemed surprised, and the councilman noticed.

"Vardoran is there something wrong?" the councilman asked.

Shuran turned his head to Vardoran. He was shorter than the average man; he had some dwarvish features, could this be the same Vardoran, Moona and Codger's son.

"Nothing; Good to see you about Nagutan, you have been holding up in that tower for some time now," Vardoran answered.

Shuran now looked at the man called Nagutan to find him looking back with just a slight smile. Something is amiss here, Shuran thought.

"Let us get on with this," Vardoran said.

"You stand accused of being a mixed blood weaver and wielder. Speak your name and prepare to be tested!" Vardoran said.

"My name is unimportant if you are to execute me. I will tell you my name when you have completed you test," Shuran said.

"You will tell us your name!" ordered another member.

"He has the right to hold his tongue," Nagutan said.

Vardoran was seething. "So be it!" he said. "Bring in the A'Su!" he called.

The doors opened and the woman from the night before came in with a tray containing instruments. She placed the tray on a small table, brought out by a guard. A second guard moved a chair over and pushed Shuran into it.

"Hold still," the woman said. Then she whispered so only Shuran could hear her, "I can see that you pass the test, but I will require a favor when next we meet," she smiled.

"Penelle… proceed!" Vardoran said.

Penelle rolled up Shuran's sleeve and tied a long string tightly around his upper arm. "Make a fist," she requested.

Shuran clenched his fingers closed around the green gemstone that he had been holding when they came in. He forgot he even held it until now.

She thumped his inner elbow several times and probed for a vein with her finger. She lifted a tube with a small animal quill affixed to the end. She jabbed the hollow quill into his arm.

Shuran focused his thoughts on the blood that flowed from his vein, warping it.

Penelle began to look excited, Shuran noticed. Her gaze widened as she stared into the blood pooling into a waiting vessel below the crude tool funneling the blood from his arm. She continued to let it flow and Shuran was starting to feel discomfort and strain from weaving the transformation into his blood.

"Enough Penelle, get on with it. You have more blood than is required," Nagutan commanded.

Penelle regained her composure and pulled the quill from Shuran's arm and handed him a bandage to apply pressure where she stuck him. She moved the blood to the table and put a glass rod into the blood and then moved it into another glass jar containing a clear liquid. She stirred the rod around, waited to see what would happen. The liquid in the container turned pink.

"He is human," Penelle said with a look of confusion.

"What?" Vardoran roared.

"He is human," she repeated louder.

Vardoran shot up from his seat and quickly crossed the room to examine the test results. He probed the contents with the Essence.

"Impossible! I have seen this pattern before. It belongs to that weaver boy from Birchshire!"

Shuran just learned two things from what he had just heard. Foremost, Bastien is alive. Vardoran referred to him in the present tense. Also, Vardoran was in league with the Order if he knew of Bastien. Shuran became angry.

Vardoran turned to him. "Who are you?" he demanded. Vardoran stared into Shuran's eyes and watched them flash over with rage.

Shuran stood from the chair and stepped back to join Mallick and Orian, who discarded their assumed costumes.

"I am Shuran, son of Dalgon and Sulura, friend to Bastien of Birchshire. What I am is the Shin'Ar reborn," he yelled. Shuran spared a glance at Nagutan who nodded slightly and gave him a smile.

"What you are, is a dead man." Vardoran lifted his hand to cast a spell.

Shuran did not wait for him to complete it. He reached into the forces that twisted the gug-lined wall to his side and shifted them. Instantly the wall burst outward then Shuran, Mallick, and Orian ran through as a ball of fire hit the wall beside them.

"Move," Shuran said. "I cannot find a line leaving the island. We need to get away from these gug-lined walls!" he yelled.

"How did you get Codger back to the boat before?" Mallick asked.

"I was down on a much lower level near the main entrance. The construction there is ordinary stone."

They ran through corridors avoiding soldiers and knocking down apprentices who were leaving rooms or walking the halls.

Every hall they went down led to another intersection. They were running blindly without direction.

"Stop," Shuran shouted.

Mallick and Orian skidded to a halt and turned to Shuran. "What is it?" Mallick asked.

"This is pointless, hold a moment," Shuran said and closed his eyes. He reached out with elemental Earth Essence. He was able to map out the academy halls, at least those outside the concentrated area where gug was mixed into the stonework. He searched for a path to escape quickly.

"Shuran Shin'Ar! Hurry they are coming!" Orian said.

"Got it. Follow me!" Shuran took off down the hall with two of his Zidu'Si at heel. He led them down halls and up more stairs until they reached a dead end. "I do not understand!" Shuran said looking at the wall coming up. He started to probe the wall as he approached only to stop short when it began to slide open.

"Inside. Hurry. Questions later," Nagutan whispered.

After the three of them passed through, Nagutan waved his hand and the door sealed behind them. With another pass of his hand, he activated a rune that disguised the door as a solid wall.

"Now then, shall we go up? You will find it easier to exit from my towers; I had them built long ago from basic stone. There is a balcony as well," he added with a wink and directed them up the winding stairs.

"Nagutan is it?" Shuran asked.

"Yes, that is my current name. And you are Shuran Shin'Ar!" Nagutan answered with a bow of his head. "Questions when we reach the top, I am too old to climb and concentrate on conversation together."

They reached the top of the tower stairs, where the wall slid back and they entered Nagutan's tower room from behind his desk.

Shuran looked around to see nothing remarkable about the room. The furnishings were modest but there were paintings, tapestries, and various pieces of ancient artifacts.

"You have quite the collection," Orian observed.

"Thank you, I have been collecting them for… a long time."

Shuran did not miss the pause in his response. "Thank you for your assistance Nagutan," Shuran said. "You risk too much."

"I have risked nothing truly. Those fools on the council can barely see far enough to make the chamber pot, never mind what is good for the realm. The things they have been allowing are wretched," Nagutan responded.

"I believe it is Vardoran pulling the strings," Shuran offered.

"That and more Shin'Ar, you are wise to see."

"Mallick, stop petting the imp, we should be leaving. Moona would be readying the canons if the Mellamu Nanna had any!" Shuran said.

Mallick stopped petting the large red-eyed black cat on the bad. When it transformed into a small creature with large ears and head, Mallick jumped back.

The imp smiled, showing his rows of tiny pointed teeth in a devilish grin.

"You will find an open balcony through the drapery, there beyond the bed. Watch that you do not knock over my new statue as you exit," Nagutan grinned.

"It looks so life like." Orian then noticed the eyes moving and looked at Nagutan.

"He tried to poison me. Now he stands guard at my window. The fact that birds find him a good place to rest and shit is just amusing," he laughed.

Shuran smiled, though he felt for the soldier a little. Shuran signaled Codger with his communication stone and told him where to bring the vessel. "How can we repay your assistance, Nagutan?" Shuran asked.

"One day I will ask a small favor perhaps, but for now your friendship is a gift."

"Will you be safe once we leave?" Mallick asked.

"Safe enough, I have faced far worse than Vardoran's like in my long lifetime. Beside I will be needed here to keep an eye, now that the kashshaptu is taking back her seat on the council," Nagutan said disdainfully.

"Penelle, she is a witch?" Shuran deduced. "I thought I smelled a slight rot about her."

A rope ladder dropped out of thin air onto the balcony. Mallick started up followed by Orian.

"I stand impressed again. A cloaked magurmu I suspect?" Nagutan asked.

"You have seen one before?" Shuran asked.

"Not for thousands of years," Nagutan winked. "Take care Shuran Shin'Ar, you have a large burden upon your young shoulders. But I feel you will do what is required when the time comes."

Nagutan turned and left Shuran with more questions.

He had not the time to question, as he saw soldiers entering the Academy below. He quickly climbed the ladder and disappeared behind the cloak before pulling up the rope. "Engage the shields and get us back home," Shuran said. "Please," he added not meaning to sound ungrateful.

"Better!" Moona scolded. "'Bout time you decided to join us." Then she smacked him in the back on the head before sitting on a crate and drawing on her pipe.

***

Vardoran seethed with anger at Shuran's escape. He was more than a bit embarrassed at being surprised by Shuran's strength and ability to escape the room. "Can someone explain to me how an inexperienced boy and his two lackeys managed to escape this academy?" he howled. "They had to have help, no one can manipulate a gug lined wall, unless someone tampered with it," he continued.

Penelle stepped forward and placed a calming hand upon his shoulder. "Do not be over angry, there was nothing you could have done to stop his escape. He only allowed us this trial to gather information I think," she said.

"What do you know of this, kashshaptu!" Vardoran demanded.

"If he truly is the Shin'Ar returned or reborn, which I have little doubt he is not, then he could have left any time he wished," Penelle said.

The look in Vardoran's eyes told her he needed more explanation.

"The Shin'Ar of old wielded all the seven powers of the Essence. He also had access to the vast knowledge of ancient ways for using it. If this young man is who he claims, then we have more to worry about." She paused and held a look of hatred. "He will be rebuilding his Zidu'Si!"

Chapter Forty

Shuran called on the wind to speed the journey back to Durangug. Within a few hours, they would be nearing home. Shuran was tired and strained from Essence. He did not use an Abnu Emuq much any longer as he built up his abilities and stamina.

"How do you suppose the old man knew to find us when he did? And why would he help us?" Orian asked.

"I have not a thought on it, but there is more to him than is met by eyes," Shuran answered. "I am more concerned with someone else at the moment," Shuran said as he turned to Moona and Codger. "Vardoran is the leader of the council, and I fear the Order of Chaos in secret as well."

Moona's expression was unreadable.

Codger, on the other hand, went ashen in the face.

"How do you know it was him?" Moona asked.

"Nagutan called his name directly, intentionally I believe. I think he was trying to help me identify who I needed to see as the biggest threat to Aurderia," Shuran started. "Then there was the fact I could feel him attempt to reach into my shi and pull upon it," he finished.

"Then it is Vardoran true. Only our son was capable of stealing another's Essence." Codger said.

"That monster is not my son," Moona cried, leaving the deck and going below deck.

"She has always felt that it was something we did as parents. She thinks we failed him, and that is why he turned out the way he did," Codger said. "Stealin' people's power to increase his own, it is not what we wanted for him." Codger went to the pilot deck to be alone.

"If we can find how he does it, then maybe we can stop him from doing it to more innocents. I bet this is why abisu have been disappearing. They are getting those death walkers from somewhere?" Mallick said as he twirled the ring of knowledge around his finger.

"I already know a way to stop him, but it would make me no better than he," Shuran answered.

"Then there is only one other way," Mallick said. "You must complete the Zidu'Si. There is a spell to hobble him, make him mundane, but it requires the united force and strength of a full Zidu'Si," he recalled from the vast knowledge of the library in the Vault.

"What knowledge does the library contain on the Kashshaptu?" Shuran asked, knowing the Zidu'Si would not be required to hobble Vardoran.

Mallick paused while he mentally searched. "Just one book, but it is blocked from me somehow. It is somehow sealed," he said with confusion.

Shuran reached into the vault to identify any 'secured' items. He found a chamber that was meant only for the Shin'Ar.

***

They landed back at Durangug late in the evening, tired and hungry. Dvargan and Grafdrik met them.

"What are you two mimic birds doing here?" Mallick asked.

"We have a message for the Shin'Ar. An envoy from Drakkfoth has contacted the King requesting he arrange a meeting. He says he has information, and gift," they spoke in turn.

"Where is this envoy?" Shuran asked looking around. The chamber in the Vault would have to wait.

"We did not bring him here, though he already knew of Durangug, or at least the ruins located here," they said.

"We are tired and hungry, can this wait?" Avrank asked.

"It may be important, but I could do with a meal and wash before receiving anyone," Shuran began. "When can this messenger be led here, the ruined tower, to meet?" Shuran asked.

"Rather quickly I would imagine once we send a guinea hawk. He arrived by drakkon!" they said with wide eyes.

"Wash first, then we can receive our guest for a late meal. Send the bird." Shuran stated then entered the Vault.

Shuran had just completed his ablutions, changed clothing, and stepped outside to setup a table and seating when he heard the heavy beating of massive wings coming in from the East. When his eyes met the sight of his arriving guest, he was breath-taken.

The moonlight gleamed off the bright green scales of the massive beast now landing before him with a grace that belied its size.

The beauty before him transfixed Shuran. The drakkon bowed its head in greeting as its rider lithely jumped down and bowed as well.

"Greetings Shuran Shin'Ar, Son of Dalgon and Sulura," he began. "My name is Gregoran, and I am honored to meet you cousin," he said.

Shuran bowed his head, and then stopped when the statement registered. "Cousin? Because I share Drakkonian blood, you mean?" Shuran asked.

"In part but more so that my adda is half brother to yours, Dalgon," he answered.

Shuran had many questions but did not know where to begin.

Gregoran could sense Shuran's need for answers. "Let me tell you my tale and what brings me to you. Perhaps this will answer some or more of your questions," Gregoran said.

"We have been following your progress. The Drakkonian people have known for some time of the prophecy, your mother shared it with us when she conceived. She had a vision of the possible outcomes and that her children would take part." Gregoran spoke of many things Shuran already knew, but he did not speak until Gregoran paused.

"How is it you come to know of my location?" Shuran asked knowing that the area was long forgotten and he could not be scried without sensing it.

Gregoran knew this as well. "It is far easier for a bloodline to find kin, scrying is not used," he provided. "The first part of my message is to send your mother's love and wish to meet."

Shuran was dizzy with disbelief. "My mother lives?" he stood and began pacing.

Moona stopped puffing her pipe. "Speak dragon boy afore I swallow you up in the ground!" she ordered.

Shuran took her by the shoulders to calm her.

"Where has she been? Why has she not sent word in all this time?" Shuran asked.

"At first she was too weak. She nearly died after... Well, you know the details. My father sent trusted servants of the barony to retrieve her. They were nearly too late.

"It took many months before Sulura was well enough to awaken from a healing sleep, even longer to remember who she was and what had happened. The rest of her decisions are hers alone to explain, but I believe things happened the way that was necessary," Gregoran said.

"And what else brings you here now?" Shuran asked pointedly.

"The Order of Chaos has your friend Bastien."

"I already discovered this, what I do not understand is how you know any of this." Shuran began to anger.

"It is through a deceptive alliance of my father Fallon, Baron of Drakkfoth, with the Order that we keep apprised of all the movements of their work. The Order has kept house within our borders for centuries. The Baron is preparing to break ties with them and force them from our land, but he wants you to save your friend while there is time."

Shuran was feeling even dizzier than before and needed to sit back down.

"Shin' for brains; eat something before you pass out," Mallick said.

A sharp shrill broke through the silence of the night.

"What in Damkianna's name was that?" Moona shrieked.

"Ah, that would be your gift Shin'Ar," Gregoran said.

288

"Shuran, please, you are among friends and apparent family. What is this gift?" Shuran asked skeptically.

Gregoran let out a whistle and a dark shadow appeared from the trees. Once in the open, the gleaming form of a bright red young drakkon came into view.

"He is to be yours, a bonded drakkon, friend, and protector," Gregoran said.

Shuran walked up to the beast that stood half the height of the great green drakkon that carried Gregoran. The young drakkon lowered to the ground in submission. "What is his name?" Shuran asked.

"He will only tell his name first to you, as they are without the gift of open speech or weaving until bonded," Mallick said. "I just looked it up," he said with a smile.

Shuran placed a hand on the beast's head and was swallowed in a bath of fire from all around him.

In the flames, Shuran just saw himself and the drakkon.

"Greetings Lugaldur, bonded master, Shuran Shin'Ar. I am called Moltar in human tongue, I am at your service," the drakkon said in Shuran's mind.

"I accept the honor and welcome you into my heart as well as my Zidu'Si," Shuran answered somehow knowing the correct way to accept.

Instantly a spark passed between them.

As Shuran gained the strength and endurance of the drakkon, Moltar gained not only the traditional ability to work elemental fire, but all of Shuran's abilities. He would be the first of his kind to do so, a new breed.

With the new abilities, Moltar raised his head to the skies and roared into the heavens. His bulk increased three-fold and he was suddenly larger by far than the green.

To all else assembled, they witnessed Shuran silently touch the beast that suddenly grew immensely.

"It is done, they are bonded and we have witnessed the birth of a new breed," Gregoran elated.

The Zidu'Si, yet incomplete, also felt the addition of Moltar and his strength, to the collective.

Shuran spent some time speaking with Gregoran and Moltar about his mother and her state before returning to the table to his ignored family of Zidu'Si. "I apologize for having gotten carried away with all this," he said.

"Understandable Shuran Shin'Ar, it is not every day that you find out your mother still lives, and someone gives you a sizable new pet!" Avrank said.

"You are responsible for cleaning up after this thing!" Moona said with a huff as Moltar landed with a large mountain yak in his jaws, end-trails falling everywhere. "That includes mess from both ends!" she finished before taking another puff of her pipe.

"I am afraid we did not bring a saddle, we would not have one to fit his size as it is. He is by far, the largest and now mightiest, of all the drakkon," Gregoran said.

A puffing of pride in Moltar followed the statement, then a slap of the green drakkon's tail.

"Do not get overly inflated, hatchling!" the green drakkon, Jade said.

"I assume you are his mother?" Shuran was answered by a proud smile from her.

"We have the materials required, I am sure the shoemaker here and myself can fashion something befitting Shin'Ar's mighty friend," Avrank said looking at Orian, who smiled and sent a shock of electricity into Avrank's backside.

"Indeed!" Orian responded.

"Now shall we decide what to do about the Order and Vardoran?" Moona, of all, said. "Don' look at me like that, he is not the sprat I raised. That sweet boy died when touched by the evil that drives what remains!" she added.

Codger remained oddly silent, Shuran noticed. "First we must worry about getting Bastien safely away," he said.

"Fallon, my adda, plans on moving against them soon, in hopes of casting them from our lands. He hopes you might bring the force of your current Zidu'Si to bolster our forces?" he added.

"Yes, we will of course come if you stand with us?" Shuran requested. "I would join you with us my cousin, and make you sheesh to the Zidu'Si."

Gregoran, unable to find words, nodded his acceptance.

"I ain' cleanin' up after the green one neither!" Moona yelled from the end of the table.

They all gathered in the Vault for the evening and spoke on plans for the next day. The space would have allowed the bulk of Jade, but Moltar was far too large to enter through the tunnel entrance.

That did not stop him, Shuran used his bond to transport Moltar directly into the vast Vault, though he had few places he could maneuver.

"Well, this is cozy." Codger said after an evening of silence.

"We leave in the morning for Drakkfoth. I would add to our forces still. Codger, if I provided the crystals, would Aknard and his guild join us?" Shuran asked.

"If you provide him crystals he would follow you into Hell's Mouth without question. But where will you find the correct type of shard in sufficient quantity?" Codger asked.

"We will stop at the Napalkua falls, Zig'Mada, on the way to Drakkfoth. They exist within a cavern behind the falling waters along with veins of gold and some other power deep in the caverns. With the added energy of the Zudi'Si, we can charge enough to power his fleet for some time.

"I will send them here and you can leave for Smuggler's Cove when they arrive. We will wait one cycle before our siege, no more." Shuran set out a plan and they went about preparing.

Chapter Forty-One

"What are we to do now, Isten? What is this Shin'Ar, Shuran claims to be?" Salmetu asked. She was a bit on edge, which was unlike her normally calm and deliberate manner.

"It is of no matter. I have found a few histories of a man once calling himself the Shin'Ar, watcher of the lands. It is old tales and that Shin'Ar could not stand against the darkness then. Shuran as Shin'Ar will not stand now!" Vardoran said.

"Our first move will be to bolster your death walkers with the students of the academy." Vardoran moved to the window and looked out to the night. There was nothing but petrified trees and rock. A lone black bird sat upon a branch in a nearby tree. "With that old witless fool Nagutan disappeared, Penelle can claim the rightful seat of the kashshaptu. Add to her my trusted followers on the council, and we have the numbers needed to take unquestioned control of the academy, and do as we see fit."

Salmetu grinned at his implied meaning.

"What of the Ogres and Trolls?" Vardoran asked her.

"The ogres have committed to our side. The trolls have yet to respond to any requests," she said angrily.

"Do not be so easily angered at their silence. Although they are witless creatures, they will answer once they are able to understand the request. Besides, trolls serve the needs of the Kashshaptu above all, as it was the witches of old that created them. I will have Penelle reach out to them," he added.

Vardoran smiled maniacally as he stood over Salmetu stroking her flowing jet-black hair. "Things are moving along better than I had hoped. Shuran is but a blemish, soon enough cleared up with a well-played move. How is our guest from Birchshire?" he asked.

"He clings to life. I do not understand how, but it will not hinder us."

Vardoran called an emergency meeting of the council the next day. He already had Penelle placed upon the council when Nagutan was not found. Vardoran assumed his paid assassin finally achieved his objective. Now that he controlled the majority of the members, it would be short work to move his plans along.

"Esteemed colleagues, I have called you here so that we may take decisive action against the growing threat to the realm, most importantly New Draven and her surrounding lands!" he started. "We find ourselves in a dire time indeed. Anzillu, they run rampant throughout the lands. They cavort with dwarves and elves. They cause havoc and bring destruction upon the Northern villages." Vardoran was being purposely over dramatic.

Penelle fought the urge to roll her eyes in frustration.

"What do you suggest we do?" she asked as instructed.

"We need to take control of the situation, for that we need the Academy and all its resources," he said with authority that found no objection.

The council had only just finished signing the documents authorizing the seizure of the academy including recruiting all students and apprentices into service of the realm, when a knock at the door came.

An inquisitor entered with a parchment bearing the seal of Baron Fallon of Drakkfoth.

Vardoran opened the message and read through it a number of times before he let his anger surface. The parchment burst into flames and he howled with anger.

"What is it, Vardoran?" Penelle asked.

"That pompous Baron of the rocks, has declared the council corrupt and withdrawn from service!" It was then that Vardoran finally noticed the vacant seat where the member from Drakkfoth had normally held station. "He will pay for this when we are through here!" he spat in rage.

The Council agreed unanimously to take over the Academy as a military installation. This included all students and their instructors; they would all serve the realm and ultimately the Order of Chaos, unknowingly.

Vardoran and the Council members already in collusion with the Order, made short work of gathering all the occupants of the Academy. They tested their abilities, and loyalty to the realm. Many of the students were found only mediocre based on Vardoran's standards.

They were sent to the lower levels and placed in cells so that Salmetu could 'enlist' them into the death walkers. Weavers sat in huddled groups, terrified as they heard the screams from the cells around them.

Salmetu went from apprentice to the next, drawing out their shi to then be replaced with darkness. Those found strong enough, were allowed to retain enough of their spirit to then be possessed by a demon, so they might control the others. Once she completed her task, she transported herself and the new undead back to the secret keep of the Order in Drakkfoth.

Vardoran sent the Inquisitors out again, this time seeking any who had the spark of Essence. Vardoran would require all the power he could muster. Something bothered him about Shuran, though he would not admit it to the others. Outwardly he saw Shuran and his traitorous band of miscreants as nothing more than a minor distraction. Inside, Vardoran was jealous of the upbringing Shuran had with Elvaria.

In private he knew there was something more to him than his up bringing. He also know decided his mother was in league with the upstart wielder. Did she plan to use the child she stole away from the Altar of Chaos, as a means of enacting revenge?

He felt duality in what happened so long ago, when a spell gone horribly wrong, siphoned the Essence through his mother and into himself. The effect left his mother without ability to weave nor wield, but it strengthened his own hobbled abilities. Since that day, the day his parents disowned him, he had only grown stronger. He was not about to let sentimentality get in his way.

***

Shuran presented Gregoran with the ancestral Zidu'Si gug weapon of the Drakkian, the Mi-Ib Ag, before departing the next morning. The sword of fire was a fitting weapon for Gregoran. He accepted it with grace and awe as the powers of the Zidu'Si melded with his own.

By accepting the honor, Gregoran and his drakkon, called Jade, added to the Zidu'si and profited from the exchange of energies. Immediately after the initial shock of joining their Essence wielding abilities, the Zidu'Si went about practicing their new gift.

"Can you imagine the surge when we collect a giant!" Avrank jested. "I still say this will never get old!" Avrank continued as he lit Orian's pant leg aflame.

"I very much doubt you can expect a growth spurt, Turd," Orian said dousing his flaming pants.

Shuran and his Zidu'Si arrived at Zig'Mada falls late the next day. The size of Moltar allowed him to carry not only Shuran, but Mallick and Avrank as well. Orian rode astride Jade with Gregoran.

They dismounted and as the drakkon drank deeply from the waters, Shuran led the men up to the falls and around to a cavern set behind the raging water that fell from high above.

The falls were formed during a great upheaval of the land, hundreds of years past. Superstition and the jagged landscape kept all but the most foolish of adventurers away. Vessels carrying trade goods from the North stopped at a transfer port far before the waters turned rapid and deadly. Goods were then taken by land around the area of the falls to calmer, southern waters where they were loaded back on another vessel to continue on south to various ports of trade.

Inside the cavern, Shuran and his men were met by pitch darkness.

Orian conjured a ball of electric force that he confined to a sphere the size of an average man's head. The light that resulted illuminated the vast cavern. The group ventured deeper into the tunnel leading down into the ground to find a smaller chamber filled with millions of dancing points of light and swirls of golden brilliance. The walls of the far end of the cavern were covered in veins of gold and the shards of quarts crystal speckled with a multitude of colored minerals.

Shuran inspected the shards and began selecting suitable pieces to imbue and send back to Codger at the Vault. Once he collected enough and coaxed them from the rock using the Essence, he and the others used their collective power and surged Essence into them.

It was tiring work but no longer did it require draining one-self only to rest for the strength to continue. Shuran now found that he was capable of channeling mixed Elemental forces and funnel them through himself and into his Zidu'Si and thus the stones, without draining his own shi.

With the task completed, and extra shards to spare, Shuran transported them back to the Vault. Shuran was about to explore more as he felt something deeper in the tunnels, when Moltar stuck his sizable head into the cavern through the falling water.

"Are you done now? Can we go!" Moltar asked. He was eager to preen and prance his new form in front of the other drakkon back in Drakkfoth.

"Okay everyone back on the dragons!" Avrank said purposely misspeaking. Seeing Shuran ready to correct him he added, "You do not mind me calling you a dragon do you?"

"Not if you do not mind us calling you lunch!" Jade answered with a toothy grin.

Shuran and comrades, climbed aboard the drakkon then headed east for Drakkfoth. They traveled through the night and arrived before the dawn of Utu over the Eastern Highlands.

Shuran was feeling anxious. His mother has been alive this entire time. He felt joy and betrayal at the same time. Soon he hoped to have all his answers. As they flew for his father's homeland, he allowed himself to relax and enjoy the crisp air and wind in his face as they flew high above the clouds.

"It is peaceful up here above the world of troubles," Shuran commented.

"Just wait Shin'Ar, when we arrive we can go through drills and see how quickly you lose your lunch!" Moltar offered.

"I cannot wait," Shuran jested back as he placed an affectionate hand on his Lugaldur.

"We have arrived!" Jade roared.

The drakkon both stopped pumping their massive wings and stalled in the air for a brief moment of weightlessness. They pulled their wings in and pointed their noses in an angle down toward the approaching mountain. After gaining teeth-jarring speed, they spread their wings to full stretch and broke into a steady and effortless glide toward an on-coming squadron of drakkon riders.

They all hailed Shuran Shin'Ar, and his Zidu'Si arriving. More than one drakkon nearly collided as they caught site of Moltar.

Shuran and the Zidu'Si were met in the drakkon practice field by the captains of the riders. Greetings and bows were exchanged quickly but dutifully, as they all seemed to sense Shuran's impatience to see his mother.

"Nephew! Welcome to your family home!" The lean yet strong man said as he took Shuran in a rib-cracking embrace.

Chapter Forty-Two

Shuran stepped back from the man to allow room for a proper bow to the Baron.

"You are among friends and family here, we do not stand on ceremony! You shall call me Fallon or Uncle. After all your father is my half brother!" Fallon said.

Shuran wondered how long the man could talk without a need of air.

"Uncle then, I do not mean to seem ungrateful for the warm welcome but-"

"Not another word my boy, she is waiting for you within."

Fallon led Shuran through the tunnels and stairs carved in the mountain. As they approached the room where his mother was, a large white wolf exited the room and transformed into a young woman.

"Shuran this is my daughter, Barurbe."

She nodded to Shuran.

"It is she who found your mother and began to heal her before we were able to transport her here safely," Fallon added.

"You have my gratitude," he smiled. Shuran felt something stir in him he had never felt. He immediately felt awkward and it showed.

Fallon caught on immediately and bent close to his ear. "She was informally adopted as my ward when I found her years ago injured," Fallon said with a knowing wink.

Shuran relaxed some as he realized he was not having feelings for a cousin, though he was unsure what to make of it.

Barurbe smiled at him sweetly and left him to meet his mother alone.

Fallon encouraged Shuran to go on in alone. "I will be but a shout away should you need for anything. I will have meals sent in for you both."

Shuran turned and entered the room.

Across the room, Shuran could see that his mother sat in a high-backed chair near the fireplace. He trembled.

"Please come, let me look upon you my son. I have waited far too long for this moment," she said breathlessly.

Shuran moved closer and began to see the frailness of his mother's form. "Mother," he whispered coming around to face her.

"My beautiful boy, how I have watched you grow and yearned to hold you!" she spoke through tears and sobs.

Shuran fell to her feet and laid his head in her lap crying with joy. Shuran spent the entire morning and afternoon with his mother sharing memories.

Sulura explained how she attempted to give her shi to save his sister that was being sacrificed, but something went wrong. She had been left on the verge of death, most of her Essence burnt through her to fuel the spell.

Tianna, the fair-haired sister disappeared in a flash of light and her star dimmed. Barurbe found her and began her healing, by licking the wound closed. For many moons she lay unconscious, and then years barely able to speak without tiring. The one thing that stayed with her was her connection to her children.

"I have been able to watch you all," she said.

"But Tianna is gone!" Shuran said.

"Not gone my boy, she is just lost. She wanders the realms disembodied and searching." Sulura said.

"I have seen her! In Britengate she said she knew I would come and she cursed an evil woman!" Shuran realized.

"That would be your sister Salmetu. Tianna taunts her as we speak," she said with deep sadness. "I am very tired my sweet boy. Will you come back for dinner and bring that sharp-tongued moon mother of mine if she is here," she asked with drooping lids and a tired smile.

"Rest, I will see you this evening and bring Moona when she arrives." Shuran left with a spring in his step but an ache in his heart.

Shuran spent as much time as he could with his mother while she was strong enough to have visits. The rest of the time he spent with his Zidu'Si and the drakkon practicing various methods of using Fire, Earth, and Electricity. These were the strongest powers among them as the combined blood abilities of the Zidu'Si currently in the collective.

Shuran could wield the other elements, but they were not shared among his trusted companions. The bond only joined the bloodlines together and strengthened the collective. The Shin'Ar could lend strength to his Zidu'Si, but his full blending of gifts was his and now Moltar's alone.

Shuran ran through drills with the Drakkian riders and their drakkon. He was a natural rider. He learned that never before had a non-pure blood Drakkian ever been bonded with a drakkon.

Moltar was affected in a way that had never happened before. Unlike Jade, who could only wield elemental flame as her bonded could, Moltar showed remarkable new gifts. While hunting he reached for a moose that was running from his grasp when suddenly, lightning shot from his outstretched claws and struck the prey dead on the spot. It also partially cooked it.

"We are running out of time Shuran, the magurmu should be here by now." Mallick stated.

"They will be here. They will have needed time to provision, and according to Codger, they had some additional passengers to pick-up," Shuran said. "The dwarves insisted on joining the battle as did the elves. I am not certain how the elves found out," Shuran said looking to Orian.

"In truth, I only advised where we were to first engage the Order," Orian said with a less than innocent look.

"Save it cobbler, he is not buying that lame horse of yours!" Avrank said.

"Oh, stuff it turd!" Orian said as he walked off.

"I think you go too far with the shoe making jokes dwarf!" Mallick said.

Avrank went shuffling off after Orian. "Hold on elf, you know I… HEY, slow down…" his voice trailed off.

"UGH!" Mallick sounded. "I bet the twin pains in my arse will be on one of those boats!" Mallick complained.

Shuran laughed and led his friend out to the drakkon fields. "Come see what Moltar has learned to do," Shuran said.

"What is worse than mimicking dwarfs?" Mallick asked.

Shuran shrugged.

"Drakkon pet tricks!" he laughed.

"You call him a pet and see how much I laugh!" Shuran smiled back.

They never had a chance to see the mighty drakkon perform his newest skill. As they approached the field, a scout flew in to alert them of an attack.

"Death Walkers. They approach from the Northwest. They arrive in the thousands."

The war horns sounded and the night thundered with riders on drakkon launching into the sky.

Shuran ordered Mallick, Orian, and Avrank to man the castle walls and wield Essence at the front lines of the enemy. "I will send you messages by thought as to what is happening in the field and you do the same here. Mallick, check if you can find what is keeping our backup!" And with that last command he launched into the air upon Moltar's mighty back.

"I am glad to not be on that creature's back!" Avrank said.

"Or in his mother's gut!" Orian jested. "Let's get moving sheesh!"

The drakkon riders dove and swerved to avoid the dark bolts of energy being sent from the death walkers. The riders and drakkon sent streams of fire into the encroaching undead army. The wielders in their ranks to great affect deflected their attacks. They were not making much headway in diminishing the enemy ranks.

"Look for an isolated master, they will be consumed with controlling the mindless death walkers. Take one out and you render those they control useless!" Shuran called out.

Word spread quickly as the riders began to take closer passes at the outer perimeters. Someone must have found one. What looked like one hundred or more death walker's halted their forward attack and wandered without direction.

The Earth below them opened, and swallowed them up. The riders attacked with added zeal. Then the fighting grew.

Clouds roiled and flashed as the first of the magurmu came into view. Lightening flashed and cracked as it slammed into the ground amidst the death walkers. The flying boats began lowering to the ground where they could safely drop warriors to engage the enemy on foot.

Elf and dwarf warriors launched headlong into the fray, hacking at the death walkers and wielding Essence to attack the spell casters. The fighting went on with wild abandon. The death walker numbers were being reduced more as the fighting went on.

Suddenly the center of the now halted enemy army cleared at the arrival of a demon-possessed wielder of greater strength.

"Shuran! Show yourself! It is time you face me after all these years hunting you!" Telalsu said.

Shuran roared through Moltar and dove from the sky at the demon.

Telalsu was not expecting this.

Moltar and Shuran came to a ground-shaking landing before the demon.

"Well, this is unexpected, the prophecies do not speak of this!" Telalsu said.

"If I have learned anything about prophecy is that they are poorly interpreted and often self fulfilling! I plan to design my own ending demon, you shall not see it!" Shuran instructed Moltar to show off his latest 'trick'.

Moltar swung back his wings and quickly flapped them ahead three quarters forward. The result was, the ground along the path of movement rippling and rolling in a concussive wave of earth and wind pushing everything forward in the direction of Telalsu.

The demon had no time to react and went sailing over one hundred paces back.

Shuran jumped from Moltar's back and gave chase. "You took my friend from Birchshire, demon. You were looking for me, well now you have found me. I will end this fruitless hunt for you now!" Shuran shouted.

All the death walkers appeared to just be watching and waiting for something. This was because the demon possessed weavers controlling them, stood in shocked surprise when Telalsu went flailing from the drakkon attack.

"Impressive, you teach your beast new tricks! Ultimately ineffectual, Ersetu mutt!" the demon spat from the ruined body he currently inhabited.

"You lay there dying and you still mock?" Shuran asked.

"Your ignorance will be your undoing no matter what power you posses. Only this body dies fool. I have another waiting for me back at the keep." The body shook and heaved, then breathed no more. A shadowy black mist slowly seeped from every orifice and made its way northwest toward the Orders's keep.

Shuran jumped back on Moltar and called out to Gregoran. "Meet me at the Order's secret keep!" Shuran shouted.

"How will I find you?" Gregoran asked.

Shuran just grinned and sent the image to indicate Moltar. "You will find it difficult to not find us. Now hurry, time does not march within our ranks!" Shuran turned Moltar toward his destination. Shuran followed the void in the Essence that was Telalsu's disembodied form slithering off toward the keep. He must get there to prevent what he suspected was to happen.

***

"Get away from me wraith!" Salmetu shouted as she sent sparks flying around the room.

"He comes, he comes, HE COMES!" The apparition mocked as the bolts of Essence passed through her.

"Why do you keep saying that?" Salmetu asked.

"It is true. He comes and he will not be happy with you! My brother comes!" Tianna shrieked as she shot from the room up through the ceiling.

Salmetu suddenly realized what was happening. She has been haunted by the sister that would have been. The one who died so that she might live to serve the darkness. And now her brother, Shuran was coming.

A tear welled up in her eye. She lifted it to her finger and looked at it momentarily, then anger took hold and the tear evaporated in a small puff of steam.

"Welcome, brother. Do come in, I have so very much wanted to meet you!" she said aloud as the foundation of the keep shook and cracks formed along the walls. "Oh dear I must have left the door locked, I will have to go let him in." Salmetu said talking to herself. An evil laugh escaped her as she left the room to go meet Shuran.

Chapter Forty-Three

Shuran could not find a way into the keep so he decided that he and Moltar would have to make a way. They flew around the natural formed tower, searching out with the Essence for occupants. He was able to pick up on where the faint signature of Bastien was.

"May I, Shuran?" Moltar asked wanting to pull the rock face away, exposing the room to the outside world.

"I think it best that I do it this time, I am less a novice and this will require some finesse to prevent injuring Bastien." Shuran felt Moltar's disappointment. "After we achieve our goal of saving Bastien, you can raze this tower to the ground!" Shuran compromised to Moltar's satisfaction.

Shuran began to match his Essence to the rhythm of the earth and focused on the rock wall before him. The tower began to tremble, and the wall started to crack. With a final push of energies, the wall burst outward and hit the shield Shuran constructed just in time. Inside, he saw Bastien lying alone on a cot.

Moltar flew over and clung to the side of the tower.

Shuran climbed along his body and into the room. He began to approach Bastien and was stopped by force of invisible power.

"Did you believe it to be that simple, brother?" Salmetu said as she appeared in the doorway. "I must say I do not understand what Isten has been so worked up about," she continued to walk closer, assessing Shuran.

"It would appear that you have been meddled with as have I. We are what now, seven or eight summers of age? Yet here we are in the prime of early human youth!" She walked closer, but Shuran did not move.

He followed her with his eyes, all the while extending his shi to sense her intentions. He felt it coming before she was able to launch an assault.

Salmetu loosed a ball of undulating dark force directly at him.

Shuran sent a counter attack of electricity that deflected it away.

Shuran and his sister sparred back and forth, testing one another. Neither of them seemed to have been attempting to intend true harm. As much as Shuran wanted to end this, he was hesitant to harm his own flesh and blood. There had to be something of his true sister in there somewhere.

"Why do you fight me sister, you must know your actions only serve Vardoran and he uses you as a tool?" Shuran tried to distract her.

"A tool? To that old fool? Do not disillusion yourself brother. He is nothing! This world is nothing! I have seen the power that fills me and it is eternal!" she said with a mad voice.

Shuran saw a dark mist entering the room through the floor and walls. It was heading toward Bastien. He had to get past this shield of hers. He searched for weaknesses but found none. What he did find was that it did not extend below the floor.

Shuran reached into the energies of the lines and found a way in. He plunged into the line and out into the space beyond the wall.

"Well, that was unexpected!" Salmetu said. She watched him head for Bastien and noticed that Telalsu was arriving to claim Bastien's prepared body. She made to stop him. "HAZA!" She shouted and Shuran froze in place.

He fought against the spell but was unable to break it.

Salmetu slowly walked around his form and paused in front of him pretending to freeze in place then laugh. Salmetu prepared to spell him again when there was a flash of light just out of Shuran's limited field of vision.

"You will not hurt him, you evil bitch!" came the resounding and familiar girlish voice.

Shuran could see the color drain from Salmetu's face.

"Leave me alone!" she said and vanished in a swirl of darkness.

Shuran struggled to free himself but could not. The dark mist was now collected and moving toward Bastien. "Tianna, help me!" Shuran said in his mind. She walk into view and smiled at him.

"You know me?" she asked.

"I have spoken to mother, she told me about you and I knew we had met."

Tianna smiled and then her face saddened. "I cannot help you from this spell," she said, passing her hands through him. He could somehow feel it. "You have only to reach out to your worried friend outside," she said with a sudden smile before she vanished.

Shuran did not know at first what she meant. He then realized, Moltar was his bonded; he could spell him a release from this state. "Moltar can you hear me!" Shuran shouted inside his head.

"YES, no need to shout! I heard the wispy girl also," he answered. "What do you need Shin'Ar!" he asked anxiously.

Shuran shared the thoughts of the spell with Moltar who had to run it over in his mind several times before he was ready to try it. Then with a determined roar, Moltar let out the spell. "SUBAR!" Moltar directed at his Shuran who was more than a friend and bonded master.

The effect was immediate. Shuran fell to the floor upon release.

Moltar began clawing at the walls trying to widen them so he might climb inside.

"I am fine," Shuran said as he climbed to his feet. He looked to Bastien and then around the room. He no longer saw the dark mists in the room. He thought, no hoped, that they left with Salmetu's sudden departure. He ran to Bastien's side and tried to wake him. "Bastien! Bastien it is me Shuran. It is good now I am here!" Shuran cried.

"Shuran?" he finally heard in a soft forced whisper.

"Yes, Bastien it is I!"

Bastien opened his eyes and looked around the room before his eyes finally settled on Shuran. "Shuran, it is you," he said.

Shuran squeezed his friend with all the love and joy he held for his lost best friend and sheesh. "I thought we had lost you!" Shuran said.

"Oh, but you have!" was all Shuran heard before he was sent flying across the room by a blast of force. "FOOL! Did you think I left?" The twisted voice of Telalsu struggled against that of Bastien's. "Oh this one is stronger than expected!" the demon announced. "It will vex you greater to attempt destroying this host we think!" he said with an evil laugh. "We shall meet again when I have gathered my strength, Shuran Shin'Ar!" the demon possessed Bastien said just before dispiriting into a swirl of darkness.

***

The fighting suddenly ended as the death walkers quickly disappeared into the night. They lost two of the magurmu and seven drakkon along with their respective riders. The enemy lost hundreds of their undead army. The flying vessels and drakkon all collected the ground fighters and headed back to the training fields of the Baron's castle.

They arrived with mixed feelings of victory and loss. Drakkon all gathered to morn the loss of their breed.

Although he had lost two of his new flying ships, Aknard was in high spirits. "We beat those unholy bastards into the ground!" he yelled.

His guild all cheered along with many of the Drakkians, Elves, and Dwarfs. The cheering began to die down as the bulking form of Moltar cast a shadow upon them. When they realized what they saw, the cheering resumed ten fold.

"Moltar and his Lugaldur the Shuran Shin'Ar!" they shouted. The crowd spread as Moltar came to land in the center of the gathered masses of mixed races.

"Where is Gregoran?" Fallon asked.

Shuran only now noticed his and Jade's absence. "We got separated at the Order's keep." Shuran said guiltily.

As if upon request, Jade roared and the crowd turned to watch them come it to land.

"What happened to you back there?" Shuran asked.

"We saw you had matters in hand at the tower. Jade noticed zealots leaving the keep so we thought to follow them. They got as far as the Stone Forest before we were attacked. We fought for some time before Jade took a wound to her wing and we had to land so I might focus on healing her," Gregoran said. "I am sorry Shin'Ar but we lost their trail by the time came we could regain the air," the Drakkian Zidu'Si said.

"They have but one place to go now sheesh, do not call blame upon yourself," Shuran said as he took his trusted companion in arm.

***

That evening those involved in the fighting celebrated their first victory.

"Not in my lifetime has there been such a joining of even two races toward a common cause Shuran. You represent a new beginning to this world. Perhaps old wounds can find healing with the events of this day!" Fallon said raising a goblet of ale.

Shuran met the toast with little joy.

"What troubles you nephew? I understand the loss of your friend. But it seems there is something more?" Fallon asked.

"I felt something in my sister Salmetu. Something conflicted and at the same time darker than anything I ever felt in Vardoran, Telalsu, or the death walkers," Shuran responded. "Excuse me Uncle, I must go to my mother."

Fallon nodded in understanding.

"Mother, are you well?" Shuran asked as he approached her bed. He found it empty.

"I am over here," she said from the window.

Shuran noticed her standing by the window under her own strength and was happy to find her in better health. "Mother you are up!" he said.

"Yes, I am stronger. Tianna was here, she said you did well against Salmetu."

Shuran sensed the hesitation in her voice.

"You should have destroyed her!" his mother spat.

Shuran was shocked at hearing this from Sulura. "Mother, you cannot mean this?" Shuran asked.

"She is consumed Shuran, taken by something more dark than we can comprehend," Sulura spoke to her son as tears ran freely.

"She is not beyond saving," a wispy voice sounded from behind them.

***

The next morning was full of many emotions. It was a wondrous event to have Dwarf, Human, Drakkian, and Elf, all working together. They all however, felt the loss of life.

Shuran was feeling the worst of all, having witness his friend Bastien, taken from him again. "I find little to celebrate, however I see the need to recognize that we took a stand against the dark." Shuran said and everyone silenced.

"We have come to a point where we take a new path to the repeating of history in Aurderia, where future people will judge our actions against what has happened before," Shuran started before the assembly of thousands. "For too long, we as a people have ignored the plight of others. In ancient times the Anzillu trials lead to the Sikil Mah, this left the lands divided." Shuran continued.

"No more! I will not allow this to continue. This is not a fight for mixed blood. It is not about the fear of who can wield more Essence," Shuran paused. "This is about what is right and wrong... no middle ground. We can debate what we once believed, but times are changed and we must change with them or be left behind to only have this cycle repeat in the future if our people survive the present."

Shuran paused at the cheers of those in attendance. "It is time we decide here and now! Do we fight for all that is good and worth saving? Then we fight for the survival of Aurderia and all of Ersetu!"

<u>Epilogue</u>

The Zidu'Si left Drakkfoth for their home of Durangug. Elves and Dwarfs were taken home by magurmu with a communication crystal for giving to their leaders. These stones would activate with instructions on where next the races must assemble in common cause. It was now a fight for the good of all Ersetu, the world.

Shuran had time to spend learning what it meant to have a bond and be Lugaldur, but Moltar made it easy. His youthful exuberance and desire to please Shuran made progress expeditious. Together they learned what it meant to become something new to the lands; something more powerful, and at the same time feared more than anything seen in millennia. Shuran had his Zidu'Si to rely upon, but they were not yet complete.

Shuran also had time now to check the hidden room in the Vault, which only he could enter. When he approached the wall where the room was hidden behind, he felt a sense of warning. He began to raise his hand to the wall and felt a sense of dread come upon him. He decided to shake it off and pushed his hand to the stone. The wall slid aside and Shuran entered the space as the wall closed behind him.

***

Deep in the tunnels below the Zig'Mada, something stirred…

Glossary of Terms

Abnu Emuq - Power Stone
Abzu Mu - deep source of water
Adda - Father
Agal Kastu - Mighty Bow /Weapon of gug held by the Zidu'Si elf
Alla - Evil God
Anse - Donkey / Ass
Anzillu - Abomination
Asipu - Wizard / Mage / Magic Worker
Assinnu Isten - First of the Order / Cult Leader
Bad - Wall / Ground
Baduruku (BA-DUR-UKU)- Water People
Bal - Transform
Bil - burn
Bitmu - Tree house
DAMKIANNA (DAM-KI-ANNA) - Mistress of Heaven and Earth
Diri - Huge
Dug - Heal
Dur - Jackass
Durani - Fortress
Ekur (E-KUR) - House that is like a Mountain
ELITUR (ELI-TUR) - Sacrilege
Emmuku'Gu (Emmuku-Gu) Ersetu - Power River (lei line) of Ersetu (World)

Emuku - Power
Ersetu (ER-SE-TU) - World
Gabara (Gaba-Ra-A) - Offering
Galla - Devil
Gug - Lodestone
Gugtu (GUG-TU) \ Zisuragug (ZI-SU)RA-GUG) - Magic Stone
Haza - Hold (used to immobilize something)
Iniminim Ma (Inim Inim Ma) - Book of Spells
Kalag-Ga - To Invigorate (Strength)
Kashshaptu (KASH-SHAP-TU) - Witch
Kes - Bind
Kigalba (KI-GAL-BA) - Great Fire Below / Hell
Ki'Ta (KI-TA) - Below
Kimmatu'Du (Kim-Ma-Tu'Du) - Son of the Clan/Family (adopted or honorary)
Kin'Ge - Send message
Kin'Su - Accept Message
Kuliana - Mermaid
Lalli Mah (Lal-Li Mah) - Great Balance
Lam Mudutu - Abundant Knowledge
Lil - Air
Lugaldur - Bonded master of a drakkon
Maaddir (Ma-Addir) - Ferry Boat
Magurmu (Ma-Gur-Mu) - Flying Boat
Masku - Hide
Mellamu Nanna - Bright Moon (Steam powered Water ship that also flies under Crystal Shard power - Codgers Ship)
Menasutur (Me-Na-Su-Tur) - Sacred War Hammer of the Dwarves / Weapon of gug held by the Dwarven Zidu'Si
Miib Ag (Mi-Ib Ag) - Fire Sword / Weapon of gug wielded by the Drakk Zidu'Si
Mu - Flying Machine
Pad - Break into Pieces
Padiri - Explode / release restrained power
Peta - Open (for me)

Sheesh (She-Esh) - Brother
Shin'Ar - Watcher of the Lands
Sikil Mah - great purge of abominations
TAMU - To Swear Oath
Tartur Mamitu - Oath Breaker
Tel - Land
Telal - Warrior Demon
Telukukal (Telu-Kuk-Al) - First Land People (First People)
Tul - Altar or Well
Tur - Sacred
Tur - Small (to be) / Derogatory term used by dwarfs naming those smaller than themselves.
Xul - Devil / Evil
Zidu'Si - Faithful Companions
Zisuragug (ZI-SU-RA-GUG) \ Gugtu (GUG-TU) - Magic Stone

<u>Spells</u>

"BEL GIBIDALAL, SISITU MUZU EMUQ, PULHU ES-INA LAMAGIRI, LASANAN EMUQ ADI ANNU ABANASQUPPATU, ZU ASSINNA ILEQQE BILTU, SEMU!"
Lord of Chaos, We Summon Thy Power. Terror to those who do not submit, Unrivaled Energy upon this Threshold. Your Followers pay Tribute, HEAR US (Obey)!

"NINTI DUL-INA GISHTIL, NADANUTE SHI BALU SARRATUM."
Lady of Life, Protect the Child (vehicle) of Light, I give my soul without falsehood.

"KUKU-MA, SI NE BUR, TAMUSU BAMU"
Gods of Darkness, fill this vessel, Make him my instrument.

Maps

***

Edinzabar
Frozen North
Duranekur
Durangug
Birchshire
Rivenwood
Entensiama
Highlands
Elmwood
Tarangale
Britengate
Great Sea
Zig'Mada
Hells's Mouth
Stone
Forest
Drakkfoth
Foresworn Territories
Altar
of
Chaos
Serpent's
Fangs
Two Bridges Middleton
Academy
Castleton
Smuggler's
Cove
New
Draven
Hakkisuru
Mist
Swamps

Preview River of Souls

Prologue

The balance of dark and light is again threatened in Ersetu. The land of Aurderia is at the center of the struggle between the forces aligned with the dark, and the rest of the world. Shuran, a young man grown from powers beyond his comprehension, faces his sister who is consumed by darkness. With his growing powers, Shuran travels the realms gathering allies and building his Zidu'Si, a collective of the races of man who serve the Shin'Ar. As Shin'Ar, Shuran has been thrust into the position as 'Watcher of the Lands', an ancient title that goes back to the Telukukal, the first people of Ersetu.

Shuran's father is missing and his best friend, Bastien, has been possessed. Shuran fights against the darkness of the Order of Chaos in an effort to find a way to balance the Essence of Ersetu. In Durangug, Shuran and the Zidu'Si, gather to gain knowledge and understanding of their part in this prophecy. While the Zidu'Si research to locate the three remaining races of man, Shuran explores a hidden chamber within the Vault.

Chapter One

P

Shuran found himself surrounded by such darkness, he felt himself melting into a shadowy nothingness. He was cut off from the Zidu'Si, not completely, but enough so that he was utterly alone. Shuran felt relief in being alone with his thoughts. All else was shut off, and he let out a sigh that allowed the weight of his responsibilities to fall from his young shoulders. His solitude would not last as he remembered where he was, the previously unknown chamber hidden within the Vault.

Shuran created an orb and closed his eyes in response to the flood of light that pulsed forth from his open palm. The darkness swallowed the light, leaving a soft glow when Shuran finally opened his eyes. The room was circular and smaller than he expected. Arms extended at his sides Shuran sized the room up as approximately four arm spans across. He could see no ceiling in the darkness so he let the sphere of light lift from his palm into the space above him.

The ceiling was half his height above his head. The walls were covered in carvings unlike anything he had ever seen or read about. As he traced his fingers across the intricately worked stone walls, he took in scenes of beings performing what must have been rituals of varying kinds. What these acts were meant to accomplish, Shuran could not begin to understand.

The human-like people were dressed in ornate robes and hats. They carried odd tools or weapons and communed with creatures unknown to him. As he continued to gingerly stroke his fingers across the works, he came to find a series of indentations in the wall. There were ten holes that if connected would resemble two half moons facing one another. Inside were two stars on the same plane. Without hesitation, Shuran reached out with his hands and found that his fingers all fit in the holes. With a slight pull, he lifted the section of wall away.

A small compartment behind the section contained a cloth wrapped bundle. Shuran set the rock panel down to investigate the contents of the wrapping. As soon as he lifted the heavy bundle, the cloth disintegrated into a pile of musty grit and powder. In his hands, he held a book that was beautifully crafted of pure gold.

As Shuran stepped back with the book, a pillar rose from the floor just below the compartment. The top of the pillar was carved to hold the book so Shuran set it down. A new light shone down from the ceiling upon the book, casting golden rays of reflecting light all over the chamber. What Shuran saw upon page after page was more of the same scenes from the walls. He turned to open the door and realized it would not budge.

***

"What is keepin' that boy?" Moona complained.

"Don' suppose that room is some privy for the Shin'Ar? Or perhaps a bottomless trap?" Codger began to wonder aloud.

"Clap your trap Codge! Ol' fool!" Moona said as she whacked him in the back of the head.

"I am certain Shuran is fine, I can sense him on the edge of my consciousness," Moltar reassured Moona from his limited space on the other side of the Vault. "If he needed our assistance, I would be able to feel his need."

"Well, that makes me feel better," Moona mumbled. "Shouldn' someone take them beasts out for a walk or somethin'!"

Moona walked over to the hidden door and reached out toward it as if to knock.

"I wouldn' do that Moony!" Codger warned.

Not to be told what to do, Moona reached further and made contact with the door. The resulting jolt sent her flailing back several paces to land between Moltar's feet. Her stringy thin hair standing straight on end, she looked dazed and confused. Her eyes focused to see Moltar staring down at her ready to give her a good lick.

Reaching up with a fist Moona stopped him as his tongue began to slither out. "If you value that particular part o' your body, you best keep it ta ya' self!"

***

Shuran struggled to pull the lever to release the door. No matter how he tried it would not move and Essence was less effective than brute force. Shuran stopped short when he saw a pattern to the reflections on the wall. Symbols formed upon particular sections of the wall. This was the ancient language of the Telukukal but in a form he had never seen.

Somehow Shuran was able to sense that it was the First Ones original form of writing, though he was unsure what it meant. There was no pattern to the placement. He reached for the book and turned the golden pages with great care. The reflections changed as did their placement on the walls.

As he studied the glyphs and symbols, he sensed a familiar pattern to them and was mesmerized by them as the reflections danced around the walls. Page after page, he watched as the patterns moved and shifted.

Shuran lost track of time as he watched the patterns change and move around the room. He did not know what to make of any of this and needed help. Shuran thought to use his communication crystal finding that it worked.

"SHURAN!" Moona screeched. "What has kept you? Gonna send me to an early grave, you are!"

"Too late for that!" Codger managed before getting another whack.

"I have found the most amazing golden book," Shuran answered.

"So bring it out. You missed a meal while distracted Shin'Ar," Orian stated.

"I have tried to exit but-" Shuran started.

"A trap! I knew it!" Moona interrupted.

"No Moona, I believe that it is a safety built into the room," Shuran began. "The place was hidden from us for a reason. Perhaps the book is not meant to leave."

Shuran explained his experience in the room and how he came across the book. As he described the scenes he observed, Codger took notes and the others discussed possible meanings. Shuran continued to describe the ways in which the symbols reflected upon the walls, changing form and position as the pages of the book were turned.

"You can continue your tale out here boy! Now put the fancy book back and get your tail out here. This pet o' yours needs walkin'," Moona barked.

"What has gotten into her?" Avrank asked Orian.

"I think she is run out of her frost moss."

Shuran slid the book back in the wall and replaced the panel. The pedestal lowered back into the floor and the strange light dimmed. When the light completely left the room in darkness again, the lever moved in Shuran's hand easily.

The door slid open to reveal a wiry-haired old woman standing ready to yank him from the chamber. Her hand could not pass the threshold. She dared not perform a repeat of the tumbling act that had the others already giggling as she pulled back her hand. Frustrated she stomped off toward her work table.

Shuran exited the room and continued into the night describing all he saw as best he could remember.

More than once Codger would stop him to ask questions or to repeat descriptions.

Mallick and the other Zidu'Si listened quietly to everything Shuran had to tell.

"Something I am certain of is a symbol I saw that represents knowledge. The symbols and their placement upon a picture depicting a treasure, lead me to believe it describes a compendium of some sort," Shuran sighed. His frustration stemmed from the awareness on the edge of his mind that was just out of reach. He did not understand where the knowledge and intuition came from and that confused him further.

"Perhaps it refers to the Vault?" Gregoran asked.

"Doubtful, since it would be redundant to reference a treasure of knowledge from within that very place," Mallick said. "I think that since it is in the language of the Telukukal, perhaps it refers to a Compendium of Telukukal knowledge. The room and book together may be a vast library in code of some sort."

"Code yes, but that room is not the Compendium. There is indication that this treasury of knowledge somehow moves or can be moved. I am still unclear on that bit. I think the room may be a means of locating where and when it will be accessible," Avrank said matter-of-factly.

"Yes, well that may be difficult since we have little reference of how to translate the ancient symbols," Mallick pointed out. "The Vault library contains no mention of the ancient script, only a few drawings with no correlated meaning."

"The images depicted on the walls are also confusing," Shuran added. "They make no sense, unless the meaning is hidden or symbolic as well."

Moona left the boys to their debates and went about working her herbs and mixing potions. She enjoyed having her ability back to sense the potency of plants and other ingredients of her mixtures. During the long years she lived with her Essence wielding abilities hobbled, Moona had to make mixtures for others on memory and experience. She trusted her knowledge, but having the power to reach her mind into a poultice and feel the potency, allowed her to definitively decide the dosage and length of effectiveness. Having her spark to activate charms back was what she was most happy about.

She was working on something that came to mind after hearing Shuran talk about exploding rocks when he was feeling frustrated. The Melammu Nanna and Aknard's fleet of magurmu could use better offensive weapons after the battle in Drakkfoth. Instead of relying on individual power, Moona thought to create ready-made Essence exploders. She was working on her first prototype while the men all talked of Compendiums and symbols.

She had been working through a rather difficult spell on setting a two-part trigger. First, she needed a spell to activate the device. Second, a spell that would cause the device to explode when in range of darkness was required. She was having trouble with the proper wording for the second spell.

"PAD - TEGE - NERI!" Moona spoke to no effect. "Blast! Still not right."

"PAD-TE'GA-NERU," whispered a voice just barely audible to Moona.

"Yes! That's it…" she started before looking to see who had given her the words.

Moona looked around to see the men all still on the opposite side of the Vault. The drakkon were both outside hunting. Moona was alone. She shook her head and fingered her ear clean of wax.

"PAD-TE'GA-NERU," she heard again.

"Who's there?" Moona called.

She looked around and saw nothing but the looming figure of an Ancient carved from gug. It was one of the many statues placed all alone the Vault's perimeter walls. Moona dismissed her unease, until she saw a faint shimmer glide across the surface of the large statue before her. It was not until that moment, Moona took more than passing notice of the statues. She retrieved a stool to gain height enough to examine the figure closer.

The features seen under close inspection were that of a female. Large eyes with a thin nose and lips dominated the narrow face. The statue wore elaborately carved robes with inlaid decorations of stars, leaves, acorns, and other heavenly and earthly objects. Her hands rested across her chest with long thin fingers clasped. Moona's eyes scanned the likeness of this other-worldly looking creature, until she noticed the pendant around its neck.

"DAMKIANNA!" Moona yelled as she lost her footing and fell to the hard ground with a grunt.

Hearing the clatter of instruments followed by a loud thud, the others ended their debate and looked for the source of the commotion. What they found was Moona laying upon the floor and a multitude of her bottles and herbs splayed out around her.

"What on Ersetu has gotten into you ol' woman!" Codger came

rushing over to help her as he saw her fall.

"Damkianna…" was all Moona could mumble as she pointed to the statue.

Shuran and Mallick soon came to assist, lifting Moona to her feet. Mallick simply thought Moona was shaky from too much work and not enough rest. Shuran felt it was more than that.

"Moona, what is wrong?" Shuran asked, concerned. He took her hands in his and felt their tremble. When she did not answer, he finally looked up at the statue. At first he did not notice anything, but he, like the others had never given them much thought. Hanging around the neck, was a golden chain with a pendant. In the center of the pendant was a clear crystal with a symbol etched inside. The face of the statue was familiar.

"Mallick, what do we know about these statues?" Shuran asked.

"Little to nothing is recorded. I just assumed they were representations of the original Zidu'Si and Shin'Ar since there are eight of them," Mallick answered.

"But there should be nine…" Avrank started, "one for each of the seven races, the Shin'Ar, and his Isten."

"There are six statues and five empty alcoves," Orian observed. "It would appear as though there are missing statues. What do you suppose this means Shin'Ar?"

"I am uncertain, but this female idol before me is not likely of the seven races of man or the Zidu'Si of old. I believe it is the Lady Damkianna." Shuran stated pointing to the pendant.

"Damn right it is! And she spoke to me!" Moona added.

"There goes our quiet time boys!" Codger said as he ducked out of Moona's reach. "Have you been hittin' the kegs woman? What would one o' the old gods be havin' to say to you?"

Moona explained, with great animation, how she had trouble with a spell when a voice whispered to her. She spoke of the glimmer of a face that drifted across the statue, and then finding the pendant with Damkianna's sigil appear inside the crystal.

"Perhaps the Shin'Ar of old and his Zidu'Si were more devout in their practice of religion. I see no other reason for the statues' presence,"

Mallick said trying to play down Moona's experience. He did not believe for a moment that one of the ancient Gods was talking to her. "Perhaps it was Tianna who spoke to you?"

Moona grumbled at that possible explanation, but her eyes never left the statue's, until the others led her back to her table.

Shuran was skeptical about Mallick's explanation. Tianna rarely appeared and when she did it was to Shuran or at least in his presence.

"What is it you are doing here?" Gregoran asked, trying to change the subject.

"A WEAPON!" Moona became excited and motioned her boys to come closer. "This here is a darkness triggered exploder. Got the idea from Shuran," she added with a smile to her young foster son. "Two spells work it. First one sets it with a word. The second spell triggers when it comes in close contact to the dark. I thought the Mellamu Nanna and Aknard's vessels could do with something what could be dropped from up high. Not gettin' so close as last time when fightin' might save a ship or more," Moona finished.

"How big of a boom are we talkin' 'bout Moony?" Codger asked.

"Take out all them death walkers within forty paces or so. I could make 'em stronger, but they would get too heavy." Moona showed them her diagrams and continued talking about how to make them.

They all agreed that those who stayed back from the trip to locate the giants would help create as many as they could. Their discussion was interrupted by the sudden appearance of Jade.

<u>Author</u>

Check out the Epic and Series website:
http://www.essenceofersetu.com

Follow on Facebook at:
http://fb.com/Author.JStevenYoung
http://fb.com/EssnceOfErsetu

Chronicles of Aurderia (Trilogy)
The Balance
River of Souls
Queen of Shadow

Hashtag Magic (series)
Blue Screen of Death
Control ALT Delete
Web of Trolls (late 2015)